Praise for Laura Pedersen

"Pedersen writes vividly of characters so interesting, so funny, and warm that they defy staying on the page." —Hartford *Courant*

"A fresh and funny look at not fitting in." —*Seventeen*

"Prepare to fall in love. . . . In a story as wise as it is witty, Pedersen captures the joy of love found, the ache of love lost, and how friends can get you through it all—win or lose."
—SARAH BIRD, author of *The Yokota Officers Club*

"Smart, funny, and chocked with fascinating tidbits and surprises . . . Laura Pedersen's lively imagination has created a cast of zany characters and an unforgettable heroine in Hallie Palmer . . . an enchanting read."
—BEV MARSHALL, author of *Right as Rain* and *Walking Through Shadows*

"Funny, sweet-natured, and well-crafted . . . Pedersen has created a wonderful assemblage of . . . whimsical characters and charm."
—*Kirkus Reviews*

"Laura Pedersen's newest work is as fresh and inviting as iced tea in August. If only I had friends as sweet and quirky and unpredictable as the characters in *Heart's Desire*!"
—AD HUDLER, author of *Househusband* and *Southern Living*

"[*Beginner's Luck*] is funny and just quirky enough to become a word-of-mouth favorite. . . . Pedersen has a knack for cap~~turing~~ ~~teenage~~ observations in witty asides, a~~~~ ~~~~er gambling and numbers savvy, ~~~~ ~~~~ly

"This book will make you laugh ~~~~ ~~~~'ll be happy to have made its acquaintance."
—LORNA LANDVIK, author of *Angry Housewives Eating Bon Bons* and *Oh My Stars*

ALSO BY LAURA PEDERSEN

Fiction

Last Call
Beginner's Luck
Heart's Desire
Going Away Party

Nonfiction

Play Money

THE BIG
SHUFFLE

THE BIG
SHUFFLE

a novel

Laura Pedersen

BALLANTINE BOOKS
NEW YORK

A Ballantine Books Trade Paperback Original

Copyright © 2006 by Laura Pedersen
Reading group guide copyright © 2006 by Random House, Inc.

Published in the United States by Ballantine Books, an imprint of The Random House Publishing Group, a division of Random House, Inc., New York.

BALLANTINE and colophon are registered trademarks of Random House, Inc.
READER's CIRCLE and colophon are trademarks of Random House, Inc.

ISBN 0-345-47956-4

Printed in the United States of America

www.thereaderscircle.com

9 8 7 6 5 4 3 2 1

Text design by Lisa Sloane

For two darling little girls,

Laurel Catherine and Sarah Amelia,
wishing you lives of magic and wonder.

Success seems to be largely a matter of
hanging on after others have let go.

William Feather (1889–1981)

THE BIG
SHUFFLE

ONE

IT'S A COLD AND WINDLESS JANUARY NIGHT FOLLOWING A TWO-DAY winter storm. All across the campus of the Cleveland Art Institute a blanket of snow sparkles as if encrusted with tiny diamonds. Thick clouds blot out the moonlight and for a moment it feels that all of nature is hushed.

Suzy, Robin, and I walk the half mile to the Theta Chi frat house, a box-shaped building with dark brown vinyl siding that looks like it could be the back part of a church where the priests reside, were it not for the large wooden Greek letters hanging between the second and third floors. Theta Chi is hosting a Welcome Back keg party and all comers are indeed welcome, so long as they can produce an ID, real or otherwise, along with twenty bucks to be paid in cash at the door.

I have to go because my roommate Suzy has a huge crush on the president, and she convinces Robin and me to be her accomplices in the manhunt. But being that it's a new semester, and a brand-new year, I'm certainly open for adventure. When you're eighteen, the possibilities seem endless. At the same time, I'm feeling a bit lonely, since Craig, the guy I really like, attends college in Minnesota. We're eleven hundred miles apart, and he and I both agreed that it's best not to be exclusive with each other, at least for now.

Once inside the front door we pay our cover charge and a guy wearing a multicolored felt jester hat uses a stamp to emblazon the backs of our hands with big purple beavers. In the strobe-lit entrance hall Billy Joel blares from speakers that seem to be everywhere. The jacked-up bass causes the wooden floorboards to thump so it feels as if there's a heartbeat in each foot. The couches are pushed back against the walls and from the ceiling of the large living room hang dozens of strings of chili pepper lights that cast a crazy quilt of patterns onto the guests. Young people stand around holding big red plastic cups, occasionally leaning in close to yell something at one other. They nod or laugh and over near the fireplace a few dance.

A guy wearing a T-shirt that says, FRESHMEN GIRLS—GET 'EM WHILE THEY'RE SKINNY, rolls a fresh keg past us and catches my eye. He's heading toward a place underneath a mangy bison head where participants in a Chug for Charity contest appear to be making excellent progress.

Oh my gosh—it's Josh! He's a junior in the art department whom I had a crush on the entire first semester of my freshman year, while he didn't even know I was alive.

After dropping off the keg he comes over and hands me a beer. "Do I know you?"

"Hallie Palmer," I reply, trying not to feel devastated that he doesn't remember my name.

We begin a shouted exchange and I remind him of the shared computer graphics class.

"Oh yeah," he says and nods.

Though whether he means that he remembers the class or me is impossible to tell. Our talk segues to general stuff like movies and families. Only the problem is that now, after so much fantasizing about our nonexistent relationship, and sev-

eral beers, I'm experiencing difficulty separating the real conversation from all the imaginary ones I had with him last fall.
For instance, Josh looks surprised when I talk about having
nine brothers and sisters, whereas I'm thinking we covered that
months ago.

I act interested in everything that Josh says about where he's
from and what he's studying even though I already know all of
this from looking up his campus profile on the Internet. I may
be majoring in graphic arts, but like most college women, I
minor in stalking.

Just when I fear we've run out of conversation, he says, "Hey,
wanna dance?"

We put down our plastic cups and move to the area in front
of the fireplace where throngs of intoxicated students dance to
Jason Mraz's "I'll Do Anything." I'm probably reading too much
into the situation, as usual, but it's as if every line of the song has
a double, or even triple meaning.

When the next song begins Josh appears to be finished with
the dancing part of the evening. He stands still while everyone
begins jumping around to "Heat Wave." Meantime, Suzy pushes
her way toward us through the closely packed gyrating crowd,
carefully ducking and maneuvering so as not to disturb any of
the headgear with beer cans attached to the top and plastic
tubes running into the mouths of thirsty revelers. Her cheeks
are flushed. "I found Ross! He's upstairs!"

"This is Josh," I lean in close and say to Suzy.

"Hey Josh," she shouts, barely glancing over at him. "Hallie,
they're playing strip poker upstairs and you have to come because I don't know how to play and—" Suzy stops midstream
and looks back at Josh. "Is that *Josh*?" she asks me. The emphasis is code for: the guy you were so obsessed with that I thought
a counselor was going to have to be brought in for an assist?

"Yes," I bob my head up and down to indicate it's *that* Josh.

Suzy smiles. This translates to: He's really cute and you're going to get lucky tonight!

"You said that you found *Ross*," I remind her.

Suzy grabs both our hands. "Come teach me how to play strip poker."

"Actually I'm not much of a poker player," says Josh, holding his ground.

"Me neither," I lie. I've been playing poker since I was seven, but why appear anxious when Suzy is going to close this deal for me?

"*Please,* you guys." She pulls us in the direction of the wide staircase that empties into the back of the living room. What might soon qualify as a three-alarm blaze is now roaring in the fireplace. The room was already hot and redolent of spilled beer, and now it's becoming filled with thick gray smoke.

Suzy is giddy with excitement, turning back and smiling every few seconds as she directs us to the second floor, and then up a narrow staircase that leads to a refinished attic. Eight kids are lounging around on oversized pillows in a dimly lit room with a lava lamp in the corner and music wailing from a CD player on the floor. Everyone is still fully dressed, and if the loud laughing and joking is anything to go by, no longer fully sober. A guy wearing khaki shorts, a frat house T-shirt, and a cowboy hat shuffles a deck of cards. There's the faint but distinctive aroma of marijuana, though given that the one hexagonal window in the room doesn't open, it's impossible to tell whether the scent is from tonight's group or previous parties.

"Are you outlaws here to play poker or are you delivering the pizza?" says the guy nearest the boom box, whom I recognize as Ross, Suzy's big crush.

Everyone laughs uproariously at this stupid joke. Suzy releases our hands and I come out from behind her. A girl named

Jennifer and a guy named Kevin, both of whom I recognize from my freshman dorm, say, "I didn't know I was going to play against Hallie Palmer," and "Now things are really getting exciting."

It's not unknown for me to sit in on a dorm game and clean up a pot or two. Most of the kids aren't exactly strong opponents to begin with; however, they usually drink while playing, giving me an even greater advantage. People who booze while they bet tend not to fold nearly as early or often as they should.

The cowboy-hat guy calls for a game of five-card draw with deuces wild. Ross announces that we all have to start with our shoes and socks either on or off.

Jennifer holds up her hand and says, "We didn't decide about underwear."

The four guys yell *"no"* to underwear while the five women shout *"yes."* "I'll do odds or evens with one of the girls," states Ross. The girls could argue this but they don't because some secretly want to play down to the nude. Let's face it, a girl doesn't join a game of strip poker unless she likes one of the guy players or she's incredibly drunk.

Suzy volunteers to throw out fingers against Ross, promptly loses the underwear option, and then conveniently remains sitting next to him.

Picking up my cards I find a pair of sixes and a wild two. With the chance to replace two cards, this means the prospect of four sixes! Though I don't receive another six or wild card, an ace comes my way. Kevin's three sixes made with a wild two have only a queen high and so I'm the winner. The others good-naturedly remove an article of clothing and throw it into the center of the circle. After four more rounds I've lost only my pants, while almost everyone else is down to their underwear, and Jennifer has also lost her bra. The girls nervously alternate puffs on cigarettes with long sips of beer. Between the cloud formed by their cigarettes and the stream of smoke rising from downstairs, the room is becoming more than hazy, and so I don't know how much we'll actually be able to see when people are fully naked.

Mr. Cowboy Hat, whom I've since found out is named Justin, is the first one required to throw in his underwear, but removes his Stetson instead. The girls cry foul.

"You'd better show us more than your side part!" exclaims Christine.

"There's no rule against hats," insists Justin. "You could have worn one."

"If that's the case then my ring and necklace count as articles of clothing," argues a braless Jennifer.

The more those two bicker the more everyone else roars with laughter. Between Josh placing his hand on my knee every few minutes and the good cards that keep coming my way, I decide that this must indeed be my lucky night.

"*Hall-ie . . .*" I hear my name echoing somewhere within the swirl of music, shouts of laughter, and a gauzy but pleasant alcoholic haze.

It can't be. It *cannot* be the voice that boomerangs through the garden at the Stocktons' and calls me in for dinner at the end of the day.

TWO

SURE ENOUGH, BERNARD STOCKTON, MY LONGTIME MENTOR AND summer employer, crawls toward the circle on his hands and knees, panting with exhaustion. Oh no—could there have been another breakup with Gil? They've seemed so happy since getting back together and adopting the two little Chinese girls. Or worse, maybe something terrible has happened to Olivia and Ottavio on their trip to Italy. A plane crash?

Bernard drops to the floor as if he's been crawling through the desert and finally reached an oasis. Covered in a heavy down parka with a scarf wrapped around his neck and carrying a fleece hat in hand, sweat pours off Bernard's face, his eyes are rimmed with red, and he's gasping for air. But something else is odd. Those aren't his usual gabardine wool winter slacks. They're navy blue silk pajama bottoms! Bernard *never* goes out of the house unless he's immaculately dressed and every salt and pepper hair is in place.

"Hallie!"

"Bernard!" Whatever is *he* doing *here,* right *now?*

"Heavens to Betsy Bloomingdale." Bernard begins coughing uncontrollably and pounds his hand on the floor while catching his breath. "I'm tipsy and tripping and dying of asphyxiation without having imbibed nor inhaled." Bernard raises his head an inch. "And possibly betrothed—some woman thinks I'm George Clooney and kissed me solidly on the mouth. She has eyes like cherry strudel and appears to be riding high on everything but skates."

"Kimberly," everyone says in unison.

Jennifer grabs a T-shirt off the mound of clothes in the center of the circle and covers her bare chest. Otherwise the group doesn't appear bothered by the adult intrusion, at least after making certain it's no one from the dean's office or else the campus police on the prowl for underage drinkers.

"Hallie, I've been searching absolutely *everywhere* for you. Come on—we have to go!" Bernard doesn't so much as say hello to the rest of the kids, which is totally unlike him. "I don't want you to be alarmed," he says in a voice that suggests I should be very alarmed indeed, "but your father had a heart attack."

Huh? My dad—a heart attack—impossible! He's young and strong and not even forty! I sit there stunned.

With a certain amount of dramatic huffing and puffing Bernard rises to his feet. "We must go to the hospital *now!*" He enunciates the words as if talking to someone who can only lip read.

Not knowing what to say I stand up and walk toward him like an automaton. It's only when I reach the door that Bernard says, "It's rather chilly outside, you might want to consider pants."

Josh has anticipated this and dug my jeans from out of the clothing pile. After handing them to me he retrieves my socks and shoes from the corner of the room.

I quickly dress and we head toward the main floor. The entire house is now chock-full of people partying, swaying to music, and propped up against walls, their outstretched legs blocking the hallways and stairwells. Bernard is *pardonnez-moi*-ing every step of the way through this obstacle course while towing me along behind him. We finally reach the front door, but it takes another moment to push through a crowd of rowdy women who claim to have paid earlier. The heavyset doorman is effectively blocking their entrance and shouting, "Show me your beavers!"

Bernard looks questioningly at me. "Hand stamp," I explain. But it's too loud to hear anything, and so I hold mine up to Bernard's face and he nods in understanding.

Once we're outside Bernard continues to yell as if he's still competing with the music. "Gil is waiting in the car with the girls. I've been to so many different parties I don't even know where I am anymore."

"What did you park in front of?" I holler back, though it's quiet now but for a few shouts coming from a late-night snowball fight across the quad.

"There was a sculpture out front—like a giant toadstool."

"That's the science building," I say. "It's supposed to be a molecule or something."

I hurry Bernard in the correct direction and the fresh air clears my head slightly. "Is it serious?" I ask.

"I'm not sure. Your sister Louise phoned." We've been jogging for a few minutes, and it's not so easy to catch our breath. "You . . . can . . . call her . . . from . . . the car."

I locate the maroon Volvo that Bernard recently traded for his vintage silver Alfa Romeo parked across from the science building with its engine running, the exhaust puffing a cloud of gray smoke into the cold winter air.

The girls are asleep in their car seats in the back and I climb between them while Bernard dives into the passenger side. The moment I pull the door closed Gil shoves a cell phone in my ear and puts the car into gear so that we jump away from the curb.

My sister Louise is frantic on the other end of the line. "Hallie? Is that you?"

"Yeah," I exhale heavily.

"*Thank God* they found you! *Please* go to the hospital right away and find out what's going on. I'm stuck here with the kids. Every time the phone rings I practically faint." Louise sounds as if she's starting to cry, and that it's not for the first time over the past few hours. "I woke up and the paramedics were flying down the stairs with Dad on a stretcher and Mom threw a coat over her nightgown and yelled for me to watch the kids. Reggie's been screaming bloody murder. I finally gave him a bottle of regular milk. It'll probably kill him. Tell Bernard and Gil that I'm sorry to have woken them up, but I didn't know what else to do."

"No, it's fine." I'm suddenly feeling incredibly sober.

"I got hold of Eric about an hour ago," reports Louise. "He's taking a bus from Indiana."

"I'll go to the hospital, find out what's happening, and then call you right back." I click off the phone and let my head tip over backward.

"Don't worry," says Gil. "The new hospital has a terrific cardiac unit—state of the art."

"How old is your dad?" asks Bernard.

"Both my parents are thirty-nine." It's easy to remember because I just have to add nineteen to Eric's age.

"Oh, that's *young*," says Bernard. "He'll be fine. They can do quadruple bypasses and even replace valves with animal parts. We eat too much ham and bacon and then the surgeons give us pig aortas. It's one giant recycling system. If your heart can't be salvaged, then they just throw it away and stitch in a whole new one."

I certainly hope Bernard is right, but I fear that he's just trying to make me feel better.

THREE

WE QUICKLY DELIVER GIL AND THE GIRLS BACK TO THE STOCK-tons, and then Bernard drives me to the hospital. The big glass doors automatically slide open as if someone is expecting us. When I ask the woman at the desk about my father, she says he was taken to cardiac care, but if I'll take a seat the doctor will come out and speak to me. I ask to go back, insisting that my mother is all alone. The receptionist explains that the cardiac care unit is different and that I'll have to wait.

Bernard and I slump down into the armless blue molded plastic chairs so that our shoulders meet and we're leaning against each other. Having basically moved in with him when I was sixteen, and then worked two summers as a yard person, we've become so close that we can read each other's thoughts most of the time. At least Bernard always seems to get mine exactly right. But since neither of us dare speak what's on both our minds, we say nothing at all.

There's nobody else in the brightly lit room and all the magazines have been arranged into neat stacks on the attached Formica end tables. The beige linoleum floor is spotless but for the gray puddles under our shoes. It's oddly quiet for a hospital. There aren't any gunshot victims or passengers who were just pried out of car wrecks with gaping wounds hurtling past us on stretchers, nor are sweaty blue-smocked doctors diving at patients with paddles while yelling "clear," the way one regularly sees on television shows. Cosgrove County is filled with people descended from solid midwestern farming stock who go around declaring they're "fine" until the moment when they are no longer *fine*, but in fact seriously *dead*. If you inquire about someone's chronic pain, they're likely to tell you that it helps pass the time.

"You don't have to wait here with me," I tell Bernard.

"Don't be ridiculous," he says.

A tired-looking doctor emerges from the swinging doors wearing a white coat and carrying a clipboard. It's like a scene out of a movie. We both rise to our feet as he approaches. The doctor's mouth is expressionless, but his dark brown eyes appear anxious and his furrowed brow telegraphs tragedy.

"Are you Mr. Palmer's brother?" he asks Bernard.

"No, just a friend of the family." Bernard nods toward me. "Hallie is his oldest daughter."

The doctor glances down at his clipboard and then back up to Bernard in his blue button-down shirt and neat gray slacks, as if given the choice between the two of us, Bernard is the official representative. Obviously my Lucky Charms T-shirt with the torn jeans does not exactly exude an air of responsibility. But I thought I was only going to a frat party.

"There are ten children?" The doctor asks this as if maybe there's a typo in his notes.

Bernard nods his head up and down. "Eric, the oldest, is twenty, and the twin boys just turned two months old," he explains in his new capacity as Palmer family spokesperson.

The doctor sighs as if this is going to be worse than he thought. He squints into the fluorescent light and then shifts his gaze back to me. "I'm very sorry but I have some bad news. Your father succumbed to a massive coronary. And your mother is in a state of shock. We're going to have to keep her here, at least for a day or two."

It's way too much to comprehend. Life without dad is unfathomable. My mind comes to a crashing halt, suddenly there is no oxygen, and I feel something tear deep inside of me.

"Is there a relative who can help you in the meantime?" asks the doctor.

"Mom has a sister." I somehow manage to get this out even though my mouth is now the Sahara Desert and my stomach continues to experience an elevator-drop sensation.

"All right then. Why don't you go home and try to get some rest and come back tomorrow to see your mother."

"Can't I see her now?" I ask.

"I'm afraid it wouldn't be a good idea. We've given her some medication to help her sleep. Come back tomorrow and hopefully she'll be feeling better." He pats me on the shoulder and turns to leave. On the way out I see him exchange looks with the receptionist that seem to say, "Oh God, is this ever a bad one." Which is not nearly so reassuring as his gentle tone of voice and comforting pat on my shoulder.

FOUR

BERNARD AND I SLOWLY WALK OUT TO THE CAR. THE SKY IS STILL dark and snow swirls and spins under the glare of the parking lot lights like bits of lost soul. No one else is on the road and the town is covered in a deep blanket of white. It's as if someone suddenly took the needle off the record player and the world went silent. I open the window on the passenger side and let the cold wet flakes melt on my face.

Bernard turns down Main Street and we pass all the darkened stores locked up for the night. A light glows in the back of the card and stationery store, but that's only because Mrs. Jamison thinks the three live-in cats need it to navigate at night. We pass Bernard's antiques store, The Sweet Buy and Buy, and a silver tea service glints in the display window.

A few houses still have Christmas lights up and plastic Santas on the front lawns. Alongside the curb lie discarded trees with half their needles missing, patiently waiting for the garbagemen to take them away.

Bernard offers to come inside, even to stay overnight if I want. And if he didn't have the girls to look after I might take him up on it. But I tell him that Louise and I can manage. He gives me a hug and it's at that moment I finally start to cry, heaving big sobs that make me lose my breath.

Bernard switches off the engine and accompanies me into the house after all. The second Louise sees us she knows that dad is dead. Her eyes are already red from crying and her face is blotchy, but the tears come all over again. We hug each other and it feels as if all of our childhood fights and other sibling nonsense was such a long time ago. Another lifetime.

I try to describe what's going on with mom but can't even remember what the doctor said was wrong with her. Bernard is the one who explains to Louise that she's in shock and will probably be okay tomorrow. He goes into the kitchen and, after a few minutes of kitchen noises, returns with two mugs of hot cocoa. As we sit looking at each other across the dining room table it grows cold.

"Eric will be here in a few hours." Louise finally breaks the silence. "Aunt Lala is flying in from London tomorrow."

"So what do we do?" I ask Bernard, since he's the full-fledged grown-up. Louise also looks to Bernard for counsel.

"You go to bed," he states firmly. "When the little ones wake up, your hands will be full. I'll come back tomorrow to help you sort things out." Before leaving, Bernard gives us both big hugs and kisses, but I notice he doesn't say anything while doing so, such as "Don't worry" or "Everything will be okay." It's pretty obvious that there's a *lot* to worry about and that everything will *not* be okay.

As Louise and I trudge up the stairs it dawns on me that I no longer have a place to sleep in this house. With eight children still living at home, space is rather at a premium. Darlene now has my bed, Teddy and Davy share a tiny room with bunk beds, and Francie and Lillian have a converted attic space with a sloped roof in which they share a trundle bed. The youngest twins, Reginald and Rodney, have one crib in Mom and Dad's room and another opposite their bedroom door in the hallway.

"I guess you'd better sleep in Mom and Dad's room," says Louise.

Before going to bed I check on the babies, who are sound asleep, and quickly realize it's impossible to spend the night in that room. Dad's watch is on the bedside table and his wallet and black pocket comb sit atop the dresser, all waiting for him to get up in the morning. Eventually I grab a blanket out of the linen closet and hunker down on the couch in the living room. There's nothing left to do but sit and try not to think anymore and wait for morning.

However, sleep doesn't come for a long time. The house creaks as if it's badly docked at a rickety old pier and about to come loose. And tears continue to roll down my cheeks as I stare up at the ceiling.

FIVE

THE TWINS CRYING IN STEREO WAKES ME FROM A DEEP BUT DIS-
turbed sleep filled with upsetting dreams. There's a foggy moment when I'm not registering all that has just happened
and then it quickly rushes back and I remember that Dad is
dead. Those howling children will never know their father.
Maybe they're the lucky ones, since you can't miss what you
didn't really have in the first place.

Their cries grow and it doesn't appear to be the moment to
philosophize about the rest of our lives. Climbing off the couch
I feel like the monster being raised from the dead in a late-night
creature feature, as if I haven't moved a muscle in years and it's
an effort just to lift my arms. Thrumming inside my head over
and over like the bass notes in a heavy metal song are the words:
"Dad is dead, Dad is dead, Dad is dead."

I turn on the hall light and peer down at the red faces
and grasping fingers. There's no point in trying to isolate the
problem—they both need to be changed, held, and fed. The hall
clock says half past seven. At least I had a solid fifty minutes of
sleep.

To Mom's credit she doesn't dress the identical-looking boys alike, and she also keeps a little blue ribbon around the ankle of one of them. Though that's for Dad, since Mom can always tell her kids apart. Only I can't, and therefore don't know which one is Rodney and which is Reginald, nor are there any labels on the cribs. But I suppose at this age they don't know the difference either and so "Hey, you" won't exactly trigger an identity crisis.

Dawn is tinting the horizon pink and I'm halfway through feeding the second twin his bottle when ten-year-old Davy comes crawling into the kitchen on all fours, apparently motivated by his Spider-Man pajamas.

"Where's Mommy?" He quickly glances around the room as if she may be trying to hide somewhere.

"She took Daddy to the hospital." I give the reply that I've been going over and over in my head all morning. "He doesn't feel well."

I have absolutely no desire to break this news to the kids. Hopefully Mom will be home this afternoon and she can do it.

"Oh," says Davy as he climbs up the counter in Spider-Man fashion to retrieve a bowl for his cereal. "Does Daddy have a stomachache?"

"Yeah." I wipe the faces of the boys with their bibs. "He has a stomachache."

"That's because it was Francie's birthday last night and we ate cake and ice cream," Davy informs me. "It was really good."

"Hey Davy, do you know which one of the twins is wearing the blue ribbon on his ankle?"

"Roddy," answers Davy.

He scoops generic cereal into his bowl from a big plastic bin on the counter. The minute Davy tips the full gallon of milk toward the bowl I can see what's going to happen, only I'm trying to burp Roddy and don't make the save in time.

"Whoops," says Davy as the milk washes over the top of the bowl like a giant wave, taking half the cereal with it.

"Don't worry, I can still eat it," he assures me while sliding the bowl through the puddle, which is now trickling between the leaves in the table and creating rivulets across the linoleum floor.

I put Roddy back in his cradle and look on the counter for paper towels, briefly forgetting that the only disposable items allowed in this house are diapers, and reach for one of the many neatly folded rags under the sink.

Darlene comes bounding into the kitchen trailing six-year-old Francie and twenty-month-old Lillian. The two youngest girls have purple Magic Marker covering their hands and faces.

"Hallie ith back!" exclaims Darlene. "Where'th Mommy?" There's a faint note of concern in her voice.

"Mommy took Daddy to the doctor because he doesn't feel well." I eject the words "hospital" and "sick" from my story.

The front door opens. It must be Mom! Thank goodness.

"How's Dad?" Eric shouts before he's even through the door.

S I X

Eric's hulking frame takes up practically the entire archway. Though he may not resemble Dad when it comes to physical features like hair color and jaw construction, Eric is built exactly like Dad—big, strong, and square. His cheeks are flushed from the cold and snowflakes dot his brown crew cut.

"Oh my God!" Eric correctly guesses the worst.

He and I escape to the living room so that we can talk. However, Teddy is plunked in front of the PlayStation blowing up a city. Eric follows me upstairs to the room that Louise now shares with Darlene, and I switch on the overhead light. Louise is the only person I haven't seen yet this morning. She's in bed looking every bit the shot-down pilot, lying on her back with eyes closed and enormous earphones covering the sides of her head.

I yank off the headset. "Louise, get up! Eric is home."

She opens her eyes and stares up at us, blinking into the light.

We fill Eric in on the details of last night, bursting into tears at the end. He sits there on the edge of Darlene's bed in stunned silence, as if we might eventually revise the story to have a happier ending.

"Someone has to go and pick up Mom at the hospital," I finally say. "I guess it should be Eric."

Louise raises no objections. But then Louise has never been what one would call an avid volunteer when it comes to family life.

"We'll get all the kids dressed, clean up the kitchen, and shovel the driveway," I say.

The next two hours are spent scrambling eggs, giving baths to the twins, and doing several loads of wash. It's amazing that one day of clothes and nightwear for this family can result in two full loads of laundry. A repairman once informed my mother that she was the first person he ever knew to actually *wear out* a lint trap. There's an ironing board in the corner but I decide that, under the circumstances, gravity will have to take care of the wrinkles.

When that's finished it's already eleven o'clock, the twins are hungry again, and it's time to figure out what's for lunch. I tell Louise to call the pizza parlor and order two pies because I don't want the kitchen messed up just as Mom is arriving home.

"But Eric's got the station wagon," she says.

At first I assume this is just another one of Louise's excuses to get out of doing something. But then I realize that Dad's minivan, which no else one but Mom was ever allowed to drive, has taken on a sacred air. Only there's too much to do and not enough time or money to be become superstitious.

"Take the van." I hand her the keys off the rack next to the refrigerator as if we toss them back and forth all the time. She doesn't take her road test for another month, but under the circumstances I can't imagine that anyone will make a fuss.

Before Louise can take a step toward the garage the phone rings, and for some reason we're both equally startled by this, jumping slightly and then staring at each other rather than lunging for the receiver.

"Maybe it's Mom," I say hopefully.

Louise grabs the receiver. After listening to some high-pitched squawking on the other end, she places her hand over the mouthpiece and whispers, "Aunt Vi." We both give each other the Aunt Vi eye roll. She's a talker, as Mom likes to say about her mother's vivacious younger sister, our Great-Aunt Vivian.

Aunt Vi must finally take a breath, because I watch as Louise quietly says, "He passed away." It's eerie to hear the phrase actually spoken, at least in reference to our dad, and I'm impressed that Louise has opted for the more churchlike version. I probably would have just said that he died.

There's a tremendous crash in the living room followed by a cry of pain and then shouts of accusation. Running toward the noise, I find Francie on the floor with her mouth wide open in protest, eyes squeezed shut in pain, and hands gripping a spot slightly to the left of her forehead.

I lift Francie in my arms and carry her to the downstairs bathroom, which I know from experience has the best combination of outdoor and artificial light for inspecting wounds and removing slivers. There's a nice gash right along her hairline, but it doesn't appear wide enough or deep enough to merit stitches.

Meantime, the phone rings again. Louise must have picked it up because there was only one ring.

While I'm wiping away the blood on Francie's head, Louise pokes her head into the bathroom. "What happened?"

"The girls were walking across the furniture in the living room and she fell." Francie doesn't dispute this version of events. Nor does Louise ask questions because the younger ones had of course learned the game from us in the first place.

"Uncle Alan is on the phone," reports Louise. "He wants to know when the funeral is."

Funeral? Such a thing had never occurred to me. But yes, I suppose there would have to be a funeral.

"Should I just tell him we'll call back when we know more?" suggests Louise.

"Yeah, that's good. Do that." I find a Band-Aid and place it on Francie's gashed forehead.

The doorbell rings. It must be Mom—I'll bet she didn't know that Eric was on his way, so she took a cab but doesn't have her keys. Eric must have accidentally locked the door when he left.

SEVEN

THROWING OPEN THE FRONT DOOR, I FIND A WOMAN WHO LOOKS remarkably like my mother, only her hair is coppery red instead of chestnut brown, she's about three inches shorter than Mom, and she's wearing two different gloves—one black and one red.

"Aunt Lala!" I shout, and hug her tightly right there on the threshold. Her name is really Lorraine, but when my mother was young she couldn't pronounce it, and thus ended up with Lala. No one ever called her anything else after that.

"How's your father?" she asks hopefully.

I suddenly realize that Aunt Lala's been on a plane from London and hasn't heard the news. But from the way I stop hugging and start staring she immediately understands.

"Oh dear Lord!" The corners of her mouth tremble and she closes her eyes tightly, as if preparing for a storm. Long drawn-out sobs begin to shake her body. I help her through to the dining room and into a seat at the table. Tears stream from her eyes and she covers her mouth with her hands. A high-pitched screech comes from the kitchen and I realize the twins are still perched atop the table out there. Not that they can go anywhere, but I think I'm supposed to keep an eye and not just an ear on them. And where have the older boys disappeared to? I wonder.

"Hang on—I have to get the babies."

The doorbell rings again.

Bernard is standing on the front porch holding a casserole dish and a laundry bag, which he immediately sets down in the entrance hall table to give me the kind of hug reserved for people who have just experienced a major loss. "Gil is going to stay home and watch the girls today. And I packed up your clothes that were in the summerhouse."

The phone starts ringing again. Louise must have picked it up again because it stops.

Bernard lifts the casserole dish and follows me toward the kitchen. "I brought leftover baby back ribs à la Bernard and my super-special Stockton shrimp scampi—hardly enough to feed everybody, but perhaps good for a little snack."

Over time one begins to notice that most of Bernard's recipes manage to work his name in there somewhere.

"Unfortunately we finished all the cauliflower," continues Bernard.

"The kids hate cauliflower," I say.

"I must admit, I couldn't eat it for a year after what happened."

There's no doubt that I'm distracted at the moment; however, a cauliflower tragedy just isn't ringing a bell.

"Excuse me?"

"The brilliant French chef Bernard Loiseau searched non-stop for a way to transform cauliflower from an unsophisticated vegetable into a dazzling side dish by caramelizing it. He blanched, strained, puréed, and then finally committed suicide after it failed to impress the critics." Bernard stares at me as if he can't believe a civilized human being could not know such a thing. He harrumphs loudly and adds, "Yet you never find any award-winning dishes named after critics, now do you?"

Louise appears in the front hallway. She gives Bernard a nod and dutifully reports, "Eric called from the hospital. Mom is still in shock and she isn't coming home."

"What?" I might be in shock, too. Nothing makes sense anymore.

"She's not yet recovered from the blow," Bernard translates.

"I know, I mean, what are we supposed to do?"

"Eric says the hospital wants to know what to do with the body," Louise somberly continues.

A loud sob comes from the dining room. Louise and Bernard appear startled.

"Aunt Lala is here," I explain. "She just found out."

"Maybe she knows what to tell them," suggests Louise. "Eric is waiting on the other end."

I walk into the dining room where Aunt Lala is still wearing her purple coat with an enormous handbag strapped across her chest. Strands of frizzy red hair hang down over florid cheeks, and her face is streaked with mascara, lending a clownlike atmosphere to the scene. Aunt Lala's naturally bright coloring goes a long way in explaining the red hair and freckled skin that pops up in every second or third Palmer child. Aunt Lala leans forward until she runs out of breath and then leans way back and loudly blows her nose into a fast-disintegrating tissue.

"Mom is sort of in shock and so they want to know what we should do with Dad's body," I say.

Aunt Lala's eyes open wide and it looks as if she's about to say something but all that comes out is another huge wail.

I step back into the front hall where Louise and Bernard are waiting. "She's not sure," I say as we hear her get started on another round of weeping.

"I know," says Bernard. "Call Pastor Costello!"

Bernard isn't a churchgoer, but he's quite fond of the regular poker games that Pastor Costello holds with some of the guys in the church basement.

"I thought of that," I say. "He's on that mission to Cambodia."

"That's right," says Bernard. "I've been so busy recovering from the holidays that I haven't been to play poker in weeks."

"Does he have an assistant or a temporary replacement?" I ask.

Louise brightens. "Yeah, there's some woman filling in. Mom really likes her."

"Tell Eric to stay at the hospital with Mom and call us back about the other stuff in a little while," I say to Louise. "Then find out what happened to the rest of the kids."

Louise disappears into the living room and Bernard brings the casserole to the kitchen. Aunt Lala has quieted down a bit and I decide it's a good time to explain to her that we haven't yet told the kids, especially since they'll all be gathering for lunch soon. That is, if I can ever get some lunch on the table.

When I return to the kitchen in order to make Aunt Lala a cup of tea, Bernard is examining the contents of the refrigerator and frowning.

"Aunt Lala is really jet-lagged—she took a train to London, caught an overnight flight to New York, and then flew to Cleveland and didn't sleep a wink." I don't know why I'm bothering to make excuses for her. Aunt Lala is very sweet and kind, but the truth is that she can't manage anything. It takes her an hour to get ready for a trip to the store and then she usually forgets the shopping list and goes to the bus station instead. According to Aunt Vi, if my mother hadn't taken her to school and back every day, it's entirely possible that Aunt Lala would still be in the tenth grade.

"Yes, she must refresh herself after an international flight," says Bernard. "Do you have a number for the church office?"

I find Mom's address book on a shelf underneath the counter. "It must be in here somewhere. Do you mind? I have to change the twins."

"It's Sunday," says Bernard. He looks down at his wrist-watch. "Church will be letting out any minute."

Bernard knows when all the churches let out because often-times people stop in his store afterward to browse or pick up a gift.

"You're right," I say. "Maybe I should just run over there now."

The phone goes off again but Louise must answer it from upstairs.

"I'll go with you," says Bernard.

Louise appears in the doorway to the kitchen. "Eric needs some insurance papers that he says should be in Dad's filing cabinet."

"Oh great," I say. "I don't know anything about insurance."

"The kids are out in the back having a snowball war with their coats unzipped and most of them aren't wearing hats or scarves," reports Louise.

"Call them inside," I say. "It's time to eat anyway."

"Okay," says Bernard in his best team leader voice. "Why doesn't Hallie show me where the insurance forms are kept and I'll sort that out, Louise can go consult with the minister, and Hallie will serve the lunch."

The phone rings.

"I'll answer the phone," Bernard says to Louise, "and you call the children in to wash up for lunch."

The twins begin crying from their new location on the din-ing room table. Apparently Aunt Lala's tears are contagious. The whole scene is like a public service ad for birth control.

The front doorbell rings. Louise disappears, in the opposite direction.

"I'll take care of the twins," says Bernard, though now sounding slightly frantic, "and you answer the door." Meantime the phone is still ringing.

I open the front door and six women between the ages of forty and sixty all seize upon me at once. "Oh, you poor little darlings!" One of them practically shouts as she gives me a half nelson of a hug while the others bustle past and begin removing their coats. Within minutes their things are neatly hung in the front hall closet and there's a row of sturdy pocketbooks lined up next to the door. They wear wool suits with large brooches on the collar or patterned dresses that fall slightly below the knee. The fact that they travel under a cloud of pungent perfume and on the weekend basically rules out social workers. I vaguely recognize one woman from a long-ago Sunday school class. I'm pretty sure she was the teacher who, when you burped without excusing yourself, used to loudly declare, "That was well brought up, but apparently you were not."

Then it dawns on me—churchwomen!

EIGHT

THE HALF-DOZEN WOMEN IN CREPE-SOLED SHOES PULL APRONS over their church clothes and instantly go into battle formation. The smiling plump one takes a fussy twin from Bernard. The taller one who wears her hair in a bun grabs the other. They make sounds of clucking and cooing, but their expressions clearly state bathing and feeding. A third woman, the one with her glasses hanging on a gold chain, moves for the ringing phone, scanning for a pen and message pad on the way, but bringing her pocketbook along just in case. Two more veer off in the direction of the kitchen.

The last woman, whom I vaguely recognize as someone who once presided over a table of holiday wreaths for sale in the church basement and wore a bracelet of weapon's-grade masking tape, explains that the interim minister, Nancy Gordon, will be along soon.

"How many of you will be taking meals at the house?" she asks.

"I've lost track," I say with embarrassment.

She's off to take a head count, sensible shoes going *squeakety-squeak* across the wooden floor. The entire front hall is now filled to capacity with huge plastic containers, the contents of which, there's no doubt in my mind, could keep a large family in good working order for several weeks.

It's like being liberated by a powerful but friendly army. This is the amazingly organized and energetic militia that runs the church school, craft group, bake sale, white elephant sale, and charity auction—basically everything except the buildings and grounds committee. (That's left to the husbands, who use the meetings as an excuse to play poker.)

These capable women belong to a parallel universe of babies, PTA meetings, Scouts, and Little League. They know instinctively where the peanut butter and jelly are kept without having to ask. They've presided over many an illness, bereavement, wedding, shower, christening, and accident recovery. Their numbers move rapidly, speak in code, and hum with a Situation Room sense of purpose. The only groups of women who might present a more skilled front in the face of tragedy are the wives of soldiers and miners.

"Well! I guess we can go and search for the insurance now." Bernard is also recovering from the surprise attack, but equally relieved.

Together we thread our way through the cooing, bustling, and clanging of the twins being changed, cleaning supplies inventoried, and meals being prepared. On the way up the stairs Bernard is close behind me and sniffing the air loudly. Finally he says, "Hallie, I've been smelling mildew or *something* ever since I arrived, and I believe it's coming from you!"

Putting my hands up to my hair, which is hanging loose almost to my waist, I say, "Oh no! My hair stinks from the party last night. Is it okay if I take a quick shower? The minister is coming..."

"Of course, just point me in the direction of the files," says Bernard, now pinching his nose with his fingers.

Looking through my parents' closet I find that Dad's paperwork is not quite as organized as Mom's kitchen. In the corner sits a file cabinet chockablock with bills, bank statements, appliance manuals, envelopes for weekly church donations, loose receipts, and even a few old magazines on house construction.

Bernard digs through the mess and in a somber voice announces, "This might take a while."

"Yeah. I guess when you arrive home every evening to all these kids and an urgent to-do list of home repairs, it's not that easy to maintain a system."

There are signs that Dad planned to eventually become organized: an unopened pack of file folders and labels, some empty three-ring binders, and a blank ledger. In the meantime, most papers have been stuffed back into the envelopes in which they arrived. Check stubs fill the cracks between the piles of envelopes.

Tackling the mess with great gusto, Bernard waves me off in the direction of the shower. When I return twenty minutes later, he's humming "When You Walk Through a Storm" from *Carousel* and sitting in front of three neat stacks of papers with his back toward me.

"I've made a separate pile for anything that has either the logo of an insurance company or a government return address, since your dad worked for the state of Ohio and they have their own benefit scheme," he explains.

While describing the new system Bernard looks up at me and knocks over a freshly organized tower of files so that the papers scatter across the floor. "Whatever have you done?" he asks.

"Nothing. I haven't touched one envelope."

"No, I mean to your hair!" exclaims Bernard.

I look in the mirror and indeed, my head resembles a strawberry blond Chia pet.

"There wasn't any conditioner," I inform him. "And the hair dryer is broken."

"I'll pick up both at the drugstore," says Bernard. "In the meantime you're going to have to do a Jackie O. headscarf because *that* is not a good look unless you're planning to audition for the musical *Annie.*"

"But you always say that women who are tall and thin can get away with anything."

"I meant anything short of making people think that Halloween has come nine months early this year."

The search continues. I find a handful of papers that are yellow with age. One is an award that Dad received for being an Eagle Scout. Another is for perfect attendance in high school, which is pretty amazing since Dad grew up on a farm about six miles outside of town. Then there are his varsity letters for everything that ends with the word *ball*—baseball, football, and basketball. I was aware that Dad had been a star athlete, since there's a box of trophies in the garage, but it's disconcerting to see all these things now that he's gone.

Bernard finishes sorting through one pile and starts on another. "It appears that your father sends the checks on time, even if it's only a day before they're due. So there's a good chance whatever coverage he has is up-to-date." Bernard looks over at me, stares at my hair again, and begins to laugh. "It's a good thing Craig isn't here."

"I'll pull it back as soon as it's dry," I promise him.

"You know what they say," Bernard replies mysteriously.

"No, what do they say? That no one has ever let their hair dry naturally?"

"Same old coiffure, boyfriend secure. Brand-new hair, boyfriend beware." Bernard gives me a knowing glance.

Last night is a blur, only I can't help but wonder how long

Bernard was in the doorway of the attic before we noticed him. Is it possible that he saw something—Josh's hand on my knee? Or does Bernard simply know me too well? I feel my face flush and decide the best strategy for now is to ignore him.

Bernard clutches his chest and breathes deeply. "Ever since we left the hospital I've been experiencing chest pains. Gil says I'm going to be the first person to have a psychosomatic heart attack."

"Hey, look at this!" I dump out an envelope containing all of our birth certificates.

"*Incroyable*," says Bernard. "Your tribe has created a full-time job for someone down at the county clerk's office."

I arrange them in chronological order before returning them to the envelope, with Mom's and Dad's on top.

"Keep your dad's out in case we need it for something," instructs Bernard.

In removing Dad's birth certificate I can't help but notice the birth year is not the same as Mom's—hers is two years later—and yet that's impossible because they're both the same age.

"Can they make a mistake on your birth certificate?" I ask Bernard.

"I suppose anything is possible," he says. "You constantly read stories about people who go into the hospital for a kidney transplant and come out with an amputated leg instead."

"Here's something!" I pull out what appear to be policies from a big manila envelope.

Bernard flips through to hospitalization coverage. "This is pretty good—only a ten percent deductible." Then he moves on to another sheaf of stapled papers and points to a section with the heading Death Benefit.

I instinctively turn my head away.

"I'll read it," he offers. "In the event of . . ." then he switches to mumble, mumble, mumble, ". . . the sum of fifty thousand dollars shall be paid to the family of . . ." mumble, mumble, mumble. "It's not much money."

"We don't have much money."

"Look through here for anything about additional coverage." He hands me a stack of papers. "Sometimes people have a supplemental policy or one with another company."

After a few minutes of sifting through papers Bernard reports, "He borrowed ten thousand dollars from the credit union last August."

"Oh gosh, part of that was money he gave me for college!"

"Don't worry, it doesn't have to be paid back anytime soon."

I flip through the pages of the insurance policy. In the health section I find that Mom and Dad both received extra points for being nonsmokers. However, at the bottom is Mom's birthday across from Dad's, and once again it's two years later.

"Excuse me for a minute," I say.

Bernard looks up to make sure I'm not having some sort of an episode. "Are you okay?"

"Yeah, I mean, there's something strange going on here with Mom's birthday. I just want to ask Aunt Lala. She's the youngest sister. Mom is the middle and Aunt Florence was the oldest."

"Now that your hair is almost dry, may I suggest a babushka?"

Glancing in the mirror I note that my fright wig looks even worse now and grab a baseball cap out of Teddy's room. Then I twist up the bottom, stick it all underneath, and tuck the loose strands behind my ears.

I find Aunt Lala on the couch having tea with one of the church ladies, who introduces herself as Vera Armstrong. Heaven only knows what they're talking about, but they both stop the moment they see me and look horrified, as if I'm a ghost. In fact, their looks are so disconcerting that I quickly check the front of my sweatshirt for boogers and food stains.

"I, uh, I just wanted to ask about Mom's birthday," I say to Aunt Lala. "Because I always thought that she and Dad were the same age." I hold up the insurance policy.

A look of panic crosses Aunt Lala's face. "Yes, well . . ." She takes a swallow of her tea and pauses for a moment. "I think you'd better talk to your mother about that."

"What do you mean? Aren't you—I mean, how old—"

The doorbell rings and the woman sitting next to Aunt Lala rises and steers me toward the door. "That will be the minister who's coming to speak with you, Hallie."

NINE

MRS. ARMSTRONG IS INDEED CORRECT AND AT THE DOOR STANDS Father Costello's temporary replacement, a woman in her late twenties with long sandy-brown hair and gentle eyes.

"Hello, I'm Reverend Nancy Gordon," she says. "I'm very sorry to hear about your loss. I only met your dad a few times, but he was obviously a very fine man."

The churchwomen usher the two of us into the living room. Reverend Gordon says that she stopped by the hospital to visit Mom. She's sympathetic sounding, yet doesn't speak to me as if I'm a child, the way some adults still do. If anything it's the reverse, and Reverend Gordon talks to me as if we're the same age.

"So you asked my mother about the arrangements?" I'm hopeful since I really have no idea about what to do. I mean, I assume Dad wanted to be buried, but I'm not sure if we own plots anywhere and how one goes about arranging such a thing. I haven't even been a regular churchgoer since age fourteen. If God is everywhere, the way my parents claim, it doesn't seem necessary to have a designated time and place for chewing the fat each week.

I sit down on the couch and Reverend Gordon seats herself

alongside of me. She looks me directly in the eyes and says, "Hallie, your mom is still in shock . . . and it may take a while . . . later today they're going to transfer her to the Dalewood Rehabilitation Center about five miles from—"

I leap up and shout, "Dalewood—that's where the crazy people are. My mother isn't *crazy!*"

Reverend Gordon rises, too, as if we're playing Simon Says. "Of course she's not crazy. Your mom is just experiencing some depression and they can help her there."

"Dalewood!" I drop back down on the couch and so does Reverend Gordon, though much more gracefully than I. That used to be the big joke in school, "Did you just get out of Dalewood?" Even the teachers would threaten to ship us off to Dalewood.

"I think we should proceed with the funeral arrangements," Reverend Gordon suggests. "If your mother is able to come, that's fine, and if not, then there can always be a memorial service later on—even a year from now."

I just stare at her. Funeral? Memorial Service? *Dalewood!* The words start to lose their meanings. Snow is whirling outside the window and I feel like walking out into the middle of it.

"How about this coming Thursday?" she suggests. "Perhaps you can send something about your father over to the newspaper and say the funeral will be held at the church on Thursday at two P.M. Or if you'd rather, I can stop back here tonight and then fax it from my office."

"Okay. I'll—I'll send something over."

Reverend Gordon asks me a number of questions about the service—who Dad might have wanted to speak, his favorite scripture, songs, or poems. But unfortunately I don't have any answers for her. The dinner table conversation usually revolved around reprimanding whoever was dropping peas into someone else's milk or shoving bacon down his throat like a sword swallower, rather than recitations of anyone's favorite verse. Dad's favorite *phrases,* on the other hand, are a cinch: *Who* is going to pay for that? *What* were you thinking? *Don't* make me pull over! What do I look like to you, a *bank?* Somehow I doubt they're the kinds of things generally incorporated into eulogies. Placing head in hands, I attempt to come up with something slightly more inspired.

The Reverend Gordon must interpret my loss for words as a sign that it's time for an evaluation of my own mental state, obviously concerned that a mother-daughter suite at Dalewood might be on the horizon.

"Are you all right?" She places a comforting hand on my shoulder and her eyes search to meet mine.

What choice do I have? If I lose it, then all these kids get dumped on Louise. Speaking of which, "Where *is* Louise?" I shout out to no one in particular. She should probably be in on this stuff.

A churchwoman appears from around the corner and, while wiping her hands on one of my mother's aprons, gives a quick report on the state of the household. "Louise is upstairs having a rest, the children are downstairs being led in games by Agatha, the twins were fed and are down for a nap, and Eric will be home for dinner after accompanying your mother to the rest facility."

So that's going to be our euphemism for the acorn academy— a *rest facility.*

Bernard comes downstairs to say that he wasn't able to find any supplemental insurance policies. However, he did locate a map of the cemetery where Dad's parents are buried, and it would appear that my folks filled out some forms and intended to buy plots there as well, but never did.

"Eric and I had better go over there tomorrow," I say.

Bernard leans in close in case anyone is listening. "Don't pay extra for monthly flowers. It's one red geranium after the next. We'll do it ourselves."

"Mom's in Dalewood," I tell him. My voice quivers and I can feel tears burning the corners of my eyes.

Without missing a beat Bernard says, "A little R and R is probably the best thing."

"But it's a mental hospital!" My voice involuntarily rises an octave.

"It doesn't mean anything is wrong," he states with conviction. "Why, when the great Broadway lyricist Lorenz Hart was institutionalized at Doctors Hospital in New York, his partner Richard Rodgers simply moved into the next room, had them send up the piano Cole Porter used when he was a patient, and they wrote a show together!"

As always, Bernard, the King of Denial, has a theatrical anecdote for the situation. Only *he* could think to suggest that going to Dalewood might be just the thing to spark Mom's creativity.

Reverend Gordon chimes in with words of encouragement, but doesn't go so far as to suggest that Mom might very well pen the next *Pal Joey* during her confinement.

After giving me an Ethel Merman–sized hug, Bernard gathers his things and promises to call after the girls are in bed. Reverend Gordon follows him out the front door, and I can see that they stop in the driveway together to talk for a moment.

Soon afterward the churchwomen exit as well, though not before leaving dinner on the table and pledging to check on us in the morning and drop off some more hot dishes then, too. Apparently they've evaluated Aunt Lala for proficiency in the core competencies of running a household and taken the view that after recuperating from the long journey, she'll be able to handle things until Mom returns. Well, I've got some news for them. While Aunt Lala might talk a good domestic game, anything she finally manages to do always has to be redone. Or as Uncle Fred likes to say about her master's degree in medievalism that's been in the works for almost two decades, Aunt Lala seems to be several knights short of a crusade.

TEN

Once the twins are down for the night and the younger children are put to bed, or at least imprisoned in their rooms and operating handheld video games beneath the covers, Eric turns to Aunt Lala, Louise, and me, and states, "We need to have a family meeting." The four of us sit down around the dining room table and Teddy silently hovers in the entranceway.

"What about Teddy?" I ask Eric.

Teddy is twelve now and definitely not stupid. He may not look very imposing, being string-bean thin with jug-handle ears; however, his wide, keen eyes don't miss much. Teddy is quiet, too, in the same way that Mom can be. You're never really sure if he's okay and just thinking, or if he's really worried about something and not saying anything. Once he waited four hours to tell anyone that his arm was broken.

When Eric arrived back from the hospital he took Teddy out for a burger and broke the news to him. I sure didn't have the strength. And it's hard to tell if Louise is still freaking out about Dad, or if she's just trying to avoid doing any work. For every hour that Louise spends downstairs, she's up in the bedroom for three, instant messaging with her boyfriend, Brandt, or lying on her bed and writing in a journal.

"We're going to try and figure out what to do," Eric calls over to Teddy. "Would you like to join us?"

I'm sort of amazed to hear Eric sounding so grown-up. Usually when the two of us are together we fall back into our old patterns of making fun of each other—I tease him about being a hulking sports star and he jibes me about being the black sheep of the family.

Teddy continues to stand in the archway without acknowledging Eric's invitation and so we decide to go ahead. Only where do you start when time has been shattered into splinters and grief sits as immovable as the dining room table.

Aunt Lala finally begins, "Your dad's brother, Alan, is going to fly from Camp Drum in upstate New York where he's running the army base."

I can only *hope* that she told him the right day.

"Aunt Vi—your great-aunt—can't leave Uncle Russ since he had the stroke," says Aunt Lala. "I suppose that's it for the relatives."

Mom and Aunt Lala had an older sister named Florence but she died in some sort of swimming accident in her twenties. At least that's what we kids have always been told. Every time the name *Florence* is spoken they immediately say "God rest her soul."

"There's no way of telling how long Mom might be at Dalewood," says Eric. "No one over there will get anywhere close to giving an answer. You'd think I was asking for the nuclear launch codes." He pauses and then looks directly at me. "But I'm sure she won't be there for more than a week or two."

Eric keeps a measured tone in making his responses and observations, the way Dad always did when talking to adults. It's obvious that he's been very upset the past couple days—since arriving home he's worn that same set jaw and furrowed brow that he gets only when about to make a crucial play in a football game. Eric has been leading sports teams since playing T-ball when he was six, and he instinctively knows that whatever feelings or emotions are expressed by the captain, so goes the team. This is good because the little kids are definitely taking their cues from his calm demeanor. Yet it also serves to make me wary of his optimism.

It becomes apparent that either Eric or I will have to stay at home for a while. And it becomes even more apparent that the leading candidate is *me*. Not so much because I'm the girl, though perhaps there's a little of that, but because Eric is on a full scholarship and studying accounting—a field that actually pays good money. Worst case, in two and a half years he'll graduate and help support the family if need be. My prospects in graphic design aren't nearly as good.

"Okay," I say. "I'll phone the bursar's office tomorrow to see if I can withdraw from my current classes and get a refund."

Eric claims to be aware that I'm drawing the short straw on this one, as he'll go back to Indiana on Monday, play football, and life will continue on much as it had before. He places his hand on mine, something he's never done before, looks directly into my eyes, as if we're making a blood pact, and says, "I promise that I'll make sure you finish school, even if I have to live at home after graduation."

"I'm sure it won't come to that," Aunt Lala chimes in.

"Money is going to be pretty tight." Eric states the obvious. "We can't afford baby-sitters or day care. I mean, just with what we spend on food and mortgage payments—"

"I'll take care of the kids," I assure him. Ever since Rev. Gordon uttered the word *Dalewood,* I guess I've known it would end up like this.

"I'll check on your mother in the morning," says Aunt Lala. "I'm sure she'll be fine in a day or two. It was just such a sudden shock is all."

"I'll go with you," Teddy announces from his place in the doorway. He's such a quiet shadowy kid it's easy to forget that he's in the room.

We look at one another but nobody objects.

"I suppose it's okay," says Eric. "In the morning I'd better call my coach and tell him that I'll be back Friday night. There's a championship game on Saturday."

It's true that Eric enjoys football, and Dad certainly loved the fact that he had a superstar son, but we both realize he's not returning for his dedication to the game so much as the necessity of hanging on to that four-year scholarship. A fifty-thousand-dollar insurance policy is hardly enough money to pay for one education, forget ten of them.

ELEVEN

SLEEPING ARRANGEMENTS ARE DISCUSSED AND WE TURN MOM and Dad's room over to Aunt Lala. I continue to crash on the living room couch and Eric uses the one in the basement. Before going to bed he helps me move the twins' cribs downstairs in case they wake up during the night.

It's after eleven when I finally tumble onto the couch, still in my clothes. Sleep is elusive and I decide if I'm still not drowsy in another twenty minutes, I'll take some of that knockout cold medicine Mom keeps in the cabinet above the refrigerator, though I don't want to be completely stoned if the boys start crying in the middle of the night.

Winter has frosted the living room windows with its icy blue breath and headlights move across the far wall whenever a car passes. One set of beams grows larger and I can hear the sound of tires crunching snow in the driveway.

The hall clock chimes midnight. I suddenly recall this TV show about a robber with a friend who worked at a hospital and tipped him off whenever the man of the house died so he could break in and steal stuff while everyone was preoccupied. Once the crook strolled right into a house after the

funeral with all the guests still there and looted the entire upstairs.

Sure enough, instead of hearing a knock or the doorbell, I
see a large shadowy figure attempting to peep in the windows. I
jump up to call for Eric when a light shines through the long
pane of glass next to the door. It occurs to me that a robber
probably wouldn't park the getaway car in the driveway, and I
remember the one person who has been visibly absent throughout this entire drama.

I open the front door and there's the bulky but familiar
Officer Rich standing with hat in one hand and heavy-duty
flashlight that doubles as a nightstick in the other. Officer Rich
has always been my safety net in times of trouble, and even
though there's nothing he can pull out of his law enforcement
bag of tricks to right this particular wrong, it's still a huge relief
to see him standing there.

After pushing the door open the rest of the way to accom-
modate his hefty frame, Officer Rich steps inside and we stand
in the dark front hall staring at each other for a moment.
Though he's known to be a warm and affectionate family man,
Officer Rich doesn't exactly go around hugging people. Finally
he puts his big arm around my shoulders and I switch on the
overhead light.

"I was testifying at a case in Cleveland for two days," he says.
"Jeanette called and told me what happened and I came as soon
as I could."

"Thanks," I say.

"How you holding up, kiddo?" he asks.

If another person called me "kiddo" I'd definitely be an-
noyed, but Officer Rich has never treated me like a child. If anything, it's always been just the opposite—he lets me in on stuff
that a lot of grown-ups don't even know about. At the end of the

day it's obvious that he really cares about the town, and after being the main patrolman here for thirty years, Officer Rich views us all as his personal charges, wanting us to be not only safe but happy.

"There's just so much to do that I haven't really stopped to think about it," I say. "I mean, I don't want to stop and think about it because I'm afraid I won't be able to get going again."

He nods with understanding and doesn't say anything, like when people are describing a crime and you don't want to cut them off before they've had a chance to rummage through their memory for all the details.

"Mom is taking it especially hard. They put her in . . . Dalewood." Only it's clear from the way I say the name that he's aware of what I'm really thinking.

"It's just until she's rested," he says in that deep, reassuring voice. "I know you kids always joke about Dalewood being the loony bin, but it's really a good place."

We sit down on the couch and Officer Rich continues, "Far be it from me to name names, but I could give you a list of people in this town who have spent time at Dalewood for everything from eating and sleeping disorders to drug and alcohol rehab to personality disorders and even bad cases of postpartum depression, and you'd be *very* surprised indeed. Not everyone who claims to be on vacation in this town is in the Bahamas." He italicizes the word *vacation*.

"I suppose," I say.

"You've watched too many movies about people being locked up in dark cells and pulling their hair out."

He's certainly right about that. And it dawns on me that he probably knows a lot about something else, too. Officer Rich often deals with records for the town clerk, especially with regard to deaths. "I always thought my parents were the same age—Dad's birthday is in April and Mom's is two weeks later in May of the same year. Dad used to joke about it—saying that April showers bring May flowers."

The normally perceptive Officer Rich looks at me as if he's totally flummoxed.

"But when I was sorting through the papers to find our insurance policies, I found their birth certificates and Mom's says she was born two years later than Dad!"

"Look." I hand the papers to Officer Rich and turn on the nearby lamp.

He takes out his reading glasses and examines the two documents.

"Do you think Mom changed it for some reason?" I ask.

"Changed her age or the certificate?" asks Officer Rich.

"The certificate—you know, like teenagers change their ID so they can get into bars." I suddenly realize that this probably isn't the kind of thing one should be mentioning to the local constabulary, especially considering that at eighteen and a half I'm firmly among the population of underaged. "I mean, that's what I've heard."

Officer Rich gives me a crooked smile to suggest that indeed he did not spring up with the flowers after yesterday's rain.

Holding the document up to the light, he squints at it. "No, this here is the real McCoy."

"Then why—"

"Maybe your parents were too young to marry without parental permission and so they pushed his age up a little higher to avoid having to wait." Officer Rich takes another look at my dad's birth certificate to see if the year has been altered.

"Are you kidding—my mother was the daughter his parents never had. In fact, I'm pretty sure I remember hearing that they gave the money for the down payment on our house!"

He starts to chuckle while handing me back the certificates. "What's so funny?" I ask.

"Folks can be peculiar about their age. There was a time not too long ago when a woman didn't want to be older than her husband. And then last week I had a lady down at the hospital insisting she was fifty-nine. She didn't have insurance, so they called her son to ask who was paying for the operation. He said, '*Insurance?* She's seventy-two years old and completely covered by Medicare!' "

"But Mom is claiming to be two years *older* than she actually is, not younger."

"Then probably she was the one who couldn't get permission from her parents," he suggests. "So they told a white lie."

"I suppose that's what happened." It would explain Aunt Lala's reaction. Though my mother isn't in favor of any kind of lying, no matter what the color.

"It's late," says Officer Rich as he rises. "And I've got to stop by the station to see the reports made while I was away and get a list of any lunatics who may be loose in our area."

This is meant to be a joke because rarely anything criminal ever happens around here, but I can tell Officer Rich is sorry he used the word *lunatics* under the circumstances.

We walk to the front door and he says, "I'll come by to check on things. The synagogue is just up the street." To anyone who doesn't live in town this might sound like an odd statement since Officer Rich, who is African American and has a St. Christopher statue on his dashboard, is the last person you would guess to be Jewish. And he isn't. There aren't more than a dozen Jewish families in town, and that's the problem. At least ten are required in order to hold daily prayers, and so he swings by the synagogue right before lunch every day and often makes up the tenth.

Fortunately he doesn't say "Call if you need anything," because I don't know what to say to that one anymore. Basically what I *need* is: Dad alive, Mom home, a lot of money, and, failing all of that, someone who wants to change diapers and feed and bathe twins all day long. Oh yeah, and someone to keep Aunt Lala from burning the house to the ground by putting bottles in a pot of water on the stove, turning the burner on high, and then taking the twins downstairs to the playroom and forgetting all about the bottles.

It's impossible to sleep. And I can't exactly call Bernard at one o'clock in the morning. Craig! He'd left several messages during the day, but it had been difficult to talk with all of the commotion around here. I curl up on the couch and dial his dorm room at the University of Minnesota. He sounds relieved to hear from me and still completely flabbergasted by what's happened. I tell him that the funeral is on Thursday afternoon.

"Then I'll fly home on Thursday morning," he announces.

It's a sweet offer, but I tell him no because he can't afford to miss all those science labs and lacrosse practices.

"I already told my professors that I have to go home for a few days," Craig insists.

Of course I'm secretly thrilled. It will be so nice to have a shoulder to cry on and a hand to hold. Eric and Louise are as gobsmacked as I am right now and it's useless for us to complain to one another. If anything, we're trying *not* to express our worst fears—the main one being that Mom doesn't ever come home.

"And I quit lacrosse," Craig adds in a nonchalant voice.

"*Why?*" I ask. "Did you get hurt?" It would be just like Craig to be sitting there with his leg in a cast and not say anything.

"No, nothing like that," he says. "It just took up too much time."

Still, I find this odd. Craig has always been a good student and never had to work all that hard to get A's and B's. But I'm too preoccupied with my own family tragedy to pursue the matter. It's just so good to hear the sound of his comforting and familiar voice. We talk for a long time—Craig recounts how he and another guy got lost in the woods while collecting mold samples for botany and had to be rescued by a platoon of ROTC students who made it into a reconnaissance exercise.

Then I tell him about Mom being transferred to Dalewood and how Aunt Lala made sticky buns with Francie to cheer her up, but forgot to add the yeast and so they never rose any higher than the pan. And the way the church ladies force the kids to play Bible Scattergories for hours on end. They're quite the linguists, too, never seeming to tire of pointing out how the words SILENT and LISTEN contain the exact same letters and that DANGER is ANGER with a D.

TWELVE

A SNOWPLOW ROARS DOWN THE STREET AT FIVE IN THE MORNING and I wake up still trapped inside the same horrible after-school special that doesn't seem to want to end. In fact, it gets worse when I hear the heavy metal blade scrape up against my front porch. Obviously the driver has passed out at the wheel and lost complete control of his vehicle.

I open the front door to find Al Santora lurching up the driveway in a big town plow and clearing the two feet of snow in minutes. He waves his hat from the cab, and I pull on a pair of Mom's boots that are by the door.

A pale winter sun is rising in the distance and the trees had taken on a thick coating of ice during the night. The rooftops are blanketed with fluffy layers of snow that make the houses appear as if they belong in a gingerbread village. The entire neighborhood has a gauzy, dreamlike quality.

Al shifts the rumbling machine down to idle, leans out the window, and shouts over the still-growling engine. "It's terrible about your dad. I'm really sorry."

"Yeah, it's a nightmare." Thick flakes of snow stick to my eyelashes and dissolve on my lips as we talk. "Mom is at Dalewood."

Al nods as if he's heard all the details.

"Nice set of wheels." I nod at the orange plow with the gold Cosgrove County seal painted on the side. Last I'd heard, Al had been laid off from the water authority and was collecting unemployment.

"It's my new job until April." He gives me a half smile that I take to mean, *When you have a stay-at-home wife and four kids, you take what you can get.* "One of the guys is out on disability and this way I keep up my benefits."

Al had a nice gig before—he wore a suit and scheduled inspections. Now I see there are bags under his eyes and his lips are chapped and cracked from the cold.

"We had six more inches since midnight." Al points to the section of the road where he's plowed.

When I look down the block, it's impossible to tell where the street ends and the sky begins.

"A big storm is coming in from Erie," he warns. "I've got to keep moving." He cranks the engine back up and throws his plow into reverse. "Turn on the radio," he shouts over the noise of gears crunching. "The superintendent just called my boss and they might close the schools."

What Al doesn't say is that he shouldn't be seen plowing individual driveways with taxpayer dollars or, worse, make someone think that he's earning a little extra on the side. But it's a huge relief for me right now. Teddy can clear up the front walk easily enough after breakfast, though Dad always liked to say that the hardest math problem ever invented was how to get five feet of boy to shovel one foot of snow.

While mouthing "thanks" I wave at Al and then dash back into the house.

The twins are still sleeping soundly and so I head toward the kitchen to make some coffee and switch on the radio. Though it doesn't really matter if school is closed because our gang wasn't going anyway. Today Eric and I somehow have to break the news.

When I open the fridge, I notice that the churchwomen have reorganized the whole interior and left two dozen sandwiches, complete with labels describing the contents, date made, and expiration. What's not there is the milk, and I know we had a full gallon. When things are missing in the kitchen, all roads lead to Aunt Lala.

Gently knocking on Mom's door, I say, "Aunt Lala—have you seen the gallon of milk that was in the fridge last night?"

"Oh dear," comes the frazzled voice from inside the bedroom. The door opens to reveal Aunt Lala in her nightgown with a complicated set of hair rollers dangling in front of her face and a large circle of pale green cream surrounding each eye.

"Did you check the freezer?" she asks.

"First thing," I say.

"What could have happened to it?" she asks. "I wasn't able to sleep and went down for some tea in the middle of the night. Do you think I may have put it back in the cupboard with the cookies?"

"I think you could have," I say with fake cheerfulness. Aunt Lala always feels terrible about making so many mistakes. We hate for her to feel bad and so hide her oversights whenever possible. A knightly quest if there ever was one.

Sure enough, the milk is in the cabinet above the sink, next to the cookies. I sniff it to determine whether it's spoiled. Smells okay to me. Just to be sure, I'll use the first child to arrive for breakfast as a taste tester and if that one vomits or collapses I'll mix up a batch of powdered milk for the rest.

The radio announcer reads a list of local closings in alphabetical order—a 4H club meeting, most of the area private schools, some church activities, and a Hebrew school class. It's a local joke that the world would have to be ending for our public school system to close. Most of the administrators were once public school students around here, so I often think they want to make sure that today's kids suffer as much as they did before the invention of fleece jackets and waterproof boots.

Darlene shuffles into the kitchen wearing her footsie pajamas. She starts to say something, but I place my finger to my lips and point to the radio just as the announcer says, "Here it is, folks—Patrick Henry School District is closed!" He says this like a game show host declaring a big winner.

Darlene looks up at me expectantly.

"Yup," I say. "That's you. No school today."

She races through the house screeching, "Thcool ith clofed, thchool ith clofed!"

I'm reminded that this means there won't be any speech therapy for Darlene today. The lisp is definitely improving, but there's still a ways to go before she's knocking back, Silly Sally sells seashells by the seashore.

THIRTEEN

By LUNCHTIME I FEEL AS IF I'M SLEEPWALKING AND THE KIDS' voices are coming from an echo chamber.

Bernard arrives shortly after one o'clock with a bottle of designer conditioner and a brand-new blow dryer. He hugs and kisses me like we're acting out a tragedy in a movie scene. "Are you surviving?"

"It's really weird." I grope for the right words to describe the surrealism of the past two days, how it's as if I'm standing at a distance from life. "I keep thinking I'm going to wake up and everything will be back to how it was—but instead it's like being stuck in a science-fiction movie. Only there aren't any killer robots to beat back, no magic ring to get rid of, no time machine to repair, and therefore no way to travel back to yesterday."

"*Courage, mon brave!*" says Bernard, and places his hands on my shoulders while tipping his forehead toward mine as if he's knighting me or transferring some sort of secret powers.

Gazing out the window only adds to the bizarreness of my current situation. It's no longer possible to see the houses across the street, or even the street, for that matter.

"How on earth did you get over here?" I ask.

"It certainly wouldn't have been possible in that fantastically stylish but reliably unreliable vintage Alfa Romeo. Whereas my new Volvo zips right through the snow and ice. It's even moose-proof!"

"Moose-proof?"

"My family will survive hitting a moose," Bernard states with authority.

"There aren't any moose around here that I'm aware of, aside from the guys who own the lodge up on Route 5."

"We have plenty of deer," says the unsinkable Bernard. "Now I hate to turn your attention back to the events at hand, but I've come to measure the children for their outfits. Thank Goddess it's early winter and the stores are still carrying some black and navy."

"I didn't even think of clothes," I said. "Try not to spend much." Bernard is constantly buying expensive dresses for his daughters. Gigi doesn't mind, but Rose tends to start pulling hers apart the minute he's out of sight.

"Don't worry about a thing," says Bernard. He glances at all the flowers and fruit baskets from Dad's office coworkers pushed off in the corner. "It will be my contribution instead of a fruit basket." He spots the family photo on the mantel, sighs, and adds, "Life is so laissez unfaire."

"We haven't told the little kids yet," I explain. "Only Teddy knows."

"I see," says Bernard. "I'll simply eyeball the measurements and hedge on the larger side. If need be, we'll just do a nip and tuck here and there. Can your Aunt Lala sew?"

Aunt Lala has just walked out of the kitchen, teary-eyed after watching Lillian crawl around saying, "Mama, Mama."

"I wouldn't count on it," I whisper to Bernard. "If Aunt Lala manages to get dressed and visit my mom at Dalewood this morning, it will be a minor miracle." As if on cue the toaster begins to smolder and I discover that Aunt Lala has put two thin slices of bread in there and then switched it on high before exiting.

"If only Mother were here." From the sigh in Bernard's voice I can tell that he wishes Olivia were back for a lot more than just sewing alterations. The constant bickering aside, they really do depend on each other, and it's obvious that he's been a bit lost with her away for an extended period of time.

"Have you heard anything from Olivia and Ottavio lately?" I ask. "She sent me a postcard from Florence around Christmastime."

Bernard perks up at the subject. "They finally left Italy after visiting Ottavio's family. And of course they had to go see all of Bernini's fountains and the great piazza in front of St. Peter's in Rome. Now they're on some Greek island, where Mother is immersing herself in poetry. Next stop are the pyramids in Egypt and the library of Alexandria, and then they'll be home in April."

"Wow, it sounds like a great trip."

"I suppose I'm happy for her," says Bernard. "Mother always loved to travel, and then Father became ill and she didn't go anywhere for years, except that quick trip to Florida."

"I suppose it's best to go places whenever you can." I don't mean to refer to the fact that I might be stuck here in this house raising these kids for the next ten years, but I guess that's how it sounds. And who knows, maybe it is what I mean. I keep telling myself that it's horribly wrong and selfish to be thinking about my own life at a terrible time like this, but it does creep into the back of my mind.

"Yes, one never knows what tomorrow will bring," Bernard

says philosophically. "Now why don't you fix your hair while I find the children."

After washing my hair again, only this time with a half bottle of conditioner, I struggle with a brush and the hair dryer to try to bring it under control. Instead I end up looking like the Cowardly Lion from *The Wizard of Oz*.

When I finally give up and switch off the dryer, the phone is ringing. I swear the thing starts at seven in the morning and doesn't stop until eleven o'clock at night. We had an answering machine for about a week, until Davy attempted to convert it into a two-way radio. I go to pick up the phone in Mom and Dad's room, but the handset is nowhere in sight, so I hurry downstairs to the kitchen. A disheveled Aunt Lala comes around the corner buttoning up her coat, the belt dragging along the floor behind her. "That must be the taxi company calling."

A taxi in this weather? I wonder about that. As I grab the telephone the doorbell rings. Perhaps there is a cab out front. Only the dispatcher is telling me he can't get a driver out to us until later this afternoon. And that's when I hear the scream in the front hall followed by the door banging shut.

FOURTEEN

Racing into the living room, I find Aunt Lala shrieking, one hand covering her face, the other pointed at the closed front door. The bell rings again. Assuming that her histrionics are the result of general anxiety, I open the door. I, too, start screaming bloody murder. It's Dad! Only he's a lot older and has a huge mustache and beard covered with icicles like the Abominable Snowman! Chunks of white hair stick out below a stiff white hat with a black visor and a big gold anchor on the front. After slamming the door closed I quickly lock it. Dad's a ghost and has come back to haunt the house!

Bernard arrives on the scene trailed by a bunch of curious kids while Aunt Lala and I babble from hysteria. He intuitively understands that the cause of our consternation lies on the other side of the door. Glancing out a side window, Bernard announces, "Heavens to Häagen-Dazs! It's the Ancient Mariner! He must be lost in the storm."

Bernard opens the door and speaks the way he does to strangers who enter his antiques shop. "Hello there, and how may I help you this afternoon?"

"Lenny Palmer—Robert's uncle," says the Abominable Snowman. "There weren't any cabs at the station." He reports this news as if he didn't mind the challenge of walking a mile in a blizzard and the two icicles that are his eyebrows rise slightly.

"Oh my goodness, come in!" says Bernard. "You must be frozen half to death."

The great big bear of a man with a chest like an oil drum makes the room seem to shrink down to the size of a doll's house.

"If I were a case of herring I guess I'd still be pretty fresh," he says in a gruff voice seasoned by wind and water. Great-Uncle Lenny removes a pair of old-fashioned black wool gloves that look as if they were abandoned by a street musician and takes off his skipper's cap to reveal a wild mane of white hair.

Aunt Lala is the first to recover from the fright. Extending her hand, she introduces herself. "I'm Lorraine, Robert's sister-in-law. I met you and a twin brother at the wedding."

"Yep, that was us. Only Barnacle Bill departed for Davy Jones's locker shortly after the nuptials—had a heart attack while reeling in a sailfish," says Lenny. "Apparently it runs in the family. I'm sorry to hear about my nephew. I took a flight from the Virgin Islands and the train from Cleveland. Alan left a message at the bar."

His address is a bar? My eyes are fixed on this man who looks like an older, shaggy, ice-covered version of my father. So this is Great-Uncle Lenny. I'd come to think of him as a character out of a novel—chasing pirates through the Caribbean and catching fish of mythical proportions. When I was little, my dad brought home a magazine containing a story on his two identical-twin seafaring uncles.

Lenny extends his hand. It's strong, ugly, rough, callused, and scarred. The skin is like leather that's been left outside for a decade, and no longer has the steer attached to keep it hydrated and smooth. He's a man from another world. The world of the ocean, I have to assume. Living my entire life in Ohio, I've never seen the ocean.

Eric comes up from the basement rubbing his eyes after a short nap. He also does a double take upon seeing Uncle Lenny but doesn't start screaming like a girl.

"This is our great-uncle Lenny," I fill him in. "*Remember Dad's father had two younger brothers who were identical twins.*"

"Sure," Eric says and extends his hand. Even though Eric and I aren't twins, we can do a pretty good sibling telepathy when necessary.

"Oh dear," says Aunt Lala, and peers out the window. "I wonder what happened to my taxi?"

"Sorry," I say. "That was the cab company on the phone, and they're not coming until later because of the weather."

"I'll drive you to the hospital," says Eric. "Let me take a quick shower."

"Hospital?" inquires Uncle Lenny. "But I thought—"

"Their mother is in shock," explains Bernard.

"Great Caesar's ghost!" roars Uncle Lenny so that we all jump back a step. "What next?"

Teddy appears from around the corner, where he was listening the entire time. The protruding ears give him an unmistakable silhouette.

"Can I go with them?" asks Teddy.

"Sure," I say.

"I'm off shopping." Bernard heads toward the door. He scrutinizes my new hairstyle and grimaces. "I'll be sure to pick up a black hat for you."

"Your parents have such wonderful friends," says Aunt Lala.

It's not the time to explain that Bernard is actually my friend a lot more than Mom and Dad's.

Just then there's a horrible crash on the stairs followed by a loud shriek.

"Man overboard!" Uncle Lenny calls out in his booming bass.

Aunt Lala and I dash toward the first-floor landing, where Francie, the family daredevil, is lying curled up at the bottom and Louise is approaching from the top.

"I *told* you to stop sledding on the stairs!" yells an irritated Louise.

There's blood running down Francie's chin, and I can't tell if it's coming from her nose or her mouth or the fingers she's using to cover her face. It's not until we finally manage to get her hair and hands out of the way that it's possible to see the gash below her bottom lip.

Aunt Lala recoils at the sight of the open wound, grabs onto the railing, and looks as if she's going to pass out. "Oh dear Lord!"

By the sound of Francie's howls one would think I was performing a skin graft, but it actually appears not to be that bad. And she doesn't seem to have knocked any more teeth out.

"We'd better go to the emergency room just to be on the safe side," I say. "She may need a few stitches."

Francie screams even louder upon hearing my unwelcome diagnosis.

"You and I can take Francie to the emergency room, and Aunt Lala can go with Louise to see Mom," says Eric.

"Who is going to watch the rest of the kids?" I ask.

The phone starts ringing in the background. Now what? Are we supposed to evacuate the area due to nuclear fallout?

"Louise will have to stay here and watch the kids," I say.

Louise gives me a look indicating that she's *over* child care.

I put a Band-Aid over Francie's cut and bundle her up.

"Darlene, Davy, and Lillian can go outside, but not for more than an hour. Be sure to put Wonder bread bags over their socks since their boots leak." I sound like Mom.

Uncle Lenny is standing in the living room. I'd forgotten about the surprise sailor situation. "Make yourself at home," I say as we hurtle out of the door.

It's cold and the roads to the hospital are still icy. The good news is that the storm has slowed down business at the emergency room. There's just one guy with chest pains whose wife is yelling at him about being too cheap to hire a plow service.

After a quick examination we're given some baby aspirin and a butterfly bandage is applied to Francie's lip. The doctor makes some notations about Francie's various scars, the knocked-out front teeth, and the still-fresh lump on her forehead from the living room fall the other day. I can tell he's wondering whether she's really this accident-prone or if we're throwing her down the stairs on a regular basis. Then he asks me to leave the room for a moment. Great. She'd better not tell one of her crazy stories and land me in jail.

Apparently the doctor is satisfied with their conversation. At least for now. And thus the big surprise turns out not to be what happens at the hospital but the scene awaiting me back at the house.

FIFTEEN

"LOUISE!" I CALL OUT. THERE'S NO SIGN OF DINNER BEING STARTED and the table isn't set. Not only that, there are no signs of children. I look out the basement window to the backyard. No one. Racing up the stairs to the second floor, I'm relieved to see light coming from underneath the closed door of Louise and Darlene's room.

Louise is alone, totally engrossed in reorganizing the closet.

"Louise! Where *is* everybody?" Panic edges my voice.

"Francie and Lillian's room," she replies without looking up from her pile of sweaters.

I dash down the hall and open the door to the girls' room. Uncle Lenny is seated on Lillian's small bed, leaning forward so that thick muscled arms balance on tree trunk legs, telling them a story. Three little faces stare up at him transfixed, while the twins lie sleeping in their car seats. Great, the man whose address is a bar somewhere in the Caribbean is not only baby-sitting the little kids but also the ten-week-old twins.

Catching my breath I manage to say, "Okay, we're back. Lunch in half an hour."

Davy excitedly fills me in on what I've missed. "Hallie! There was a man and his dog shitwrecked on an island—"

"Thipwrecked," Darlene corrects him. Sort of.

Davy doesn't miss a beat. "And when they found the man's clothes and the dog's bones they couldn't tell which eated the other!"

Davy reaches out and touches Uncle Lenny's beard. "You're God, aren't you?"

"Don't be stupid," says Darlene. "He's Santa Claus."

"You're stupid," says Davy. "Because Santa is back at the North Pole. He only comes at Christmas. Everyone knows *that.*"

Uncle Lenny shakes with laughter. Not unlike Santa Claus. Or perhaps God after hearing a really funny joke.

The doorbell rings. I've made it only to the landing when I hear the cheerful voices of the church ladies. They unpack casseroles and fruit salads and pineapple upside-down cakes.

I'm grateful they've come to the rescue once again. However, I'm also aware that their visits will become fewer and further between. They have their own families to get off to work and school in the mornings, and a list of community activities that require constant attention. Plus, they view Aunt Lala as one of them, probably due to her print dress, and believe that things are more or less under control.

If only the church ladies knew that a large portion of Aunt Lala's day is spent playing Memory with packets of herbal tea and artificial sweeteners. Honestly, if that's all she did, I wouldn't care. But every time our paths cross Aunt Lala asks, "What's going to happen? Whatever will you do?"

The churchwomen, on the other hand, instinctively understand that no matter what calamity is playing itself out, you keep repeating, "It's all going to be just fine! You'll see." And though I don't believe them for a second, it's really the only thing I'm interested in hearing right now.

As the churchwomen march past me and into the kitchen with their bright smiles and hair pulled neatly back, I wish I could be more like them, absorbing life's unexpected turns as easily as they adjust to changes in the weather.

SIXTEEN

ON THE MORNING OF THE FUNERAL I WAKE UP JUST AFTER four a.m. I'm ground down by exhaustion and sorrow and yet it's impossible to sleep.

Finally a sliver of pink dawn begins to creep over the horizon. Outside the window snow falls softly through the bare trees and onto the empty yards and rooftops.

I rise and drag myself through the paces of feeding and bathing the younger children while Eric heads off to the hospital to see if Mom will be able to attend the funeral.

At half past one I start herding the kids into the car. "Come on, it's time to leave for the church," I announce in my best let's-sound-like-Mom voice. Eric has the station wagon and there's no way we can fit ten people and two babies into the van, so Aunt Lala, Uncle Lenny, Davy, and Darlene have to ride in a taxi.

As we're going out the door the phone rings and I rush to answer it.

"Mom's not going to be able to make it," says Eric.

While backing out of the driveway it comes to my attention that Louise is missing. I rush back inside and almost rip the slacks to my new black pantsuit while taking the steps two at a time.

Louise is lying across the bed and talking on the phone. Clothed all in black, she looks stunningly beautiful, with her swan-necked elegance and ballerina body.

"C'mon, Louise," I say impatiently. "We have to go!"

Louise draws her slender shoulders together as if she's cold and gives me the one-minute sign with her finger. Meantime, one of the kids starts leaning on the horn in the driveway. They know they're not supposed to do that unless it's an emergency. Oh no! What if the exhaust pipe is blocked with ice and they're all suffocating to death?

"Louise, *now!*"

She gives me a nasty look, whispers something into the receiver, and tosses the phone onto the bed. I grab her arm and start pulling her toward the door.

"It was Brandt!" she says, as if this explains everything.

"What can the two of you possibly have to talk about for six hours straight every single day?" Whenever I ask Louise to help, she's on the phone with Brandt, who is studying at the Massachusetts Institute of Technology.

"Just lunar phases, solar system debris, and the fate of our sun, for your information," she replies haughtily.

"You're kidding me, right?" I ask as we hurry out the front door. It's an obscure collection of problems to be brooding about right before our father's funeral.

"The sun will end up a compact white dwarf held in place by strange quantum-mechanical forces after expelling its outer layers to form a bubble of flowing gas," continues Louise.

"And I'll be roasting hot dogs for eight kids over the flames," I say. "Get in the car!"

Finally we're under way. The snowstorm has passed and the

carpet of white is now broken by the tracks of newspaper carriers, mailpersons, and children building forts and snowmen. The church parking lot overflows with cars. Men in dark overcoats and plaid scarves hold up women wearing black-netted pillbox hats and long wool coats so that they don't slip on the ice while making their way to the main entrance.

Bernard and Gil are waiting for us in the vestibule. Taking Reggie out of my arms, Bernard asks, "How did the younger children take the news?"

"They think Uncle Lenny is God and had to take Dad away and aren't interested in any other version of the story at this particular time."

"*Très intéressant,*" says Bernard.

Strong arms grab me from behind and what feels like the start of a takedown turns out to be my athletic friend Jane. "Oh Hallie, this is *so* terrible! I tried to get here sooner, but the driving was horrible."

"Mom's in *Dalewood,*" I whisper.

My friend Gwen's parents rush forward. Mrs. Thompson is easily recognizable by the silk leopard print scarf that adorns her black wool dress. Gwen's mother exudes grief the way other people give off the scent of perfume. She attempts to say something but immediately begins sobbing and then practically falls forward, wrapping her arms around me and sinking that Mount Rushmore bosom directly into my rib cage as a violent burst of Chanel No. 5 further stifles my breathing. If I was wearing high heels and not flats, we'd both be on the floor with Gwen's mom on top.

Fortunately Mr. Thompson rescues the situation by taking his wife's arm and gently drawing her to his side. Turning to me, he says, "We're so sorry that Gwen couldn't make it from California for the funeral. She's been trying to call you, but it's impossible to get through." What is unspoken here is that my dad was the only person in Cosgrove County who would not pay for call waiting. Or caller ID. Or cable TV.

It's impossible for me to take a single step without someone known or unknown speaking very close to my face. One woman describes Dad as being "taken from us," as if he's been kidnapped by aliens.

Bernard steers me to a place in the front row where he's organized the children. There's a clear view of the highly polished black casket with gold handles. It's difficult to comprehend that Dad is inside that . . . that *box,* while we're over here lining the pew.

Aunt Lala and Uncle Lenny are each holding one of the twins, both of whom are sound asleep. Teddy sits somberly in the pew while Davy, Darlene, and Francie push and poke one another. Only tiny Lillian sits quietly in her little navy dress and stockings, with her legs dangling over the edge of the pew, looking wide-eyed at the enormous stained-glass window of the angel whispering to Mary. Lillian looks like a "mini-me," with the same long strawberry-blond hair, pink skin, and hazel eyes. The only other difference is that her freckles are just emerging, whereas mine have begun to fade.

Eric hurries up the aisle as the minister approaches the podium. There's a commotion next to me that results in Davy, Darlene, and Francie all elbowing one another.

"Stop messing around *this instant!*" Eric hisses in a deep stage whisper.

The children immediately obey him, sitting meekly and staring down at their laps. This is in striking contrast to the way they basically ignore my directives, no matter how much I yell and threaten them.

Turning my head, I scan the back of the sanctuary for Craig.

He said there was a flight from Minneapolis this morning that had plenty of room. Surely he would know to look for us up front. The church is almost filled to capacity, but pale-faced mourners continue to spill through the doors. Ushers in dark gray suits scurry up and down the aisles trying to find seats for those gathered at the back. Some of the men drift about like museum goers, uncertain of how long to stay in a certain place or exactly how to comment upon the events, taking their cues from others. Yet the women move efficiently, quickly taking in who is here, where they're seated, and probably even what they're wearing.

Suddenly I wish that I'd worn the long black gloves Bernard brought over, which I decided were just a bit too Audrey Hepburn in *Breakfast at Tiffany's*. My hands are freezing and my fingers practically numb. Whether it's from the cold or my nerves I don't know. It's no longer possible to feel where I end and the world begins.

SEVENTEEN

NANCY GORDON, THE INTERIM MINISTER, RISES FROM HER HIGH-backed chair and approaches the dais. The crowd settles, with just a few heavy bronchial coughs echoing throughout the sanctuary.

"We're gathered here today in the spirit of Christ to celebrate the life of Robert Palmer," she announces, as if some of us may have put on our black clothes and rolled up at the wrong church. No one rises to leave and so she continues, "And to offer worship, praise, and thanksgiving to God for the gift of life, which has now been returned to God, the author of life and the hope of the just."

In no time at all scripture is swirling through the air the same way that hunks of wet snow were flying around yesterday. "God loves you, abides with you, and will not forsake you in these moments and in the days of readjustment and reorientation that lie ahead of you," she informs us. "This is surely the message of the Jesus."

Sometimes I can hear what's being said and other times I can't. A roar like the bottom of a waterfall is inside my head, and I just barely manage to make it from one heartbeat to the next.

At the other end of the pew I hear sniffing and the rustling of tissues and look down to see Louise with tears streaming down her face. This has the effect of making Darlene cry. Aunt Lala has raccoon eyes from wiping at her mascara, while little red rivers of burst capillaries stand out on her nose and cheeks in the places where she's swabbed off her foundation makeup.

A man who worked with Dad talks about what a devoted family man and wonderful coworker my father was. Certainly no one is going to jump up and dispute that.

Eric strides up to the podium and reads Psalm 46. His voice comes across clear and strong, especially during the part about "therefore we will not fear, though the Earth give way and the mountains fall into the heart of the sea." I hear sniffles and sobs reverberating throughout the sanctuary. Although Eric is as big and powerful as Dad, he doesn't bear a strong resemblance to our father. But Eric *sounds* exactly like Dad.

I was asked to speak but said no. Basically everyone here is aware that I left home at fifteen, play cards, and then there was all that nonsense about the missing money. Besides, what would I say? I doubt that a Bible verse from an underage gambler would go down real well today.

Reverend Gordon hugs Eric solidly before he returns to our pew. Then she asks the assembled mourners, "Where could we find stronger words of comfort? And not with just any God, mind you, but with the one true God, the creating, redeeming, and loving God . . ."

Off to the side I catch a glimpse of Jane's mother nodding her head up and down in vigorous agreement. I've never really thought much about funerals, having been to only one in my life, at the age of six, when Mom's father died. Now I begin to wonder if these rituals are supposed to make a mourner feel better or worse? I mean, maybe they're intended to land a person at rock bottom so after you leave it's possible to start climbing back up again. I don't know. All that's clear right now is that the kids are getting itchy in these fancy clothes, they're starting to fidget, and it seems as if the service might actually overlap with the Second Coming.

"The Book of John speaks of our heavenly Father's house," continues Reverend Gordon, her voice rising in that ministerial way that indicates we're finally coming in for a landing.

She closes her eyes tight and raises her hands, palms upward. "In our Father's house there are many rooms. Right now I imagine Robert Palmer is settling into his new home. We feel sorry for ourselves, but we must not feel sorry for him."

I know it's terrible, but I can't help think that no one in the Palmer family is going to feel especially sorry for anyone getting his own room in a nice big house.

"Robert Palmer would not want our sympathy, because he is happy in the presence of Jesus. And that same mighty power is among us today in the person of the Holy Spirit, to bring his love and comfort to us all."

We rise for "There Is a Land of Pure Delight" and a rock-solid soprano directly behind me undertakes the singing for our entire section. She comes across particularly loud and clear on the subject of "removing these gloomy doubts that rise," as if she has never experienced this personally but is happy to explicate the matter for the benefit of the rest of us.

Finally the benediction. The congregation adds their own murmured and scattered "amens," the organist lays into some dirge, and we begin to file out. After being crowded with so many people the sanctuary is now warm. Walking directly behind the casket I can briefly see my silhouette reflected in the high gloss finish. Suddenly a wave of anxiety begins in my feet, then travels up to my stomach, through my chest and throat, and bursts out the top of my head.

EIGHTEEN

IN FRONT OF THE CHURCH WAIT A HEARSE AND BLACK LIMOUSINE with engines struggling against the cold. Steady streams of white smoke spill from their tailpipes and melt into the late winter afternoon air. People going to the cemetery are offered a flag to place on their car. Toward the back of the parking lot Officer Rich and Al help the town's one full-time librarian start her car with jumper cables. Mom has been taking the little kids to story time there every Thursday mornings at ten as far back as I can remember.

Eric and I are both surprised when Bernard points us in the direction of the limousine. Neither of us has ever ridden in one before. A few kids rented them for the prom but certainly never any Palmer children. Dad would have lain down in the driveway underneath the wheels if we'd hired a limo. It's a good thing he isn't here to see this. Bernard nudges me forward and whispers, "You can't ride in a *taxi* to the graveyard!"

Gil takes their Volvo and Bernard drives our car with Aunt Lala and the little kids back to the house. It's been decided that the burial might be too traumatic for them.

Uncle Lenny stands by the open car door until Eric, Louise, Teddy, and I are safely inside. Eric digs something out of his coat pocket and hands it to the driver through the partition. In a minute the haunting words of Leonard Cohen drift through the back of the car: *I did my best, it wasn't much, I couldn't feel, so I tried to touch* and then the droning chorus of *"Hallelujah."* The limo has a really great sound system with speakers on all sides of us. Music has always defined the moment for Eric. He can tell you where he was and what he was doing when he first heard any song. In fact, I often think he would have enjoyed playing an instrument in the school band if Dad hadn't always been so rah-rah about sports.

I glance over at Uncle Lenny to see if he's going to disapprove of the unusual music selection by either saying something or just giving us a look. However, with his great beard and mustache all neatly combed out for the occasion, he takes on the appearance of an old philosopher who has been to many different kinds of funerals and finds that they all pretty much get the job done in the end.

"Were you in the navy?" Teddy asks Uncle Lenny.

I had also assumed this was the case because he's wearing a blue military uniform with brass buttons and a white cap with a black visor that has a gold anchor on the front. Dad's family is mad for uniforms. At one point they had someone in just about every branch of the service.

"Thirty years in the United States Coast Guard," Uncle Lenny replies in his gruff voice. "After retirement my brother Bill and I set up a charter fishing business in St. Thomas."

"Is that where you live?" asks Teddy.

"Most of the time. Unless I'm driving a boat for someone, working with a wreck crew, or running down pirates." Uncle Lenny winks at Teddy on the word *pirates*.

"Cool," says Teddy. Though it's obvious by his furrowed brow that he's not sure whether or not to believe Uncle Lenny about the pirates. "I'm going to be a navy SEAL—they always bring back their dead."

A *navy SEAL*? This is the first I've heard about Teddy's military aspirations. Last I knew he wanted to be a baseball player.

"Uncle Sam would be mighty lucky to land such a strong intelligent young man as yourself," Uncle Lenny says with great seriousness.

Teddy sits up straighter in his seat. With jug ears that stick out like shutters even with a hat on and a gangly frame that seems to bend with the wind, Teddy is used to being mercilessly teased about his career opportunities, not complimented.

The limousine rolls past houses that have drifts of snow reaching practically up to the roofs. Clouds of smoke bellow from chimneys and rise toward the heavens like holy offerings. The snowbanks along the sides of the street are so high that, when there's no traffic light, it's necessary to inch out into the intersection to check for oncoming cars.

At last we turn down the road that runs adjacent to the cemetery and pass headstones that look like rows of gray mailboxes surrounded by a chain-link fence. The long car comes to a slow stop a few yards away from where a crowd with winter coats buttoned up tight and scarves wrapped around their faces has gathered.

The driver comes around to open the door, and a gust of wind rushes inside the back of the car. Suddenly there's a splinter in my heart and I feel faint. I don't think I can make it. I tell Eric to go ahead without me. But he takes my arm and practically holds me up as we walk toward the grave. A crust of ice covers the ground and crunches under our feet as we pass the gray skeletons of trees.

I don't hear a word of what the minister says as she recites above the gaping hole, a dark gash in the white landscape. Eric stands next to me with his head bent and his eyes lowered. Louise is across from us, looking effortlessly pretty even while grieving. Without makeup her skin is pure ivory and her lips are the deep and velvety red of roses. Yet as the coffin is lowered her features become tense, as if she's suddenly in pain.

Only Uncle Lenny is looking up now, his craggy and weather-worn face resolutely staring at the sky, studying the wind and the clouds. His soup strainer of a mustache has little icicles forming at the bottom.

Off to the side, behind some people I don't recognize, is the familiar trademark boating cap that belongs to my old pal Cappy, the local bookie. Like most citizens who make their living in the gaming professions, Cappy believes that you don't change anything, including your clothes, when you're beating the odds in life. His restless eyes dart from person to person as if he's searching the crowd for a card cheat.

Cappy must have read about the funeral in the newspaper. Still, I'm more than a little surprised to see him here. Cappy tends not to attend such community functions where he'll run into his clients and, more important, their wives. Most townspeople are aware that he's a bookmaker, organizer of card games, and general fixer. Though Cappy considers himself more of a therapist, in that he keeps people from depression and even suicide by helping to maintain their hope of cleaning up on a long shot.

I'm vaguely conscious that the drone of human words has finally trailed off. A smoke-blue veil of dusk settles over the graveyard to make it hazy and ethereal, like a dream dissolving, and the cold breeze sounds full of whispers. It's as if the rustling trees are saying this will be the first of many funerals, that the distance between the dead and the living is no more than a heartbeat and a breath.

Who will be next? I can't help but wonder. Will it be our resident daredevil, Francie? In a family as large as ours, sometimes shouting "Look at me" isn't quite enough. And who will be the last, departing the cemetery alone, leaving behind eleven Palmer grave markers all in a row? Maybe one of the twins, seeing as they're the youngest. Whoever it is, I can almost hear Dad reminding the last one to turn out the lights.

The crowd begins to disperse and I realize it's finally over.

Cappy catches up with me as I'm about to climb into the limo. "Hanging in there?" His breath makes smoke in the wintry air.

I shake my head as if it's too early in the game to be setting any firm probabilities.

"Tough break," says Cappy. "The Big Casino." He nods up toward the sky. "You know that you only have to pick up the horn if you need some lettuce."

"Much obliged, Cappy," I say. And I really do appreciate his offer. Cappy is not exactly known for extending interest-free lines of credit. In fact, it's usually quite the opposite. However, if you insist upon calling Cappy a con artist, then it would have to be with the emphasis on the second word, given that it's highly creative how he separates people from their money. Afterward his customers often leave feeling good, or at the very least with a philosophical air, the way one might exit a gallery.

Only Cappy isn't satisfied that he's done enough to improve my psyche. He takes my elbow, leans in close, and says, "Listen, two frogs fell into a pitcher of milk and it was too slippery to climb out. The first gave up and drowned. But the second one had gumption, and he kicked until eventually the cream turned to butter and he climbed out."

I assume this is Cappy's version of when the going gets

tough, the tough get going. Fortunately he makes his money betting on sports and not as a motivational speaker.

Everyone else is in the limo by now, and the driver is waiting for me. I give Cappy a quick hug and climb inside the warm car. The snow along the winding road has been packed down hard from all the traffic and it squeaks under the tires. As we slowly make our way through the cemetery gates it's hard not to feel I've left my childhood behind along with my father.

NINETEEN

WHEN WE TURN INTO OUR STREET, THERE ARE CARS PARKED everywhere. The drapes in my front window have been pulled wide open and people are milling about in the living room. For some reason it didn't occur to me that the general public would be coming back to the house. But apparently this is how funerals work.

I discover that Mom and Dad's bedroom has been turned into a coatroom, the long wooden kitchen table is now covered with a white linen cloth and holds a buffet that has Bernard's fingerprints all over it. Big carafes of coffee and hot water for tea sit on a silver tray atop the sideboard.

Uncle Lenny and Aunt Lala come over to me. Between dabbing underneath her nose with a tissue, Aunt Lala manages to get out, "Your dad's brother Alan is snowed in at his army base in upstate New York. The storm we had yesterday is moving east. And your boyfriend, Clive, left a message that his flight was canceled due to a mechanical failure or something of the sort."

"Craig," I gently correct her.

"Yes, he said to tell you that he's awfully sorry."

Uncle Lenny shakes his head from side to side and mutters, "Ship outta luck."

Aunt Lala's eyes are still red from crying. "It was a beautiful service."

"A-1 at Lloyd's," adds Uncle Lenny. From the way he beams at me I take it that this is positive.

Adults stand around the living room whispering to one another like members of a secret society. It's not possible for me to turn around without someone hugging me and telling me how sorry he or she is. In fact, it begins to feels like we're playing hot potato and tossing me from one set of arms to the next between waves of coffee breath. When a woman asks me how I tell the twins apart, I feel sort of stupid admitting that it's only by the little blue ribbon tied around Roddy's ankle.

Suddenly I start to feel my stomach rising up inside of me. I run to the bathroom and throw up. Vomit gets in my hair, and this reminds me of how when I was a little girl my mother always held my hair back when I puked.

There's a knock on the bathroom door. "Hallie, are you all right?"

It's Aunt Lala. I open the door and race past her toward the kitchen, where Bernard is rinsing off a platter. Without a word I grab his hand and pull him along behind me as I search for a place where we can talk privately. Only everywhere I turn there's a clogged artery of mourners and the minute they see me they start saying how sorry they are and patting me like a lost puppy dog. It's too cold to go outside without digging our coats out from under that mountain on my parents' bed.

Eventually I drag Bernard into the coat closet under the stairs and slide the door closed. It's where I used to hide from Mom and Dad when I was little. Mittens on strings and snowsuit arms are hitting us in the face. I'm practically hyperventilating.

"Hallie, what on *earth* is the matter?" says Bernard. "If you're upset that I didn't consult you about the buffet, it's just because I thought it was the last thing you needed to be bothered with right now."

Tears stream down my face as I collapse onto a pile of boots. "What am I supposed to *do* with these people—to *say* to them all?"

Bernard settles down on the mud mat across from me and our knees interlock. "Just listen to them for a moment, say thank you, and then move on."

"But why do they all want to talk to *me*?"

"Because you're the de facto lady of the house right now."

I let out an involuntarily snort at "lady of the house." That'll be the day!

"They're being polite and paying their respects," continues Bernard.

"How about the ones who ask what's going to happen?"

"Simply tell them that you're busy making arrangements."

"What about the people who ask about Mom? Some haven't even heard she's at Dalewood!"

"Just say she'll be fine," counsels Bernard. "And she will be."

Suddenly there's a knock on the closet door.

"Who is it?" Bernard calls out in the singsong way he answers the door at home.

"Pamela Brunner."

Bernard slides open the closet door a few inches and looks out from his place on the floor with his back up against a sled. "Yes, Mrs. Brunner, how may I assist you?"

"I was just wondering," Mrs. Brunner says in a tone suggesting that it's perfectly normal to be sitting on the closet floor after a funeral, "since the cold cuts are almost finished, if you'd like me to put out the fruit plate."

"If you would be so kind," says Bernard. "There are some

mint sprigs for garnish in a plastic bag in the refrigerator and a box of chocolates on the counter."

Mrs. Brunner nods and Bernard slides the door closed again.

"They keep saying that Dad's been laid to rest," I continue. "Or worse, that we *lost* Dad."

"Those are just nice ways of saying he died," says Bernard. "Like *passed away.*"

My nose is running so ferociously that I have to blow it on a scarf that's dangling from a hook above. "But it sounds as if he's suddenly going to turn up somewhere—in a corner of the garage or down at the bus depot!" I raise my arms to gesture and a wool pom-pom scrapes my eyeball. "I can't take it anymore—the funeral, the graveyard, and now all these people!"

"We'll go and sit together on the couch and I'll help you. They shouldn't be here much longer. Worst case, you'll go upstairs and I'll simply say that you're exhausted."

"I look terrible."

"It's a funeral, you're supposed to look terrible," Bernard says emphatically. "Why do you think women wear hats and veils and dark sunglasses?"

We exit the closet and go into the kitchen, where Bernard hands me a tissue and a glass of ice water. Then he sits down next to me on the couch in the living room. With his arm resting on my back, Bernard does the talking while I just nod as if I'm his tongue-tied dummy.

Cheap old Mr. Exner, the owner of the sporting goods store, stands in front of us and says, "Your dad was one heck of a ballplayer. I remember him pitching a perfect game when he was knee-high to a grasshopper, and I said to myself, That boy is going places."

"Yes, indeed," replies Bernard. "He was so many things to so many people."

Others take turns coming over and saying how sorry they are, and Bernard nods with understanding and says how much the family appreciates their condolences and thanks them for attending the service. He's actually very good at this and no one stays for more than a few minutes. It's as if Bernard is a priest handing out absolution. Each person walks away looking very much relieved. And no one seems to mind that they're actually talking to him and not me.

It's going pretty well until one woman who worked for Dad starts in about my being "a poor lamb," and asking "Whatever will you do?" before bursting into tears. Bernard places his arm around the woman's shoulders and ends up comforting *her.* "There, there, Hallie is a lot like her father—very strong. She is our *legionnaire!*" He switches to French for a bit of dramatic flair and then he hugs her with all the subtlety of a silent film star. Finally the woman ratchets the waterworks down to a sniffle and scuttles away.

Bernard leans over and whispers, "If you can't be a winner, then at least be a martyr."

We survive this receiving line of mourners and eventually they head out, passing Eric at the front door; he shakes all the men's hands and politely hugs the women. Louise must have gone straight up to her room. I haven't seen her since we arrived back from the graveyard. And knowing her aversion to providing unpaid child care, it's doubtful she went to the basement with all the kids.

Bernard and Gil not only help clean up and rinse all the glasses, but also put the kids to bed. We decide that even though tomorrow is Friday, they should probably go back to school. Sitting at home for another day isn't going to do any good, and it will be easier for me to get organized with them out of my hair for a few hours. As Bernard keeps reminding me, all these flowers and fruit baskets will require thank-you notes. It's too bad there's no way to exchange them for diapers and lunch meat. I'd definitely be more enthusiastic about the thank-you notes.

By the time I lie down on the couch it must be very late. Yet I don't bother to look at the grandfather clock directly across from me. Time no longer matters. It's as if all the hours on the clock have been painted over, leaving it blank, with the hands going round and round, indicating nothing.

Eventually I drift off from sheer exhaustion, only to be awakened by a nightmare in which I can't remember what Dad looks like. I turn on the light and locate the photo of Mom and Dad from the mantel and put it next to me on the end table. Staring intently at Dad's face, I try to recall everything about him—what he wore, how he smelled, his favorite foods, the way he picked us up and carried us over his big strong shoulders when we were tired. I burn these images into my mind so that I won't ever forget.

TWENTY

THE FOLLOWING MORNING I WAKE UP AT EXACTLY HALF PAST
five. This is amazing because in school at least two alarm clocks
were necessary if I had to rise before seven. My grand plan is to
get Davy, Darlene, and Francie ready before the twins wake up.
Lillian is almost two and I have no idea what Mom does with
her all day long, aside from try to prevent her from ruining the
house and ingesting small pieces of plastic along the way. She is
into absolutely everything!

First I go to the kitchen and make the lunches. Then I put
cereal and milk on the table. The days of everyone having what
they like for breakfast are over. Anyway, Dad always said it was
ridiculous for Mom to make four different things and that kids
should eat what's put in front of them or not eat at all.

By the time I head upstairs to wake those children targeted
for the school bus, Eric emerges from the basement, where he
and Uncle Lenny are sleeping on couches. I can hear Aunt Lala
running water in the downstairs bathroom. Eric is driving Aunt
Lala and Uncle Lenny over to visit Mom at Dalewood, and then
I'm supposed to go in the afternoon.

In the small room at the end of the upstairs hallway, Teddy

and Davy share bunk beds. On the top bunk Teddy is still sound asleep, completely wrapped up in a tan velour blanket and looking remarkably like a giant caterpillar.

Shaking Davy awake, I can't tell if his red hair has paint or glue clumping it together, and there are some new freckles on his face that could be dirt or possibly Magic Marker.

"Hey, mister, when was the last time you had a bath?"

His eyelids flip open just as I notice the unusual map on the wall next to his place in the lower bunk bed. "What is *this* on your wall?"

"A map," he says.

"I can see that. What is it made out of?"

"Gummy bears," he replies, as if only an idiot wouldn't know this.

"But they're stuck directly onto the wall—has Mom seen this?"

Davy blinks his bright green eyes at me several times as if any and all knowledge of the English language has suddenly escaped him.

"Never mind," I say. "Take a shower and get dressed for school."

As I give this order the water across the hall goes on and someone else has grabbed the shower.

I change the order. "Go eat breakfast and then come back up and take a shower. You're filthy!"

"Hallie," says Davy.

Uh-oh, I think. Here it comes—the stomachache, sore throat, whatever. Davy will use any excuse not to be on that bus. "What, sweetie?"

"My throat hurts," comes the faint reply.

"I'll write your teacher a note saying that you should sit out recess." I'd learned this one from Mom.

Next on my list is Francie, who shares a room with Lillian. With the birth of the twins Lillian was transitioned slightly early to a "big girl" bed, much to her delight. Francie's already up and sprawled out on the floor playing with her dolls. Though she treats them more like stunt dolls than babies or playmates. Instead of having tea parties or playing house, they have to jump off the bed into a bucket full of water or else leap through orange-colored paper rings of imaginary fire. At least the fire is supposed to be imaginary. Most of them don't have hair because of the one day it wasn't.

"When was the last time you had a bath?" I ask.

"Yesterday before we got all dressed up."

She looks clean enough. "Okay, then put some clothes on and go downstairs for breakfast."

"Don't want to go to school," she announces while placing her dolls all in row, facing forward, which could either be to receive Olympic medals or face a firing squad.

"Why not?" I decide to take a stab at being a child psychologist. If she's still upset from the funeral, then I guess it won't hurt to stay home another day.

"Because I hate Randy Perkins," says Francie. "He stoled my Black Beauty."

I don't know if she's talking about a book or a plastic horse. It's definitely not a lunch box. The Palmers are strictly a brown paper bag family.

"Tell him to give it back and if that doesn't work then ask the teacher to talk to him." I pull open a drawer and dig around for pants and a sweater, but all that's in there are a bunch of T-shirts and mismatched pajama tops and bottoms.

"I'm going to beat him up!" declares Francie.

"*No, you're not,*" I say in my best Mom voice while checking the closet for something wearable. When I was home for Christmas, Mom told me that Francie has already been in two fights with boys this year. "Francie, where are your school clothes?"

"Dunno."

I'd better check the laundry room. As soon as I'm out in the hallway the twins start the dawn chorus from down below. I quickly poke my head into Darlene and Louise's room. Louise is lying in bed facing the wall with the cordless phone pressed to her ear.

"*Who* are you talking to at six-thirty in the morning?" I ask. As if I don't know.

Louise turns her head enough to give me a none-of-your-business scowl before returning to her conversation.

I gently shake Darlene, who will probably go down in history as the obedient Palmer child. "Hey, Super Girl, it's time to get ready for school."

She rubs her eyes with her fists and sits up on the edge of the bed. Another set of yowls come up the staircase and both of the twins are now in full voice.

"Check and see if you have any clean clothes to wear," I instruct Darlene. "If not, go down and have breakfast in your pajamas while I get stuff from the laundry room."

Just then the doorbell rings.

"Louise, could you please bring some clothes up from the laundry room while I answer the door and change the twins?"

Louise covers the mouthpiece of the phone and angrily hisses back, "You're not my mother, you know. You can't tell me what to do!"

The doorbell rings again. Eric yells from the bathroom, "Somebody's at the door!"

"I'm not trying to tell you what to do," I say to Louise, though my voice is also rising and developing an edge to it. "I'm simply asking for a little help here. If *you'd* rather answer the door and change the twins, then *fine.*"

Louise turns away from me to face the wall and resumes her phone chat.

The twins are now bawling as if nobody has fed them for a week.

TWENTY-ONE

WITHOUT LOOKING THROUGH THE SIDE WINDOW TO SEE WHO IT is, I throw open the front door. A guy in a suit is standing there with an envelope in his hand. He looks like a salesman.

"Hi, I'm Burt." The man shifts his weight from one foot to the other while fixing his gaze squarely on the welcome mat. "I work for your dad—I mean, I worked for your dad. . . ." He becomes flustered and the sentence trails off.

"I'm Hallie." I usher him into the front hall. "You were at the funeral yesterday, right—in the back?"

"Yep. Sure was a big crowd!" Burt says this as if it speaks well for the family.

In the background only one of the twins is yowling, which means Aunt Lala must have picked up the other one. However, the sound of a shrieking child appears to discombobulate Burt, and he recognizes that it's not really a convenient time to be having a chat.

"Sorry to come by so early, but I was on my way to work and saw the lights on," he explains abruptly and then shoves the envelope toward me. "Uh, we took up a collection at work. I wish it was more, but . . . well . . ."

"Oh!" I take the envelope from him only because I have no choice—he's abandoning it in midair. My head is telling me to say thanks, but we don't need any charity. Burt appears even more uncomfortable as the one assigned to bestow the gift. He's halfway down the steps by the time I've lowered my hand back down to my side. "Okay then," he yells over his shoulder. "Call if you need anything, absolutely anything at all." He practically runs back to a car that is idling by the curb.

Tossing the envelope onto the sideboard, I hurry to fetch the twins.

Uncle Lenny appears all dressed and ready to go. "Help yourself to anything in the fridge," I offer.

"A couple of apples are just fine if you have them."

"In the dining room," I say. Lord knows, we have enough fruit to feed the entire monkey house at the Cleveland Zoo. The little kids continue to be somewhat wary of Uncle Lenny, as if he's the dark at the bottom of the stairs. I can't exactly blame them. His deep bass voice rumbles up from the bottom of his barrel chest and emerges through a froth of white whiskers like a cannon going off. When I was having a hard time getting the kids into bed last night, Uncle Lenny loudly declared that he'd kick them in the backsides so hard that their spines would come out through the tops of their heads. They scooted off to bed lickety-split.

At long last Darlene, Davy, and Francie are on their way to school, and Eric leaves to see Mom with Aunt Lala and Uncle Lenny. After lunch Eric will watch the kids while I visit Mom. He has to catch a bus at four o'clock so he can play in a championship football game tomorrow.

Teddy races through the living room and out the front door to catch up with Eric. I grab a coat out of the front hall that looks to be about the right size and dash out after him.

"I'm not sure they're going to let you in, Teddy." I toss the coat into the backseat where he's sitting next to Aunt Lala.

Eric rolls down the front window. "Then he'll have to stay in the waiting room. On the way home I'll drop him at school."

Back inside Lillian is chewing on green cellophane from one of the fruit baskets. I haul the old playpen up from the basement. Then I run a bath for the twins. It's when we're finished that I spot the little blue ribbon that had been tied around Roddy's ankle lying near the drain. I quickly look over at the naked babies crawling on the big towel spread out on the floor. Oh no! They look *exactly* alike.

Louise opens the bathroom door. She's wearing a coat and scarf. "Just thought I'd say good-bye."

"Okay," I say. "See you later."

"I left Brandt's number on the kitchen counter."

"Brandt? You're going to visit him in Massachusetts? *Now?*"

"I'm moving there. We're going to live together."

"You're *what!*" I shout. "No way!"

"You left home when you were fifteen," says Louise.

"That was *different.*" Only it was and it wasn't. I try another tactic. "Mom will kill you!"

"Mom is gone," she says as she walks away, no longer sounding angry, but more like a robot.

I finish dressing the twins just in time to see a cab pull up and Louise heading out with two stuffed garbage bags, the customary Palmer luggage set. I follow her with an unknown twin in each arm. Lillian has by now managed to throw every toy out of her playpen and is demanding that I fetch them for her.

Louise opens the front door and I stand there speechless. What am I supposed to say—that she can't leave me in this situation, what about school, what about *money?* Then I truly will be acting like Mom and Dad and her actions will be even more justified. Besides, I don't completely blame her for generating an exit strategy. Deep down I realize that if I had an out I just might take it, too.

Only Louise can get away with this. It's hard to explain, but because she's beautiful, it's as if her good looks make her extremely fragile, to the point they're actually some sort of a *handicap,* and thus people act as if she needs extra help to navigate the world. Whereas the more plain-faced among us are always expected to be strong and to sacrifice.

This has always been the case, at least in our house. If Louise didn't want to eat dinner or attend a skating lesson, it was fine. If the rest of us tried to wriggle out of something, we heard about wasted money and the need to "start what we finish." If you were ever to point out this child-rearing protocol discrepancy to my parents, they'd completely deny it. I suppose it's true what they say: that every child is born into a different house.

As the taxi pulls out of the driveway and speeds down the street the red taillights become smaller. A light snow begins to fall and low dark clouds move quickly toward us from the west, another storm on the way. It crosses my mind that luck is a lot like the weather and sometimes for no apparent reason it turns really bad.

TWENTY-TWO

THE LAUNDRY ROOM IS IN THE BACK CORNER OF THE BASEMENT, A dimly lit concrete bunker with piles of clothes reaching almost to the ceiling, and particularly attractive to spiders of the daddy-longlegs variety.

Mom has a system where she washes about three loads every day, from six different categories—baby clothes, boys' coloreds, boys' whites, girls' coloreds, girls' whites, and then a mishmash pile of sheets, towels, washcloths, bibs, and baby blankets. If one of the kids is sick and Mom gets a few days behind, it's almost necessary to go in there with a miner's hat and a steam shovel.

The next three hours disappear in a flurry of cleaning, vacuuming, and throwing away decaying fruit.

As I finish giving Lillian and the twins lunch, Eric returns home from the hospital with Aunt Lala and Uncle Lenny. "Did you give Teddy some lunch money? After you left I realized he didn't have anything to eat."

"He stayed at the hospital," says Eric. "We agreed that he'd come home with you. There's a cafeteria and some vending machines."

"Is Mom better?" I ask hopefully. Though better than what

I'm not exactly sure. I haven't seen her since leaving for school at the beginning of the year.

"Still the same," says Eric. "She doesn't respond. I mean, I know that she sees us, and I'm pretty sure she recognizes us, but she doesn't say anything."

"Then what is Teddy wanting to stay there for?"

"To be honest, it's a good thing he came along," says Eric. "After the first ten minutes of trying to pretend that everything is fine, the rest of us ran out of steam and sat there in silence or talked with one another. But Teddy just prattles on as if Mom understands every word he's saying."

So much for my plan to ask Mom about the age mystery— why her birth certificate makes her two years *younger* than we've always believed her to be.

"Well, the big excitement around here since you left is that Louise left for Boston. She's going to live with Brandt." In the old days I might actually have enjoyed the shock value of dropping such a bomb. But not anymore. We've had enough surprises for one week.

"With Brandt!" shouts Eric.

"Yes." My voice is calm. I'm too overwhelmed to get wound up about anything.

"And you let her just *leave?*"

"What was I supposed to do? Throw Lillian's potty seat around her neck and tie her to the playpen?"

"This is just great," says Eric. "What about school?"

"They have schools up there," I state the obvious, though not in a sarcastic way.

"What about *you?*" he asks. "You can't possibly manage all this by yourself." He collapses into a kitchen chair and exhales like a bear. "That's it—I can't go back to school this afternoon!"

I crumple into the chair across from him. "You have to go

back, for a lot of reasons. If Mom doesn't get better I don't know how we're all going to afford to live past next year. The checking account is down to nothing. Ten thousand is owed to the credit union and there's forty-three thousand left to pay on the house!" I've found that suddenly I do have the energy to become agitated.

"Well you can't take care of seven kids by yourself!" says Eric.

There's a crash in the next room followed by the sound of glass splintering. This serves to indicate that Lillian, who tends to operate on the theory of sustained attack, has thrown a toy out of the playpen and managed to lodge a direct hit. I know right away it was the picture of Mom and Dad that I was looking at the other night and forgot to put back on the mantelpiece. Because the house is completely childproof—compliments of the children themselves—anything the least bit fragile was either broken or stored away a long time ago, except for Mom's decoupage projects. We have plenty of backups if those get ruined.

"Aunt Lala is making her reservations to go home as we speak," says Eric. "Uncle Fred called her cell phone while we were in the car. Our cousin Marci dyed her hair purple and is threatening to get a tattoo."

"Let's face it Eric, Louise wasn't exactly a huge help to begin with. When she's not at school or cheerleading, Louise is off with her friends. She's always despised baby-sitting. You know that. And . . . and . . ."

"And what?" asks Eric.

Only his frustration at this recent turn of household events keeps me from saying it—that maybe it's better, at least for her. And that if Louise were a boy we might not even be having this discussion: Would a brother be expected to completely change his life in order to help care for younger siblings?

"Dad would kill her if he were here." Eric states the obvious. "Living with some guy and she's not even sixteen."

"Three more weeks," I say. "Besides, from the conversations I've overheard it's safe to say that Brandt's more interested in string theory than sex."

"Well, Mom is going to have a fit about this when she's better, and I only hope she doesn't blame us," continues Eric. "Don't say anything when you go to visit her!"

"I won't. But I'd better leave now if you're going to catch the bus at four. I mean, Aunt Lala . . ." I roll my eyes to indicate that she's not exactly able to keep track of the entire brood on her own. And we don't even bother to mention big gruff Uncle Lenny in the context of child care. He drinks three beers with every meal, which is apparently nothing, because according to Uncle Lenny, every sailor in Admiral Nelson's navy was issued eight pints of beer a day *by law*. The moment Uncle Lenny drains a can he crushes it in his hand like a Dixie cup, shouts, "Tide's gone out!," and pops open another. Meantime he tells the kids to eat their broccoli because "it will help to grow hair on their chests like stalks of rhubarb." In fact, with that wild white mane and walrus whiskers I'm surprised they didn't try to keep *him* at Dalewood. Retired seaman or local madman? A close call on the basis of looks alone. And when he starts talking about cooking up some snake and pygmy pie for lunch, it's anybody's guess.

"I'll be back in time to take you to the bus station." I grab my coat and keys. Darn it, I was hoping Louise could stay with the kids this afternoon so I could pick up my car at school. There are probably a hundred parking tickets stacked under the windshield wiper by now. Maybe Bernard and I can make a quick trip to get it over the weekend.

"Is there anything to eat?" asks Eric. He's bulked up even

more during his second year on the football team, if that's possible, and eats four huge meals a day.

"Bernard and the church ladies left lots of food in the refrigerator."

He grunts in acknowledgment of this statement. And suddenly I feel as if we're some old married couple complaining about the kids and wondering what's for lunch.

TWENTY-THREE

IT'S ONE OF THOSE BRILLIANTLY SUNNY WINTER AFTERNOONS, THE kind where people oftentimes can't make out the color of the traffic lights, and so you have to be extra careful at intersections, especially since they're already banked with four feet of snow. Everything glistens as the snow begins to melt, and when the temperature drops tonight the roads and sidewalks will turn to a sheet of ice. No doubt tomorrow will be a perfect day for breaking hips, just like the first big storm always means Heart Attack City as overzealous retirees head outside with their shovels.

I don't know if it's the bright white landscape or because it's the first time in days I'm completely alone that the ride has such a surreal feeling. Or if it's the fact that I'm going to visit my mother in a mental hospital for the first time. Last I saw her she was taking down the Christmas decorations and fretting that the tree had become so dry it would set the house on fire.

The grounds at Dalewood are attractively landscaped around some very old oak and maple trees with plenty of benches, walkways, and even a duck pond. The main structure is dark gray stone with small windows, rather than the red or white brick of a modern hospital, and unfortunately on a dreary day this serves to give the place more than the suggestion of being a haunted house. In fact, you could go so far as to say that in a thunderstorm it wouldn't exactly be ruled out as a location for shooting *Jane Eyre* or *Wuthering Heights.*

A young man at a school-style desk signs me in, hands me a visitor's pass, and points in the direction of room 232. The corridors are painted an institutional pale green and chrome bars line the walls. The old building has some nice touches, like wood molding along the ceilings and cornice pieces. Pleasant paintings are arranged on the walls, with little gold plaques indicating that the pieces were a donation from someone, which is clearly not your typical doctor's office crap.

Several people shuffle down the hall wearing their own bathrobes. A young woman in a white blouse, white pants, and white clogs pushes a man in a wheelchair. None of the doors are closed, and so I can hear televisions inside the rooms. The place smells like a combination of disinfectant and your grandmother's parlor on a rainy day.

Before reaching Mom's room I hear the chirpy young voice of Teddy. From outside the door I can see them sitting side by side on the edge of Mom's bed going through a stack of photos. "That's Lillian's christening party, do you remember, you made peanut butter cookies with M&M's in them? And when it started to rain we had to move everything into the garage."

"Hi, guys!" When I go around the side of the bed to kiss Mom hello, I'm startled to find her normally cheerful face is practically vacant. The bright brown eyes that always gave off a warm light have turned melancholy, while her head is bent forward slightly and her shoulders are drawn together as if she's trying not to be noticed.

"Hi, Hallie," says Teddy, the spokesperson for the duo. "We're looking at some photos from Lillian's christening. We just finished the ones of you and Craig going to the prom. You look pretty funny in a dress."

Meantime Mom is staring straight ahead, not at the photos but not out the window either. She's expressionless. Or perhaps exhausted from grief.

"So Mom . . . how are you?" I ask.

Only Teddy quickly shoots me a look as if I've used the wrong fork at a White House dinner party.

Mom doesn't respond, or even look up, and so I don't know what difference it makes.

Teddy points to another photograph. "This is Christmas last year and I got a new bike."

I'm so stunned by what's happening that I just stand there like a patient myself and watch the photo session continue. Eric hadn't prepared me for this! Mom is completely listless. She doesn't talk or move. How does she eat? What does she do all day? Where did she *go*?

And what about Teddy? He's perfectly fine sitting here for hours talking to a mute woman in her robe and slippers? Teddy was definitely a strange twelve-year-old, no doubt about it. He'd ask a teacher or a person at church his or her age and then say, "Do you ever wonder if the happiest time in your life has already passed?" or "Do you ever think about how long you'll live?" Teddy hardly uttered a word until he was eight years old, and ever since then it's only been the *big* questions.

A part of me feels like shaking her out of this trance. When I was in sociology class last semester we took personality tests and I came out as a full-blown "activist." This basically means that when I'm upset, excited, or worried, I have to do something.

Suddenly I feel as if I'm going to lose it. "Teddy, we need to go because Eric has to catch the bus."

"Why don't you just pick me up after dinner?" Teddy calmly asks.

"Because Louise," whoops, I stop myself before letting that cat out of the bag, though I don't even know if Mom understands anything we're saying. "Because it's too complicated with all the kids. Come on. Get your coat."

Teddy places the stack of photos on Mom's bedside table next to a little maroon-covered copy of the New Testament. " 'Bye, Mom," he says as he leans over and kisses her cheek. "Tomorrow is Saturday and so I'll be able to stay longer."

I follow Teddy's example by bending over and kissing Mom on her forehead. As I do it I feel like bursting into tears and so quickly turn and head for the door.

We're silent on the way home. Teddy stares out the passenger-side window, lost in his thoughts. I'm wrapped up in mine. Mom is I don't know where. Sorrow is a solitary road.

TWENTY-FOUR

WHEN WE RETURN HOME I FIND OUT THAT AUNT LALA HAS BEEN able to get a seat on the overnight flight to London from New York. I'll take her to the airport after dropping Eric at the bus station. The next hour is a whirlwind of Eric's draining the furnace in the basement and my assembling some dinner for the kids. Organizing one simple meal in this house is like planning an invasion. How my mother managed three every day is just short of a miracle.

It isn't until Aunt Lala's suitcases and Eric's backpack are in the hall that I realize Uncle Lenny's battered canvas sea bag is not among them. I just assumed he'd be leaving, too. Pulling Eric into the front hall closet, which has become the winter conference center, I say, "You can't leave me here alone with *him.*"

"C'mon, Hallie, he's a harmless old guy," says Eric. "Okay, so he's a little rough around the edges. But he's a relative."

"Eric, we hardly know *anything* about him," I say. "He could be wanted for murder in six states! Last night at dinner Uncle Lenny actually admitted that he was forced to leave the country back in the 1980s!"

"You weren't listening—he incorporated his charter fishing

company in the Bahamas because the U.S. government was killing small businesses with taxes and regulations."

"Well, find out when he's leaving," I say.

"Hallie, that's rude," says Eric. "Now come on or I'm going to miss the bus and Aunt Lala is going to be late for her flight. Are you sure it's okay to leave Teddy in charge here for a while?"

"Yeah, the twins are down," I say. "We'll put Lillian in the car seat." The way I figure it, any sibling is better than Louise, who was the anti-baby-sitter. For all she cared the kids could turn on every appliance in the kitchen and play restaurant.

As we exit the closet Aunt Lala appears with her coat over her arm. "Hallie, one of the boys is a bit fussy." She's been too polite to mention that I lost the ribbon on Roddy's ankle and there's no way to tell which twin is which, so we've been circumnavigating the identity issue by saying "one of the boys."

Ugh. Why can't they get on the same schedule? Aside from when they wake up in concert every morning, one is always dropping off just as the other is coming to life.

"I took the liberty of calling the airport taxi service and they've agreed to drop Eric at the bus station."

Eric and I both panic at the word *taxi,* much the way Dad used to shudder at the words *field trip.* Visions of dollar bills dance before our eyes.

"Don't worry," she says and smiles. "It's my treat. And I've left some money on the kitchen table to tide you over until the insurance check arrives."

"Thanks so much, Aunt Lala," says Eric. "That's very generous of you." Pride is put aside. Obviously we're in no position to be turning down assistance from a relative.

"I wish it were more," she says. "Maybe one of these days I'll win the lottery." Aunt Lala is a fanatical player of lotteries and bingo. Cappy says that lotteries are a tax on people who are bad at math and bingo is a Native American word that directly translates to: She who pays eighty dollars for a lamp worth twelve.

The taxi arrives and we all hug each other good-bye, too exhausted for tears. Uncle Lenny shakes hands with Eric while I look at my brother in a way that clearly states, "If we're all killed and chopped up for shark bait it's *your* fault."

TWENTY-FIVE

AFTER DINNER I START PUTTING THE KIDS TO BED, PATROLLING the house room by room and issuing threats like a prison warden. Without Eric around it takes longer to settle things down at night. Previously we could divide and conquer. The other problem is that a few of them are starting to sense that I might not have the control vested in me by sheer size, like Eric, or age, like Bernard. If this were the jungle, they would be the team of smaller but wily animals sizing up their chances of overpowering the larger but single elephant.

Just to be safe, I haul the twins back upstairs so Uncle Lenny doesn't get any ideas about absconding with them during the night. I'll definitely catch hell from everyone if my little brothers end up as cabin boys on a pirate ship in the South Seas. With Louise gone, I can move back into my old room upstairs, leaving an entire floor between us and Captain Ahab.

Exhausted, I finally crawl under the covers and find myself dreading the fact that tomorrow is Saturday. This is quite a contrast to the old days, or at least to a month ago, when the weekend is what I lived for, and Mom was a superhero able to heap dirty laundry in a single mound.

In the bed across from me nine-year-old Darlene is a slight figure with flame-red hair among a heap of stuffed animals, mostly of the feline variety. After the light is out a tiny voice trembles in the darkness, "Hallie . . . are Mommy and Daddy coming back?"

Obviously I'm not the only one operating in a hurricane of confusion. It would be easier to say that she'll see Dad again in heaven, or that he's watching out for us from up there. Meantime the doctors don't even know what the prognosis is for Mom, other than to say that they're optimistic and we need to give it some time. But when pressed for the definition of "time"—a week, a month, a year—Eric says they simply shrug and talk about the importance of quiet, good care, and hope.

"Daddy isn't coming back, sweetie," I say, unable to make myself go with the heaven story. "But he loved us a lot and now he's in our thoughts and memories, and that's the important thing."

There's a brief silence before I hear an ominous series of bass notes coming from the hallway.

"Ahoy there, Hallie, are you awake?"

Oh my God! He's been waiting for Eric to leave and now begins the murderous rampage. I think if there are any weapons in the room, but all that comes to mind is Darlene's baton next to the dresser. While lunging for the baton in the darkness I trip over a step stool and land flat on the floor.

The overhead light goes on, and Uncle Lenny's large figure blocks the doorway. He's wearing an old coast guard sweatshirt and worn white deck pants. "I'm afraid we're taking on water," he reports.

"Huh?" I shake my head in an attempt to recover from having almost knocked myself out.

"Downstairs," Uncle Lenny continues without remarking

on the fact that I'm lying prostrate on the floor with a step stool for a pillow. "A pipe burst and the basement is flooding."

"Oh no!" I manage to get up and limp after Uncle Lenny. Sure enough, there's an inch of water covering the basement floor with alphabet blocks and Lincoln logs floating around like little boats.

"What do we do?"

"I've already shut off the water," he reports. "We just have to call the plumber in the morning. If you have a pump I can clean this mess up pretty easily."

"A pump? No, I don't think we do."

Uncle Lenny surveys the basement. "Not a problem. There's just cement. It'll drain."

"So there's no water?" I ask. With ten people in the house there's normally a certain amount of toilet flushing during the night.

"Plenty of snow outside," says Uncle Lenny. "I'll fill a few buckets and put them in the bathrooms. Then you just pour in water to refill the tank."

"Thanks, Uncle Lenny," I say. "You're a lifesaver."

He shrugs off this praise as if a basement flood is pretty low on his list of emergencies. "I'll collect some of these toys so they don't clog the drains. Just show me the mop and buckets and get back to bed. Morning comes fast around here."

"What did you just say?" I ask.

"If you have some buckets—"

"No, after that."

"Morning comes fast around here." Uncle Lenny chuckles. "It's what our mother always said right before we went to sleep."

"It's what my dad used to say as he shooed us off to bed."

"He comes by it honestly," says Uncle Lenny.

Suddenly Uncle Lenny doesn't seem quite so sinister. In fact, he's more like a savior.

After I climb back between the sheets it's only a minute before I see Darlene slip out of her bed and stand next to mine. Wordlessly I lift the covers, and she slides in next to me.

"Hallie, do you know what would make everything a lot better?" she speaks softly in the dark.

"Yeah. If we had a plumber in the family," I say. How much is fixing the pipes going to cost? I wonder.

"No, really?" says Darlene.

"What would make everything a lot better?" I hug her tight, expecting to hear that if Mom and Dad were home and life was back to the way it used to be.

"If we had a kitten," she says.

Mom and Dad had a strict no-pets policy, reasoning that we didn't need any more mouths to feed, someone was probably allergic, and the furniture would be ruined. Though it's not as if ten kids haven't destroyed their fair share of furniture without assistance from a pet.

"Yes, I suppose that would make things a lot better," I agree.

"*Really?*" says Darlene, unable to believe where this might be leading after her five-year campaign to get a cat.

"Really. Now go to sleep," I whisper close so that my breath tickles her ear and she squirms and giggles. "Morning comes fast around here."

TWENTY-SIX

On Saturday I rise to the usual cacophony of the twins howling in stereo. It's almost eight o'clock and from the sound of things, the rest of the household is already wide awake. There's shouting in the hallway, the garage door goes up, the basement door slams shut—every conceivable noise except the shower running. Which reminds me, I have to call the plumber.

The kids will be starving for breakfast. I stumble into the kitchen to get bottles for the twins. Uncle Lenny, outfitted in his admiral's cap, a blue coast guard polo shirt, white pants, and well-worn deck shoes, looks like the skipper in *Gilligan's Island*. He sits at the kitchen table leaning over a map and appears to be preparing to take over the town as he draws lines from one dot to the next.

"The plumber will be here at oh nine hundred hours!" he announces in a reverberating bass that could do serious damage if the listener had a hangover. "I fished the number out of your mum's logbook. Meantime, the mates have suggested breakfast grub at the mall food court, and I have agreed to be their captain, if that's okay with the Home Office and you can lend me a vessel."

I'll *bet* they suggested the food court, with all its chain restaurants. Mom never lets anyone eat out unless it's a friend's birthday party. Just looking at those prices makes her dizzy.

The door leading from the garage into the kitchen swings open and Bernard enters in musical mode, performing one of his favorite numbers from *Singin' in the Rain.* "Good morning, good morning, we talked the whole night through, good morning to you!" He then points to us individually while adding, "And to you and you and you."

When Bernard sees Uncle Lenny's marine garb he salutes and shouts, "My Gallant Crew, Good Morning!"

Uncle Lenny looks up from his map and bellows, "Refrain, Audacious Tar!"

Suddenly I'm afraid they're going to have a fight. And I appear to be correct.

Bernard approaches Uncle Lenny and yells, "Can I Survive This Overbearing?"

"Never Mind the Why and Wherefore," Uncle Lenny volleys back while rising from the table, his bushy eyebrows floating above his eyes like fluffy white clouds.

Practically toe to toe with Uncle Lenny, Bernard hollers, "We Sail the Ocean Blue!"

To my great amazement they both break into lively song, *"We sail the ocean blue, and our saucy ship's a beauty; we're sober men and true, and attentive to our duty."* Never shy about performing, Bernard makes up in enthusiasm what he lacks in pitch. However, Uncle Lenny of the low register growl erupts into an opera-ready high tenor. Not only can he carry a tune, but potentially seed a few clouds with his robust projection!

After their chorus is complete Bernard notices my startled expression and casually explains, *"H.M.S. Pinafore."*

Bernard nods approvingly at Uncle Lenny. "Those are *some* pipes."

"Twelve years in the Coast Guard Glee Club," Uncle Lenny proudly states, and then salutes Bernard.

I see this as my opportunity for a conference about Uncle Lenny's plan to disembark with the kids and say, "Bernard, um, could you come and help me with the twins for a moment?"

"Of course." It's apparent that he gets my drift. "I'll leave these thank-you notes here on the counter."

Bernard follows me out of the kitchen and upstairs to my old bedroom.

"A pipe burst in the middle of the night and Uncle Lenny has offered to take the kids to the food court at the mall over in Timpany." I whisper so that Uncle Lenny doesn't overhear. Though I can't imagine he would since you practically have to shout right in his face for him to know he's being addressed. Back when Uncle Lenny was in the coast guard, they must have still been using cannons.

"I thought the kids were terrified of him," says Bernard. "And though he appears to be a jolly fellow underneath all those whiskers, I can see why they might be a bit tentative."

"With the power to access fast food he's become exponentially more appealing," I explain. "They'd follow a serial killer to the food court. All Palmer children suffer from acute Happy Meal deprivation."

When we reach the spot where the twins cribs are, I can't believe my eyes. Teddy has just finished changing both boys. I wasn't even aware that he knew *how* to change a diaper.

"I saw you were busy in the kitchen." Teddy says this as if he changes the boys all the time, which I happen to know full well he *doesn't.*

"Gee, thanks," I say. This is very strange indeed.

"Uh, Hallie," Teddy says casually, "Uncle Lenny can drop me off at the hospital on his way to the mall."

"Teddy, he doesn't even know where it is. Eric drove him there exactly once."

"Uncle Lenny says he can find any place with a map and the sun or the North Star." Teddy disappears around the corner before I can give him an answer.

"Do you think it's safe to let him take a car with the kids?" I ask Bernard.

"Anybody who knows the words to a Gilbert and Sullivan operetta is okay in my book. It's probably just more difficult for a . . . well, a bachelor man such as himself to find ways to be useful with all these children. Give him a chance."

"Not to sound like my mother, but his address is a *bar*."

"It's difficult to get mail in the middle of the ocean," says Bernard. "And having a little drink now and then is by no means a sign of derangement. Why, Edith Rockefeller was a teetotaler and yet believed herself to be the child bride of King Tutankhamen."

"I suppose," I say. "It sure would be nice to get a few things done without the carnival going full tilt."

"We can pick up your car at school," adds Bernard. "Weren't you worried about parking tickets?"

"Okay, but the plumber is coming at nine. At least I think that's what Uncle Lenny said. I can't understand what he's talking about half the time. Did you know that Oscar, Tango, Bravo, Echo is marine code for *overtaken by events*?"

"No I didn't, but it certainly goes a long way in describing your current situation. We can work on the thank-you notes until the plumber finishes."

I lean my head back and groan. "Do I have to write them *today*?"

"May as well get it over with," says Bernard. "But I suppose if you think your mother won't mind . . ."

"Fine!" I raise my hand in front of his face—the international signal to stop nagging someone before she slaps you. Bernard knows exactly what buttons to push with me. My mother would of course be horrified if thank-you notes didn't go out in a timely manner. And not just any old notes but ones properly written with *no* shortcuts, such as a form letter that begins "Dear Mourner." After all, Mom is the one who wrote a note to thank the man who smashed her rear axle for giving her a ride home after the tow truck finally arrived.

TWENTY-SEVEN

When the plumber spends ten minutes changing a fitting on a pipe and charges me $185, it's obvious that I've been going to school for the wrong occupation. As I forge Mom's name on a check, I see from the neatly kept ledger that there's only $111.43 left in the account.

Bernard and I pack the twins into the back of his Volvo and head over to his house. "Slight change in plan," he says. "It's getting late and I'm bringing the cinnamon sugar palmiers to Hattie McKenzie's retirement tea at the historical society this afternoon. Gil will drive you to Cleveland to pick up your car."

"Palmiers?" I ask.

"Puff pastry," replies Bernard. "Believe me, you don't want to know the rest—I was up until five o'clock this morning with collapsing dough. Heaven forbid the recipe says not to use whipped butter—these French dessert books assume that one was *born* knowing these things!"

Now that I take a good look, Bernard does indeed appear tired, with circles under his eyes and a slightly gray pallor.

"At two A.M. I was at the convenience store buying every stick of butter in stock." Bernard raises the back of his hand to his forehead and dramatically states, "I think I'm suffering from pastry shell shock."

Sure enough, Gil is waiting inside the front door and they switch places. Gil is the more athletic of the two, and he swings into the driver's seat with one hand on the roof of the car without even disturbing his hat. The Cleveland Indians baseball cap that he wears almost constantly is not to designate him a fan so much as to hide his receding hairline.

"Cleveland or bust!" says Gil with a cheerful smile as he checks for traffic and then pulls out of the driveway.

"The car isn't far from where you guys parked that night you picked me up," I say. And then I can't help but think, *that night,* the one when the world came off its axis.

"Bernard said we're also clearing out your apartment," says Gil.

"There really isn't time for the apartment." The truth is that I just can't bring myself to pack up. Besides, there's no chance of finding someone to take over my portion of the lease at this late date. "How's work?" I change the subject. Though it's common knowledge that Gil hates his job as a corporate trainer.

"I'm caught in a trap," says Gil, using a line from *A Streetcar Named Desire.* "The work isn't too hard, the pay is pretty good, and I absolutely hate it. But Gigi and Rose will need money for college and so I do it."

"Not for another fifteen years," I say. "And Bernard's business is doing well."

"He's told me to quit a million times," says Gil. "But I wouldn't feel right about not pulling my weight with the bills."

When we locate the dirt-covered green cabriolet, it's stuck in an ice-encrusted snowbank and there are four tickets stuck under the wipers along with an explanation of how long you have to dig out after a major storm. Oh well, it could be a lot worse. I escaped the tow truck.

Gil shovels the plow-packed snow out from around the tires while I clean the windows and make sure that it starts. As we work, kids walk past us on their way to the library and the art rooms, talking and laughing or listening to music through earphones while enjoying the privacy of their own thoughts. It's hard to believe that I was one of them just two weeks ago.

After the car is free from the hardened snow and warmed up, we transfer the sleeping twins to the backseat.

"Drive safely," says Gil. "I'm going to stop by my office and pick up some files."

It's a long ride home under a pollution-gray sky, one that I wouldn't be making until spring break if Dad hadn't died. Will I ever be able to finish school? The twins wake up in the backseat and make noises that indicate they're anticipating lunch at my earliest convenience.

On the outskirts of town I pass the Starview Drive-in, an outdoor movie theater that has been there since the 1950s. In fact, it's where my parents went on their first date. The marquee that usually reads SEE YOU IN THE SPRING in big black letters has been changed to FOR SALE, followed by a phone number. The combination of rising real estate prices and people wanting to see the stars from the comfort of their own living rooms has apparently put an end to our only drive-in. The twins might never know what it's like to attach a clunky speaker to the window and make out in row H.

When I arrive back at the house, Uncle Lenny has Teddy occupied with a bunch of wires and a big yellow balloon in the front yard. Uncle Lenny explains that Teddy is supposed to be shipwrecked and about to be rescued by using a balloon with a radar shield. Or something like that. Uncle Lenny informs us that his real calling is as an inventor. Yeah, Uncle Lenny is actually an inventor and I'm really an heiress to the sippy cup fortune.

"I called the house a couple times from the mall, but no one was here." Uncle Lenny concentrates on adjusting the radar box as he speaks.

"I had to go and pick up my car in Cleveland," I explain.

"They said you'd given permission for everything."

Number one, permission for *what*? And number two, you *never* believe children about *anything* when they're in a mall. Based on the shouts coming from inside the house, I decide it's probably better to go and see for myself rather than make further inquiries.

Inside, it all hits me at once, in a Mad Hatter Tea Party sort of way. Francie's hair was halfway down her back this morning and now it's competing with Eric's crew cut. Darlene has gone from having long red tresses to a bob that ends slightly below her ears, while Davy has a spiky gelled-up style possibly modeled after something in the cockatoo family. Lillian's hair is about three inches shorter and she now sports bangs, which I decide are rather cute. They must have stopped in that place where the high school kids get the bulldogs shaved into their heads.

No one notices my entrance, given that they're all preoccupied with a little gray and white ball of fluff. "Whose cat is that?" I ask angrily, afraid of the answer.

"You *thaid* we could get a kitten on Thaturday!" whines Darlene, tears already forming in the corners of her eyes. Her lisp always worsens the minute she becomes upset.

"I did not say *on Saturday.*"

Francie runs over and hands me a bowl with an exotic-looking bright red fish in it.

"It's a Japanese fighting fish," explains Davy. "You can't have two in the same bowl because they'll fight to the death."

"Aren't cats and fish awfully close in the food chain?" I'm distracted from my fury for a second by the simple facts of nature.

"We're not going to keep them *together*," explains Francie, as if she's addressing a complete idiot.

Now I'm ready to blow my top. What is Mom going to say about these haircuts? Yes, I'd been muttering that they needed trims . . . however, the pets have to go back *right* now. This is absolutely the wrong moment for animals. But then I watch how joyous they all are, pulling a piece of string around for the kitten to chase, exclaiming over the fish, and no longer encumbered by tangled hair. What the heck? As Mom said the time that Francie chopped off Lillian's curly mop on one side, "It will grow back."

With less than three inches of hair covering Francie's head, I notice a glint coming from her earlobes. My voice rises as I move closer. "Did you get your ears pierced?"

There was definitely no permission slip issued for this infraction. When Louise and I were younger we had to beg Dad to let us get our ears pierced, and even then he was angry for a week, acting as if streetwalkers had taken up residence in his house.

Francie quickly covers her ears with her hands as her face turns bright red. She's well aware that there's no arguing her way out of this one. On the other hand, all I have to do is tell her to take them out, the holes will close up in a few days, and no one will be the wiser. Only with her short hair they at least make her look like a girl. Actually the little pink studs are sort of pretty. Normally she's such a tomboy.

Francie catches me the moment my guard is down and hugs my knees. "Darlene was too afeard," she says proudly.

Darlene looks up upon hearing her name and, hugging the kitten close, informs me, "His name is Kitty!"

Oh well, so many things have changed recently, what's a few more? I'm suddenly cheered. Worst case, I'll simply blame everything on Uncle Lenny and say that, when all this happened, I wasn't part of "the command structure," a direct quote from him.

TWENTY-EIGHT

THE PLAN FOR SUNDAY HAD BEEN TO TAKE THE KIDS TO CHURCH and then go sledding in the park after lunch. However, there's an ice storm in progress and it sounds as if the windows are being pummeled by a thousand marbles. Opening the front door is like going in front of a BB-gun firing squad, and if you step onto the front porch without metal cleats you'll go flying all the way to Main Street.

As I'm making breakfast Eric calls from school to report that they won their game.

"That would make Dad happy," I say.

"How are things going?" he asks.

"Okay, I guess. I don't remember having this much energy as a kid. Even if you stick them in front of the television they manage to jab at each other and start fights."

"You were always off in some corner with a deck of cards," Eric reminds me.

"Actually, that's not a bad idea," I say. "Today is never going to end. Maybe I can get them to play a really long card game like War, only with five decks."

I hear a crash upstairs followed by a shriek and tell Eric that I'd better go. Francie has knocked the fishbowl over and the poor creature flops around on the floor while she screams at full volume. I grab the fish in my hands and race toward the bathroom, only she thinks I'm going to kill it and becomes hysterical. Finally I'm able to explain that it's only in the toilet until we get a bowl from downstairs. She guards the flusher to make sure.

Teddy appears in the bathroom doorway and asks if Uncle Lenny or I can drive him to see Mom. "Sorry, Teddy, but it's an ice storm. Look out the window—no one is on the road."

Davy comes flying past us carrying the kitten, heading toward the stairs, with Darlene in hot pursuit, screaming, "Give it back!"

"Teddy—huge favor—please put Francie's fish in a new bowl," I say.

"If I do that, then will you drive me to the hospital?" Teddy bargains with me. "They'll salt the roads soon."

"Teddy, I think we have to give it a rest for today," I say.

"That's not fair!" he raises his voice. "How is Mom going to get better if we don't help her!"

A howl goes up from Francie's room and, recalling Darlene running past wearing only her nightgown and socks, it's easy to guess what happened.

Charging into the bedroom I shout, "What are you doing in there with broken glass!"

But it's too late and Darlene shows me the cut on her foot. Fortunately it's not terrible and there don't seem to be any glass fragments stuck inside.

Uncle Lenny appears at the bottom of the stairs carrying Lillian under his arm like a big football. She's managed to get into the blueberry jam and it's all over her face and in her formerly strawberry-blond hair. We're approaching *Cat in the Hat*–level chaos and it's not even breakfast time. Honestly, I'm ready to burst into tears.

Uncle Lenny puts the forefinger and pinky of his right hand

into his mouth and lets fly an ear-piercing whistle. This certainly gets everyone's attention. Davy, still in his Spider-Man pajamas, stops tearing around with the kitten and comes to the top of the stairs to see what's going on, Teddy stops arguing, Francie stops crying, Lillian stops wriggling, and even the kitten looks wide-eyed with expectation.

"Parade halt!" booms Uncle Lenny.

Parade? It's more like a six-ring circus. All we need are some dancing bears and a poodle act.

"All children will be washed, dressed, booted, and spurred with hair combed in exactly one-five minutes and report to the galley for breakfast vittles!"

The kids quickly disperse, even Teddy. Uncle Lenny comes up the stairs and I nod toward the fish in the toilet while applying a Band-Aid to Darlene's foot.

"I'll work the top deck while you deal with the guppies." That's how Uncle Lenny refers to the twins.

Twenty minutes later Uncle Lenny is lining the kids up in the kitchen according to height and issuing bowls of cereal and slices of banana. There's none of the usual nonsense of complaining about this or that.

When they've finished breakfast, Lenny marches them off to learn how to tie knots, and he says if they're good he'll teach them how to play pirates and coast guard. Normally Teddy won't do anything that involves the little kids, but even he follows along.

This gives me a chance to finally do some laundry and open the huge stack of mail that's piled up over the last week. It's mostly condolence letters and hospital bills. One large flat envelope looks as if it might contain an 8-by-10 photograph and says DO NOT BEND in bright red letters on the outside. It turns out to be Dad's death certificate. The cause of death is listed as a "major cardiovascular event." They make it sound as if he died while competing in the Olympics. On the bright side, Dad always loved sports.

When I open the bill from the gas company, it's my turn to have a heart attack. Whoa—$396.43 just for heat! I race to the thermostat and twist the dial to the left at least ten degrees. Apparently there was a good reason that Mom used to tell anyone who complained of being cold to "put on a sweater."

Near the bottom of the pile is a paycheck for Dad. I should probably be thinking how creepy that is, but I'm more concerned with wondering if it's possible to deposit a dead person's check.

There's a lengthy note from my great-aunt Vi saying how sorry she is they weren't able to attend the funeral. The note takes up every available inch of the sympathy card plus both sides of an inserted piece of notebook paper. Aunt Vi can write almost as much as she talks. And suddenly I get an idea.

I look up Aunt Vi's number in Mom's address book and call her in Oklahoma City. She rambles on for at least twenty minutes about everything from "what a terrible tragedy" Dad's death is to how Uncle Russ has taken to shredding paper. It was fine when he used a pair of scissors and just worked on newspapers and old phone books, but now he has a shredding machine and any piece of paper is fair game. She's had to put the deed to the house and other important documents in a safety deposit box down at the bank.

Finally Aunt Vi takes a breath and I jump in. "Aunt Vi, the insurance company might cut us off because Mom's birth certificate doesn't match her age." It's an out-and-out lie, but how is she going to know that?

"Oh dear." There's a pause into which you could fit the entire town. "Can't you ask Lala to help sort it out?"

"She went back to London."

"Oh dear, oh dear, what to do?" Aunt Vi says again, and there's a long silence, which makes me think she may have passed out since I can't remember a time when Aunt Vi permitted an actual lapse in any conversation.

"Hallie, this is something none of us ever talk about. You're old enough to understand that every family has its little secrets and they're a private matter that no one else needs to know about."

There's another long silence and clearly she's hesitating about whether or not to proceed.

"I promise not to tell anyone," I say.

"Your mom became pregnant with Eric when she was only seventeen, in her final year of high school. And your dad was nineteen. He was a freshman in college. Your mom dropped out of school, they married, and then of course she had the baby."

My mouth hangs open as I think to myself about Mom pregnant out of wedlock—my mom who won't even talk about sex. Talk—she won't even say the word. If absolutely forced to use the word *sex* Mom actually *spells* it! And now it turns out that she was married with a baby when she was younger than I am now!

Aunt Vi audibly exhales and then lets out a little laugh, as if to say we all do foolish things when we're young, and if that's the least of it then it's not so bad. And I guess she's right in view of the fact that everything more or less worked out in the end. I mean, they were happily married and Eric became their pride and joy with his good grades, good work ethic, and good forward pass. Dad somehow managed to finish college. Though I think he switched to night classes and that explains why the sports trophies suddenly stopped. I always assumed it was because of his bad knees.

After hanging up with Aunt Vi I quickly dial Bernard's number.

"What are you up to these days?" he asks, as if I'm part of his ladies-who-lunch clientele.

"Taking over a medium-sized country," I retort. "What do you think I'm doing other than changing diapers, cleaning spit-up, and heating bottles?"

"How about some sterling silver picture frames so you can have all those adorable little faces right next to your bed-side?"

I relate to him my conversation with Aunt Vi and how my mother has been hiding becoming pregnant at seventeen and dropping out of high school by telling us she's two years older than she really is.

"You know what I always say—every one mother equals a one-hundred-step program for the offspring."

I want to talk more about this, but Bernard is obsessing about the fact that a Girl Scout troop is coming to his store the next day. "When they first made the inquiry, I was thrilled by the prospect of doing a little presentation on the finer things in life, surmising that today's girls are tomorrow's brides—the future givers and getters of crystal and hand-painted vases. But now I'm not so sure about keeping the attention of a dozen or so twelve-year-old girls."

"You'll be fine," I say. "Tell them the story about that heiress woman Louise Stotesbury who played poker against President Warren Harding in the White House, and how if he won she had to sleep with him, and if she won he had to give her a set of White House china."

"Hallie, I don't think that's a story appropriate for young ladies."

"Why not? She beat him! You're so boring since becoming a father," I say. "Then tell them how Lady Astor's dinner guests had to keep a careful eye on her while eating because when she switched from talking to the person on her left side to the person on her right side, they all had to switch, too, and so three hundred heads would all turn at once."

"I suppose there's no canceling at this late date," frets Bernard. "And someone must deliver a little culture to this wasteland. It's not as if Christo is attempting to swath Main Street in fabric."

"We could hang a quilt by Jane's mom," I offer. "Jane called last night and said that ever since the divorce her mother has become a mad quilter. Last week she sent one to Jane for her dorm room that says, 'If Life Were a Bouquet of Flowers I'd Pick You!' "

"There's no accounting for taste," says Bernard. "Edgar Degas was obsessed with painting ballet dancers and washerwomen. Why does your voice sound so far away? Are you on a cell phone?"

"No. I'm wearing Eric's old hockey mask while I change the twins. They keep peeing on me."

We hang up and I start preparing lunch. Outside the kitchen window a shower of ice crystals comes down from the trees and shatters across the frozen ground like broken glass. It looks as if a whole world disappeared overnight and a new one sprang up in its place.

TWENTY-NINE

Wʜᴇɴ Uɴᴄʟᴇ Lᴇɴɴʏ ᴀᴘᴘᴇᴀʀs ɪɴ ᴛʜᴇ ᴋɪᴛᴄʜᴇɴ ᴇᴀʀʟʏ Mᴏɴᴅᴀʏ morning, I hastily explain that Davy is claiming to be ill with a stomachache. Only I don't really believe him.

"I think Davy is faking sick," I tell Uncle Lenny. "Should I call the school psychiatrist?"

"Psychiatrist?" asks Uncle Lenny. "And if my aunt had been a man she'd have been my uncle."

I take that as a no and follow Uncle Lenny, who is marching toward the stairs.

"Did I hear that someone is dragging anchor up here?" he bellows as he enters the bedroom that Davy shares with Teddy.

Davy is huddled on the top bunk holding his stomach and moaning. Uncle Lenny leans in close so that his expansive whiskers are almost touching Davy's forehead. "What we've got here is a bad case of Cape Horn fever," he loudly proclaims.

Davy squirms in his bed while Uncle Lenny turns and secretly winks at me.

"Oh, that sounds very serious." I play along.

Uncle Lenny peers at Davy while Darlene and Francie peek in the doorway. "We're going to have to cut a hole in your big toe and remove a couple gallons of blood every hour or so," Uncle Lenny states with authority, and the little girls behind me gasp. "If that doesn't do the trick then I suppose the legs will have to come off."

Davy leaps out of the bed. "I'm fine, I'm fine!"

"Not surprising," replies Uncle Lenny. "The Cape Horn fever is a very mysterious illness and has been known to come and go inside of a minute."

With everyone now out of bed I'm able to continue mobilizing the troops so they'll be on time for the bus. And the kids' new haircuts have helped take at least ten minutes off the morning routine.

Uncle Lenny has come up with a few other morning time-savers. Davy, Darlene, and Francie—all three reluctant bathers under the best of circumstances—now put on swimsuits and he basically hoses them down in the shower. Then there's a military-style inspection of ears and nails. The reason the kids put up with the regimen is because Uncle Lenny tells amazing bedtime stories, involving plenty of blood and guts, and that's their reward for getting into bed quickly and efficiently. Plus they're assigned pirate names such as Skull Splitter, Fang Flasher, and Scurvy Dog.

Of course they also love that at least once a day Uncle Lenny releases a thunderous fart and hollers, "Fire in the engine room!" When he's not around, the kids imitate him by making armpit farts while yelling his now-infamous expression. My complaints fall upon deaf ears, or else they're met with even louder fart sounds.

Fortunately they don't quite understand when Uncle Lenny comes out of the bathroom and proclaims, "Twice the man, but half the weight!" However, it doesn't stop them from repeating this expression as well.

Francie is convinced that Uncle Lenny is Santa Claus and whenever he naps she tugs on his beard to see if it's real. It's become a game between the two of them because sometimes Uncle Lenny only pretends to be sleeping and then he roars to life and scares the heck out of her. Francie screams and runs, but at the same time she loves it and can't wait to do it again.

The kids get off to school on time this morning, and so I'm surprised when a woman from the main office at the high school calls. She's very pleasant and I can tell she assumes that I'm Mom—either because I'm home at nine o'clock on a Monday morning or because I sound harried enough to have ten kids.

"I understand you've experienced a tragedy, Mrs. Palmer, but I'm phoning to find out when we can expect Louise. A psychiatrist comes every Thursday if you think we should make an appointment."

I can't help but wonder if it's the same headshrinker they had chasing me around town after I left school, moved out of our house, and went to live with the Stocktons.

"She relocated to Boston over the weekend," I explain.

"Well, Mrs. Palmer, Louise is still a minor and has to be enrolled in school, so if you can give us the new address I'll make sure that her records are transferred."

"This is Hallie Palmer," I confess. "My mother's in the hospital."

Silence. Apparently there's no prepared script for this one.

"Oh, I see," she finally says. "Why don't I have someone call you back?"

"Fine." We both hang up.

Only call me back about what? In two weeks Louise will turn sixteen and can drop out or do whatever she wants. Having recently gone a similar route, I'm fairly up-to-date on the government's educational requirements. I go to find Louise's birth certificate because they'll surely want proof. Or else she'll need me to mail it to her in Boston. While searching through the files I notice an envelope I hadn't seen before that's labeled HOUSE.

Inside it are the rough architectural drawings for a house. Only it's definitely not ours. This house has a huge kitchen, a master bedroom with a skylight, six more big bedrooms, and *four* bathrooms. I can't believe what I'm seeing—these sketches were made by Dad. Our names are written across the different bedrooms in his neat blocklike draftsman printing. There are items with Mom's initials next to them, such as a porch swing and a laundry room that's not in a dark corner of the basement but on the main floor with a big bay window overlooking the garden. A workshop running along the side has Dad's name written on it. Surely a lot of people imagine their dream house, but I'm just so stunned that Dad actually sketched his. I mean, we kids were always complaining about needing a bigger house, especially me. And Dad was always the one saying that this house is plenty big enough, and a larger one would just be more to clean, heat, and fix.

Turning the papers over, I search for a date but there isn't one. Lillian and the twins aren't included in the names at the bottom of each bedroom, and so I assume they weren't born yet. There's only one room with two names etched at the bottom of it, Darlene and Francie. Then I see it, up the staircase, down the hallway and off to the left, a corner room with two windows and a big closet. Etched in small but neat block letters at the bottom is HALLIE.

THIRTY

THE SCHOOL DOESN'T CALL BACK FOR THREE DAYS. JUST WHEN I assume we're safe from the Education Police, the phone rings.

"This is Martha Davis calling on behalf of Dr. Collier at Patrick Henry High School," a crisp, businesslike voice announces. "Am I speaking with Hallie Palmer?"

"Yes," I reply.

"Dr. Collier wishes to see you at your earliest convenience," snaps Ms. Davis.

Apparently Dr. Collier has continued his rise in the high-flying academic attendance world and now has his very own secretary.

"How about a week from Friday?" I offer.

"How about first thing tomorrow morning?" She suggests this alternative in the way I imagine army officers *suggest* that prisoners of war march to their detention centers. We agree on tomorrow morning. Maybe Uncle Lenny can watch Lillian while Mrs. Muldoon, the next-door neighbor, wrangles the twins.

The phone rings again and I briefly consider ordering caller ID solely to weed out any more exchanges with the dreaded Martha Davis. However, it turns out to be Craig.

"Hey, stranger, I just wanted to see how things are going."

"It's so great to hear your voice! But the kids are supposed to arrive home from school any second and so I don't have time to talk, other than to tell you that I'm not so sure I want to have kids."

"How about just one?" he asks.

"No way! Everyone knows that only children are crazy." This is of course meant as a joke because Craig is an only child. I say that if he wants to call back later tonight, I'll fill him in on all the local gossip, such as how Bernard has become a Girl Scout. Apparently his session down at the shop went so well that the entire troop is going to the house next week for a tutorial on table setting and napkin folding.

The doorbell rings and we have to hang up. My poker pal Herb has arrived with a care package from the drugstore he owns. It's mostly baby stuff—diapers, wet wipes, shampoo, powder, and diaper rash cream.

After I've thanked Herb for the box he admits, "That's not the real reason I came."

I'm suddenly worried that he knows something—for instance, that the school is sending social services over here to check on us. Or maybe that doctor in the emergency room decided to launch an investigation after all. Images race through my mind of having to flee into the woods and hunt squirrels in order to keep the family together.

"Teddy stopped by the store to pick up his asthma inhaler and the insurance company rejected the claim," explains Herb. "It seems you owe them some paperwork."

Leading Herb past Lillian in her playpen, I show him the stack of medical bills on the dining room table. Herb looks at his watch, removes a pen from his pocket, and sits down in front of the mess. "I'll see how far I can get in an hour."

Davy, Darlene, Francie, and a neighborhood child come flying through the doorway chasing one another and yelling about who did what to whom on the short walk from the bus stop— knapsacks, coats, and school projects are strewn across the living room floor as they storm the kitchen for a snack. Between the punching and poking the common refrain is, "You started it!"

It soon becomes obvious to Herb why I haven't caught up on all the paperwork. Before leaving he says, "I'll stop back tomorrow and try to do a little more. In the meantime you should come by the game Friday night. It'd do you some good to get out of here for a few hours."

"Yeah, right. As soon as I finish writing a hundred thankyou notes, find a free baby-sitting service, and buy a self-cleaning bathtub."

I can't even remember the last time I washed my hair. Not that it makes much difference since the strained carrots would go right back into it as soon as the twins had their lunch. On the bright side, they practically match the color.

THIRTY-ONE

THOUGH COMMUNISM COLLAPSED SOME TIME AGO, THE HIGH school is ready to serve as the Kremlin West should bolshevism rise again. The dark gray cinder-block building manages to block out the sun and cast a shadow over anyone who dares enter its steel-framed doors. The inmates all share the same sentence—four years with no time off for good behavior and no chance of probation.

One of the first things I notice is that the traditional row of student cars in the back of the parking lot has been extended from one row to three. Either more kids are taking after-school jobs or else more parents are tossing automobiles around as sixteenth-birthday gifts. Apparently *someone* has money.

It's the first time I've walked down the halls of Patrick Henry High School since dropping out over two years ago. There still aren't any metal detectors to pass through, the way they have in some of the Cleveland schools, but it definitely feels as if the halls are narrower than when I was a student. However, I must admit, the kids moving through the halls and stopping at their lockers look pretty happy. And though you may think that nine o'clock in the morning is a bit early for making out, more than a few couples are pressed together in their favorite shadowy nooks and dark corners.

All of a sudden I'm staring into the face of my old history teacher, Mr. Wright. He recognizes me and says, "Hello there, Hallie Palmer." I go on autopilot and abruptly blurt out, "*Plessy versus Ferguson*, 1896." This isn't a complete non sequitur, since Mr. Wright had spent the better part of a week drilling five landmark Supreme Court cases into our heads.

Mr. Wright just laughs, as if I'm only one in a long line of old students to see him, panic, and start reeling off Supreme Court cases. We talk for a minute and as I'm walking away he shouts after me, "*Miranda versus Arizona!*"

For a second I freeze but muscle memory kicks in. "Before questioning suspects police must inform them of their right to remain silent!" I call down the hall.

Mr. Wright smiles back as if brainwashing young people is a good thing, and then becomes lost in a sea of pimply faces and brightly colored knapsacks.

I walk into the front office and receive a warm greeting from Mrs. Hardy, the perpetually kind and sunny office secretary whose twenty-something daughter has been in drug rehab three times. Mrs. Hardy doesn't take it upon herself to judge others.

"Well, if it isn't Hallie Palmer," she cheerily announces.

"Hi, Mrs. Hardy."

"We were all so sorry to hear that your father was called home."

She makes it sounds as if Dad's desk phone suddenly rang and a voice announced that his eternal bungalow was ready.

"Thanks," I say.

Mrs. Hardy comes out from behind her desk and gives me a hug. "You're so skinny, Hallie. I heard that the ladies' auxiliary from church was coming by with some food."

"They are." I try to sound reassuring. "We have plenty to eat. I guess I've just been getting a good workout from stress and X-treme vacuuming—it's a new sport I'm trying out."

"Well, do try and take care of yourself," says Mrs. Hardy. "And what can we help you with today? Did you come to drop off a lunch or some gym shoes?"

"I'm here to see Mr.—I mean, Dr. Collier," I say.

"Oh!" She looks surprised. I assume this is because my regular run-ins with the attendance office ended over two years ago and certainly she'd seen my name on the graduation list.

Mrs. Hardy turns to another secretary and tells her that Hallie Palmer is here for an appointment with Dr. Collier. A woman who appears a decade too young to have gray hair briefly looks me up and down as if I should probably be strip-searched, and then tersely states, "I'll tell him you're coming." She whirls around in her swivel chair and picks up a phone.

Mrs. Hardy gives the impression that she's accustomed to a lack of courtesy from her office mate and points down the hall while explaining that Dr. Collier's office is now where the janitor's closet used to be. I give her a look that says, Janitor's closet? Only she just smiles and says, "That's right, we're absolutely desperate for space around here." But from her eyes I can tell that the rest of the staff think he's an asshole, too, and probably no one would share an office with him. There's a reason that generations of kids have referred to Mr. Collier as Just Call Me Dick, and it's not just because that's what he says as soon as he meets a parent.

As soon as I step outside the office door I spot Collier's beaky profile coming down the hallway. When he sees me standing there, he rubs his hands together as if they're the feelers of an insect contemplating some long-awaited prey.

JCMD ushers me into his office, where he's done a fairly

good job disguising the fact that his lair was recently a janitor's closet, except for the big industrial-sized drain that's still visible in the corner. And the air freshener on top of his J. Edgar Hoover file cabinet can't do anything to suppress the smell of damp mops from days gone by. Just as the black swirl of a dozen carefully placed hairs does little to conceal his balding head.

"I'm sorry about your father," says JCMD as he points to an uncomfortable metal chair.

And I'm sure he is, seeing as my dad more or less sided with him in the fight to keep me in school. It was my mom who finally examined alternative solutions and then worked on my dad. Likewise, I'm prepared to fight for Louise. Even though I don't approve of what's she's done and want her back as well, there's no way I'm going to tell *him* that. I remove Louise's birth certificate from my folder and hand it across the desk.

"Louise is going to be sixteen in two weeks, and after that she doesn't have to attend school," I say. "She's planning to start in Boston as soon as she gets settled." This may or may not be true, but it's intended to avoid the drama of trying to chase her down between now and her birthday.

JCMD doesn't take the birth certificate from me or even try to look at it. Instead he slides a piece of paper with a calendar on it in my direction. "Theodore has been leaving school before lunch every day for the past week and not returning—which means he's missing math, science, and, on Tuesdays and Thursdays, physical education."

"Teddy? This is about Teddy?"

"When I asked him about the situation, Theodore refused to give an explanation, other than to pose the hypothetical question: If I knew exactly what day I was going to die, would I do anything differently?"

Dr. JCMD looks perturbed about this. And I have to keep

myself from laughing. That definitely sounds like Teddy. When Mom sends him to his room as punishment, he usually mumbles something about Kierkegaard and trying to live spontaneously without being spontaneous. He's read that book *Zen and the Art of Motorcycle Maintenance* a hundred times.

I look at the copy of Teddy's schedule and the red lines indicating where he's cut class. It's a chart very familiar to me. And it's pretty easy to figure out what's going on—he's found a way to go and visit Mom in the hospital. Still, I'm not about to tell Dr. JCMD that.

"I understand there's been a death in the family and so I'm trying to be sensitive to his needs," continues Dr. Collier. "I organized an appointment with a counselor, but he didn't show up. One of his friends offered some information that leads me to believe he's involved with a cult, which you know we have to take very seriously."

"He's not in a cult," I inform JCMD somewhat angrily. "Teddy just likes—what do you call it—metaphysics. He says he's a monist—a person who believes that everything in the universe is connected, or something along those lines." I have plenty to worry about without keeping track of Teddy's philosophical musings. But I know enough to be sure that he doesn't fit into any loner gunman profile.

Dr. JCMD sits opposite me at his desk, stares directly into my eyes, and says, "I'm worried, Hallie."

It's safe to assume that homeschooling is definitely not an option at this point in our lives. "He won't skip any more school," I promise.

"I think that problems in the home are negatively impacting the education of your siblings."

Now I'm really steamed. Because it's none of his business what goes on in our home. "I don't really think it's your concern what's going on so long as the kids are in school," I say sharply.

"Quite the contrary," says JCMD, his voice becoming more slippery than eel snot. "The state of Ohio depends on its public school system to alert the authorities about any family problems such as neglect or drug and alcohol abuse, just to cite a few possibilities."

It's like being on trial. "My mom will be home soon."

Dr. Collier trains his steely gaze on me as if he's made a few phone calls and knows otherwise. "And in the meantime what qualifies you to take care of so many children?"

"I'm their sister!"

Dr. Collier turns his head away and sighs as if this just isn't good enough.

"What? Are you going to try and have all my brothers and sisters put into foster care?" My quivery voice betrays how upset I've become.

"There's always the option that they could go and live with relatives."

"No one can take in seven kids!"

"Well, of course they'd have to be split up," continues Dr. JCMD, and I think I catch the slight glimpse of a cruel smile.

It was two years in the making, but finally his revenge is in sight.

THIRTY-TWO

UPON ARRIVING BACK AT THE HOUSE, I CAN'T HELP BUT THINK about when I would return from school in the old days. There were freshly baked cookies on the kitchen counter, or else cake and ice cream left over from a birthday party the night before. The good thing about having a mother who bakes and a large family is that there's a terrific birthday cake almost every few weeks. And no matter how much Mom scrimped and saved on meals, she always made huge cakes with lots of frosting, carefully decorated, and served with at least two flavors of ice cream.

While changing the twins I study them intently for any sort of identifying marks. Nothing. Hopefully the hospital made fingerprints or footprints just in case we ever need to know for sure who they are. When I hoist them off the table, my shoulders ache a bit and I wonder if they're growing incredibly fast or I'm just getting incredibly old.

Next I change Lillian's pull-ups. I promise myself that starting tomorrow there will be a major effort to resuscitate Lillian's potty training, which has seriously lapsed during the past few weeks. Mom has a foolproof six-week program to convert any child from diapers to underpants, only I'm not sure exactly how it works. Dad used to call it her Ministry of Potty Training.

It seems as if the minute I've finished giving Lillian and the twins lunch and put them down for naps, the rest of the gang is coming off the bus and soon it will be dinnertime. How does the day go by so fast?

After the younger kids have their snack, I take Teddy aside and spare him none of the details of my meeting with JCMD, and how his brothers and sisters are going to end up in different foster homes and it will be his fault. "You'd better shape up, mister."

He simply shrugs as if there are worse things in the world than our family being broken apart. I swear, I almost punch him. I call Eric at school and leave him a message saying, "You'd better read Teddy the riot act as soon as possible because he's cutting school and getting us *all* into big trouble."

By the time dinner is made and served, the last plate is in the dishwasher, and the twins have had their final feed, I'm not only bushed, but have a serious case of bottle fatigue. When I go to put clean sweaters in Francie and Lillian's room, I find all the kids huddled around Uncle Lenny as he's about to start a story. Deciding to relax for just a moment, I climb onto the bed next to where Darlene is curled up with Lillian and the kitten. The rest have elbows balanced on crossed legs with their chins resting on the palms of their hands, eyes fixed on Uncle Lenny. I wonder if he's going to read from a seafaring adventure such as Robert Louis Stevenson's *Treasure Island*. I mean, he must be telling some great stories for the whole gang, including Teddy, to give up Connect Four and video games.

Uncle Lenny sits on the floor with his back against the closet door and shows the kids a trick in which he cuts a piece of rope and then magically restores it. He performs another by tying a knot that keeps switching places along a length of rope. There's a coin that Uncle Lenny claims is a Spanish doubloon, which he makes disappear and then pulls out of Francie's ear, much to her delight. Finally he glances at his big silver pocket watch and says it's just about bedtime. The kids all start yelling, "No, no, tell us a story!"

Uncle Lenny gives a wonderful look of fake surprise and says, "A story? I told you that I don't know any stories."

"Yes, yes, you do!" they all shout back. And from the way everyone seems to know their lines so well, I surmise that this scene has been acted out before.

"Oh, well, I suppose I could tell you about something that *actually* happened." By the way he hesitates it's clear that he's only considering the idea.

"Yes, yes!" The crowd goes wild.

"Tell the one about the wicked witch of Tweety," says Francie.

"I think you mean Tahiti." Uncle Lenny winks at me.

"Yeah," says Davy, "the witch with the tits likes a basset hound's ears."

The kids all giggle and put their hands up to their mouths. Standards are definitely dropping.

Everyone settles in while Uncle Lenny furrows his brow and appears to dredge his memory. Finally he lowers his voice so that we all lean in just a little closer and begins, "Well, now, I was in Burma not too long after they gained independence from the British. We sailed into the port of Rangoon with a cargo ship that was supposed to take on a load of teak wood. It was during the wet season and so you had to watch out for snakes."

Uncle Lenny pauses for a second, and I look around to see all the kids wide-eyed and spellbound.

"Yes, indeed, there were lots of big tricky snakes to watch out for," continues Uncle Lenny. "Especially the Burmese python, which can grow to be more than twenty feet long and weigh over two hundred pounds. They're quiet fellows and good climbers. Excellent swimmers, too. Only if those serpents don't eat regularly they can get awfully cranky. But a python is a constrictor, which means it doesn't always slide over and start chomping on its prey."

Uncle Lenny uses his big hands to show us how a snake's mouth clamps down on a person and just narrowly misses Davy, making him jump.

"No, the python wraps its body around you and constricts until you can't breathe and your eyeballs pop out." Uncle Lenny demonstrates by squeezing his neck with his hands and all the kids inhale deeply as if they're also losing their breath.

"Do they eat *people*?" asks a fascinated Teddy.

"If they're hungry, they eat anything that has a heartbeat— a lion, a deer, even a harmless little pussycat."

Darlene shudders and hugs Kitty closer to her chest.

"A Burmese python doesn't know from people—you're dinner just like a rabbit, rat, or goat. In fact, the locals always had to be careful to make sure the pythons didn't get in the cribs of the babies. They especially like small children."

Lillian squirms.

"So the day after we docked in Rangoon most of the crew went ashore, except for a few down below sleeping off the wine, women, and song from the night before. I'm on the aft deck leaning over and working on the lines when I suddenly feel something bite into my leg and guess that it's probably a wharf rat. Looking down I see those diamond marks on that long bright yellow body—not the golden yellow of the sun, mind you, but the greenish yellow of the slick boogers you blow out when you have a cold."

"Yucky!" says Darlene.

"And I see those two flat black eyes like piss holes in the snow."

Davy giggles while Francie gasps, because Mom would definitely consider this to be "bad language." And Uncle Lenny would be branded as a "potty mouth."

"When I go to pry open his jaws, he starts wrapping that eighteen-foot body around my chest. And do you know what I said?"

"Great Caesar's ghost!" the kids shout in unison.

"Exactly!" Uncle Lenny smiles at them for making such a good guess. "So I grab a nearby machete that I've been using on some rope and hold it up against my chest with the blade pointed outward." Uncle Lenny demonstrates by taking a comb from his back pocket.

"Now I wait as the snake keeps coiling itself around me. I know that if I can only keep the blade from slipping to the side, when the devil is finished he's going to try and suffocate me by squeezing as hard as he can. Sure enough, that big old snake starts constricting and the blade cuts him in two and he falls right off me!"

Uncle Lenny pops the comb forward and the kids jump as if they can feel the blade.

"Two days later I sold him to be made into ladies' shoes in Japan."

It's hard to tell if Uncle Lenny is the most fearless entrepreneur in the world, a nutcase, or totally full of shit.

"Okay, crew, bedtime!" announces Uncle Lenny. "Let's do our group grace."

Mom and Dad used to run a police action around eight o'clock every evening to make sure the Lord's Prayer was being said, and so I assume Uncle Lenny is keeping up the tradition. The kids dutifully bow their heads and along with Uncle Lenny recite in unison:

"Now I lay me down to sleep,
I pray the Lord my soul to keep.
Grant no other sailor take,
My shoes and socks before I wake.
Lord guard me in my slumber,
And keep my hammock on its number.
May no clues nor lashings break,
And let me down before I wake.
Keep me safely in thy sight,
And grant no fire drill tonight.
And in the morning let me wake,
Breathing scents of sirloin steak."

"Aye-aye," booms Uncle Lenny instead of the more traditional "Amen."

The kids raise their heads.

"Any special intentions?" he asks the assembled crowd.

Davy volunteers, "God bless Mommy in the hospital and Daddy in heaven and all my brothers and sisters except for Francie, who stole some of my soldiers."

"Did not!" shouts Francie and pounces on him.

"Okay, off to your cabins before I send names to those Barbary pirates I told you about!"

The kids miraculously scatter. I can only imagine what *that* story is about.

THIRTY-THREE

On Sunday morning when I go to call the kids for breakfast, they're not in their rooms. Or anywhere else in the house.

Only Teddy is here, quietly reading a book on the couch.

Frantically I ask him, "Where are Darlene, Davy, and Francie?"

Without looking up from his reading Teddy says, "Outside waiting for the bus. They were bugging me, and so I told them it's a school day."

"That's it, Teddy. Eric and I talked about it and you're grounded except for school. And you'd better go to school or we're *all* going to be in a lot of trouble! I don't know who was driving you to see Mom after lunch, but there's going to be a guy stationed in the parking lot keeping an eye out for you from now on."

"*You* didn't go to school," he says.

"That was different."

Teddy stares straight at me, and it's clear to both of us that I'm losing this battle. Evil Dr. Collier's words echo in my mind and sound as if they've been put through a synthesizer. "What qualifies *you* to take care of so many children?" And the obvious answer is *nothing*.

Every time there's a knock at the door I'm afraid it's social services coming to scatter all the kids to the winds like in some made-for-TV movie.

Only it's just the usual procession—Bernard with some food, Al to check and see if the house is falling apart, Officer Rich to make sure we're not being staked out by burglars, the occasional churchwoman with a casserole, and Herb to organize the bills.

"You are, what we'd call in a poker game, *down to the felt,*" announces Herb on this particular morning.

"Tell me about it. I had to write a check to buy batteries." It reminded me of how Dad was always yelling, *Where do all the batteries I buy go? Do you kids eat them for breakfast? Batteries are expensive. Do you think they just grow on trees?*

"You only had to call and I'd have brought over some batteries from the store," says Herb.

"I appreciate all the help, but you have your own family to support," I tell him.

There is the sound of pounding feet coming up the basement stairs. Uncle Lenny emerges carrying his sea bag slung over one shoulder and unexpectedly announces that he must set sail. "The spring thaw has begun and I'm running a vessel from New York down to the Caribbean. Gotta love these Wall Street bigwigs—buying expensive yachts that they can't even steer down the Hudson River without help. They'll kill themselves and each other before doing any harm to the fish, that's for darn sure."

Wow. This is a surprise. I'd started taking Uncle Lenny for granted.

Kids converge from all over the house to give Uncle Lenny big hugs good-bye. Francie explains to the assembled crowd that he has to go back to the North Pole and start preparing for Christmas. This causes Uncle Lenny to let out one of his great bellows of laughter, which in turn only serves to convince Francie that he is indeed Santa Claus.

"Promise that you'll come back and visit soon," says little Davy, on the verge of tears.

"Right as rainwater I will," says Uncle Lenny.

We stand gathered in the driveway as Uncle Lenny loads his bag into the trunk of a taxi. It feels rather like Mary Poppins, or in our case the Ancient Mariner, is taking leave after having finished his work here, much to our dismay. The snow melts to rain in midair as Uncle Lenny addresses the kids by their pirate names one last time and then gives us all a big salute. We shout "Anchors aweigh" as the taxi turns at the corner and disappears into the encroaching fog.

THIRTY-FOUR

THE FOLLOWING WEEK IS THE FIRST TIME THE ROADS ARE DRY enough for the kids to ride their bicycles to school. This removes some of the pressure of getting ready in the mornings since we no longer have to worry about missing the bus.

After they leave for school on Monday I know that I should visit Mom, but I've just been feeling so tired all of the time. Once the kids have had breakfast and are ready to go, I'm ready for a nap.

At noon, while I attempt to spoon mushed peas into the mouths of the twins, the phone rings. It's one of those ominous rings.

"I'm sorry, but this just won't do." Dr. Collier's voice is dripping with self-satisfaction. "The parking lot monitor just witnessed Teddy leaving on a bicycle."

Before I can respond there's a click on the other end. Did the line go dead? Did he hang up on me? And if so, what is that supposed to mean?

In the moment I've been distracted, the twins have somehow managed to smear strained peas all over themselves, their high chairs, and the linoleum.

Bernard opens the door leading to the garage and gaily calls out, "Bonjour, *mon petit* sparrows! How is everything at Chez Palmer?"

A pile of dishes sits in the sink and the counter is littered with the remains of making the lunches. The far wall is covered with a crayon mural by Lillian, which she managed to accomplish in the short period of time it took to change the twins' diapers this morning. A dried puddle of chocolate syrup decorates the center of the table. The place looks more like a crime scene than a kitchen where seven kids just had breakfast.

"We're not going to win any good housekeeping awards." I use a spoon to start scraping peas off the twins' faces. "And a controlled burn isn't out of the question."

"But it's comfortable—in a sort of post-apocalyptic way." Bernard moves closer and leans in toward my forehead. "*What* happened with your bangs? Are you trying to channel former First Lady Mamie Eisenhower?"

I put my hands up to cover my forehead. "I trimmed them a little. They were in my eyes."

My plan had been for Bernard to watch the kids while I got a haircut and visited Mom, but one of the twins is fussy and feverish, and so I've made an appointment at the pediatrician's.

"Instead of seeing Mom I'm going to have to take this guy to the doctor," I say. "His color isn't very good."

"Your color isn't very good either—sort of a chartreuse. I suppose a stop at the tanning salon is out of the question."

"I'll try and work it in between my bridge game and tennis lesson."

Bernard walks over to the kitchen wall where a series of bright red blotches is splattered above Lillian's mural. "Ketchup or paint?"

"Tomato sauce, I think."

"Salvador Dalí couldn't have dreamed all this up."

I grab a dishrag to wipe up the peas on the floor.

"And look at you, Hallie—your clothes don't fit. Are you on a diet?"

"Yeah, right," I say. "I thought dropping out of school and taking care of seven kids would be the answer to having thinner thighs in thirty days."

Bernard gives me a sympathetic look.

"Whatever you do, don't pick up the phone," I warn Bernard. "We're getting obscene phone calls from Just Call Me Dick over at the high school."

I pick up Twin A, strap him into his car seat, and head over to the pediatrician's office.

"I'm so sorry about your dad," Dr. Karpen says as we enter the examining room. "Heart disease." He shakes his head from side to side. "How is your mom getting along?"

"Much better," I lie. If the doctor knows that I'm in charge, he might threaten to call social services as well.

"And who do we have here?" asks Dr. Karpen.

"Roddy." Okay, it's a guess. But one with a fifty percent chance of being correct. I wonder if there's anything on Dr. Karpen's chart that might indicate otherwise. Not knowing the names of the twins is one more sign of my incompetence.

The doctor says that "Roddy" has a cold along with an ear infection and prescribes some medication. Fortunately, he knows that we're on a tight budget and always gives us free samples.

"Watch the baby's temperature and call if he stops eating or drinking," instructs Dr. Karpen.

I listen carefully. All I need is to have something happen to one of these babies on my watch. Not only would I never forgive myself, but I'm certain that will be the end of us as a family.

THIRTY-FIVE

THE GOOD NEWS IS THAT TWIN A IS STARTING TO LOOK BETTER after throwing up and spending a long night hollering. The bad news is that Twin B is beginning to look the way Twin A did yesterday morning.

The rest of the kids are playing in the basement. Except for Teddy, who has of course gone off on his bike to see Mom. We always assumed he was too rangy to play a sport, and now it turns out he might be an ideal candidate for the Tour de France bicycle race. Going to Dalewood is at least eleven miles round-trip, and the journey doesn't seem to faze him in the least.

I straighten up Darlene's bed where the kitten has torn open a pillow. Fortunately Mom is too economical ever to buy down-stuffed pillows or comforters, so there are just streamers of nylon scattered about.

Darlene comes upstairs crying because Davy is teasing her that she has pimples. An examination of her neck, face, and hands reveal what appear to be chicken pox!

Say it isn't so. Eric, Louise, and I had it when we were in elementary school. But I'm not at all sure about the rest of the brood.

Racing down to the basement, I frantically shout, "Who here has had chicken pox?"

Davy, Darlene, Francie, and Lillian all stare back at me uncomprehendingly.

"Oh no!" I examine the rest of them for telltale red spots. If I recall correctly, Louise was the one who had it first and then Eric and I went down a few days later.

"Sorry, Darlene, but you have to go upstairs to our room." That's when I see Francie scratch her stomach. Sure enough, there are two spots on her chest and three on her back. "You've got it, too."

Francie stares curiously at the area I've just condemned and then continues scratching.

"Don't scratch! Okay, we're changing rooms. Darlene goes in with Francie and Lillian sleeps in my room."

I march the two girls off to their new quarantined quarters. The last thing I need is for the twins to get chicken pox on top of the cold they already have. I'd better call the pediatrician. But first the boys need changing, or else I'm going to be charged with reckless endangerment of children from diaper rash. I strap on the hockey mask that now doubles as a vomit shield as well as a pee protector.

As I open a new box of diapers the doorbell rings. Please let it be Bernard with the fried chicken he promised to bring over. Gil bought him a Fry Daddy along with a southern cookbook for his birthday, and he's been going to town making corn dogs, donuts, Thai fried bananas, breaded Gulf Coast shrimp, and even fried ice cream. Bernard told me that if you're really quiet while eating you can actually hear your arteries snapping shut.

On second thought, I'm not sure he should come inside if we've got chicken pox. With my hand about to turn the knob I peer through the side window before opening the door.

It's Pastor Costello! I've never been happier to see anyone in my entire life.

"Thank goodness you're back!" I dash out onto the front stoop to give him a tremendous hug.

"Hallie?" he seems to say in a questioning tone of voice.

"Of course it's me!" But then I realize I'm still wearing the hockey mask. I pull it off and we give each other big smiles. My heart is racing and I feel flushed all over. And also a little dizzy from not having had anything to eat yet.

"Come in, come in," I say and head back through the door. "Wait a second, have you had the chicken pox?"

"Yes," says Pastor Costello, "though I believe it was long before you were born." His gentle singsong voice is so reassuring, making every sentence sound as if it could be the start of a hymn.

"I have to finish changing the twins," I say.

He follows me into the hall outside the downstairs bathroom that serves as the staging area for changing and dressing the little boys.

Pastor Costello is tanned like an English saddle, giving him an especially healthy glow during the time of year when everyone in Ohio walks around pasty white, sneezing and hacking with flu, and when the suicide rate is at its highest. He's also shed the belly that wasn't visible under his clerical robes but was somewhat noticeable when he was wearing street clothes. For a few years Pastor Costello had experimented with a comb-over before finally settling upon the more distinguished silver fringe that currently surrounds his brow like a halo. Now in his early forties, I suppose people would say that Pastor Costello looks his age, not any younger and not any older. Though despite not being what one would consider attractive in the conventional sense of the word, he carries himself with the calm confidence of a man who knows that he has nothing to prove.

"You look *thin,* Hallie," says Pastor Costello.

"So do you!" I say in a complimentary way.

He smiles and admits, "I had a few pounds to lose, which isn't the same for you, I daresay."

"With all the running around—"

The doorbell rings again. "That must be Bernard," I say. "Would you mind answering it while I finish up here?"

As I pull on Twin A's shirt I begin to feel a pounding in my forehead. And when I look up there's an unfamiliar woman in the front hall holding a briefcase under her arm and shaking hands with Pastor Costello. A social worker! They're going to take the kids away and put them in different foster homes all over the state!

A great rush of heat fills the area behind my eyes so that for a moment I can't see, and then everything goes black for good.

THIRTY-SIX

SLEEP ARRIVES LIKE A KNOCKOUT BLOW. I'M ON A BEACH SOME-where with the sun beating down and I see the kids playing near the edge of the water. A big wave is heading toward the beach, but the kids are busy building a sand castle and they don't see it. I yell for them to move out of the way, but they can't hear me over the roar of the ocean.

Then I'm four years old and riding a tricycle in the driveway while Dad tosses a little orange Nerf football to Eric on the lawn. Mom comes out smiling and wearing an apron, underneath which is a bulge indicating pregnancy. She's carrying a little girl in one arm who looks exactly like Louise. Mom tells us that it's lunchtime, but when she turns to go back inside she trips and drops the baby.

Now I'm working in the yard at the Stocktons' and hear Olivia's delicate voice calling me inside for lunch. "We're having celery," she says. I think celery is an odd thing to have for lunch. But the day has become very hot and I'm hungry and thirsty and welcome the break. "Hallie, *where* are you?" she calls again. Now I'm standing directly underneath the kitchen window. She's looking straight at me but doesn't see or hear me. "I'm right *here*!" I say over and over.

Olivia's voice sounds as if it's inside the house but at the end of a long corridor. "Yes, you're here. Everything is fine."

"Olivia?" I open my eyes, but I can't tell if this is still a part of my dream. The room is so bright that I have to squint to see anything. Yet it really is Olivia, perched on the edge of the bed like a butterfly. She smiles at me and a series of tiny pleats around her blue eyes smile along with her. Her thick white hair is pulled back with a few strands hanging loose around her face.

It takes a few moments to try to make sense of things. "I thought you were coming back in April. Have I been in a coma for two months?"

"Only a day. The doctor gave you something to sleep," says Olivia. "I came back early from my trip."

"Oh." I want to ask why but I vaguely start to remember the moments before passing out—the social worker! And the house is too quiet. I don't hear kids playing or the twins crying.

"My brothers and sisters!" I manage to say, though it burns my throat to talk. I start climbing out of bed to find them.

"Whoa," says Olivia. "They're all fine. The girls are upstairs recovering from the chicken pox and the twins had a twenty-four-hour virus—they're better now."

"And you, Wonder Woman, have a doozy of a case of infectious mononucleosis."

"Mono?" I whisper. A freshman guy at school had mono and everyone called it the kissing disease.

"I know," says Olivia, correctly guessing what I'm thinking. "You may have picked it up at school, but with all the germs coming through here, the doctor said he wouldn't be at all surprised if one of the kids passed it to you."

"But are they all still here? What about the social worker?"

"Everyone is here. Pastor Costello is dealing with the agency," says Olivia. "Never underestimate the power of the clergy in Cosgrove County. Though it certainly doesn't help that Mr.

Collier is apparently still holding a grudge against you for managing to graduate without attending classes. On the other hand, there's no way the children can be taken away unless social services comes over and finds you with a drug habit or a loaded gun on the kitchen table. Even then there would have to be a trial."

"What about Mom?" I ask.

"Pastor Costello says she's making a bit of progress. I must say, I've never bothered much with the Christian community in this town, but he's a very sweet man and dedicated to social causes. He's been telling me the most fascinating stories about Cambodia. In fact, I've signed up to go on the next mission."

"But who's taking care of—"

Olivia puts her finger to my lips. "Pastor Costello has moved in—lock, stock, and barrel. Mrs. Muldoon took the twins to her place so they wouldn't catch the chicken pox. My goodness, that woman is besotted with the babies—offering to keep them night and day, for weeks if need be. She must have eighty all but surrounded, and yet she still has the energy of someone half her age."

My throat is too sore to explain to Olivia that Mrs. Muldoon has a grown daughter but she'd wanted a large family. It's too bad because she's definitely mad for kids—always inviting us in for lemonade and cookies and baking brownies for our entire school class on our birthdays. However, she also doesn't hesitate to get on our cases when we're bad and report back to Mom and Dad. To Mrs. Muldoon the community-watch signs in the windows mean that you should be monitoring the local children for bad behavior more than keeping an eye out for intruders.

"Lillian is staying with Bernard and Gil and the girls," continues Olivia. "And we found out that Teddy was skipping school to visit your mother."

I roll my eyes toward the ceiling to express the fact that I'm somewhat aware of this problem.

"We've made a deal with him so that he does a full day at school and then gets rides to and from Dalewood afterward and on weekends. They have a van service he's able to use."

"Do you think it's good for him to be there so much?"

"Pastor Costello spoke to her doctor and they don't believe it's harmful to either party."

My eyelids begin to droop. I shake my head to signify my horror at how the family almost fell apart while all I could do was stand by and watch, or, rather, fall down while watching.

"You need to stop worrying about how everyone else is doing and get some rest."

Olivia stands up. "I'll get you a nice bowl of soup. You're skinny enough to pass for a Brancusi."

"Huh?" I'm a bit groggy for one of Olivia's impromptu art history classes.

"He was the Romanian-born French sculptor known for a simple and streamlined geometric style intended to lay bare an image's underlying nature."

For some reason the word *bare* brings to mind the story of Old Mother Hubbard who went to the cupboard. "What about dinner and the lunches and—"

"Pastor Costello ran Bible camp for eight summers. You'd be amazed at how organized he is!"

Sinking my head back into the pillows, I close my eyes, but the light fixture continues to burn in my brain like a giant sun.

"When you feel a bit better you'll have to let the rest of us in on the secret of telling the twins apart. Mrs. Muldoon said there used to be a blue ribbon around the ankle of one."

Uh-oh.

THIRTY-SEVEN

WHEN I NEXT AWAKE IT'S TO THE STRAINS OF MUSIC. THIS IS ODD because our stereo conked out years ago, after the kids covered the knobs with Play-Doh. Someone is singing.

I lie in bed for about ten minutes summoning the energy to rise—using the time to go over and over the same problem that's been on my mind since the night Dad died. This infinite loop of thought has taken up the space in my brain that should have been occupied with other things—like taking better care of the kids—but obviously wasn't.

The singing continues to drift into the bedroom. How many verses can there be?

I follow the upbeat sound of "Children of the Lord" toward the kitchen. I move slowly, using the walls to guide me, stopping every few feet to rest, and then stumbling forward like a toy whose batteries are running down. Pastor Costello has an assembly line of bread to which he's applying a piece of lettuce on top of three rashers of bacon and one slice of tomato, all while letting out an enthusiastic chorus of, *"Rise and shine and give God the glory, glory, children of the Lord."*

Pastor Costello turns toward me wearing a big smile and a

blue tracksuit with J.C. STATE OF MIND emblazoned on the top. "What are you doing up so early?"

"I think I fell asleep at about seven o'clock last night."

"Yes, you missed dinner and I didn't want to wake you. How about some breakfast?"

"I am sort of starving."

"A good appetite is a good sign," says Pastor Costello. He takes a clean plate from a stack next to the sink, moves toward the stove, where there are two large square baking pans covered with aluminum foil, and asks, "Eggs and bacon or French toast or both?"

"Wow!" I say as Pastor Costello removes the foil to display a mound of scrambled eggs and a mountain of French toast triangles.

I take the plate and fill it with some of everything.

"Sorry there's no coffee, but I wasn't expecting any adults." He returns to the sandwiches, wrapping them in wax paper with practically a single flick of the wrist. Sitting next to the pile of sandwiches is a row of bookmarks with a verse from scripture written on each one. "So, what's on your mind?"

"What do you mean?" I ask.

"Looks as if something's on your mind." When Pastor Costello has finished putting a sandwich, piece of fruit, cookie, and juice container into each bag, he drops in a bookmark before folding down the top.

"I've been wondering . . . I've been thinking . . ."

He looks up from what he's doing and over at me.

"I was wondering how many verses there are in that song you were singing." I stare down at my plate.

Pastor Costello grins and says, "Believe me on this one, sometimes ignorance is bliss."

A forced laugh issues from somewhere inside me. Then I

blurt out, "I've been wondering if I did something to deserve all this."

Pastor Costello sits across from me and, though I don't look up, I can feel his kind eyes looking directly at me.

"No, you didn't do anything to deserve this. In fact, you've been heroic in coping with it all. I wish that I'd been home earlier to help. It's just life, Hallie. It's the way life goes."

"But it's so hard." I say, and look up at him with tears in my eyes.

"We keep lifting the weight and that's how we become stronger."

As long as I'm in it this far, I may as well go the rest of the way.

"Do you believe that bad things happen when you lead a bad life—you know, disobeying parents, having premarital sex, eating food in the grocery store." I attempt to mask the item I'm most concerned about by sandwiching it between some older offenses.

Pastor Costello puts his hand on mine and says, "We discourage young people from vice and bad habits so they don't end up in difficult situations before reaching their potential."

"I just mean, how many bad habits make a vice and how many vices until you're at the sin level? Is it a system of weights and measures like pints, quarts, and gallons?" I try to make sense of the problem mathematically, because that's always how I understand things best.

Pastor Costello looks at me as if this formula is one of the unknowable things about the universe. Or if he does know the answer, he's not telling. Maybe you have to go to J.C. State for the answer to that question.

"Love can never be considered a sin." Pastor Costello attempts to reassure me. "Though you have to exercise good judgment regarding the right time and place. Like the Man said:

There's a time for everything, and a season for every activity under heaven."

"That's from a Byrds song," I say. "Gil has the album."

"Yes, well, actually they borrowed their lyrics from the Book of Ecclesiastes in the Bible."

The kitchen timer goes off, and I look for smoke to start coming out of the oven. "Time to wake up the little lambs." Pastor Costello rises and glances out the window. "It's finally stopped raining."

"I slept so soundly that I didn't even know it *was* raining."

"Spring is just around the corner," he says brightly.

Is it possible? I look out the window and sure enough, the isolated patches of snow have melted and water seems to trickle everywhere, searching for lower ground. The cars parked in the street are all grime gray from the combination of salt, dirt, and slush. A single squirrel darts along the power line.

Pastor Costello heads off in the direction of the kids' rooms. On his way he says, "Sometime when we have a moment and you're feeling a bit better, I'd like to ask you about the children's prayers."

THIRTY-EIGHT

AFTER A FULL WEEK OF CONVALESCING, I MISTAKENLY BELIEVE that I possess more energy than I actually do. Pastor Costello still gets the kids off to school, rather easily I might add, and then leaves to take care of business at the church.

After wandering through the upstairs, where everything is very much in order, even the boys' room, I lie down on the couch. I'm too tired to be awake and too awake to sleep. The phone rings once and then stops. After a moment it starts ringing again. That's Bernard's secret signal to avoid calls from JCMD.

"Welcome back to the land of the living," he says.

"Is that what this is supposed to be?" I reply.

"I have a surprise for you," says Bernard. "Turn on the TV."

"I can't watch a movie with you—we get four channels and the reception is terrible!" When I was at school Bernard and I would sometimes watch old movies together over the phone late at night.

"That's the surprise!" he says gleefully. "Now you can have all Bette Davis all the time."

I switch on the TV and can actually see the people on the screen. The reception is crystal clear on every channel, and there are at least a hundred of them!

"Cable!" I yell out. "But, Bernard, we can't afford this."

"Don't be silly," he says. "It's my gift to the Palmer family. I think you'll have fewer murals in the kitchen with the Cartoon Network in the living room!"

We hang up and I watch a soap opera for the first time in my life. Today's story features gorgeous men and scheming women. One of the guys looks a lot like Craig and I decide to give him a call. He's out. Probably in a swamp somewhere. Last time we spoke he was learning to test lakes for mercury and boron. Apparently if it seeps into local drinking water, entire towns have to be evacuated.

Gwen answers her cell phone in a cavernous room where I can hear sewing machines whirring away in the background. The big fashion show is in a week and it counts as half her grade. The theme is cocktails and Gwen tells me about the red and black eveningwear she's created. Her parents are going to fly out to California just for the show.

I call Jane at Bucknell but she's rushing off to practice. She stays on the phone just long enough to tell me that her handicrafts-obsessed mother sent a horrible needlepoint pillow that says, IF YOU'RE GOING TO FIGHT, THEN USE A PILLOW. It's safely hidden in the back of her closet behind some hockey equipment.

A woman on the soap opera seems to have a split personality, or else she's a twin with an identical but diabolically evil sister. It's hard to tell. Sleep washes over me. When I wake up, Bernard is standing in the living room holding a pile of seed catalogues.

He pulls a chair up next to where my head is and announces that it's time for a new garden.

"Did Olivia finally wear you down about growing Concord grapes and fig trees?" I ask.

"Heavens, no," says Bernard. "Mother doesn't care about grapes or figs. She only wanted them because it's what Emily Dickinson grew in her garden."

"*You* wanted a white garden like Vita Sackville-West had at Sissinghurst."

Bernard gives me a dismissive wave as if to say that was *completely different.* "I want a Chinese garden in order to help the girls embrace their cultural heritage."

"You already bought willow-pattern china, hung wind chimes, put up silk paintings, organized Chinese lessons, and regularly take them to Chinatown in Cleveland."

"Well, it's one of the oldest cultures on the planet—there's a lot to embrace," counters Bernard.

"You put Ming vases in their rooms, bought eight different kinds of chopsticks, and cook bok choy at least once a week."

"I thought we'd plant a Chinese tea garden," Bernard continues undeterred.

"Can you even grow tea in Ohio?"

"It would be a tranquil place for sipping tea, reciting poetry, and doing calligraphy."

"How stupid of me," I say. "Blame the medicine."

"We'd have chrysanthemums, jasmine, wintersweet, red and pink flowering oleander, and bamboo greens. We'll build a little temple with lacquered teak doors, a graceful pavilion with glazed tile roof, and use Taihu rocks to create a little waterfall. And of course we'll have ginkgo and plum trees!"

"Of course," I say. But my real concern is why Bernard keeps saying "we."

"And who is going to install this Chinese tea garden?"

"I'll do it," says Bernard. "You know what they say: Trowel in hand, joy in heart."

"Oh, really?" That will be the day Bernard cuts back on his estate sales and auctions to do yard work. He can't stand the thought of missing out on a bargain.

"The girls can help as part of their cultural immersion."

"The *girls* are twenty-seven months and three and a half years old. You'd better hire a nanny."

"I've done even better," says Bernard in his best I've-got-a-secret tone of voice. "I now have an employee!"

"You mean an actual gardener?"

"No, silly, down at the shop. June Hennipen is going to run the store while I go to sales, take care of the girls, and post items on the Web site from home."

"Isn't she that weird woman who runs the astrology tent for the Founder's Day picnic, with the frizzy, maroonish, not-found-in-nature–colored hair, chandelier earrings, and purple peasant skirts?"

"Okay, she does herself up in a bit of a costume, but that's just to hawk those crystal necklaces and mood rings, or whatever it is she sells. In exchange for dealing with my customers, I've given her a display window and basically free rent for her kooky little business."

"I'm not sure it's an act," I say. "Officer Rich told me that she briefly worked down at the town hall but kept rearranging all the desks in the building to balance them with the universe and that she's so into horoscopes she didn't show up for work on her unlucky days."

"Plenty of accomplished architects believe in feng shui—the Eastern art of placing furniture and objects according to yin and yang," says Bernard. "Though June does have a tendency to begin every sentence with, *My therapist says* . . . in fact, before accepting the job she had to call and consult with him."

"Wouldn't it be easier just to plant more tomatoes?" I ask.

"As per usual, we're on exactly the same page!" He opens the catalogue and shows me a glossy picture of some incredible-looking tomatoes. "I thought we'd order the Brandywines again this year."

"Didn't the deer eat them all last time?"

Bernard quickly flips the page. "The deer have had a tendency to treat the vegetable garden as a salad bar in the past, but I've been reading that if you surround the plants with these sharp oyster shells, they stay away."

"It's worth a try," I say. "Playing the radio didn't scare them off the way the guy at the garden center promised it would. In fact, I think they *liked* the music. Only, where are you going to put all this stuff?" The backyard is already chock-full with three regular gardens, an herb garden, a gazebo, and the new pond. Then there's the summerhouse and the shed.

"You didn't hear?" asks Bernard, eyes wide.

Apparently it's slipped his mind that I've been just a little busy lately, not to mention unconscious a good part of the past week.

"I'm going to buy the lot behind the house!" crows Bernard.

"That's great," I say. There's a lovely wooded acre or so at the end of the property, and it'd be nice to prevent something awful from being built there.

"I'll make us some cherry grain balsam pear tea from the Yangtze River basin to celebrate." Bernard produces tea bags from his breast pocket as if pulling out a fresh hanky. "And then we'll write up the order."

Through the kitchen door Bernard continues talking and explains how he's been made interim leader of the Girl Scout troop.

"You're kidding me, right?"

"No. Melinda—she prefers Mel—broke her ankle when they went hiking along some old canal last weekend."

"How can a guy head a Girl Scout troop?"

"It's just temporary," says Bernard. "I'm working in a volunteer capacity that's officially called a Do-Dad."

"Does this mean you have to go camping and hiking and stuff like that?"

"I always had my doubts about that outdoor business," continues Bernard. "Just a lot of sprained elbows and ruined skin, if you ask me."

I look down at my own dishpan hands.

Bernard returns with two cups of tea that are clear in color but pleasant-tasting. "The kitchen is spotless!"

"Pastor Costello," I say.

"That man knows how to clean," says Bernard.

"Pastor Costello says that if Jesus was able to clean up after himself, then the rest of us are equally gifted. And all that's necessary for those hard-to-reach places is a positive attitude. He even cleans the church himself."

"Maybe he'd like to tackle my garage," says Bernard.

"I'm afraid you've made a pact with the devil on that one." The garage contains everything that Bernard ends up with when he has to buy an entire lot just to get the one or two items he really wants.

Bernard takes up his catalogues, this time with pen in hand. "It would be nice to have a spring garden this year—impatiens, petunias, and how about some white rhododendron? Wouldn't they look nice around the pool?"

"The pool! Let me get this straight. I don't have the energy to wash my hair and you're planning a spring garden, Chinese tea garden, vegetable garden, and a swimming pool?"

Bernard raises his teacup high, tilts backs his head as if gazing off at some imaginary mountaintop, and proclaims, "A garden is like a lovely memory—it should grow more glorious over time."

THIRTY-NINE

THE HOURS MELT INTO DAYS AND THE DAYS DRIFT INTO ANOTHER week. The chicken pox flies the Palmer coop, the kids are back in their regular beds, and Pastor Costello now sleeps on the couch in the living room. He sends the multitude off to school in the morning and then serves them dinner and puts them to bed at night. A duty roster now hangs on the fridge, and all the kids check off their chores every morning and every night. It's safe to say there are no more unmade beds around this house.

Mrs. Muldoon has offered to keep the twins until I'm well. She's taking some medicine for her arthritis that seems to have given her a new lease on life and insists that caring for the boys keeps her young.

Since hiring June Hennipen to mind the store, Bernard is free to work from home during the day, and so he picks up Lillian every morning and brings her to play with the girls. She's even learning a little Chinese by sitting in with Rose and Gigi's language tutor.

The doctor wasn't kidding when he said the recovery process would be three steps forward and two back. After the kids leave for school on Thursday morning I head back to bed.

There's no TV in Mom and Dad's room, I'm too tired to read, and so I drift in and out while the bedside clock radio plays a crackly R&B station.

Maybe I should become a blues singer. That way I could make money at night while the kids are asleep and then arrive home just in time to put them on the bus in the morning. I imagine myself wearing a black sequined gown in a smoky night club operating out of a shack by the river. A blind man in coveralls sits on a stool playing his guitar while I sing along:

> *I wake up in the morning*
> *Get those children dressed and fed*
> *Cause Daddy's gone to heaven*
> *And poor Momma's lost her head.*

The blind man takes a solo and everyone in the audience nods their head as if their troubles are bad, too. Then it's back to me.

> *The preacher come to help me*
> *We prayed to cure my ills*
> *But instead of being answered*
> *All I got was bills.*

I imagine the chef announces that the catfish is ready and so my set is over, whereupon I promptly fall back to sleep.

Olivia arrives in the afternoon and does some laundry. She says the basement reminds her of Dante's *Inferno*, only in this case the ninth circle of hell is reserved for colorfast sheets.

Then Olivia and Pastor Costello feed the kids their dinner. Every once in a while I can hear Pastor Costello shout "Oh phooey" when he drops or spills something.

While Pastor Costello finishes washing the dishes, Olivia sits with me and reads out loud. The play is called *Diana of Dobson's* and was written by a woman named Cicely Hamilton. It's mostly about the lack of opportunities for women in the early 1900s, particularly if they didn't marry right away. Despite winning awards and garnering acclaim, the play hasn't been performed much since it first came out. Part of Olivia's current crusade is to revive female dramatists from the early twentieth century.

At the end of Act Two Olivia and I decide that we've had enough of poor but plucky Diana for one night. Putting the book down on the bedside table, Olivia asks, "So, Hallie, who is your favorite fictional character in all of literature?"

"I guess Tom Sawyer or Huck Finn," I say. "What about you?"

"The Brontë sisters created some wonderful characters. And so did Charles Dickens, of course. But there are so many. I suppose if I had to choose just one, it would be God."

"So I guess this means you definitely don't believe in God," I say.

"I don't think it matters whether or not you believe so much as that you care."

"Care about what?" I ask.

"Whatever your heart can undertake."

Davy bursts into the room with Darlene in hot pursuit. The kitten is asleep on my bed, and so they can't be trying to kill each other over that.

Darlene shouts at me to tell Davy to give him back a piece from a game they're playing. Davy runs around to the other side of the bed so she can't catch him. Darlene dives across the bed and her left foot jabs my kidney.

Olivia, having raised an only child, doesn't possess the skill set for conflict resolution among rambunctious siblings, aside from to suggest that they "use words and not hands."

Their screams reverberate throughout the house. Pastor Costello enters the room while wiping his hands on a dish towel. "As the Irish like to say—is this a private fight or can anyone get in it?" Clapping his hands, he announces, "Okay, one cookie apiece and off to bed. Truce is better than friction." Pastor Costello has a quiet authority and an arsenal of aphorisms that make children instinctively stop hitting each other and want to start hitting him.

"Will you tell us a story?" asks Darlene.

"Yeah, one with a snake in it!" says Davy.

"Why certainly, I know just the one," says Pastor Costello. "In fact, this story has a *talking* snake."

The kids race out of the room, their faces glowing with anticipation. Only I'm afraid they might be disappointed when they hear about the snake in the Garden of Eden instead of Uncle Lenny's Burmese python that had to be cut in half with a machete.

After Darlene and Davy scamper off, Olivia straightens out the blankets and says, "Look at the bright side: Rome was founded on the basis of sibling rivalry between twins."

"So in the end they got along famously and actually accomplished something?" I ask.

"Oh no!" says Olivia. "They continued fighting until Romulus killed Remus and then named the city after himself."

Eventually the house settles down and it's quiet enough to hear the heat struggling to come up through the vents in the floor. The moon lights the backyard with a blue splendor, and the night sky is pinpricked by thousands of stars.

Olivia's gaze drifts to the window. "There certainly are a lot of stars out tonight. When Bernard was young and he couldn't sleep, we'd play a game called Unitarian constellations. Oh, how he used to make me laugh!"

I'm aware that Olivia attends the Unitarian church, where

they don't seem to worry about religion nearly as much as writing their congressmen, but this is the first I've heard about any deities. "What's a Unitarian constellation?"

"Let me try and remember some of them," says Olivia as she studies the patch of universe visible through the bedroom window. "See those four stars that form a square—that's an aluminum can belonging to Sunbeam, the Great Recycler." She points to the left side of the window. "And those six bright dots over there make up the edge of Moonbeam's skirt. She believed world peace could be achieved through interpretive dance."

"What about that shape to the right of the moon?" I ask.

"That must be the scissors used by Thomas Jefferson to remove references to God and miracles from the Bible."

"Wrong, wrong, wrong!" Bernard is standing in the doorway. "That's the comfortable shoe of Susan B. Anthony. And above it is the long, *long* belt that went around the enormous waist of Unitarian President William Howard Taft."

Olivia claps her hands with delight. "I've always felt that Bernard missed his calling as an astronomer."

"I brought over a big dish of chicken à la king left over from Girl Scouts," says Bernard. "You should have seen the horrific concoctions they were eating—why, the Red Cross wouldn't serve such fare to disaster victims."

"When Bernard was a boy, he was so talented and had such a plethora of interests that I often wondered what he'd do as an adult," says Olivia. "However, Girl Scout troop leader is possibly the one vocation that eluded me."

"It's only temporary—until Mel's ankle is better," says Bernard. "Oh, Mother, I almost forgot—a man named Darius came by the house looking for you."

For a moment Olivia looks completely stunned, but she quickly regains her composure. "Oh, what a surprise!"

The ever-inquisitive Bernard senses a story. "And exactly *who* is Darius?"

"Just a nice young man I met in Greece. He's planning to open a restaurant in the States, and so I gave him our number," she says offhandedly.

"Oh." Bernard brightens. "He's a chef then?"

"Darius is an excellent cook. His family owns a café overlooking the sea on the Greek island of Folegandros. Why don't you go on ahead and I'll be along in a few minutes." Olivia looks downcast, her natural gaiety having fled.

Once Bernard is out of earshot, I ask, "Is something wrong?"

"I came home early because Ottavio and I had a fight," says Olivia. "It was silly, really. We went to the café every morning. They had the best coffee and raki—the Greek equivalent of a hot toddy. Anyway, one day Darius invited us for a sunrise sail on this lovely old wooden boat he owns with his brother. The island of Folegandros is famous for its sunrises the way Santorini is known for its sunsets."

Olivia pauses and looks dreamy, as if she's momentarily transported back to the breathtaking beauty of it all. Then she apparently recalls that paradise didn't last. "Ottavio tends to feel seasick on small boats, and so he didn't want to come along. When I agreed to go alone, Ottavio became angry."

Olivia sighs, glances down at her now bare hands, and unconsciously rubs the place her sapphire and diamond ring used to be. I can still see the faint outline of where the skin wasn't exposed to the sun.

"I thought he was being unreasonable," she continues. "Others were invited. And besides, it was clear to everyone that I was there with Ottavio. Just because we weren't married

doesn't mean that I would ever betray him. Anyway, I went by myself. When I arrived back Ottavio wouldn't speak to me and so after two days I left."

"Did this Darius guy have a crush on you?" I ask.

"I highly doubt that," says Olivia. "He flirted with *all* the female customers. Darius is extraordinarily handsome—the tourists called him Adonis. In fact, Ottavio and I used to joke about it, at least before we argued. If Darius was busy talking to a pretty woman, it could take half an hour to get the bill."

"And you haven't heard from Ottavio since then?" I ask.

Nodding her head to indicate that she hasn't, Olivia rises from her chair by the side of the bed. "I'd better go." She leans over and kisses my forehead. "Do you want me to close the shade?"

"No thanks," I say.

Olivia departs and I stare out the window at the bright panoply of stars that make up heaven's floor. The big dipper looks like a kite at the end of its string. But all I can think of is how the brightest star in the Palmer constellation has gone out.

FORTY

ONCE THE KIDS ARE OFF TO SCHOOL, PASTOR COSTELLO GENER-ally heads over to his office. Fund-raising has fallen off since his trip to Cambodia, and the church roof is leaking in more places than usual. This morning he looks particularly hurried and pre-occupied, as if he has more important things to do than scrub the oatmeal off the kitchen table.

I sit on the living room floor and try to attach Lillian's sneak-ers to her body so that Bernard can pick her up to play with Rose and Gigi, whom he happily refers to as his "lunachicks." Only she's more interested in luring the kitten out of its hiding place underneath the couch than being bogged down with footwear.

"Lillian! Will you please hold still so I can put your shoes on?"

"I don't like those shoes, Mommy," she retorts. Oh God! I cover my face with my hands. It's like a bad episode of *Little House on the Prairie*.

Pastor Costello comes through the room searching for his spectacles.

"I feel bad that you've wasted so much time over here," I say to him. "I'm fine now and can handle things on my own." Hell, the kids are even calling me Mommy, I almost add, but don't.

Pastor Costello stops directly in front of me, and his mournful countenance instantly changes to alarm. "Whatever would make you say that? I'm enjoying this challenge and feel very blessed to have the opportunity to be of service."

"Oh, well, it's just that you look sort of anxious. Obviously we're keeping you from a lot of stuff—your life, for instance. I appreciate all your help, but there's really no reason to spend the night anymore."

"Now I remember why you're such a good poker player—you read the people instead of the cards." Pastor Costello sighs and sits down on the couch. "My mother died a year ago today. She was quite ill and suffering, and so I can't say I wish she'd carried on in that condition. But I'm still not used to an empty house."

The back door opens and Lillian shouts with glee as she runs through the kitchen to meet Bernard and the girls.

"You came home to an empty house and I've arrived home to a full one." I nod my head in the direction of the noise.

"Yes, I suppose so," says Pastor Costello. "What we can't cure we must endure. I'll light a candle and say a prayer for her when I get to the church."

"Do you really believe that prayers help?" I ask. "Olivia says that people change things, not prayer."

"But prayer changes people." Pastor Costello rises to leave. "I'll see you this afternoon."

It's easy to pray for my mom, because I just pray that she'll get better. When it comes to Dad it's not nearly as straightforward. Do I pray that he's happy wherever he is, that his soul is at peace? Although I know what *he* always used to pray for at the beginning of April—a big tax refund. In fact, that's a good idea. I'll pray for the things I'm certain would have made Dad happy—good health, especially for Eric, since if he gets injured we're all in trouble, good grades, and a good refund.

FORTY-ONE

AﬀﬀﬀFTER TWO MORE WEEKS OF DIVIDING MY TIME BETWEEN THE bed and the couch, I'm finally ready to tackle a full day. The first thing on my list is to recover the twins from Mrs. Muldoon. Only when I go next door to fetch them, she actually appears heartbroken. It doesn't take much for her to convince me to let her watch them every afternoon. That way she can do her cleaning, shopping, and errands in the morning and I'll do mine later in the day. It's easy to see why in ancient times village women gathered at a central location with all their tools and kids in order to get anything accomplished.

"I'm sorry that I can't pay you for all of this baby-sitting," I say. And I mean it, because Mrs. Muldoon should probably be receiving a hundred dollars a day for taking care of not one, but two, babies.

Mrs. Muldoon looks horrified. "Don't be ridiculous, Hallie. I should be paying *you*. My daughter Barbara wants me to move out to Scottsdale and live with her. She made a ton of money with those computer things. I tell her, 'Barbara, I may not be as good in the kitchen as I once was, but I can still manage.' You should have heard Barbara when I told her about taking care of

twins! I finally said, 'Barbara, they're just babies, like you were once, and I'm not dead yet!' "

"Arizona is supposed to be nice," I say. Honestly, it wouldn't take much to interest me in a trip to someplace warm and sunny right about now.

"It's not for me," scoffs Mrs. Muldoon. "This is my home, right here." She points to the living room with the plastic covers over the couches (probably a good thing with the twins around). "And now I have the perfect excuse for not going without hurting her feelings. Barbara knows how I just adore children."

"Where's George these days?" Mrs. Muldoon's younger brother had lived with her most of the time I was growing up.

"Somewhere in New Hampshire," says Mrs. Muldoon. "George is still finding himself."

I'm tempted to say that if a guy in his late seventies has not yet found himself, then he may not be looking in the right places.

Taking a twin under each arm I walk back across the lawn, through the garage door, and into the kitchen.

"Surprise!" None other than Craig is sitting at the kitchen table.

I'm so surprised that I almost drop both the boys onto the linoleum floor.

"I thought you weren't coming until next week! I'm a wreck!" I hold one of the boys up to cover my face and attempt to smooth my wild hair. "You can't see me like this!"

"I finished early." Craig rises and kisses me on the forehead, right between the two boys. Taking one of them into his arms, he says, "You look terrific. I expected to find you in bed."

Craig's yellow hair is wavy now that he's let it grow out of the crew cut he had while playing football in high school. And

FORTY-ONE

AFTER TWO MORE WEEKS OF DIVIDING MY TIME BETWEEN THE bed and the couch, I'm finally ready to tackle a full day. The first thing on my list is to recover the twins from Mrs. Muldoon. Only when I go next door to fetch them, she actually appears heartbroken. It doesn't take much for her to convince me to let her watch them every afternoon. That way she can do her cleaning, shopping, and errands in the morning and I'll do mine later in the day. It's easy to see why in ancient times village women gathered at a central location with all their tools and kids in order to get anything accomplished.

"I'm sorry that I can't pay you for all of this baby-sitting," I say. And I mean it, because Mrs. Muldoon should probably be receiving a hundred dollars a day for taking care of not one, but two, babies.

Mrs. Muldoon looks horrified. "Don't be ridiculous, Hallie. I should be paying *you*. My daughter Barbara wants me to move out to Scottsdale and live with her. She made a ton of money with those computer things. I tell her, 'Barbara, I may not be as good in the kitchen as I once was, but I can still manage.' You should have heard Barbara when I told her about taking care of

twins! I finally said, 'Barbara, they're just babies, like you were once, and I'm not dead yet!' "

"Arizona is supposed to be nice," I say. Honestly, it wouldn't take much to interest me in a trip to someplace warm and sunny right about now.

"It's not for me," scoffs Mrs. Muldoon. "This is my home, right here." She points to the living room with the plastic covers over the couches (probably a good thing with the twins around). "And now I have the perfect excuse for not going without hurting her feelings. Barbara knows how I just adore children."

"Where's George these days?" Mrs. Muldoon's younger brother had lived with her most of the time I was growing up.

"Somewhere in New Hampshire," says Mrs. Muldoon. "George is still finding himself."

I'm tempted to say that if a guy in his late seventies has not yet found himself, then he may not be looking in the right places.

Taking a twin under each arm I walk back across the lawn, through the garage door, and into the kitchen.

"Surprise!" None other than Craig is sitting at the kitchen table.

I'm so surprised that I almost drop both the boys onto the linoleum floor.

"I thought you weren't coming until next week! I'm a wreck!" I hold one of the boys up to cover my face and attempt to smooth my wild hair. "You can't see me like this!"

"I finished early." Craig rises and kisses me on the forehead, right between the two boys. Taking one of them into his arms, he says, "You look terrific. I expected to find you in bed."

Craig's yellow hair is wavy now that he's let it grow out of the crew cut he had while playing football in high school. And

FORTY-ONE

AFTER TWO MORE WEEKS OF DIVIDING MY TIME BETWEEN THE bed and the couch, I'm finally ready to tackle a full day. The first thing on my list is to recover the twins from Mrs. Muldoon. Only when I go next door to fetch them, she actually appears heartbroken. It doesn't take much for her to convince me to let her watch them every afternoon. That way she can do her cleaning, shopping, and errands in the morning and I'll do mine later in the day. It's easy to see why in ancient times village women gathered at a central location with all their tools and kids in order to get anything accomplished.

"I'm sorry that I can't pay you for all of this baby-sitting," I say. And I mean it, because Mrs. Muldoon should probably be receiving a hundred dollars a day for taking care of not one, but two, babies.

Mrs. Muldoon looks horrified. "Don't be ridiculous, Hallie. I should be paying *you*. My daughter Barbara wants me to move out to Scottsdale and live with her. She made a ton of money with those computer things. I tell her, 'Barbara, I may not be as good in the kitchen as I once was, but I can still manage.' You should have heard Barbara when I told her about taking care of

twins! I finally said, 'Barbara, they're just babies, like you were once, and I'm not dead yet!' "

"Arizona is supposed to be nice," I say. Honestly, it wouldn't take much to interest me in a trip to someplace warm and sunny right about now.

"It's not for me," scoffs Mrs. Muldoon. "This is my home, right here." She points to the living room with the plastic covers over the couches (probably a good thing with the twins around). "And now I have the perfect excuse for not going without hurting her feelings. Barbara knows how I just adore children."

"Where's George these days?" Mrs. Muldoon's younger brother had lived with her most of the time I was growing up.

"Somewhere in New Hampshire," says Mrs. Muldoon. "George is still finding himself."

I'm tempted to say that if a guy in his late seventies has not yet found himself, then he may not be looking in the right places.

Taking a twin under each arm I walk back across the lawn, through the garage door, and into the kitchen.

"Surprise!" None other than Craig is sitting at the kitchen table.

I'm so surprised that I almost drop both the boys onto the linoleum floor.

"I thought you weren't coming until next week! I'm a wreck!" I hold one of the boys up to cover my face and attempt to smooth my wild hair. "You can't see me like this!"

"I finished early." Craig rises and kisses me on the forehead, right between the two boys. Taking one of them into his arms, he says, "You look terrific. I expected to find you in bed."

Craig's yellow hair is wavy now that he's let it grow out of the crew cut he had while playing football in high school. And

he's not as built up as when he went to the weight room several times a week. But his restless green eyes are the same, and you could probably cut glass on those cheekbones.

He helps me settle the boys into their portable car seats on the kitchen table. "It's just so great to finally see you!"

We both feel how much has happened since we were together over the holidays. It was only three months ago but seems more like several years.

"How come I didn't see your car pull up?"

"I parked down the street in order to surprise you. I haven't even been home yet. Why don't I go unpack and then pick you up later this evening?"

"Pick me up?" I want to laugh, but it's so *not* funny that I can't.

"Uh, Craig, my brothers and sisters will be arriving home from school starting at three, and they have to do homework, eat dinner, get ready for bed, you know . . . I mean, Pastor Costello comes by every day to help, but I can't just leave him here to do everything. He's already been incredibly generous with his time while I was sick."

"Of course," Craig enthuses, and his eyes give out a lively light. "I'll come over and help."

"Okay, that would be great."

Suddenly things are looking up. And the prospect of doing six loads of laundry doesn't seem nearly so bad.

FORTY-TWO

WHEN CRAIG RETURNS AT FIVE O'CLOCK, I DON'T HEAR HIM
come through the front door because of all the noise. Darlene,
Davy, and Francie are playing some game that involves screaming as loud as they can. In fact, that's all it seems to involve. Lillian has found a kazoo, and the twins have turned into sheep,
going "Bah!" every few seconds. Meantime Teddy is accusing
Francie and Darlene of leaving the caps off of his Magic Markers *again*. The twins are loudly proclaiming their innocence as
Teddy threatens to wallop them. One might well ask, "Where
are the parents?"

Pastor Costello removes the chipped-beef casserole from the
oven while I set the table. When I poke my head into the living
room to tell Lillian to quit it with the kazoo, Craig is standing in
the front hall like a deer caught in headlights, unable to take a
step without landing on top of toy soldiers set up for battle, scattered checkers, various pieces of Mr. Potato Head, and an abandoned game of Candyland. Francie's favorite Raffi CD is blasting
from a boom box, and the kitten is happily tearing apart a mit-
ten under the coffee table. Craig has never spent any time at the
Palmer household, aside from the day we stopped by before the
prom, and apparently wasn't expecting this level of critical mass.

"Come on in," I shout over Raffi singing "Willoughby Wallaby Woo" accompanied by Lillian's kazoo. "We're in the kitchen." To the kids, I say, "Clean up this stuff, wash your hands for dinner, and turn that CD off or Willoughby Wallaby Woo the elephant is going to sit on you, too!" A county fair couldn't make more commotion.

Craig makes his way through the mess. "Wow. These are all your brothers and sisters?"

"No, I've taken hostages." Granted, when they're gathered in one room and not spread out in the backyard it does look like a much larger group.

At dinner Pastor Costello leads the prayer. In the past few weeks he's Jesused us all up with a full-length grace at each meal, complete with special intentions from *everyone*. Then during dinner each child must tell one good thing and one bad thing about his or her day. Francie goes last because she harbors grudges against almost every boy in her class and it takes at least ten minutes to work through them all. Pastor Costello feels the need to invest a substantial amount of time deconstructing her anger, with a focus on forgiveness. Meantime, I, the less charitable among us, think we should pursue a different line of inquiry: What is Francie doing to make these boys so angry in the first place?

After dinner Craig and I clear the table and start in on the stacks of dishes.

"Wow, it's sort of like working in a restaurant, isn't it?" Craig asks good-naturedly.

"Welcome to my world," I say. "The best part is that you don't have to worry about quality since everyone is a repeat customer. The bad news is that the tips are lousy and the floor needs mopping after each meal."

Pastor Costello comes over to the sink with his trademark white dish towel slung over his shoulder and says, "Why don't you kids go and get some fresh air while I keep watch over the flock? According to St. Thérèse of Lisieux, God is in the pots and pans."

Despite the fact that I feel like anything but a kid these days, I'm thrilled to have the chance to escape. Pastor Costello is the one who should be sainted.

Craig and I attempt to look guilty as we quickly relinquish our places in front of the sink. We head toward the door, eager to spend time alone together.

"Be careful," he says.

I take this to mean that we're supposed to remember that sex is for procreation and not recreation. However, no actual abstinence pledges are called for, and so we mumble "Okay."

FORTY-THREE

THE EVENING SKY IS WATERCOLOR GRAY AND THE CLOUDS ARE full of rain. As the gravel crushes softly under our tires in the old familiar driveway, I realize that several months have passed since I've been at the Stocktons'. The white Victorian house with its black shutters and gingerbread trim appears welcoming. And the row of silver poplar trees practically glows in the cool stillness of the shadows.

The prospect of being alone with Craig is thrilling. Just the sight of him sitting next to me in the car causes a rush of delight throughout my entire body. Our plan is to sneak into the summerhouse. In a small town, trying to have sex with someone you're not married to is a lot like trying to sneak hot-fudge sundaes into diet camp.

"It's only a quarter past seven," says Craig. "They're probably finishing dinner."

"I guess we'd better go in and say hello first."

I knock on the heavy front door before opening it and call out, "Hello there, it's Hallie."

Gil comes around the corner carrying a storybook and is the first to greet us. "Welcome to bedtime! I'm offering a bounty of a hundred dollars for every child captured." Gil stretches his hand out toward Craig. "Hey, big guy! It's great to see you."

Craig is only an inch or two taller than Gil, but he's much broader, especially since playing football in high school and lacrosse in college. Gil has more of a baseball player's lanky grace and the sinuous build of a long-distance runner.

"I've got one!" Bernard announces as he enters the front hall swinging Rose in his arms. "Welcome home, Craig. How's school going?"

Craig appears caught off guard by the question. "Oh . . . you know, school. Same as ever, I guess."

"Where's your little sister?" Gil waves a finger at the giggling and writhing pajama-clad Rose.

Rose wriggles free and manages to make her escape. She's growing up tall and athletic—any developmental issues she had when she first arrived nine months ago have entirely disappeared.

"That's what happens when you capture one in a half stockton instead of a full stockton," says Gil.

"She's adorable," says Craig, and smiles.

"And fast," Gil adds as Rose practically flies up the stairs.

"Those pajamas are gorgeous," I say of the pink silk brocaded with ivory flowers.

"They're imported from China," says Bernard. "It's part of their cultural heritage."

Gil rolls his eyes.

Only Bernard catches him. "If you would stop showing them music videos, they might actually absorb some of it rather than dancing around like David Byrne!"

"*Stop Making Sense* is not a music video but a landmark film made by a world-class director. And an important part of *American* culture. If I leave everything to you, the girls will be laughed out of school for having lunch boxes stuffed with chopsticks, General Tso's chicken, and green tea."

"Is Olivia around?" asks Craig. "I was hoping to ask her something."

He was? This is news to me. Then suddenly I understand— Craig is providing an excuse for our coming over. This way it won't look as if our only intention was to shack up in the summerhouse.

"She went out," says Gil.

"Church?" I ask.

"Don't get me started!" says Bernard.

"Darius," says Gil.

"Who's Darius?" asks Craig.

"Some con-artist gigolo she met in the Greek Islands who is using Mother to get citizenship and then start a business with her money."

Gil lets out a sigh to indicate this may not exactly be the story, as Bernard is prone not only to dramatization, but also exaggeration.

"He hasn't asked Livvy for anything," says Gil.

"That we know of," Bernard shoots back.

Rose comes zooming by and Gil makes an unsuccessful grab for her. "And stop straight-bashing in front of the children."

"Gay or straight, he's an *opportunist*," says Bernard.

"May I remind you that *she's* the one who convinced him to stay here? Darius had already checked into a motel. You just don't like him because he's handsome and looks young for his age," says Gil. "Which is not much more than *your* age."

Bernard responds with a look that indicates Gil has no idea what he's talking about and will probably be committed by morning.

Rose comes around again and this time Gil manages to catch her. "Let's find your sister so we can read a story."

"I've looked everywhere," says Bernard. "Rocky must have taken her to the summerhouse." Bernard removes a coat from the front hall closet while explaining, "With the space heater it's more or less become a playroom, especially since *you know who* has been staying rent-free in the den."

Craig and I follow Bernard out to the summerhouse. Dark clouds scuttle toward us, sheeting the sky with an eerie greenish-gray. I can't help but notice that the gardens are ready to be turned, and how little green buds dot the branches of the rose-bushes that haven't been pruned.

"The swimming pool will go back there." Bernard points to an area near the front of the woods marked off by wooden stakes with red flags on top. "A Neptune pool like William Randolph Hearst had at San Simeon, complete with colonnades, statues of nymphs, and of course a slide for the children."

"Better go easy on the nymphs if you want my brothers and sisters to be allowed to swim in it."

"The Chinese tea garden will go over there." He indicates a spot to the right of the summerhouse where it used to be just grass, but now there are several mounds of dirt and a large wooden platform.

We stop to check on the pond that Craig built last summer, which seems to have survived the harsh winter in good shape, complete with the majority of fish alive and swimming. As Bernard opens the door to the summerhouse the wind picks up and rustles the branches above. I shiver not with cold so much as enthusiasm.

"Rocky and Gigi are inseparable," explains Bernard. "I don't know what he's going to do when she eventually starts pre-school."

The summerhouse is the same as I left it, except for some toys scattered about. And sure enough, Rocky and Gigi are snuggled up together asleep on one of the couches. It's probably a good thing the adoption agency doesn't know that the girls' nanny is a recovering alcoholic chimpanzee, even if he was trained to assist paraplegics.

The two look awfully cute lying there together. Gigi has a thick, full head of hair now, rather than the short punk-rock do she sported when the girls first arrived.

"I'd hire a sitter, but Rocky is amazing with the children," says Bernard. "And you don't have to worry about coming home to him on the phone with his girlfriend."

"How is his girlfriend, by the way?" I refer to Lulu the Great Dane, who lives next door.

"Didn't I tell you?" asks Bernard. "She had puppies on New Year's Day. Sometimes we get all the kids together for a play date."

"Is Rocky still desperately in love with her?" asks Craig.

"I believe they're just good friends nowadays," says Bernard. "As in most relationships, things change after the children arrive."

"Having recently found myself in the family way, I can certainly see how that's possible," I reply.

After glancing back toward the sleeping child, Bernard whispers, "Gigi can already say the alphabet. I'm quite certain that she's a genius."

Craig and I both nod vigorously, as if this is undoubtedly the case. Taking another look around, it appears that all the children's toys are indeed educational ones. Not exactly like our basement playroom, the place where homemade sock puppets go to die.

Bernard wakes Rocky by tapping him on the shoulder.

Rocky is excited to see Craig and me, and after placing big smacking kisses on both of our cheeks, he gently lifts Gigi without waking her and heads out the door with the sleeping child in his furry arms.

Once they've exited Bernard says, "It's no use trying to take her away from Rocky. *He* gets angry and *she* starts screaming. I had to bring him with me to the pediatrician one day. *That* made for an interesting waiting room experience."

"I'll bet," says Craig.

"Why don't I ask Gil to read the girls a story while I fix us some hot chocolate?" suggests Bernard. "I have a wonderful new creation called orange zest hot cocoa—it sounds *terrible* but tastes *magnifique*! Especially with a pinch of cinnamon and fresh whipped cream."

Looking down at my feet, I mutter, "Craig just arrived back and I was wondering if maybe the two of us could just sit and talk out here for a while."

Bernard gives an expressive, "Oh," to indicate that he gets it. "Yes, yes, of course. Why don't the two of you catch up on all the local gossip. I have a lot of work to do on my new weekly antiques newsletter—*Decorators Without Borders*."

Once Bernard is gone, Craig and I stand awkwardly in front of each other.

I finally say, "Remember when you came over before leaving for school and—"

"And we kissed on the couch and then made love on the bed," Craig finishes the sentence for me.

"I never could have made it through these past two months without you," I tell him. And it's the truth.

"Sure you could have," says Craig. "You're strong."

"No matter how bad things got I always knew that at the end of the day I could call and you'd be there for me."

Craig kisses me. His lips are smooth and cool, and I feel that old tingle all through my body. I kiss him back hard. We shed our clothes and climb under the covers. He rubs my back with those big strong hands and it feels so good. I close my eyes and release a deep breath.

"Hallie, wake up!"

"Huh?" I have no idea where I am.

"It's almost eleven o'clock!"

"Oh my gosh, I crashed. I'm so sorry."

Craig laughs. "Me too. We slept for two and a half hours! I guess I was tired from all that driving."

We crawl out from under the covers and quickly dress. "I meant to ask, why *did* you drive home rather than fly?"

"I had a lot of stuff to bring back."

Craig drops me in front of the house, promising to come by tomorrow so that while the kids are at school we can finally get a chance to be together—just the two of us.

Pastor Costello is lying on the couch reading and doesn't hear me come in. When he looks up and sees me, he quickly shoves his book behind the couch pillow as if it's pornography.

"Sorry I'm so late." I pretend not to notice that he deep-sixed the book.

Only it was so obvious that he removes the book and shows it to me. "Mystery novel," Pastor Costello explains sheepishly. "Guilty pleasure."

I laugh. "What's there to be guilty about? It's not as if the church has banned reading novels."

"I know. It's just that . . . well, I feel as if people expect me to be perusing the Bible or something more high-minded." He nods toward the cover where a bloody knife rests atop a hand mirror and next to a heart-shaped bottle of spilled perfume.

"Your secret is safe with me," I say.

"Amen to that." Pastor Costello rises from the couch in the way that middle-aged people do, slowly and checking to make sure everything still works before applying too much pressure. "How was your date?"

"Great," I say. I'm tempted to add that the best way to achieve abstinence is not with a pledge, but through extensive child care.

"The Larkins are a nice family—longtime members of the Methodist church, though Craig's father was raised Lutheran."

"I wasn't aware that you preachers kept score."

"In a town this size you eventually get to know just about everyone. Besides, most of these trains are heading for the same station. We're on slightly different tracks is all."

As Pastor Costello gets his things together, he says, "It's nice to see you with a little color back in your cheeks."

Yeah, nothing like a good nap with your boyfriend, I think.

"I thought I'd go home tonight, now that you're better," says Pastor Costello.

I assume it will be a nice change for him to wake up in his own bed, except something in his tone makes me say, "Either way is fine."

"I'll be back in time to make breakfast. And the lunches are in the fridge," he says. "Call if you need anything. We're open twenty-four hours a day, just like heaven."

FORTY-FOUR

SOMETIMES THE RAIN IS SO LOUD DURING THE NIGHT THAT IT wakes me up with a start. Water gushes from the gutters and cascades off the roof onto the driveway and back porch. At one point I find little Lillian trembling at the edge of my bed and open the covers so she can crawl in beside me.

When I look out the window in the morning, the downpour has let up and steel-gray clouds scud across the sky heading toward Cleveland. What I *don't* see are any big yellow buses. By sixty-thirty A.M. the high school is normally picking up the early birds who practice for swim team, work out in the gym, or volunteer for safety patrol. Also missing are cars. I soon realize there's a good reason for this: There don't appear to be roads anymore.

Water swirls in the street while the lawns are a marsh with only the tops of bushes poking up like scrubby little islands. Big green garbage cans and plastic planters bob along the surface, accompanied by plastic toys.

There's no point in waking the kids for school. I check the basement for water and discover some trickles here and there, but nothing major yet. When we used to complain about needing a bigger house, Dad always said that we were lucky to be in this one because it's built on high ground compared to the rest of the neighborhood.

Swinging open the front door I'm hit with a powerful but unusual smell—a combination of raw sewage and spring. The air is about twenty degrees warmer than it was yesterday. At the end of the street I hear a buzzing sound, as if a large mosquito is approaching. Zipping around the corner in an inflatable boat comes Officer Rich and Al, both wearing blue caps with gold badges on the front. Al must have been deputized for the emergency. A rowboat emerges from between the two houses across the street. And at the other end of the block a kayak glides into view.

I step out onto the front porch and Officer Rich pulls his boat alongside as if the stoop is a dock.

"Ship to shore," Al calls out to me as he grabs the iron railing.

"Guess you don't need your snowplow today," I say.

"We reached the high-water mark about two hours ago," explains Officer Rich. "It's starting to go down."

"But there's no school, right?" I ask.

"Roger that," says Officer Rich. "Spring break is starting a day early. But don't let the kids out to mess around in the water. It's not all that clean."

"And don't let them touch any wires in the basement," says Al. "Call me if it doesn't drain by tomorrow and I'll bring the electric pump over."

"So far it's mostly dry," I report.

Al looks up and down the street to survey our chances of being flooded. "You're lucky, because on the other side of Main Street water is sloshing around in people's living rooms."

Mr. Cavanaugh waves as he floats by in an old beat-up tin horse trough. Then he returns to scanning the surface of the water while holding a crab net over his shoulder.

From behind my house seventy-year-old Mr. Blakely from the hardware store comes bobbing along in a washtub, using a broom to propel himself through the brackish water. His eyes are also fixed on the swirling surface.

"What's everyone doing out here so early?" I ask. "It's not even seven o'clock."

Officer Rich smiles. "Cappy's father had a secret stash that the flood brought up."

I don't know if it's the early hour or the mist, but I don't get it.

"You know that Cappy's father was a legendary bootlegger, right?" asks Al.

I nod my head. I'd heard stories, but never really asked him about them. Being that we live so close to one of the Great Lakes and Canada had looser regulations during prohibition, there'd certainly been a lot of action around here in the 1920s and '30s.

Officer Rich holds up a brown bottle with no label while Al continues, "Things got pretty hot near the end, and he was constantly changing hiding places right up until the minute he was shot."

Shot? I definitely didn't know about that.

"There's always been a rumor that Pappy Cappy had fifty or so cases of whiskey made by a distillery in Canada in 1932, really good stuff, not the rotgut they sold to the public," says Al.

"The flood opened up the hiding place, which appears to be around Main and Swan streets. At least that's where most of the bottles have been found," says Officer Rich. "Probably in a back room or basement of one of the old buildings along that stretch."

From his horse trough Mr. Cavanaugh lets out a huge whoop and hauls something in with his net. Mr. Blakely looks over from his washtub with envy. Up the street I can see cheap old Mr. Exner paddling along in an old birch bark canoe.

I look down and count three bottles lying in the bottom of Officer Rich's boat. "So are you guys confiscating it?"

"Hell no!" says Al. "We're *collecting* it. This is almost hundred-year-old hootch!"

"I talked to Cappy this morning," says Officer Rich, who always does the right thing in such circumstances. "He said finders keepers."

Some men outfitted in waders and yellow slickers ride by in an inflatable pool toy shaped like a giant lobster, obviously drunk from the way they're shouting and stumbling about.

Pastor Costello paddles up in the rowboat that's always been used for the Sunday school production of *Noah's Ark*. It still has some of the cardboard animals in front and a giraffe neck leans out over the side. His cheeks are flushed from rowing, and he's trying to catch his breath enough to speak. "I just wanted to make sure that you're okay."

I see a bottle tucked under a cardboard cutout of a squirrel in the middle of the boat.

"There's trash everywhere," he explains. "Just trying to do my part."

Inside the house the phone rings. I wave to the brave seafarers and wish them luck as they cast off again.

When I answer it, Craig says, "Would you believe me if I told you that the reason I can't come over and make love to you is because of a flood?"

"You don't expect me to fall for that old excuse again, do you?" I ask.

"Sorry, Hallie. We must be the only family in town without a boat. I was going to swim over, but my mother put a stop to that. She insists that I'll die from typhus."

"It doesn't matter since school is closed." Our big plan had been to drop Lillian at the Stocktons', send the twins over to Mrs. Muldoon's, and then have the house to ourselves.

"Officer Rich says the water is starting to go down and so maybe you can come over later," I say hopefully.

"Did you hear about the whiskey?" asks Craig. "My uncle Joe called at five o'clock this morning. He's out there on his son's surfboard and wanted my dad to join him."

The twins start making noises in the other room, and I hear the scuffle of pajama-clad feet on the stairs. "I have to get the twins ready and make breakfast. Come over as soon as you can."

Francie skids into the kitchen, yelling, "Uncle Lenny made the whole world flood!" Then her eyes grow wide and searching as she looks up at me. "Is it because we've been bad?"

My own theory is slightly different—that someone up there is trying to keep Craig and me from being alone together.

FORTY-FIVE

AFTER TWO DAYS THE WATER RECEDES ENTIRELY, LEAVING BEHIND a bitter springlike smell in the air. The earth has once again performed its miraculous annual ritual of renewal, with bright green buds almost everywhere. Off in the distance spring sunlight threads through soft, fluffy clouds. And soon there will be prairie dog–sized mosquitoes dive-bombing us from every direction.

Bernard has invited the whole family over for Easter dinner, but I decide there are too many of us. Eric and I agree to take Pastor Costello up on his invitation to be part of the church supper. No one mentions that it's for the parishioners who don't have anyplace to go.

On Friday I finally call Louise to see if she's coming home for the holiday. As Eric had said when we talked about it, "She's still part of the family."

Louise informs me that she has a job waitressing at a catering hall and that working on Easter Sunday will pay time and a half, in addition to big tips. Apparently the Resurrection of Jesus is a cause for great generosity among the brunch crowd. From the hours she claims to be working it's obvious that

Louise isn't in school, so I ask about her taking an equivalency exam. Louise explains that she's not allowed to sign up for it until she turns eighteen, because the government doesn't want to encourage kids to drop out of high school, so her plan is just to earn some money between now and then. It must be working because she has her own car and a cell phone.

The majority of the parishioners who come to the church supper are old, and so next to almost every chair is a cane or aluminum walker. People love saying this town is a good place to raise children. But most young people finish high school, go away to college, and then off to the cities to build careers. Maybe after the new commuter train is up and running, things will change. It's supposed to be really fast—cutting the trip to downtown Cleveland from an hour and a half to fifty minutes.

At first not celebrating Easter in our own home seems strange—like we're an orphan family. But in the end I'm glad we decide to go to the church. It's better to stand behind a table and serve creamed onions to the cane and crutch crowd than to sit at Bernard's perfectly laid table trying to make all the little kids behave and keep them from breaking stuff. At church there's a playroom with a couple teenagers in charge where the kids are served some chunks of ham with French fries, followed by chocolate pudding. So they're happy, unable to cause a public disturbance, and I get a break from them until it's time to leave.

Eric is home, but he's with his new girlfriend, Elizabeth, and after the church supper they head off to a party with all his old football friends. He's going to visit Mom in the morning and then they're driving to see Elizabeth's family in Indianapolis. Elizabeth is pretty with short dark hair, large expressive doe eyes, and creamy skin. My only complaint is that she smells as if she's been dipped in a vat of perfume. On the other hand, Eric always reeks of Ben-Gay, so maybe she's just trying to counter-act his own distinctive stink.

Later that night, after the kids are all in bed and I've cleaned up most of the Easter grass that the kitten has dragged *all* over the house, Gwen and Jane stop by for a visit. Originally Jane had said to meet them at the pizza parlor. That's a laugh. It was nec-essary to explain that life has changed just slightly since the days when I used to ride my bike around at all hours.

I admit that for a while I was kind of mad at them. They haven't called much since Dad died and I've been under serious house arrest. But I eventually decided that Gwen and Jane prob-ably didn't want to have to tell me about all of the fun they were having, knowing it would only make me feel bad. And I didn't exactly phone them a lot either, not wanting to tell them how miserable I was, knowing it would just make *them* feel bad. It was easier not to call than to lie.

The great thing is that now I can honestly tell my friends that even if money is tight, life is much better since Pastor Costello arrived and Craig came back for spring break. And also that Mom is coming home soon.

"So when can you go back to school?" asks Jane.

There it is, the million-dollar question. "I guess I might have to wait until Eric graduates next year," I manage to say without bursting into tears.

Fortunately Gwen, who is always looking to get the low-down on everyone's love life, changes the subject. "I thought that Craig would be here tonight."

"He had to go to his aunt Dolly's in Akron," I explain.

Both girls then proceed to say what a fantastic guy Craig is and how lucky I am to have him as my boyfriend.

"Because we know what total *jerks* guys that age can be," adds Gwen.

Jane and I are aware that she's referring to her ex-boyfriend, who is now sleeping with her roommate. But we don't say anything, afraid that she'll start crying over that one, again.

I know they're right about Craig. And if I can finally see him alone, if only for an hour, everything will be even better.

FORTY-SIX

WHEN SPRING BREAK ENDS, LIFE RETURNS TO BEING MEASURED not in days or months, but by the number of lunches packed and spoonfuls of strained squash with rice launched into the mouths of the twins. Sometimes between loads of laundry and vacuuming Cheerios out of the rug, I'll stop and interview myself with the furniture wand.

So, Ms. Palmer, what do you do with all of your spare time?

Mostly I knit blankets for earthquake victims and shop for the housebound elderly after I've finished up at the women's shelter. Though when it's autumn here, that means spring in East Africa and so I'm of course busy sending over packets of seed corn and organizing local bake-offs to raise money for basic farm implements. My altruistic reverie is interrupted by a phone call from Mrs. Muldoon. She's at the Star-Mart and Land O Lakes butter is on sale. Should she pick up one of the large tubs for me?

These days Davy and Darlene don't arrive home until five o'clock due to various after-school activities. Francie is now attending a program at the YMCA where the kids are allowed to play games and roughhouse on mats in the gym. It was suggested by her school nurse—okay, threat or recommendation, everybody has a different take on things. It's a little more driving for me and costs twenty-five dollars a week, but I must admit the new routine has certainly helped reduce Francie's excess energy and cut down on fights and injuries, self-inflicted or otherwise.

The only problem now is that every time one of the kids walks out the door he or she needs money for something—activity fees, uniforms, field trips—or some type of baked good for the never-ending stream of fund-raisers and class parties. Plus all the kids are now required to have organizers (which they lose during every vacation) that cost eight dollars apiece.

On top of all that, Darlene's speech therapist had the brilliant idea that she should take up the clarinet—which costs forty-four dollars a month to rent, after a one-hundred-dollar deposit, and that doesn't include sheet music and reeds.

And then Teddy needed train fare every day during vacation. He'd spent practically the entire week researching depression at Case Western Reserve's medical library in Cleveland.

Thank goodness the insurance money finally arrived. But that goes in the bank for paying the mortgage. And we now get a social security check every month. Only after the groceries there's not a dollar left over. Forget putting money aside for educations, Mom's old age, and another minivan. The guy at the garage said the station wagon will never pass inspection without our putting at least eight hundred dollars into it.

The only bright spot on the financial horizon is that Eric landed a job at his university to be assistant coach for a girls' basketball camp this summer. I'd hoped he was going to help with the kids, but right now the money is more important.

Pastor Costello comes by during the morning rush, and if he doesn't have vespers or a counseling session, then he stops back for dinner. Craig usually arrives around ten in the morning, and while I clean the house he's been getting the yard in shape and fixing some shingles on the roof.

Finally, on Wednesday, Craig and I actually find an hour to spend together, just the two of us. With the house empty of children and the windows open to usher in the spring, we merge effortlessly like two raindrops. It feels like Craig has pulled my body out of the swirling floodwaters and resuscitated me by placing his lips to mine. An almost physical sense of lightness washes over me, as if all the boxes and bags I was carrying have been put into ministorage.

FORTY-SEVEN

ON THE DAYS THAT BERNARD TAKES LILLIAN, CRAIG ACCOMPA-nies me to the grocery store and afterward we usually stop at Custard's Last Stand for ice cream. If the weather is good, we'll drive around before heading home, stopping on a dirt road to make out in the car like teenagers. I guess that technically I still am a teenager, even if I sure don't feel like one anymore.

Friday afternoon is a particularly nice day. Once we're a mile outside of town, it looks like a scene from an Andrew Wyeth painting—windswept, golden, and lonely.

Craig and I lie across the roof of the car and hold hands while staring up at the gauzy clouds hanging in the air over-head.

"You're going to be twenty next week," I say. "In another year you'll be old enough to have your first beer."

He laughs. "I drank so much beer the first two years of col-lege that I'm planning on giving it up for my twenty-first birth-day. When the guys in the frat house tell you they have a three-point-oh, you'd better be sure to ask whether that's a grade-point average or their blood alcohol content."

"What do you want for a present?" I ask. "Anything in the world—so long as it doesn't cost more than five dollars."

"Just you," he says.

"How about a small child?" I joke. "I have all different shapes and sizes, and the best thing is that they're just like pets—they all have their own little personalities."

"Then I'll take Roddy," says Craig.

I've let him in on my little secret about losing track of the identities of the boys.

"I have a better idea," I play along. "I'll put the twins behind my back and you'll pick one."

"Deal." He shakes my hand and then seals the bargain with a kiss.

We get back into the car and head for home to put away the groceries before the eggs start to hatch.

"Why don't we have a birthday party at my place," I suggest. This is something I might actually be able to do. Mom has all sorts of decorations, and I can bake a cake from a mix. (Who am I kidding? I'll just invite the Stocktons and Bernard will take care of everything.)

"That would be terrific," says Craig. "My mother will call you for a list of vaccinations they should get before coming over."

The kids have given Craig two colds back to back and one stomach flu in the three weeks he's been home.

"How about Saturday night?" I ask. "What time do you have to leave for school on Sunday?"

Craig looks out the window for a long while. Eventually he mumbles, "School already started."

"What do you mean it started?" Is Craig taking a semester off to stay and help me?

"I dropped out," says Craig. "It's not for me." And then he laughs as if it's all a joke.

"But *why*?" I ask. "I thought you liked college, and your parents are paying for everything."

"Well, I don't," he says. "I cleaned out my room at the fraternity house and I'm not going back."

"If it's the school you don't like, then just transfer," I say. "Your parents could easily afford a private college anywhere in the country."

"I don't want to go to another school. I have no idea what I'm doing there or what I should be studying. As soon as I pick a major I change my mind."

"Take more classes until you find something you like," I say. "You can always go for a summer session or an extra year to earn enough credits to graduate."

"But I don't want to do the whole corporate thing like my dad, and I don't want to spend all my time gathering samples and looking at slides under a microscope."

"That's the whole point of college—to find out what you *do* like," I argue.

Craig's face becomes red and he balls his big hands into fists. "Hallie, will you listen to me? I dropped out! I would think that *you* of all people might understand."

I'm becoming angry as well. Though I don't know if it's more because Craig quit or that he didn't tell me until now.

"Why did you wait until *now* to tell me?" I think back to all those nights we talked on the phone until one o'clock in the morning. "Surely you've been planning this for some time."

"Because you had your own problems," says Craig.

"But we're together!" I practically shout. "That's why I felt okay bothering you with my problems, and not Gwen and Jane."

"Okay then, because I knew what you would say." Craig stares straight ahead.

Instinctively I realize that this is the critical hand right now and whatever I do could substantially impact my future fortunes. It's the moment to be supportive. Only I can't bring my-self to play that card. Not while I'm sitting at home while every-one else is in school, where I desperately want to be, and Craig is dropping out for no apparent reason.

In a calm voice I say, "Why don't you at least finish the se-mester and then make the final decision. That way you won't waste any money."

"Everything isn't always about money, Hallie! What about being happy? Sorry if it sounds cliché to you, but I'm trying to find myself."

"Dammit, Craig, you're right *here*. And you have parents who not only gave you a new car, but will pay for college and even graduate school. I'm sorry if I just don't understand the problem."

"You had *your* phase," says Craig.

"I was sixteen. And at no point was I not earning any money, I might add."

"So what does *that* mean?" asks Craig.

"It means how are you going to be responsible if you can't do something just because it's not providing you with maxi-mum enjoyment? It means that you're going to be twenty in a week and you're throwing your whole life away!"

"Thanks for all your understanding!"

We drive along in silence until it becomes so uncomfortable that I hit the button on the CD player. It's a secondhand car and the radio never worked to begin with.

"The Wheels on the Bus Go Round and Round" blares from the dashboard. I switch it off and we continue with only the noise of the wind rushing in through the open windows.

The shortest way home involves driving past several new de-velopments where it appears the contractors are all working from a single set of plans. Soon families will be moving in and grass will be growing out front. Meantime, the elusive riddle that is *my* future seems further away right now than ever before.

Once we're in the driveway Craig gets out of the car and leaves without saying a word. After all this worry about a long-distance relationship, it was the short-distance one that killed us.

FORTY-EIGHT

W HEN BERNARD ARRIVES WITH LILLIAN, HE TAKES ONE LOOK AT me and says, "Your aura suggests that you've recently been tossed about in a hurricane."

"Craig and I had a fight," I explain. "He dropped out of school. But it really wasn't about that so much as making money, I guess."

"That great lady of letters Edith Wharton said that the only way not to think about money is to have a great deal of it," says Bernard.

"We're just so broke right now that it's scary," I explain. "This morning I was seriously looking at a job in the paper to be a lunch lady. There aren't many careers that only need you between ten in the morning and three in the afternoon."

"I know one!" says Bernard. "I thought I'd be able to tend the yard by hiring June to mind the shop. But with keeping up my Web site, the newsletter, and being a stay-at-home dad, it's just too much. The girls are starting dance class. The Girl Scouts come every Thursday. Gil is working these incredibly long hours and all day on Saturday."

"I don't think so," I say. "Mrs. Muldoon loves baby-sitting the twins, but I can't turn her into an indentured servant."

"Twenty dollars an hour; make your own schedule," says Bernard. "And lunch. You're thinner than an Amish phone book."

"Believe me, I'd love nothing more." I glance at the scattered building blocks on the floor, the dirty dishes in the sink, and the lineup of unfinished science projects on the kitchen table. "But Mom is supposed to come home on Friday, and the doctor said that she needs a lot of rest."

Lillian comes screeching past, chasing after the kitten. I look at Bernard as if to say, I rest my case.

"Oh, I almost forgot." Bernard reaches into his pocket and hands me an envelope. "Ta-da! It's the first copy of my newsletter, where I discuss everything that's currently hot in the antiques market and the next big trends in art and decorating."

"Baron Heinrich Von Boogenhagen, art expert extraordinaire from Lichtenburg." I read the biography aloud. "Who is that?"

"My nom de plume," says Bernard.

"And where is Lichtenburg?"

"Don't you *remember*? It's the fictional country where Ethel Merman was appointed ambassador in *Call Me Madam*."

"Won't people know it's a fake place?"

Bernard waves a dismissive hand. "Americans are useless at geography. The only time they learn the whereabouts of a country is when our government decides to bomb it."

"Now you sound just like Olivia," I say. "Why not write under your own name?"

"Who would listen to Bernard Stockton from Cosgrove County?"

"People are always asking you to give lectures about antiques and other dealers constantly call to find out how to price stuff."

"*Exactly!* Everyone will assume I'm promoting my own

wares, or favoring one dealer over another with a positive mention."

"So now you can promote *your* stuff under someone else's name." I have to laugh. Bernard is almost always working an angle. And it usually doesn't involve a cut for the United Way.

"Don't be such a cynic," Bernard scolds. "Baron Von Boogenhagen has a completely legitimate, though somewhat distant claim to the Austrian throne."

"But there isn't really a Baron Von Boogenhagen, right?" I ask. "It's you."

"I prefer to think of it the way the editor of the *New York Sun* explained Santa Claus to Virginia—that he exists as certainly as love and generosity and devotion exist." Bernard clutches his hands to his heart and gives an emotional performance for the appliances, as if they're his imaginary audience.

I clap because the stove and refrigerator are limited when it comes to their ability to express appreciation. "Once again, you've managed to raise art to a whole new level."

"The word *artifice,* after all, begins with *art,*" says Bernard. "But more important, my dream of royalty has finally been realized, if only on the Internet!" He bows deeply to the sink and the dishwasher.

FORTY-NINE

IT'S A WARM, SUNNY EVENING AND THE KIDS ARE EXHAUSTED FROM playing outside until dark, so they fall into bed without my having to take them down like calves at a rodeo. Pastor Costello called to say he's staying late at church to lead a Bible study group. Better him than me.

This leaves plenty of time to lie on the couch eating chocolate ice cream out of the carton and dwell on how I've ruined my life. It's not as if I had elaborate fantasies about marrying Craig, but I can't honestly say that it never crossed my mind as a possibility for the future, after we'd both finished school and started working at real jobs.

The back door opens and I hear a commotion in the kitchen. Only it's not kids or church ladies but deep male voices and the heavy clunky steps of size-twelve boots.

"Who do you have to know to get a game going around here?" comes a shout.

It's Al's voice.

"The children are sleeping," Pastor Costello shushes him.

Dashing into the kitchen, I find Herb, Al, Officer Rich, Pastor Costello, and Bernard all removing their jackets.

"Surprise!" Bernard says as he unloads two shopping bags full of snacks.

"Hey, Poker Face," Herb calls to me.

"The mountain has come to Muhammad," says Pastor Costello.

"That's *so* sweet of you guys," I say.

"Spare me the group hug," says Herb.

"This kitchen table is perfect," declares Officer Rich as he sits down at the head of the long wooden table in the big chair that was my dad's. Granted, it's safe to say that the other seats wouldn't hold his ample girth.

"Gather round, ye brave knights of the green table," calls out Bernard.

"No set, no bet." Al makes himself at home in the middle and organizes the chips.

Herb glares at Al because he despises stupid poker expressions. "Lose the patter, will you?"

"Kiss my ace," retorts Al.

"Some Bible study," I say to Pastor Costello.

"The family that plays together stays together." He pulls two decks of cards out of his pockets and tosses them in my direction.

Officer Rich opens a bag of potato chips and the tangy smell of vinegar fills the room. "It's not candy and sugar that's my downfall," says Officer Rich as he inhales deeply, "but salt and grease."

Within minutes the kitchen has been transformed into our old poker stomping grounds, with cards being dealt and chips sliding in and out of the pot. Only Al isn't allowed to smoke inside, and so every half hour he sits out a hand and heads to the backyard.

"For some reason having a poker game in my kitchen is making me feel old," I say to no one in particular.

"Old!" barks Herb. "When I was a kid, playing cards were carved out of granite."

Bernard chimes in, "What I miss about the old days is that you could tell someone you'd been trying to phone them for *weeks,* when you really weren't at all!"

Officer Rich tells us a story about a woman who locked her keys in her car at the supermarket and then got stuck in the back window trying to crawl through to retrieve them from the ignition. To pry her loose he'd needed to place one arm around her chest and the other across her butt.

Pastor Costello takes us by surprise when he manages to top Officer Rich by recounting a wedding he was supposed to perform on a ship. As everyone was boarding, the mother of the bride slipped on the gangway and fell into the lake. The woman's husband jumped in after her, but he had a history of heart problems and so the bride jumped in to save them, only to be promptly dragged under by the weight of all her finery. The groom went in after her. Then the captain dove in, but he was corpulent and almost seventy. A sailor jumped in and eventually the entire wedding party was pulled out at various points along the shore.

"Did they still get married?" I ask.

"Oh yes!" says Pastor Costello. "Though not on the ship. We went back to the hotel so they could change and had the ceremony there. If it's meant to be, then it's meant to be."

"I'm not sure I agree with that," pipes Bernard. He complains about having trouble closing on the land he needs for his new pool due to zoning problems.

Al suggests they meet at the town hall and look at the deeds and property maps together since sometimes there's a loophole.

"Al is very creative when it comes to resource management," says Pastor Costello. It's a well-known fact that somehow Al manages to borrow the town's only fire truck for the church picnic every year and raises a thousand dollars by auctioning off rides to kids (and dads).

Al tosses a bunch of chips into the pot, but it's a bad throw and they land between Herb and Pastor Costello.

"Hey!" barks Herb. "Quit splashing the pot, dammit!" He quickly follows with "Sorry, Father" for the curse word.

Herb firmly believes that anything done to upset the equilibrium of the game might adversely affect the hand he's about to be dealt.

I complain about the high cost of all the stuff the kids need for school and how I feel like a bus driver with so many of their activities happening in different places. "On top of everything, there's a horrible smell coming from the corner of the backyard. When I called the plumber this afternoon he said 'uh-oh' in a very ominous way."

Only the guys just laugh at me.

"Yeah, uh-oh for you and five hundred dollars for him," says Al.

"I think I preferred it when you were a juvenile delinquent, rather than a homeowner with a failing septic tank," says Officer Rich.

"Yeah," says Herb. "Now you sound just like my wife. And the whole reason I come to poker is to escape all that for a few hours."

By midnight I've won a few hands worth a total of sixty dollars, but with each deal I'm feeling increasingly drowsy. At one point Al sneaks out for a cigarette while Herb goes to the bathroom, and I put my head down on my arms for a moment.

The next thing I know Officer Rich is covering me on the couch. Sounds of running water come from the kitchen. Waking slightly, I ask him, "Is the game over?"

"It is for you," says Officer Rich.

"I'm awake," I reply sleepily.

"Best to quit while you're ahead," says Officer Rich. "Just be sure to snag your winnings from Pastor Costello before the mail goes out tomorrow, or you might find they've been donated to that school he helped build in Cambodia."

FIFTY

On the day that mom is supposed to come home teddy pretends to be sick so that he can be here when she arrives.

"If you're really sick, then you'll have to stay in your room all day and night. We can't risk giving Mom the flu on her first day out of the hospital," I respond with a straight face. Before he can answer I quickly throw in my insurance policy. "And I'm sure Mom will agree."

Off goes Teddy, shoulders sagging and feet dragging, but nonetheless in a schoolwardly direction. The *last* thing I need is Dr. Dick harassing me today, just when we may finally be getting sorted out.

Dalewood is sending Mom home in their special ramp-equipped van. I can't decide whether this is because they take responsibility right up until the patient is back in her own bed or, more likely, they're coming to do a home inspection. In case it's the latter I spend the morning dusting and vacuuming, putting clean sheets on all the beds, and arranging a vase full of daisies on Mom's dresser. I also make certain that the condoms left over from my short-lived reunion with Craig are no longer in her night-table drawer. Yes, he had been the first. And from the way things are going, probably the last.

I'm not sure what to expect. I haven't seen Mom in such a long time. Teddy claims that she now talks and responds to questions, though she doesn't laugh much and becomes tired easily. My biggest fear is that the first thing she's going to do is ask about Louise. Bernard suggested saying that we'd lost Louise to long distance, the way Amanda Wingfield describes her husband's departure in Tennessee Williams's play *The Glass Menagerie*. I've decided to go with the more mundane excuse that she's visiting Brandt in Boston and looking at a few colleges around there.

Last but not least, I sit Lillian down (on the toilet) for a heart-to-heart. "If you'll be a big girl and use the potty all the time from now on, Mommy said she'd come home right away."

Lillian eagerly agrees, so we trade in her pull-ups for "big girl" cotton panties.

Mom enters the house escorted by Dr. Lewis, her regular physician at Dalewood. She's a slightly older version of herself. Not dramatically changed, or even particularly tired-looking. Certainly her figure is as slim as ever—Mom loses baby weight in about eight minutes. Maybe there's a little sadness to her eyes, but she's smiling while surveying her new surroundings, or rather her old ones. I decide I'll have to settle for Cappy's description of an ordinarily good gambler who's just experienced a streak of bad luck—Mom looks like she's had a pretty tough paper route.

"Welcome home," I say. My first instinct is to take her coat and offer to make some tea, as if she's a guest.

Mom gives me a long hug and then takes a good look around the living room. "It's nice to be home," she finally says. "It doesn't appear that anything has changed."

Are you kidding me? *Everything* has changed, I want to tell her. But this doesn't seem like a good first conversation, so I return to my initial plan of offering everybody tea and coffee.

Mom leads the van driver upstairs to show him where to put her suitcase while Dr. Lewis takes me into the kitchen so we can speak privately.

"Your mother needs peace and quiet," explains the doctor. "I can't emphasize that enough."

It's a good thing the kids aren't home from school yet; otherwise, he'd certainly march Mom right back into the van and it'd be the last we'd ever see of her. I'm going to have to put them down like a prison riot—no shouting, no horsing around, and no talking back. It'd be nice to threaten them with a loss of privileges, but at this point in the budget they don't really have any. And grounding will just mean having them inside when I want them expending all of their excess energy *outside.*

"I've left your mom's medication on the counter," continues Dr. Lewis. "It will probably have to be changed in six months. Or she may no longer need anything. You never know."

Huh? This is a *doctor* talking. Aren't they supposed to *know*?

"Why is that?" I ask. While I was sick I'd watched a television news show that said you're supposed to ask doctors lots of questions so they know you're paying attention.

"This type of depression seems more circumstantial rather than a permanent chemical condition."

Oh gosh. No pressure there.

Pastor Costello comes through the back door huffing. "Sorry I'm late."

"Late for what?" I ask.

"The van is out front," he says. "Your mom is home!"

"Well, yeah," I say. "Only you haven't exactly missed anything. She just went upstairs to her bedroom."

From the way Pastor Costello and Dr. Lewis exchange a few remarks, I can tell this isn't the first time they've spoken to each other.

There's a knock at the front door, and from the kitchen I yell, "Come in!"

Dr. Lewis looks at me as if this is exactly the kind of noise we *don't* need.

Whoops. "Sorry," I say. It's going to be a challenge for *all* of us to reduce the energy level in the dynamic Palmer household, self included.

It's three of the church ladies. They quickly head for the upstairs bedroom like hunting dogs that know where the bones are buried.

I don't seem to be needed and decide it's as good a time as any to pick up the twins. Mrs. Muldoon has a four o'clock podiatrist appointment to have her toenails cut. It's kind of scary how we've become so well informed about the intimate details of each other's private lives.

When I return with the boys, Mom is sitting in the living room with Pastor Costello and the church ladies. It looks like a little tea party. Everyone has a steaming cup nearby, and there's a plate of dainty cookies on the coffee table that definitely didn't emerge from any of our kitchen cupboards. Unless they were hidden behind the Sunny Doodles.

Mom's face lights up when she sees the twins and she stretches out her arms. I realize that I can't hand them both to her at once, but the church ladies are two steps ahead of me and they each take a child and sit next to her on the couch so she can coo over both without exerting herself.

I'm careful to refer to each one as "he" or both boys together as "they."

"They certainly are growing," I say.

"Look, Roddy is reaching out to me with his left hand," says my mother. "I wonder if we have our first lefty in the family."

Pastor Costello and I exchange surprised glances. Can she really tell them apart? Or is it the antipsychotics talking?

"My father was left-handed," says Mom. "Though he always referred to himself as *southpaw.*"

"You can tell them apart?" I ask in as casual a tone as possible.

"Of course!" says my mother.

"Okay, but how?" They still look like clones to me.

Mom glances from one to the other and says, "I just can."

"A mother always knows her own children," offers the church lady on the right.

The back door flies open and the onslaught begins. Pastor Costello speed-walks to the kitchen to head off the mob, I take the twins, and the church ladies escort Mom up to her bedroom. It's been decided that the children will visit one at a time after they've had a snack and settled down.

Teddy breaks through the barricade and gives Mom a huge hug and kiss, the kind of greeting I should have given her, instead of a light peck on the cheek.

The rest of the afternoon and evening is spent keeping the kids at low volume. I let them watch the Cartoon Network or whatever else they want, just so long as there aren't any broken bones, broken furniture, or breaking of the sound barrier. My goal is to allow just enough activity to disguise the fact that Louise is gone. I had the feeling that, when Dr. Lewis said Mom is to avoid stress at all costs, discovering that Louise dropped out of high school and moved in with her boyfriend just might fall into that category.

FIFTY-ONE

AUNT LALA ARRIVES FROM LONDON ON MONDAY MORNING, ONLY this time she's planning to stay for three weeks. Her thesis on the Fourth Crusade is finally finished and daughter Marci has been shipped off to a boarding school for problem children somewhere in the English countryside. Pastor Costello stops by early each morning to help get the kids ready for school before heading over to the church. He returns in time for dinner and doesn't leave until the last child is tucked safely into bed and prayed over at night.

The church ladies also come and go like clockwork, making sure the little ones don't make too much noise or get in Mom's hair, and that we're all eating our vegetables and changing our underwear. The kids are told that Mom needs a lot of rest if she's going to continue to get better. They assume her illness is something more akin to a cold or a stomachache. Teddy is glued to Mom's side whenever he's not in school. They watch afternoon talk shows together, page through magazines, and share this whole world that I don't belong to. It's not that I'm jealous, exactly. But the more I become aware of this intense bond between the two of them, the more it makes me feel as if I've somehow failed.

Mom doesn't say anything about suddenly having a hundred channels on the television along with terrific reception. Perhaps she forgot that we used to live in the Stone Age of mass media. Mom also doesn't complain about the addition of a cat. I guess any creature that arrives fully housebroken is okay in her book.

In no time at all the house is back to the way it was right after Dad died, with people coming and going, flowers and fruit baskets arriving, and Jell-O salads miraculously appearing on the kitchen counter. Did Pastor Costello place an announcement in the church bulletin? More likely all the traffic is a result of what Bernard calls, "Telephone, Television, Tell-a-Woman."

Quite frankly, the whole situation is just plain bizarre. I'm not sure what my place is anymore. Mom is here but she doesn't do much. When the kids have an argument, they want her to rule in their favor, but she just looks helplessly at me. Only they don't listen to me as much now that there's a court of appeals. To make matters worse, I can no longer use my best form of crowd control, which was to light a kitchen match and threaten to set them on fire.

On Friday morning I'm in the kitchen washing out all the Tupperware containers. At one point there are at least ten different tops and bottoms, none of them matching. I hate Tupperware. And I hate this kitchen. I hurl the mismatched pieces across the room and head out the back door. It would be a good time to start smoking. I don't know what it's like to crave a cigarette, but I'm pretty sure this is how it feels.

The minivan is blocked in by somebody else's minivan. And a Dodge Dart is behind my cabriolet. Eric took the station wagon to college when he went back after Easter. His motorhead friends are going to fix it up enough to pass inspection. Besides, with Louise gone, I'm the only one who can drive.

To hell with everything. I dig my old bike out of the garage and ride over to the Stocktons'.

Bernard is working on the computer while Rose, Gigi, Lillian, and Rocky play on the floor with Legos. The kids are awfully loud, and when Bernard sees me and says something, I can't hear him.

He claps his hands at Rocky and the girls. "It's time for mime! Let's show Hallie how good we are."

They gleefully begin gesturing at one another and acting out everything they want to say. The room goes silent. Amazing. I can't help but wonder if it would work with my gang.

"So do you still have a job for me?" I ask.

"I thought you'd thrown in the trowel," Bernard replies smugly, as if he knew this would happen. "What changed your mind?"

"Tupperware."

Bernard looks intrigued.

"I couldn't get the tops and bottoms to match."

"Promise you won't change your mind if I tell you that there are corresponding numbers and letters on each top and bottom so they can be easily matched up."

"I never want to see them again!" I say.

"Good!" says Bernard. "Let me show you the Chinese tea garden. I hired one of the men from the nursery to get things started, just until I have time to do some work out there myself."

FIFTY-TWO

Bernard and I stroll down the flagstone path, past the three main gardens, until we come to a teak pagoda, two benches, and a curved walkway leading to a small shrine. The earth has been turned so that Bernard can plant flowers and some small trees. I also notice the area originally marked off for the pool has been extended farther back. "Are you allowed to build into the woods like that?"

"The property is finally all mine!" says Bernard. "Al helped me buy it from the town."

Olivia wanders into the garden looking greatly altered in appearance since I saw her two weeks ago. Her hairstyle is completely different, her makeup is a bit brighter, and I've never seen that jewelry before.

"Ah, the roofless church of Henry David Thoreau," she remarks while surveying the empty gardens. "He said the worst thing is to get to the end of life and find you haven't lived."

"Mother, I've been looking for you," Bernard says sternly.

Olivia more or less ignores him. "I thought that was Hallie's old bike in the driveway." She gives me a hug. "How's your mom doing?"

"Okay," I say. "Aunt Lala is staying for a while and she's good company for Mom."

Bernard waits impatiently for us to finish. "Mother, *where* did Aries sleep last night?"

"His name is *Darius,* as you know full well," Olivia replies sharply.

"Well, it's certainly not *Aristotle,*" says an agitated Bernard. "So where did he sleep last night?"

"I don't know, I assume on the pullout bed in the sunroom."

"Then how is it that when I came down to get some juice for Gigi at three o'clock in the morning, he *wasn't* there?" Bernard sounds as if he's a lawyer for the prosecution.

"Perhaps he went out for a walk," suggests Olivia. "When I came down at seven, I saw him in there."

"That's what I thought the last two times," Bernard says with great suspicion in his voice. "Only now I believe that maybe he was in your room."

"Maybe *you* drove him in there with your cold stares and constant playing of Nancy Sinatra's 'These Boots Are Made for Walkin'.'"

Bernard's eyes appear as if they're going to pop out of his head. "Mother, the boy is half your age!"

"Darius happens to be forty-three," says Olivia. "He just looks very good for his age. And if you'd take the time to get to know him, you'd see how nice he is. Talented, too! Darius is a marvelous cook."

"A cook?" Bernard actually snorts. "He doesn't know the difference between Teflon and Tiffany."

"And back home he sang in the church choir," adds Olivia.

"So did Hitler and Stalin."

"That's *not* funny."

Dictators, in any context, rarely amuse Olivia.

"Just look at you!" Bernard points an accusatory finger. "With your hair cut short and harlot's lipstick."

"You've been begging me to update my look for years." She calmly adjusts the strands of hair that make up her bangs. Olivia's silvery-white hair has been cut so that it frames her face and makes her pretty blue eyes and high cheekbones stand out. She always wore lipstick, but this one is a shade darker than her usual pink. And she has on some pretty silver Paloma Picasso earrings rather than the single strand of pearls she used to wear. Otherwise, age just seems to agree with Olivia. It's as if she'd been spun from an enchanted cloth whose threads are only enhanced by the passage of time.

"When I suggested a makeover I meant twenty-first-century-grandma chic, not the noctivagous strumpetocracy."

"The *what*?" I ask.

"That's how Walt Whitman referred to nineteenth-century streetwalkers in Manhattan," a bemused Olivia informs me.

"Cut it out!" I say to Bernard. "She looks fantastic."

"She's dressed like a teenager," says Bernard.

With her trim figure outfitted in a pale purple short-sleeved sweater and navy slacks, Olivia does look younger.

Olivia pretends to scrutinize a place directly behind Bernard's left shoulder, as if there's something growing there. "Go to the tower and ring the bell."

Bernard quickly reaches back and covers his neck with his hands. "I do *not* have a dowager's hump. This shirt is just puffy because my sleeves are rolled up." He yanks down his shirt-sleeves. "I don't understand what's wrong with you, Mother. Why can't you become a man-hating late-in-life lesbian? Find a nice woman your own age and we'll tell everyone it's your sister from Cambridge."

"I happen to like men, same as you," says Olivia. "Besides,

I'm a failure as a lesbian. The one time a woman kissed me like that I spent the whole time thinking about how I was going to remove a tea stain from the front of my new white sweater."

"But you're from *Massachusetts*," insists Bernard. "Give it more time. She just wasn't the right one. You could take a carpentry course."

"Sorry, darling, but I think that gene skipped a generation. However, your uncle Danforth would be proud that you share his penchant for Flemish sculpture, Italian Baroque painters, and Baccarat Medallion candelabrum from the 1860s. Before making a big impulse purchase he used to love saying, *Why not go for baroque!*"

"Yes, apparently Uncle Danforth was quite a character prior to being institutionalized for dropping trou during an auction," offers Bernard.

"It wasn't exhibitionism so much as an early example of performance art," says Olivia. "The Burwood side of the family was always rather infamous for being ahead of the times."

"Mother, if I can't convince you to become a lesbian, then you're forcing me to tell you the brutal but honest-to-God truth. Now, I wasn't eavesdropping or anything like that. . . ."

Olivia and I look at each other as if to say, That will be the day!

Ignoring our exchanged glance, Bernard continues, "But I happened to overhear a few of Darius's phone conversations. And this *enfant terrible* is only after what every Hellenic immigrant wants—a green card so he can open a diner."

"First off, do not stereotype immigrants," states Olivia. "Half the founders of this country were themselves immigrants, or else the children of immigrants. Thomas Paine had lived in America for only two years when he wrote his famous political pamphlet *Common Sense*—of which you seem to possess precious little. Second, how *dare* you insinuate that Darius is court-ing my affections simply to advance his own agenda!" Olivia ap-pears truly hurt that Bernard won't acknowledge that Darius might be in love with her for herself. "It's true that Darius wants to open a restaurant. He's a culinary artiste. But the fact of the matter is that *you* simply don't like having any competition around."

"Competition, hah!" scoffs Bernard. "The man could be in charge of a salad bar, *maybe*."

"You'll see! Darius is going to open a wonderful vegetarian restaurant serving Mediterranean-style cuisine," insists Olivia.

"Once he gets his rabbit-food restaurant you'll see how fast he leaves you. And after the salad palace closes he'll be running back to Greece with a gang of creditors chasing him all the way to the dock."

"I highly doubt that," says Olivia. "Vegetarianism was in-vented in Greece. Plato was a vegetarian. Same with Aristotle, Diogenes, Socrates, and Pythagoras. Pythagoras lived to be over a hundred!"

"And Socrates killed himself by drinking hemlock!" inter-jects Bernard.

Fortunately Gil arrives in the backyard and acts as if he's been looking everywhere for Bernard. "Intervention," Gil an-nounces as he pulls Bernard away.

"He's half her age!" Bernard now directs his complaints to Gil.

"Not true," says Gil. "Perhaps twenty years younger. Though your mother's exact age is rather an algebra problem in itself, with her birth year being the variable X."

"He's a disgrace!" insists Bernard. "Ottavio was age-appropriate, dignified, and respectable."

"And you didn't like *him* at first either," Gil reminds him.

Bernard raises his hands above his head. "I'll never understand her no matter how long I live."

"You don't have to—you *are* her." Gil steers Bernard toward the house.

"If you want to be young and tacky, why not go all the way and buy some fun fur!" shouts Bernard.

Olivia turns to me and says, "Whereas some are born destined for glory and others to serve, I do believe that Bernard was born to fill the silences."

FIFTY-THREE

ONCE AGAIN A NEW ROUTINE IS ESTABLISHED AND THE DAYS quickly mount into weeks. In the mornings I get the kids off to school and then race to start the laundry and do some house-keeping. Then I drop the twins at Mrs. Muldoon's and make any necessary supply runs. Now that Mom has officially identified them, I've placed the blue ribbon back around Roddy's ankle and a green one on Reggie, just to be safe.

At about half past nine I take Lillian with me to the Stock-tons' and leave her inside to play with the girls while Bernard works on his inventory or writes the latest edition of his news-letter. Apparently it's going gangbusters and the Baron Heinrich Von Boogenhagen has been invited to speak at conferences as far away as Hong Kong.

More often than not Bernard piles the kids in the car at around noon to check out an estate sale, because he doesn't like to be around when Olivia and Darius are having their lunch to-gether in the dining room.

Today I arrive at the Stocktons' just as Darius and Olivia are leaving for an organic food market in Cleveland. Darius has thick sculpted black hair and flashing dark eyes, and he wears his starched white shirt open to reveal an extremely muscular chest. I know that Olivia has never been one to go by looks alone, but he really is godlike handsome.

"Now do you see what I have to put up with?" Bernard hisses after they go out the front door together chatting and laughing.

"Darius seems nice enough," I say. "Besides, I thought he was moving to New Jersey to open a restaurant."

"*Supposedly* he's waiting for a cousin in Englewood to finalize a lease," says Bernard. "Frankly, I don't believe a word of it."

I escape to the yard and inhale the deep perfume of damp earth, which has the ability to make the past and future fall away in a single moment. The sun hangs like a pink gumball above the trees, and particles of dust dance in the air beneath canopies of bright green leaves. By the time I open the doors to the shed I've never been so thrilled to see a lawn mower in my entire life.

When afternoon comes, I run the program in reverse, shanghaiing Lillian from inside, fetching the twins from Mrs. Muldoon, and then sorting out the other kids as they clamber off the late bus or pedal home on their bicycles. Pastor Costello picks up Francie from her hyperactive child program when he finishes his hospital rounds.

On Friday morning after the kids have caught the bus, Mom comes into the kitchen in her robe and slippers and says, "Hallie, Teddy told me that Louise dropped out of school and moved to Boston. Is this true?"

The good news is that Mom doesn't include how Louise is "living in sin." The bad news is that the story about Louise being on a trip to look at colleges appears to have worn a bit thin. "Only in a manner of speaking," I hedge. "Teddy was mistaken in saying *dropped out.* The only thing preventing Louise from taking the equivalency exam is that she has to be eighteen."

"I want you to call her right this minute and tell her I said to come home."

"Mom, it's not that simple," I say. "She has a pretty good job and a car."

"Hallie," Mom continues, "please don't think I don't appreciate how hard you've been working, but I'm still the mother and Louise is my daughter."

Ouch. My first solid scolding in about two years.

I go into the other room and try to reach Louise on her cell phone. There's a lot of clanging and hollering in the background. "Hang on a minute," she shouts into the receiver.

A door slams and there's silence. "Okay, I'm in the refrigerator."

"Mom insisted that I call you and tell you to come home immediately," I say.

"Why?" asks Louise. "Did something happen?"

"Because she's the mother and you're the daughter."

"Okay," says Louise.

"Okay what?" I ask.

"Okay, I'll come home."

What? Louise is coming home just like that. How is this possible?

"But only if I can live in the basement," Louise quickly adds.

Aha! I knew it couldn't be that simple. Let the negotiations begin. "I can't imagine that Darlene will miss listening to *Bone Machine* by the Pixies all night long."

"And I want cable TV," says Louise. But her voice is more hopeful than demanding.

"You're in luck on that score. While the kids had chicken pox and I was sick, Bernard gave us the gift that keeps on giving cartoons twenty-four-seven. And now that Mom is supposed to rest, she's hooked on those cooking shows. All you have to do is put a TV in the basement."

"Okay," says Louise.

I suddenly realize that this was way too easy.

"What's wrong?" I ask.

"I'm bored out of my mind. And the customers treat you as if you're going to be a waitress forever. To them I'm just another servant."

"What about Brandt?"

"Brandt is fine," says Louise. "But he's busy with school. His scholarship gives him a job in the lab, which he loves, but sometimes he's there all night. Are you mad at me for leaving you in the lurch like that?"

"Of course not," I say. "Pastor Costello has been helping."

"Everything at home reminded me that Dad was dead," says Louise.

There's pounding and yelling on her end of the line.

"I have to get back to work," says Louise. "See you on Saturday."

I return to the kitchen and report back to Mom. "Louise will be home on Saturday."

Mom smiles as if she knew all along.

"She's moving into the basement because she sleeps better down there." I make it a point not to add, "Away from all the kids."

The phone rings and I fear that Louise has changed her mind. Maybe her boss offered her a raise. With her double-take good looks, I'm sure that Louise is good for business. There's no shortage of older men swooning over Louise who, with some makeup and heels, can easily pass for twenty-five.

"I'm going to kill him!" comes Bernard's voice. "He doesn't lift a finger unless Mother is watching. Meantime, she claims that his good looks are so natural—well, I found *under-eye cream* in the bathroom! I have a *bad* feeling about this one, Hallie."

It's safe to assume he's talking about Darius. Mom is standing a few feet away and so I reply, "WWJD?" This is our code for, What Would Judy Do?

"I don't know—I'm so riled up I can't channel Judy Garland *or* Ethel Merman," says Bernard. "What would you do?"

Pastor Costello's number at the church is next to the phone, and so I recite one of his favorite lines, "Hate the sin but not the sinner."

"Thanks a lot!" says Bernard and hangs up.

However, Mom looks over at me and appears to be quite pleased, as if her lost sheep has returned to the flock.

FIFTY-FOUR

THE TOWN IS OVERBURDENED WITH SPRING. RAIN HAS LEFT THE grass bright green and as soft as velvet while the light falls in great sheets through the trees. The dandelions are in full flower, and among the bushes hover orange butterflies trimmed in black.

Mom now has enough energy to deal with Darlene and Davy when they come off the bus, and so I'm able to stay and work in the garden until late afternoon.

On Thursday I plant cucumbers, cauliflower, and green beans. Bernard has decided to start home pickling this summer. At around half past three cars begin pulling up and eleven-year-old girls skip toward the house. I assume that Troop Bernard is assembling for a crash course in braising, blanching, or bread making.

After an hour it begins to rain, and so I head inside to scrub up and collect Lillian. From the dining room I hear Bernard announcing, "Permit me, if you will, to quote that great British lady of screen and stage, Isabel Jeans, in the musical *Gigi*—'Bad table manners have broken up more households than infidelity.' "

Peering through the archway I see ten girls seated around

the table and four more in chairs set off to the sides. They wear white shirts or blouses with khaki pants or jeans, and a few have green sashes containing an array of badges and gold pins. Underneath their seats are thick Scout handbooks and small spiral notepads.

Hunched over a three-ring binder in the corner is a solitary boy hanging on to Bernard's every word. The table is set for a dinner party, complete with individual saltcellars, napkins folded like swans, and beeswax candles in the center. Bernard's hectic cheerfulness is infectious, and the kids lean forward with big smiles on their faces.

Olivia comes up behind me and we both watch as Bernard holds forth on the correct way to lay the silverware.

I whisper, "I thought the Girl Scouts are supposed to go camping and braid leather into key chains."

"Not Bernard's troop," says Olivia as we watch him demonstrate how to fold a napkin into a swan. "I think this is the closest they'll get to any actual wildlife. Besides, I'd much rather Bernard be a Girl Scout leader. They're very inclusive compared to the Boy Scouts."

"What's with the boy in the corner?" I ask. He looks about two years younger than the girls.

"That's Andrew. His sister Gretchen is in the troop and claims that he has to come along because no one is home to watch him." Olivia gives me a knowing look and then adds, "It would appear that Bernard has awakened Andrew's dinner party gene."

I go into the kitchen, remove a chocolate Yoo-hoo from the fridge, and relax at the kitchen table for a moment. In the next room I can hear Bernard calling his troop to attention, "Listen up, ladies, gentlemen, undecideds." He claps his hands. "We're working to create the appropriate *atmosphere* for a dinner party. Who can tell me why we dim the lights?"

"So people can't see the food," says one girl.

I briefly choke on my Yoo-hoo and a little bit trickles out of my nose.

Bernard quickly retorts, "I hope that's not the case, Samantha, unless something has gone horribly wrong in the kitchen! But every cook knows that you can cover a number of errors and doubts beneath a good sauce."

Another girlish voice chimes in, "To create the mood?"

"Yes," Bernard enthuses. "In large part. And what else?"

"So we appear more attractive," says Andrew.

"Indeed, indeed." Bernard claps excitedly as if the boy has correctly answered the final question on a quiz show. "Because we often invite people we wish to impress—your future law firm colleagues or the parents of your significant other or—"

"But how do we know if he's the right one to be our husband?" a girl interrupts Bernard. "I mean, significant other."

I imagine Bernard starting to stutter and turn red in the face. But he sails on effortlessly, without missing a beat. If anything, he becomes even more articulate.

"It's the same way you feel when you experience a piece of great art," he says. "Giovanni Bellini's *Madonna of the Trees,* Giorgione's *Sleeping Venus,* or Mary Cassatt's *The Mirror.* Sometimes you feel disturbed by it, like Francisco de Goya's *Disasters of War* and Picasso's *Guernica.* And occasionally we desire a painting or piece of sculpture because we know that someone else wants it."

"My mother says it's best to marry a doctor or a lawyer," offers one girl.

"The thing to remember is that the *right one* is not necessarily the most expensive, raved about by the critics, or displayed in a gallery or museum. It might be at a local shop or even a garage sale. It doesn't matter if it's new or old, though of course you don't want to look foolish by having a child's toy."

I'm quite certain this was said for Olivia's benefit, as Bernard emphasizes the last line.

Bernard dramatically wraps up his soliloquy. "It's the one that makes you feel good inside, and you know that if it hangs on your wall for the next sixty years you'll never become tired of it."

First one tear falls onto the kitchen table and then another. It suddenly becomes crystal clear that I've gone and ruined the best thing that's ever happened to me.

Another young voice in the other room pipes up. "What's the right age to get married?"

"It's not like a soufflé. You can't time these things," says Bernard. "Now let's concentrate for a moment on candles. The wicks must be trimmed to a quarter of an inch so flames aren't licking the ceiling and leaving black smoke on the brows of your guests."

The grandfather clock in the hall chimes four times. "Where *do* the hours go?" asks Bernard. "Next week we'll be discussing proper skin care, and so everyone bring a pumice stone."

FIFTY-FIVE

On MONDAY MORNING I'M ABOUT TO LEAVE FOR THE STOCK-tons' when Bernard calls and asks me to stop at his store. He's sold a tortoiseshell scent bottle over the Internet and says that June will have it all packed up.

I park in front of the plaque marking the spot where two generals faced off during the War of 1812. Something is different and I realize that the Curl Up and Dye Beauty Salon next door has a new neon sign.

When I enter Bernard's shop, little bells tinkle above my head. The sound of New Age music more or less disguises the noise from all the clocks ticking. The harp and guitar combination is pleasant, but I can't help think that if you listen long enough your thoughts could conceivably turn to homicide.

June has frizzy purplish red hair that ends just above long complicated wind-chime earrings. She's wearing a bright yellow knitted top over a diaphanous paisley peasant skirt with enough crystals suspended from her neck to ensure that at least one of them could paralyze Superman. June has a heavy hand with the cosmetics; it's safe to say that she doesn't just love gold-flecked purple eye shadow—she wants to marry it and have its children.

The shop is the same as ever except the glass case that was previously filled with cloisonné snuffboxes and silver cigarette cases is now home to black felt-covered trays holding different colored stones. And instead of the usual smell, which was basically your grandmother's living room, there's a forest aroma. I notice a few incense sticks burning on a refectory table that send curls of smoke into the air. June sits behind the counter bent over a piece of jewelry, using tweezers and a magnifying glass.

"Mmm, it smells nice in here," I say.

June closes her eyes, takes a deep breath, and exhales. "Roman chamomile." She points to a little blue bottle that looks like it was designed to hold a magic potion in a movie about witches. "It helps maintain alertness. I'm a Pisces, and when entering a strong sign like Cancer I become very accident prone."

I nod my head as if this makes perfect sense.

"What's *your* sign?" asks June.

"Oh, I'm not much of one for astrology." I chuckle a little bit. "I mean, what if your mother has a caesarean and the doctor schedules it on a Thursday because he wants to play golf on Friday and that ends up changing your sign?"

June looks as if she's been startled by a burglar. "The soul is always born at exactly the right time, even if there's medical intervention involved! Were you a C-section?"

"Um, no. Actually, Mom says I was right on time—September eighth."

"Virgo! How *interesting*! Virgos are creative, delicate, and intelligent."

"I thought it meant virginal," I say. Which is appropriate since I'm apparently destined for a life of celibacy. I may as well start signing myself "Sister Hallie."

"It means that the sun shone in the sixth house of Virgo,

which is an earth sign, on your birthday. So you're shy, like a virgin waiting to find the perfect lover. Virgos are responsible—you can always give a job to a Virgo and know that it will get done. And although you're idealistic, you're almost always logical when it comes to everyday life."

"I guess that sounds like me." I must admit, I'm rather intrigued.

"But you have to be careful that disappointment doesn't harden you into a cynic," June warns.

She opens a large book next to Bernard's old-fashioned cash register, which wasn't employed for charm so much as that it doesn't keep a record of sales for the IRS. June turns to a complicated diagram and points to a particular section. "Your ruling planet is Mercury, your lucky colors are green and dark brown, and your lucky numbers are two, five, and seven."

"How interesting," I say.

"If you have an hour, we can do your chart," June offers.

"What will that do?" I ask.

"Tell you more about yourself, your past lives, when you should make important decisions, when you shouldn't—those kinds of things."

"Does it say what's going to happen to me in the future, like if I'm going to get married?"

"There are indications," says June. "The romantic character of the Virgo is very complicated. Your heart can lead you into unpleasant situations and also from one affair to another. That's because you like to use your creativity and imagination in a relationship. If you're currently worried about a specific situation, then the best thing to do is wear a crystal to address that particular purpose."

"I don't know, I should get going," I say. "Bernard is waiting for that scent bottle so he can go to the post office."

However, June is already removing some pendants from the display case. "You see, the essence of the body is energy, and crystals function as transformers and amplifiers of various energies that rebalance the system on a cellular level, as well as your emotional, mental, and spiritual levels."

I'm skeptical that all this mumbo jumbo is simply an effort to make a sale.

June places a bright blue stone in my hand. "Clearing is the process of changing negative emotions into positive ones. Anyone who holds a crystal while experiencing bad energy can imprint those feelings onto the crystal. Repeat the following light invocation three times." June clasps one of the crystals hanging from her neck, closes her eyes, and chants: "I invoke the Light within. I am a clear and perfect channel. Light is my guide."

I look out the window to make sure that no one I know is walking by. And I certainly don't close my eyes or chant. But funnily enough, I also feel a tingling. Maybe it's from squeezing the stone so hard, or inhaling too much of the pine-heavy air.

"By the time you've completed the third repetition, the negative emotion should be gone!" June flips open her gold-flecked purple lids. "You see, negative emotions are transferred to the crystal, where they can no longer affect you. Bad energy, whether it's environmental or emotional, can cause you to separate from your body and feel disorientation."

"That's it!" I practically shout. "I've felt separated from my body ever since my dad died!"

"You can ground yourself back to Mother Earth by being in tune with your crystal at all times." She selects a few stones and opens a wooden box that contains silver jewelry settings. "I'll make you a pendant with a few different crystals, and that will bring the two yous back together."

It's very tempting, but all this stuff looks expensive. "Thanks, but money is sort of tight right now."

June appears horrified. "Don't be ridiculous! It's clear now that when my horoscope showed a stranger on the horizon and I was worried about something catastrophic happening, it actually meant that you were arriving with all of your bad energy! So this is quite a relief. No charge."

June begins placing different stones into my hand one by one. The first is dark black, smooth, and shiny. She gives an explanation that sounds like an earth-science course taught by a teacher dropping acid.

"Black agate brings the Great Spirit into one's life and attracts good fortune. It also helps overcome fears and loneliness, and has even been known to remove jinxes. It's a hot stone, and so it encourages fertility."

"I definitely don't think pregnancy would be a good idea at this moment in time."

Undaunted, June replaces the black agate with a light purple stone. "Amethyst calms and protects the mind. It's called 'nature's tranquilizer' by many healers."

I close my eyes and hold the stone in my hand. No matter how long my palm surrounds it I can still feel the coolness. "Yeah, this is a nice one."

June is enthusiastic. "Amethyst is also very good for dealing with edginess, emotional despair, and ineffective communication."

"Check, check, check," I say.

June places a moss agate in my hand. The stone is dark grayish-green but translucent, with specks of minerals that look like moss or foliage. "This one increases trust and is good for freckled skin."

"I don't feel anything, and freckles are the least of my problems right now."

She exchanges the moss agate for a stone that is smooth and dark red.

"Red jasper facilitates astral travel and organization," says June.

She can see from the look on my face that nothing is happening. June takes off the pendant from around her neck and removes a stunning pink crystal that captures the light from every angle. It's pale and pearly, like clouds at sunset. She places the crystal in the palm of my hand, closes my fingers around it, and bends my arm inward so that my hand is pressed against my chest.

"Rose quartz," says June in a hushed voice. "It opens and soothes a wounded heart."

My knees are suddenly weak and I think I'm going to cry.

June guides me to a nearby hoop-back Windsor armchair so that I can sit down before I fall down. I watch as June fashions a necklace with the two stones on a black silk thread and then ties it around my neck.

"You have to let me pay you," I insist.

"Good karma is my reward."

"Don't you need the rose quartz for yourself?" I ask.

"Not anymore." A big smile crosses June's face. "I've recently begun a new chapter in my romantic life and I'm ready to wear green aventurine. It's a prosperity stone that brings luck in love once you've found it."

Exiting the store in a crystal-induced daze I completely forget about Bernard's package. June has to run out to the car and hand me the little box wrapped in brown paper. So much for Virgos being responsible.

FIFTY-SIX

"OH MY PAULETTE GODDARD—JUNE GOT YOU!" SHOUTS BERNARD the moment I enter the house. "Take that nonsense off right now. You can't tell me that you actually believe in her spiritual claptrap."

Olivia and Darius are reading the newspaper in the living room, and they both look up to see if I'm wearing an Indian headdress.

When Olivia spies the crystals around my neck, she says, "Leave Hallie alone!" Although there's none of the usual bickering warmth in her voice. Ever since Darius moved in, mother and son have become increasingly frosty toward each other.

The gravel crunches in the driveway and a taxi pulls up. Between people coming for Olivia's stash of morning-after pills that she freely distributes and Bernard's antique drop-offs and pickups, this is not unusual.

A short balding man pays the driver and collects his suitcase from the trunk.

"If it isn't Ottavio!" exclaims Bernard.

Only I get the feeling he's not nearly as surprised as he pretends to be.

Olivia rushes to the window. "What is *he* doing here?"

"He's here for Gil's birthday, of course," says Bernard.

"That's not for another two months!" she replies.

"The airlines are so unpredictable," counters Bernard.

Olivia is staring daggers at Bernard, and I honestly think she's considering sonicide. "That's it. We're leaving."

"What?" says Bernard.

"Darius and I are moving out!" Olivia heads for the stairs.

Bernard looks stunned. He turns toward me.

"The plants are going to die if I don't water them right away!" I race toward the back door.

FIFTY-SEVEN

Louise arrives home the following Saturday. She was able to work out a deal where if she attends summer school and goes to gym class four days a week instead of two, she can graduate with her class.

Dinnertime feels almost like the old days, except, of course, Dad isn't here. And Pastor Costello is dashing around the kitchen in his T-shirt that says, JESUS IS COMING—EVERYONE LOOK BUSY.

Mom even makes two birthday cakes—one for Teddy, who is turning thirteen today, and the other for Louise, whose birthday we all missed.

There's a knock on the front door at half past eight and I'm surprised to see Gil standing on the front porch. "Enter at your own risk," I say.

He winces at all the commotion coming from inside the house. The kids are supposed to be getting ready for bed but run around chasing each other instead. "Any chance you can go AWOL for a little while?"

"Meet me in the backyard in ten minutes." I point toward the open gate on the side of the house that's clogged with bicycles and a plastic slide.

Mom is in the living room picking up crayons, and I tell her that I'll be out in the backyard talking to Gil.

"Is everything okay with the children?" she immediately asks.

"If you mean children as in Gigi and Rose, they're fine," I say. "If you're talking about Olivia's child, Bernard, I'm afraid that's a different matter."

Gil has brought his boom box along and sets it on top of the weathered picnic table. "What was Bernard thinking?" he asks, sounding somewhere between incredibly angry and extremely exhausted.

"I guess he wants to get them back together."

"Well, this time he has gone *too* far. Olivia and Darius packed up and moved to a bed-and-breakfast over in Timpany." Gil takes two beers from the cooler bag he brought along and hands me one. "I'm the vice squad tonight."

The trees and bushes and anthills begin to disappear one by one, whisked away under the magical cloak of evening, and so I don't worry about Mom or Pastor Costello seeing us through a window. The night is warm and a gentle balmy breeze tussles the leaves in the trees. There's the occasional slamming of a screen door as cats and dogs are let in and out, and the *plink plink* of a beginner practicing piano a few houses away. In the next breath it will be summer.

Gil takes out a bag of Mallomars, two quarts of chocolate fudge ice cream, and two large spoons. "Believe it or not, I didn't actually come here to complain about Bernard. He told me about the breakup with Craig, and I've been so busy at work that I never had a chance to tell you that, you know, I'm sorry. . . ."

My hand automatically reaches for the crystals that hang from around my neck. Though whether it's to hide them or make sure they're still there, I'm not exactly sure.

"Anyway, I've made you a CD of the best breakup songs," says Gil.

"Please tell me 'The Man That Got Away' isn't on it," I say. "It's all Bernard played when you were gone."

"Heavens, no! This has Fleetwood Mac's 'Songbird,' '17 Again' by the Eurythmics, a few from Sinéad O'Connor, an entire Melissa Etheridge breakup album, and Dido singing 'My Lover's Gone.'" He pulls out another CD. "Once you finish with that there's *The Best of Bonnie Raitt.* Basically everything of hers counts."

Gil cracks open two more beers and hands me one. We sit in silence for a moment staring up at the faraway moon. It looks as if someone took a machete and sliced it into two equal pieces.

"Cool—it's a perfect half," I finally say.

"If this were one of my horrible training classes, someone would ask if it was half empty or half full," says Gil.

In the distance the courthouse clock tolls ten times.

"Bernard says you've turned to the occult to get you through these difficult times."

"Not exactly. June just gave me a few crystals to wear."

Gil nods and I can't tell if he thinks they're foolish or not.

"I know that I used to complain when Bernard was in charge of my love life, but it was better then," I say. "During this recent mess with Craig, he hasn't said anything about my being stupid, right, wrong, or otherwise."

"He's preoccupied with the Darius situation. Actually, I think he's about to have a nervous breakdown." Then Gil looks as if he shouldn't have said that around me because of Mom.

"Where's *my* nervous breakdown?" I ask, though not necessarily to Gil, more to the moon.

"So what happened with Craig, if you don't mind my asking. Bernard was a bit sketchy on the details."

"He dropped out of school. And if you love someone, doesn't it mean that you want certain things for that person, and for you, too, for your life together? Or does it mean you should unconditionally support their dreams? I don't know."

"My parents had a lot of hopes and dreams for me that I didn't fulfill." Gil is referring to the fact that they disowned him when he came out of the closet.

"I know this sounds terrible, Gil. But I don't want to be poor. I don't want to wonder if we'll be able to pay the mortgage and worry that if someone gets sick we may lose our house or car."

"I'm with you," Gil raises his beer toward me. "I hate my job. But I like my car and being able to check out of the grocery store without tallying up the items first. When Bernard and I had our problems I had enough money to rent an apartment for a while."

"I'm so tired of money!" I say.

"Maybe you and Craig are just one of those couples destined to have a love/hate relationship," offers Gil.

"I think it's more that I love him and he hates me," I say.

Gil's boom box is playing "Born Under a Bad Sign" by Cream, and we hear the lyrics, *If it wasn't for bad luck I wouldn't have no luck at all.* Only this particular coincidence doesn't make us laugh.

The windows of the house glow orange, and I occasionally see the silhouettes of family members going through their bedtime routine.

"What's your gaydar reading on Pastor Costello?" I ask.

"Church, candles, incense, and robes—all rather theatrical, isn't it?"

"I feel bad for him because how can he ever have a boyfriend without the people in his congregation finding out?" I say. "Sure, they talk about tolerance, but you *know* that doesn't apply to their minister."

"Cleveland has a big gay population and he could have a social life there."

"I guess so," I say.

"Either I've had too many beers or there's someone on top of your garage." Gil looks toward the roof.

"That's Teddy sneaking in," I say without having to look up.

"What's he doing out this late?" asks Gil. "It's not as if this town has so much as an all-night diner."

"Setting up a meth lab in an abandoned barn for all I know. They way I figure it, if the ones under ten don't die of starvation or get run over on my watch, then I'm doing my job. I don't get paid enough to worry about teenagers."

Gil leans in and clinks his beer can against mine.

"Did you ever have a bad breakup?" I ask him. "I mean, other than the one with Bernard?"

"What isn't a bad breakup?" asks Gil. "The only thing worse than the breakups was the sneaking around. I'd bring boyfriends home from college and they'd stay in the guest room— at least theoretically. One night my mother was up and caught a man leaving my room, and we told her the ceiling fan in the guest room was broken. Of course she went in and it worked just fine."

"I slept with this guy Mike at school last October," I confess.

"Mmm," says Gil.

I'm not sure what "mmm" means. Gwen asks *very* specific relationship questions. She would want to know why why why? Did I like the guy, did I no longer care about Craig, did we have a fight, and so on. "Craig and I didn't have an exclusive arrangement or anything. I mean, he was probably with some other people, too."

"Mmm," says Gil.

"It's just that I thought if we got married, I mean Craig and me, then he'd be the only guy I'd ever been with, and for some reason I decided that was bad—you know, that we'd have a better shot if I had an idea of what else was out there. That sounds stupid, right?"

"Comparison shopping is as old as searching for new spices and exotic clothes in foreign lands," says Gil.

"It wasn't very good," I say.

"Mmm," says Gil.

"Though he had a terrific butt," I add and let out a giggle.

"ROTC?" asks Gil.

"Yeah, how did you know?"

"They always do," Gil says knowingly.

The band Green Day comes on with the song "Good Riddance," and for a moment Gil sings along: *So make the best of this test and don't ask why.*

When the song is finished, he asks, "Do you still love Craig?"

"How can you love someone when you don't want the same things?"

"Mmm," says Gil.

FIFTY-EIGHT

"TODAY IS THE BIG DAY!" MOM ANNOUNCES AT THE BREAKFAST TABLE on Wednesday morning.

Francie graduates from kindergarten at noon. Only a mother could be excited about such a thing. And would someone care to enlighten me as to why kindergarteners require graduation ceremonies complete with cap, gown, and diploma. Are we celebrating the fact that they've finally stopped counting paste as a food group? Because it's not as if they're about to start jobs down at the auto plant the following week.

Unfortunately Mrs. Muldoon isn't able to share our joy. Her arthritis flared up, and so I'm in charge of both the twins and Lillian. And with the current situation at the Stocktons', I don't feel it's appropriate to park Lillian over there.

While organizing Francie's miniature mortarboard and tiny blue gown I find a crumpled note explaining that she's supposed to bring cupcakes for the party. Mom says she's fine watching the kids while I go to the convenience store. Pastor Costello has already left for church, and I decide four is a bit much, so I take Lillian with me in the car, along with a large plate and some plastic wrap.

There's another woman in the parking lot transferring cookies from a flimsy cardboard box to one of her own platters. And when I go to throw away the bakery box I see quite a few boxes in the big plastic garbage bin.

Going back to the car I notice a really cute guy about my age or maybe a year or two older standing next to a pickup truck with Ohio plates.

"Bake those yourself?" he jokes, and nods at the plate now filled with cupcakes on the hood of the car. Obviously he'd seen me remove them from the box.

"Yeah, I love nothing more than to get up at six in the morning and put the oven on preheat," I flirt back. "Where you headed?"

"Out west—Montana maybe," he says.

"What's wrong, the mountains around here aren't high enough?" This is of course a joke because most of Ohio is so flat that if it weren't for all the trees you could see from one end of it to the other.

Lillian, my ambassador of goodwill, waves at him from her car seat in the back.

"Sweet little girl," he says.

"Oh, she's not mine," I say. "I mean, she's mine, but she's my sister." I briefly consider asking him to be my date to the kindergarten graduation. Surely it will be tons of fun, complete with Juicy Juice and Nilla wafers and all the kids singing "I Believe I Can Fly." And then there are always the one or two kids who actually attempt flight, like my sister Francie.

At that moment his girlfriend comes out with a pack of cigarettes and they take off, just the pair of them, heading west. She's stunning, tall and slim with wide-set eyes the size of dinner plates and perfectly windblown chestnut-colored hair.

Those two will be sorry, I can't help but think. They'll get married and it will all be romantic for a year or so. Then the kids will come and they'll start to fight about the bills and whose turn it is to change the baby.

I meet Mom and the twins at school. All the parents are running video cameras and couldn't be happier. There's no doubt in my mind that this whole thing is a conspiracy created by greeting card companies, bakeries, and electronics manufacturers.

Francie's kindergarten teacher, Miss Ward, is the approximate size of a small bungalow and from the School of Dieting that says if you can't lose it, then accessorize it. However, she plays a darn good piano, and those kids march around in lockstep as if a drill sergeant had worked them over. And a certain uniformity to the baked goods would suggest that we weren't the only ones to have indulged in a box of convenience store helper.

FIFTY-NINE

I HEAR PASTOR COSTELLO DOWNSTAIRS SINGING *YOU'VE GOT TO accentuate the positive, eliminate the negative* while preparing lunches for the kids who are starting camp today. His latest thing is to write little inspirational sayings on the outsides of the banana peels, such as "A true friend is the best possession" and "Well done is better than well said." Francie's messages usually pertain to conflict resolution, along the lines of "Quarrels never can last long if on one side lay all the wrong."

Pastor Costello has enrolled Francie, Davy, and Darlene into a nearby Christian summer camp. Davy wants to explore the local woods and informs me that he's not going. Pastor Costello has been so good to us that I feel we can't reasonably appeal the decision, especially after he went to the trouble of getting all three kids scholarships. I bargain with Davy—we'll buy him some hiking boots. He wants a two-hundred-dollar global positioning device. No deal.

I can see that Davy is preparing to escape by running out the back door. Not being much of a churchgoer myself, I hate to employ Christianity in my arguments the way Pastor Costello does, but in this case I make an exception. I grab Davy by his shirt, basically lifting him off the ground three or four inches, and say, "Listen, buster, I dropped out of college to take care of you. And if you don't get your rear end to camp, I'll hit you so hard that you'll really do some exploring, of the stratosphere, because you'll go up in the air like a homesick angel." Tears form in the corner of Davy's eyes and I feel his body go limp with defeat.

Teddy is leaving to go around the neighborhood with our lawn mower and offer to cut people's grass. He hasn't bothered with any advertising. If a lawn is overgrown he just rings the bell and quotes a reasonable price. When the person answers, usually a woman, and looks at her yard in comparison with her neighbor's, she's overcome with suburban shame and Teddy is off and mowing. What she doesn't know is that Teddy has a habit of drawing the Druid symbol for "Earth" in the middle of the front yard with weed killer so that it seems to just magically appear a few days later.

The month of July passes quickly. On the weekends the kids go over to the elementary school playground for baseball and kickball. They basically only show up when they want lunch or Band-Aids.

At least that's the routine until Bernard opens the new pool on the first day of August. He purchases a van (which instantly becomes a tax deduction when the name of the shop is painted on the side), and picks everyone up at nine o'clock sharp for a day of frolicking in the water. Bernard has hired two teenagers from the high school swim team as lifeguards and swimming instructors.

There's an ice chest by the side of the pool chock-full of juice boxes and Popsicles, while a stream of delicious snacks comes out of the kitchen. Despite the addition of the girls and all the extra work caring for them, Bernard has not lost his ability to turn ordinary daily events into celebrations. If any-thing, he's more engaged in doing so now that he has children. In fact, the sheer delight he gets from watching everyone else enjoy themselves occasionally makes me wonder if I want a family of my own someday.

Mom often sits by the pool while the kids scream and splash while playing Marco Polo or singing "The Littlest Worm" at full volume. Though she's not quite back to her old is-*that*-what-you're-wearing self, Mom can manage the kids on her own when necessary. Sometimes she even holds Lillian and Gigi in the shallow end, one under each arm, so they can practice kick-ing. It's terrific to see her laughing and absorbing a bit of sun-shine, held firm and secure by the extraordinary gravitational pull of Bernard's own personal planet. Mom actually thinks it's funny the way Bernard refers to God as the "Great Stage Man-ager" when he prays for the rain to hold off and dances a little jig on the patio.

Ottavio spends his time giving diving lessons in the deep end, and when Olivia comes by to visit her granddaughters, she ignores him. Meantime, Rocky makes delicious blender drinks with fresh peaches, strawberries, and ice cream, topped off with three maraschino cherries.

Gwen and Jane come home for a few weeks, and if Pastor Costello stays at the house after dinner, then I'm actually able to go and hang out with them at the pizza parlor. I know I'm tak-ing advantage of Pastor Costello's generosity, but he insists that he doesn't mind. Besides, it's not going to be for very long. Gwen leaves soon for an internship at a costume shop in Chicago, and Jane is off to try out for the women's Olympic soc-cer team. And though they're careful not to talk much about these upcoming adventures, it's clear that certain people are moving on while others remain behind.

SIXTY

After my siblings have gone home for dinner Ottavio and I pull all the toys out of the pool and hang the wet towels over the fence. Tonight is Gil's birthday dinner, and so Bernard called the girls in early. Ottavio and I sit on the bench in the Chinese tea garden commiserating like two jilted lovers, even though the dilemmas we now find ourselves in are basically our own stupid faults. Ottavio's mouth sags at the corner as he stares at the marble and granite statues of the animals that are known as Lucky Beasts in China because they supposedly bring good fortune to a garden. Scattered among the peonies and peach blossoms are snapping turtles, snails, horses, frogs, winged cats, and two pale pink dragons.

We're surrounded by a yard that has exploded into a riot of summer. The birds bathe and splash in the low pool and have melodious arguments, accompanied by the constant thrum of insects. Shadows creep across the lawn and the quiet surface of the pool.

I honestly don't know what Bernard was hoping to accomplish by importing Ottavio. Well, I know what he was aiming for, but the scheme certainly failed—Olivia didn't exactly leap into Ottavio's arms now, did she?

"Itsa no use," Ottavio finally says and looks up.

"Maybe you can do something to impress Olivia," I suggest. "You know how she likes those Greek, I mean Roman, myths— something knightly, chivalrous."

He's not getting it.

"You need to be a hero," I explain.

"Ah si, *eroe.*"

Though I can't really think of any knightly quests appropriate for twenty-first-century Ohio. These days the really useful tasks—hooking up computers, programming cell phones, and downloading music off the Internet—are mostly undertaken by teenagers.

"Bernardo says he has idea," announces Ottavio.

I'm aware that Olivia has agreed to come to Gil's birthday dinner and wonder if Bernard is planning to lock the two of them in a closet or else sprinkle their food with some sort of aphrodisiac.

I go inside and find Bernard busy chopping vegetables, slaving over steaming pots and sizzling woks while gaily singing "Blame It on My Youth."

Bernard is smiling and in a wonderful mood. "Two cannibals were cooking dinner in a big pot out in the middle of the jungle and one says to the other, 'I don't like my mother-in-law.' The other cannibal replies, 'So then just eat the vegetable.' "

I look around the kitchen for anything strange, but everything appears to be in order. The minute Olivia's cherry-red Buick pulls into the driveway, Bernard announces, "I forgot the bread."

I offer to run to the bakery but Bernard insists that he'll go, though not before whispering to me, "The center cannot hold."

"Huh?" I ask. "Can't hold what?"

"It's from William Butler Yeats's poem 'The Second Coming,' " he says, and rushes out the back door.

There's something doubly mysterious about this errand, because in all the years I've known Bernard he's never forgotten
anything for a party. The man has more lists for six people to
come for dinner than most people make for an entire wedding.
Just out of curiosity, I go into the kitchen and peek under the
napkin covering the breadbasket. Sure enough—there are a
dozen rolls.

When Bernard returns, we begin serving his version of a traditional Chinese dinner. While plating the dim sum he explains
to us that in Cantonese these words mean, "To touch your heart."

With Olivia and Ottavio not speaking to each other, the
conversation lags slightly when Gil and Rocky go upstairs to put
the girls to bed. Bernard takes the opportunity to regale us with
a story about how the French singer Edith Piaf had once been a
police suspect for the murder of her manager.

No one else really has a view on the matter so Bernard turns
to ridiculing my T-shirt, which happens to be a giveaway from a
pool installation company.

"Hallie, didn't you ever play dress-up as a child and put on
your mother's clothes, makeup, and jewelry?" asks Bernard.

"Can't say that I did."

"That was you, Bernard," Olivia says icily.

We have a delicious German chocolate cake for dessert,
which is Gil's favorite. Fortunately he managed to nix the green
tea ice cream and honey walnuts that Bernard had originally
planned.

I offer everyone coffee, but Olivia rises and announces that
she'd better get going, seeing that she has to *drive home*. She and
Ottavio exchange a terse farewell.

Just as his mother is leaving, Bernard appears in the front
hall with a sheaf of papers in his hand. "Oh Mother, I thought
you'd be interested to know that Darius is wanted in Athens for
arson."

"That's a lie!" declares Olivia.

"Scout's honor." Bernard puts up three fingers on his right hand. "It's all here—the report from the insurance company, an arrest warrant, a prior conviction for a hotel fire. I've even gone to the trouble of having everything translated into English for you."

Olivia switches the hall light on and looks carefully at the papers, as if it would not surprise her in the slightest if Bernard had hired someone to create all these documents on a computer just for the purpose of chasing Darius off. "And exactly how did these come into your possession?"

It just so happens that Baron Von Boogenhagen is very popular with some prominent antiques dealers in Athens, and they were more than happy to do a little research in exchange for the baron's advice on a few matters.

But rather than thank Bernard for all his hard work, Olivia hurls the papers at him and storms off to her car.

He glances down at his watch and says, "She'll be back."

"How do you know?" I ask.

Bernard stands in the vestibule staring out at the empty driveway, watching the cloud of dust settle. Suddenly he doesn't look nearly as pleased with himself, but actually rather sad. "Because this is her home."

SIXTY-ONE

BERNARD WASN'T KIDDING. I'VE JUST FINISHED DOING THE dishes and putting away the platters when a car pulls into the driveway.

Olivia tosses a black leather case onto the couch and opens the lid to reveal two antique pistols resting on a lining of plush but worn blue velvet. "What are *these*?" she demands to know.

"Why, they would appear to be pistols," says Bernard.

"And this?" she waves a piece of paper in Bernard's face.

"I believe that's a note challenging Darius to a duel with Ottavio at sunrise," he says calmly.

"A *duel*?" Olivia repeats incredulously.

"Well, of course," says Bernard. "That's the way two gentlemen typically resolve their claims on a lady."

"Bernard, you can't manipulate people's emotions," Olivia states sternly.

"I'd never do anything of the sort," insists Bernard. "Wasn't it your beloved Franklin Delano Roosevelt who said, 'Remember you're just an extra in everyone else's play'?"

Olivia scowls at him the way she does whenever Bernard uses his mother's own favorite quotes against her.

"Please, Mother, you can't make me believe that you're going to stand by a convicted criminal!"

Ottavio enters the room and appears puzzled, though I can't tell if it's a language barrier or the actual drama that he finds confusing.

"Ottavio, did you challenge Darius to a duel?" asks Olivia, rather brusquely.

"Non!" answers Ottavio, and frantically waves his hands in front of his chest while looking at the pistols.

"I didn't think so," says Olivia.

"What's the big deal?" asks Bernard. "It was a little joke. I'll call Darius right now and apologize."

However, I detect a gleam in Bernard's eye.

"Darius is gone!" states Olivia.

"Then when he gets back," says Bernard, oozing nonchalance.

"He's left for good," says Olivia.

"Oh my!" Bernard claps his hand to his mouth. "If he's absconded, then you'd better check your valuables."

"Nothing is missing," says Olivia. "Only your head is going to be missing, Bernard, you snake in the grass, you . . ."

"I believe it was Winston Churchill who so famously said, 'We are all worms. But I do believe I am a glow-worm.' "

Olivia, normally the one with a quotable quote for every occasion and situation is speechless.

Ottavio uses the moment of silence to produce out of his pocket the engagement ring that Olivia used to wear.

"Per piacere Oh-leevia!" Ottavio drops down before her on bended knee. *"Mi dispiace!"*

"Oh Ottavio, not *now!*" Olivia turns and heads out the door again.

Ottavio dashes after her.

However, I notice that this time she doesn't immediately get into her car. In fact, they turn at the side of the house and walk in the direction of the gardens. And why not? The night air is warm and fragrant and full of cricket concerts and frog serenades.

SIXTY-TWO

THE COUNTY FAIR SETS UP SHOP EIGHT MILES NORTH OF TOWN
the last week in August, as it's been doing for over a hundred
years. Attending the fair has been a Palmer family tradition as
far back as I can remember.

Mom says that she's going, but over breakfast changes her
mind. I suppose it's because Dad isn't here and she's afraid that
it will only make her sad. Mom has never missed a fair. In fact,
the first set of twins, Darlene and Davy, were almost born there
when they arrived five weeks early. As Dad liked to tell the story,
they went directly from the midway to the maternity ward.

We all clamber into the minivan following a big lunch at
home, the thinking being that we'll save money on food and still
get to enjoy the fair at night when all the lights are on. I review
the troops and decide that between Louise and Teddy and me,
we should be able to handle Darlene, Davy, Francie, and Lillian.

As soon as the Ferris wheel comes into sight the kids are
squirming and ready to jump out of the car. "Don't unlock the
doors until we're parked!" I yell at them at least three times.

Teddy disappears the second I hand him ten dollars, and the
moment Louise sees a gang of her friends she begs to go and

join them. The little kids, of course, want to go on all the rides first thing.

After being twirled and flown around in miniature airplanes and rocked and smashed in small boats, they're finally ready for some of the more tranquil pursuits the fair has to offer. We head to where the contests are held for dung throwing, best bread, biggest boar, and longest beard (45 inches). The kids marvel at the 875-pound pumpkin and the chickens with wild hairdos. In the refrigerator gallery a big crowd is gathered around 600 pounds of butter sculpted into a motorcycle on one side and the Last Supper on the other. I can only imagine what kind of remark Bernard would have for that—the things you see when you don't have a blowtorch.

Then it's time for snacks, which consist of everything you can shake a stick at on a stick, as Dad used to say. There are pickles, sausage, pork chops, and caramel apples. The men and women serving grilled corn wear caps and T-shirts that say, I'M SO CORNY. Then there's the hiss, fizzle, and splatter coming from the enormous vat of oil that produces the kids' favorites— deep-fried Twinkies and Snickers bars. I'm more of a funnel cake person myself.

Davy orders a blue Slushee and then he can't hold his Twinkie, so while I'm carrying the drink for him, Darlene knocks into my leg and it spills down my shirt. Now it looks as if I have blue vomit all down my front.

We pass by the tent where the gospel choir alternates singing "It's Me, O Lord" and "Give Me the Wings of Faith" with a fiery sermon by one of those hell-and-damnation revival preachers attempting to convert the sinning masses. Oddly enough, it's right next to the beer tent, where men (and a few women) regularly stumble out and appear disoriented for a moment as they shield their eyes from the bright afternoon light.

Next stop is the Mooternity Barn and the Swine Shed, which

is a collection of stalls and pens that house livestock of the bovine and porcine variety. People stand by their animals wearing cowboy boots and work boots—real ones, the kind used for riding and roping, not for creating a fashion statement.

This is where Eric used to hang out, trying to make time with the farm girls. In the first aisle we run into Gwen's younger brother Billy, who won a prize for the steer he raised on their farmette, only now he's miserable because it's going to be slaughtered. Gwen's parents are both trying to console Billy. His grandfather has even offered to buy the beast, but apparently such interventions are against the rules.

"Glad you could all make it," says Mr. Thompson. "Your dad was always a judge for the heifers."

"A blessed memory," says Mrs. Thompson. I assume she's referring to my dad and not all the cows that ended up as hamburger.

"He was a darn good judge, and we miss him," says Mr. Thompson.

Dad had grown up on a farm and was regularly asked to be a livestock judge because no one in our family entered the competition. And Mom was always invited to judge the baked goods. When people asked why she didn't enter her own delicious pies and cakes, Mom always joked that with so many children underfoot they didn't last long enough to make it to the fairgrounds. Fortunately for us, this was the truth. Mom had surmounted the number one curse of baking—if it looks good then it must taste bad, and vice versa.

Davy and Francie pet the steer very gently, as if it has the same low threshold for being mauled by children as the kitten. Gwen's uncle Vernon and her aunt Sharon arrive with some shish kebabs for the family. The minute Uncle Vernon sees my little brother and sisters he tosses out one of his famous (for being bad) jokes that he's collected over the years as an elementary-school gym teacher. "Hey there, in what school do you learn to greet people?"

"Cow school?" guesses Davy.

"Horse school?" Francie also proceeds along the barnyard line of thinking.

"Good try!" Uncle Vernon says to both of them with such enthusiasm that you'd think they'd just answered correctly *and* won a million dollars. "But the answer is *Hi* school! Get it?"

I can tell that Uncle Vernon is gearing up for another twenty jokes, so I quickly announce that we'd better see if Jane is with her mom in the handicrafts barn. In truth I know that Jane would rather be dead than get caught up with the Mad Quilters, as she calls them. However, we use the excuse to move on. Outside the barn you can pay five dollars to ride in a buggy pulled by enormous golden Clydesdale horses with creamy white manes.

Admittedly, the handicrafts barn is pretty boring, but it's a good place to finish digesting all the food we've eaten. A dozen or so older women are quilting at a big table in the center. On the surrounding tables are cakes, jams, soufflés, jars of pickles, and quiches, many waiting to judged, some already displaying ribbons. These are interspersed with trophies for cherry preserves, given that it's the fruit for which the county claims to be famous. Along the far side of the barn Mennonite women in long gray dresses and white bonnets run a stand selling pies, but otherwise keep to themselves, and when not taking care of business they congregate in tents behind the barns.

Jane's mom is working at a booth showing quilted bags and embroidered pillows. They say stuff like, OLD LAWYERS NEVER DIE, THEY JUST LOSE THEIR APPEAL and I'D RATHER BE SEWING. Her own T-shirt is hand stitched with the words, SEW MANY

QUILTS, SEW LITTLE TIME. I ask if Jane is around, and Mrs. Thompson reports that she's playing Skee-Ball next to the gallery with the artwork made from seeds. Jane has a Skee-Ball addiction that's definitely more serious than any penchant I might have for playing poker.

After determining that the food is firmly anchored in the kids' stomachs, I allow them to go on the pony rides. Then we watch a pie-eating contest and are surprised to see a petite Asian woman beat a very large man for the grand prize.

Inspired by watching all that consumption, the kids beg me for cotton candy. Lillian is tired and I carry her while Davy and Francie pull at each other's pink and blue cones. Suddenly I spot Craig holding hands with Megan, heading directly toward us. Megan O'Rourke. I should have known. She's been after Craig since high school, at least according to Gwen. I hope she's happy with her sloppy seconds.

There's only an instant to decide whether to grab the kids and quickly turn around, or to stay where we are, in which case they'll surely see me. Looking down at the blue Slushee all over my T-shirt and the general grubbiness of our merry little band of fairgoers I decide to try and hide. However, Megan sees me and starts waving. There's no choice but to wait for them to pass by.

It's an awkward moment when we all say "Hello." I'm suddenly conscious of the fact that Lillian has pulled out half my ponytail while I was carrying her and that I probably have powdered sugar stuck to my face, in addition to the stained clothes. Meantime Megan looks perfect in a filmy powder-blue silk blouse and an immaculate white skirt that is shrink-wrap tight. She politely asks us to join them. I say that we have to help Jane's mom in the handicrafts barn because she's showing one of her quilts. What a stupid lie—how do you help someone show a quilt?

Craig and Megan continue in the direction of the midway. A buzzer goes off a few feet away and it startles me. A booming voice yells that he'll guess anyone's weight and if he's off by two pounds they win a prize. A woman goes by with a display of pinwheels and helium balloons. I look down and Francie is gone!

"Where is she?" I holler at Darlene and Davy. One points vaguely in the direction of the midway and the other toward the restrooms, like Tweedledum and Tweedledee. We search for twenty minutes and then head to the main office. Sure enough, Francie is sitting there eating a Popsicle and happily petting someone's rabbit.

I scold her for getting lost and suggest that if we can't stick together then maybe we should go home. The kids beg to stay for the fireworks and swear on their favorite toys not to get lost again. As we walk out of the aid station the merry-go-round kicks up its dizzying theme song. Coming around the corner I see someone who looks like Mom. It *is* Mom.

"I was hoping to find you!" she says, smiling.

We hurry over, and the kids all yell at once about the rides and the pie-eating contest. Fortunately no one finds the fact that Francie got lost exciting enough to include in their report.

Pastor Costello appears carrying two sugar waffles. "Your mom was all alone, and so I suggested we come look for you," he says cheerfully, and some powdered sugar spills down his T-shirt, which says: JESUS—THE ORIGINAL SUPERMAN.

"Hallie, maybe you can go and catch up with some of your friends," suggests Mom. "We'll take the children."

"I wouldn't mind seeing if Jane is still in the arcade," I say.

As we part ways it registers in a corner of my mind that Mom looks rather happy. I'm glad that she came to the fair. Pastor Costello has been so good to us. And I decide here and now that I should stop feeling sorry for myself. Things could be *a lot* worse. With the little bit of insurance money, Dad's modest pension, and social security, Mom will never be wealthy, but we'll manage.

By now the lights on the rides twinkle against the sky, and the smell of fresh caramel being melted onto apples fills the evening air. A barbershop quartet wearing red-and-white-striped vests and blue pants strolls past singing "Lida Rose." As I walk toward the midway, bells ring, shots go off, megaphoned barkers shout at passersby enticing them to play, and the winners whoop it up when they succeed. Above the games can be heard the screams of people riding the salt and pepper shakers as they hurtle and spin through the air. I look away. If you've been to enough fairs, you know that this is the point where "motion" equals "sickness." And in my book the only thing worse than vomit is flying vomit.

After making my way through the bustling midway and deafening arcade, I head back toward the handicrafts barn. A band made up of an accordion, banjo, and harmonica sets up on the wooden stage for the crowning of the Cherry Queen (yes, the boys have fun with that one). Bursts of raucous laughter come from the beer tent, while a few feet away strains of "Blessed Be the Ties That Bind" issue from the revival tent. Directly above the tent is the large and indifferent yellow stare of a great August moon.

Just before turning left toward the soft but insistent lowing that issues from the Mooternity barn, I spot Craig and Megan climbing onto the Ferris wheel together. The scream is silent, but it's there, all the same.

SIXTY-THREE

AT FOUR O'CLOCK IN THE MORNING I WAKE UP AND CAN'T FALL back to sleep. Not wanting to rouse anyone by starting a car, I ride my bike toward the Stocktons'. Morning is still part of night, and everything is a different shade of gray. The beauty of four in the morning is not its furnishings and décor, but its aimlessness and stolen quality. I suppose that's why Cappy always calls it "The Convict Hour."

I lean my bike against the side of the house and slip into the yard. The wind sighs in the birch trees and the butterfly bushes drip moisture from their leaves. Sitting by the edge of the pond I stare down at the fish, serene and barely moving, as if their alarm clocks haven't yet gone off.

Somewhere between the breeze and the faraway sound of a train comes a single line of birdsong. As the sun peeks above the horizon, light begins to spread like a flower of fire. A cardinal flits from one tree to another, making a bright red brushstroke in the air.

Soon the gray sky is a cool timeless blue and the golden sunshine has turned the pond surface into a hundred flashing diamonds. I hear sounds coming through the open windows of the house but no voices.

That is until a voice directly behind me says, "Don't mind me, I've just come to pick some rosemary for a loaf of bread I'm making."

I continue lying in the grass, looking up at early morning sky that's still gauzy with starlight. "Do you ever think about death, Bernard? How you're going to die? When? And what happens afterward?"

"Never. I'm very much opposed to the idea," he says. "Now come inside, and I'll make you some popes Benedict." This is Bernard's latest creation—a mushroom, goat cheese, and dill omelet cut into the shape of a cross.

I follow him inside and watch while he fills the bread machine and brews a fresh pot of coffee.

"You're up early," he says.

"Couldn't sleep." I rummage through the fridge for a chocolate Yoo-hoo.

"Well, the headline here is: Duel resolves dueling boyfriends. We have fled madness and found gladness."

"And exactly how did you know that Darius would take off rather than call your bluff?" I slump down at the kitchen table and chug directly from the bottle.

"I think the fact that I included a plane ticket helped to sway him just a teensy bit." Bernard gives me a wink. "Plus I mentioned that Ottavio was not only a master dueler, but also a war hero."

"War hero?" I ask. "He's never even been in the military."

Bernard waves his arms as if I'm trying to sabotage him, pretends to pull at his hair, and then clamps a hand over my mouth. It would be an understatement to say that he's addicted to the dramatic gesture.

"The main thing is that they're back together!" concludes Bernard. "Like two peas in a pod!"

I want to be happy about this turn of events but it's not my day for happiness. Plus I can't be sure that Bernard's not exaggerating the reconciliation. "And where is the happy couple?"

"Upstairs preparing to attend a vigil for the homeless in Cleveland." Bernard suddenly turns growly. "It's too much for Mother to admit that I was right, and so she's aggravating me by sleeping outside all night and will most likely get arrested for vagrancy. Only she's going to be surprised when I don't come to her rescue with the bail checkbook."

"She'd love nothing better," I say. It's a well-known fact that Bernard has had to literally drag Olivia out of prison on more than one occasion after she's been arrested while marching or protesting. She likes being incarcerated because it gets more publicity for her cause of the week.

Bernard stares at my face for a long moment, as if it's the first time he's noticed me in weeks. "What is going on with you? You look *terrible*." He takes my ponytail in his hand. "Holy hairpins! Are you using a two-in-one shampoo conditioner?"

"Whatever is on sale," I say, and free myself from his grip.

"Are you still wallowing? The Craig breakup was months ago! It's time for a comeback."

"I'm turning nineteen in two weeks. Isn't that a little young to make a comeback?"

"Don't be ridiculous," scoffs Bernard. "Every time Judy Garland returned from the powder room the press called it a comeback."

"It's no use," I say. "I ruined my life."

"I hardly think so," says Bernard. "Let's take a page from Dinah Washington's songbook, shall we?"

He disappears into the living room and after a few minutes I hear the song "What a Difference a Day Makes" playing on the stereo.

Bernard reappears and announces, "Dinah was accused of selling out by the critics as well as her contemporaries, and she married seven times."

"And the last marriage was terrific?" I ask hopefully.

"Not exactly. She struggled with a weight problem and died from an overdose of diet pills mixed with alcohol at age thirty-nine. But Dinah was still in peak voice, singing at a blues club in Los Angeles just two weeks before the end!"

"And what am I supposed to do with *that* information?"

"Change your perfume, find a new hobby, learn a language," Bernard reels off suggestions.

"My routine is baby-sitting and weeding," I say. "And I don't have time for hobbies or new languages."

Bernard sighs as if I'm a hopeless case. "Shop at a new mall. Do *something!*"

We hear Olivia humming as she comes down the stairs, followed by the shuffling of papers in her den.

"She's probably searching for her copy of the Declaration of Independence to read aloud at the protest," says Bernard. He pushes me toward her den. "Go have Mother give you one of her stop-cursing-the-darkness-and-light-a-candle speeches."

"But I'm not *cursing* about anything."

"You're moping. It's ten times worse, and I can't take it anymore."

I enter Olivia's den and close the accordion door behind me. Though it's more to escape Bernard's frantic cheerfulness than anything else.

"Welcome home," I say.

"Thank you, Hallie. But a lot of people don't have homes or even the basic level of housing, and that's why we're organizing an overnight vigil in front of city hall. They can no longer keep us quiet with bread and circuses." She raises her left hand above her head as if the protest has already begun and the floor lamp is the mayor.

"Is Ottavio going with you?"

"Yes, we've kissed and made up," says Olivia. "And as much as it pains me to admit this, Bertie was right. Darius was too young for me."

It sounds very much as if a self-satisfied harrumph comes from the other side of the door, even though running water can be heard in the kitchen, indicating that Bernard, the inveterate eavesdropper, is only pretending to wash dishes.

Olivia glances in the direction of the noise and adds, "It's just as well. He wasn't very good in bed."

We hear a glass drop and smash on the floor right outside the door.

SIXTY-FOUR

OLIVIA AND OTTAVIO ARE LOADING THE CAR WITH BLANKETS
and big cardboard signs as I'm getting ready to leave. Bernard
stands by the side of the driveway trying to talk her out of
spending the night on a sidewalk in downtown Cleveland.

"Mother, what is the point of all this nonsense?" he asks,
arms akimbo. "The legislature *can't* include a new shelter in the
budget—there isn't enough money for the pensions they already owe."

"Those people can advocate for themselves," Olivia says
tersely. "The homeless cannot."

"Yes, Mother, I understand all that," continues Bernard. "But
this is a done deal—your legislation is *not* going to pass. People
have already announced how they're voting. Tell your Unitarian
jihadists to turn their efforts to something that has a chance."

"We might still change some minds," says Olivia. "Convincing Americans that we needed the Civil Rights Act of 1964
didn't happen overnight."

"Then write editorials or get up another petition," says
Bernard. "Why do you have to sleep outside overnight and then
personally attend the vote?"

Olivia suddenly comes to life and switches from a measured but dismissive tone to one of tremendous valor. "*Why?* For the same reason that Eleanor Roosevelt sat through the congressional session where they voted down the Anti-Lynching Bill— *to bear witness!*"

Bernard drops his arms and throws his head back. "Fine, then what are you going to eat while *bearing witness*? It sounds like a real calorie-burner."

"We'll be homeless people," says Olivia. "Whatever we can scrounge up or nothing at all."

Olivia and Ottavio climb into the cherry-red Buick, the ends of their picket signs sticking out the back windows.

"That's where I draw the line—at the two of you Dumpster diving or starving to death on the mean streets of downtown Cleveland," says Bernard. "Wait just a minute. I made up a basket with eggplant, tomato, and mozzarella panini sandwiches, Tuscan white bean soup, and some fruit salad."

Olivia appears to consider for a moment. "I'm not sure that wouldn't be cheating."

"Don't worry," Bernard assures her, "there's plenty of extra so you can share it with all your homeless friends."

"Oh, I suppose that's all right," Olivia replies gaily, as if they're heading off on vacation.

Bernard dashes inside to fetch the food before they can escape.

I wish them both luck and hop on my bicycle. On the way home I usually stop at the Star-Mart to pick up some groceries, but since I don't have a car today it's easier to stop at the convenience store.

"Hey, Hallie!" I hear from the far end of the aisle. "It's me, Auggie."

"Oh my gosh! I-I thought you moved to Russia." Last I heard, my two dates with Auggie the previous summer had the effect of rocketing him back across the Atlantic and into the arms of his ex. Because unlike the women who drive men crazy, I drive them away. Far away.

He smiles sheepishly as if to say, *Oh yeah, that.* "I'm back," he says, holding up an apple and bottle of iced tea as if to prove it.

"*Here?*" I ask.

"No, no. Just passing through on my way to Iowa."

I look further surprised.

"School—the University of Iowa."

"Congratulations!"

"I'm going to study writing."

"You should. That's wonderful."

Only Auggie's preoccupied by the unusual necklace that June made for me. "Are those crystals?" He starts to laugh.

"Yeah, why?" I take them protectively in my hand. "You think they're stupid, right?"

"No, of course not. The universe is all about energy. It's just that, well, you're the last person I ever thought would be wearing them. You're just so—"

"So *what?*"

"I don't know . . . mathematical," says Auggie.

Frowning back at him, I uncomfortably kick at a piece of gum that's stuck to the floor.

"Come on, don't get mad. They're great," he says sincerely. "And I was really sorry to hear about your dad."

"Thanks," I say.

Auggie nods toward his beat-up tan Chevy Cavalier out front with all his stuff packed inside and a box strapped to the roof. "I'm leaving early in the morning—but, uh, do you want to go out tonight?"

"Out? Okay, sure." It's been so long that I don't even know

where out is anymore. I may as well have a court-mandated curfew.

"One of Grandpa's friends has this restaurant on a restored riverboat near Cleveland called Lolita's—ever hear of it?"

"Sure." Lolita's was famous for being high class, expensive, and, well, Italian owned and operated. "It's sort of fancy, isn't it?"

Auggie glances down at his T-shirt, jeans, and sandals. "I guess I'd better wear a jacket. But you look good in anything. What time should I pick you up?"

My mother is not especially judgmental, but I decide that in view of the last few months, her precarious mental health might be upset by Auggie's peace sign earring, long hair, and beaded necklace.

"Why don't we meet there?" I quickly suggest.

"It's kind of a long drive," says Auggie.

"How about Cappy's office at the pool hall?"

"I'm spending the night at his place," says Auggie. "Can you come over there at about six?"

"Is that on the dirt road off Millersport?"

"Yeah, it's the only turnoff. You can't miss it."

"It's a date," I say.

"Then don't be late," says Auggie.

SIXTY-FIVE

LOUISE CAN'T BELIEVE HER EARS WHEN I ASK TO BORROW A DRESS and some shoes. "If you need cash that desperately I can give you a loan," she offers.

"I'm flattered that you think I could make money as a prostitute, but I actually have a date. Only don't tell Mom. He wears an earring and has a ponytail."

"It sucks being the oldest girls," says Louise. "Mom is not going to give a shit if Francie and Lillian's boyfriends have tattoos and nose rings and do lines of cocaine on the coffee table."

"Are you kidding? Mom is so cheap, can you imagine her watching someone put five hundred bucks up their nose?"

"You're right," says Louise. "Nervous breakdown numbers two and three."

We both giggle. Of course we know it's terrible to make fun of everything that's happened. On the other hand, Louise and I have become much closer since she's moved home.

Louise holds up a green sundress that doesn't look too much like a shower curtain and hands me a pretty white silk cardigan to wear over it. She rummages around her jewelry box and pulls out some opal earrings set in gold. "Here, these will look nice with it."

I put them on and check the mirror. "Thanks," I say.

"You look really pretty," she says.

"I look as if I'm eloping in a pickup truck," I say.

"Having people always tell you that you're pretty is nice," says Louise. "But after a while you begin to wonder if they'd still want to be your friend if you weren't considered attractive, or, worse, if you were suddenly disfigured in a horrible fire. Or scarred by bad acne. Or mauled by a bear."

Obviously she's given some thought to this.

"You mean, like rich people have to wonder why people want to be their friend?" I ask.

"I suppose."

"I guess we're pretty lucky that we don't have to worry about that!" I joke.

"Amen to that!" we both imitate Pastor Costello, in word and enthusiasm.

"Why is your hair so dry? Can't you ever wear a hat when you're out in the sun?"

"My hair would be dry if I lived in an underwater cave with Ariel the mermaid," I report. "My system has a conditioner deficiency."

Louise picks through her magic potions and selects a tube of something to squeeze into her palms and apply to my straw head. She doesn't look overly pleased with the results and tries adding more.

"Oh, for God's sake," says Louise in frustration and grabs the bottle of hand lotion off her night table. She pours white glop into her palm and styles my hair anew. Suddenly she looks pleased. "Better."

I take a quick glance in the mirror. "Not bad. Definitely got rid of the frizzies and flyaways."

"Just don't let anybody touch it," she adds.

"Great, now you tell me." Putting my hands to my head I

have to admit that there's a certain Bundt-cake-mold feeling to it.

While grabbing my car keys it occurs to me that I have to tell Mom *something*. If I say that I'm going on a date, she might ask me about Craig. At first I figured one of the church ladies or Pastor Costello would spill the beans, but I've quickly learned that when you are just out of a mental institute people concentrate on delivering only happy news.

"Oh, Hallie! You look lovely!" Mom surprises me at the bottom of the stairs.

"Thanks," I say. "So do you." She's wearing a housecoat and white canvas shoes and so this is pretty stupid.

"Why, thank you," she says. "I feel well and I guess that's the main thing."

"Amen to that!" The phrase is still ringing in my head.

"You're going out, I take it?"

"A party," I lie. "With some friends from college." Another lie.

"You couldn't have a nicer night for a party," she says. "Have fun."

Interrogation over. She knows I'm lying.

S I X T Y - S I X

IT'S A WARM EVENING AFTER A HOT DAY. SUMMER IS FADING AWAY, drifting into a green haze. The sky is streaked with purple, and a fresco of light and shadows play across the lawns as the sprinklers rise and fall.

I've never been to Cappy's house before. It's the only driveway along a road that makes up the northern edge of town. Or at least it used to. Now after two hundred yards you get to a development of brand-new McMansions with names like Shady Glen and Idyllic Forest, basically a description of what was destroyed to build them.

Finally I come to a big rambling Spanish-style hacienda with wide stone walkways and a red tile roof. There's a similarly styled guesthouse in the back with Auggie's hunk-of-junk car parked in front, and so I pull up next to it.

Adjacent to the main house is an enormous swimming pool surrounded by a wrought-iron fence decorated with big bronze suns. At both ends of the pool are tiled fountains that make pleasant trickling sounds. Large painted clay pots stand in every corner decorated with glazes of intense cobalt blues, radiant yellows, and rusty reds.

It's quite a surprise, almost like a mirage. Cappy's office down at the pool hall contains some old metal furniture that looks like it was found out by the curb on garbage day. The walls there are a sickly yellow color, and whether it's paint or smoke, or more likely a toxic combination, is hard to tell.

The door to the guesthouse is ajar, and I can see Auggie standing over a mound of laundry wearing a nice black suit with a maroon shirt underneath. Now that he's showered and changed it's clear that Auggie is still as attractive as ever, with his smooth face, slim hips, and fine features. On the other hand, I don't know why I'm bothering to notice after our last date was such a disaster—me falling in love with him while he was longing for another woman. And that's not even touching on the part of the evening when he casually announced his bisexuality.

"Just give me a minute to throw in some wash," he says.

The guesthouse contains its own washer and dryer behind some tall shutters next to the bathroom. In the kitchen area hang a dozen or so bright copper pots, and along the far wall is a fireplace big enough to cook in. With the tiled floor and exposed-beam ceiling, the interior looks like a set for a movie that takes place in the old Southwest.

"This place is unbelievable!" I say.

"Grandpa has dealers in Mexico and South America send native crafts and handmade furniture. That way he freshens up his money and invests at the same time. Cappy says the stock market is up and down like a whore's drawers."

We both giggle because no one else *would* say such a thing but Cappy.

I suddenly hear what sounds like someone crying for help. I'm aware that Cappy runs a thriving bookmaking operation, but he supposedly retired from certain moneylending aspects of the business a long time ago.

Seeing the look of alarm on my face, Auggie quickly explains, "Peacocks."

"*Peacocks?*"

"That's the way the males sound. Cappy hates them. But this guy couldn't pay for a bet, so he gave Cappy peacocks instead," explains Auggie. "I told him you were coming. Go over to the house and say hi."

Everywhere I look are graceful arches, palm-dotted gardens, and big terra-cotta urns decorated with flowers, geometric patterns, and Spanish writing. If Cappy ever decides to head south of the border, he's doing a good job acclimatizing himself.

"Hey, Red, what's the word?" I hear before I've even had a chance to knock on the screen door.

SIXTY-SEVEN

CAPPY IS IN HIS STANDARD SUMMER OUTFIT OF A CHECKED BOATing cap, white shirt, white shoes, brown socks, and Bermuda shorts. He acts as if it's perfectly normal for me to be standing in a sundress at his door. "I've been meaning to stop by and see how you're getting along, but I'm terrible with stuff like that."

"Thanks for the food basket," I say. It was about ten times bigger than all the others and from some fancy place in New York.

"It was the least I could do. You can't eat flowers, right?"

Cappy doesn't ask me about Auggie. He never asks who you're dating. Cappy says that when a person comes looking for a spouse or family member, perhaps with court papers in hand or a sawed-off shotgun, he likes to be able to honestly say that he doesn't know anything.

"This is quite a place!" I say. On the far wall is a mural of galloping horses that look as if they're about to plow us right over. Leading up the spiral staircase hangs a tin mask collection. All that's missing is a herd of piñatas.

"Come on, I'll give you the grand tour."

Everywhere I look there's ornate wrought iron and delicately carved wood, colorful tiles, and arched pueblo doorways. The upstairs hallway glows from a combination of golden-hued plaster and brightly colored tapestries. The master bedroom features a wooden bed built right into the wall that's covered with a brown and red Indian blanket.

We head back down to the living room and Cappy offers me a seat on the rich chocolate-brown suede couch. There's a big bowl of onyx stones on the coffee table and stacks of woven baskets in every corner. Slightly out of place is a large black-and-white photo of a guy pitching a baseball, and the caption below it says, 1919 WORLD SERIES.

While studying the photo I ask, "So was this the biggest scam ever?"

"Heck no," replies Cappy. "Chump change."

"What then—Ponzi?" I refer to the pyramid scheme Cappy told me about that operates on the rob-Peter-to-pay-Paul principle and has practically bankrupted entire countries.

"Hardly," says Cappy.

"Then what, in your opinion, was the biggest con ever?" I ask.

"Easy," he says. "The British Empire. You've got an island less than one hundred thousand square miles in size running one quarter of the planet."

And here I always thought the reason Cappy became a bookie was because he didn't do well in school.

Cappy sits down in a worn armchair that has a huge stack of racing papers on both sides. He reads the racing papers the way women go through old decorating magazines, looking for the answers to life's eternal questions.

"Your dad was in the same grade as my son, and so I saw him play football when they were in high school. I always wondered why he didn't go pro. That's a team I wouldn't have bet against."

I'm surprised to hear all this, because Cappy doesn't normally traffic in personal details. I just nod.

"How's your mom getting along?"

"Doing better," I say. "She came home. I'll probably wait a year before going back to school. Eric will almost be finished by then."

"Well, don't let the government shake you down for any interest. I give tax-free loans for education."

"Thanks," I say. I've always felt that I could go to Cappy if things ever got really bad. I mean, as a *last resort.*

"And don't become another Ruffian."

Cappy isn't referring to an angry young person, but rather the famous filly who drove herself so hard trying to win the Triple Crown that she broke down and had to be destroyed.

Then there's a long pause, and it feels as if one of us is supposed to say something.

"So, how's business?" I finally ask.

"Business is *bueno*! I'm constantly amazed by how many people want you to take their money." Cappy points toward the mantelpiece, where there are several photos of horses with wreaths around their necks standing in the winner's circle. "A racehorse is a magnificent animal in that it can take several thousand people for a ride at one time."

"The less you bet, the more you lose when you win." I repeat Cappy's favorite expression for encouraging his customers to double their action.

The door opens and in comes a woman of about fifty carrying two grocery bags. At first I think she's the housekeeper, but she's dressed a little too fancy for that. Plus her hair is all done up and she's wearing lots of silver and turquoise jewelry.

"Sheila, I don't know if you remember Hallie," says Cappy.

"Nice to see you again," says Sheila with a sort of Texas twang to her voice. "What a lovely dress. Big date?" She winks at me, but of course we all see her do it.

Sheila? Where do I know Sheila from? The longer I look and listen to Sheila the more familiar she seems. It's the woman from last year's poker games! Only with half the makeup, a third of the upswept gold hair, and her majestic bosom now fenced in by fabric.

"Texas!" I practically shout.

"One and the same," she says, and gives me a big smile. Texas/Sheila glances down at her absent décolletage and pronounces, "or at least half the same. Cappy here don't like it when I'm auctioning off the merchandise."

"Sheila, would you do me a favor and make us some coffee?" We all know this is Cappy's code for giving him some privacy.

"I have a confession to make to you," says Cappy. "Remember when you first moved to the Stocktons' and your parents and that creepy guy from the school found you there?"

"Yeah," I say. Though it seems like a million years ago. And I can't imagine how it could matter now anyway.

"Well, it wasn't your little-old-lady neighbor Mrs. Muldoon who blew you in, the way you always thought. Sorry to be a stool pigeon, but your old man came to see me. It wasn't like turning on someone's partner—he was just a guy worried about his kid, and as a parent I understood where he was coming from. They were on the trail anyway. It's too small a town to hide something like that for very long."

I can't believe that Cappy ratted me out. I mean, at this point I'm not really mad about it, seeing as everything worked out in the end. Except of course for Dad dying. But still, what happened to the Convict's Code and all that?

"Why did my dad go to *you*?" I ask.

"Back when you were a kid and started showing up at the track, he asked if I'd keep an eye on you out there—you know, a twelve-year-old girl on her own. The place attracts a lot of sleaze." Cappy says this as if he can hardly believe the sordid characters he's forced to deal with on a regular basis.

"So how come you're telling me all this *now*?" I ask. "Are you about to die or something?"

"Not that I know of—but you'll tell me if you hear anything, right?" He smiles at his little joke.

I just stare at him.

"I figured you'd understand when you had some kids of your own to worry about." It's obvious he's referring to my re- cently inherited brood.

"Well, I knew that all along," I say.

"Yeah, right. And I just won a daily double that went off the board at a hundred to one."

"Please, the first week I was living there my dad referred to Bernard as 'that Addams guy.' And who else but *you* ever called the Stocktons the Addams Family?"

Cappy narrows his eyes, unable to determine whether I've nailed him or not. "So what about my grandson, Auggie Strind- berg? He sure as hell can't add numbers, so I guess we should be relieved that he's interested in combining letters. His story about living in Russia won a prize from a Chicago news- paper, and now he wants to write a novel. It's the American dream—bootlegger to bookmaker to book writer in three gen- erations."

"I thought you said that your father was a printer."

"He was, he was. And a damn fine one at that!" Cappy gives a gigantic Santa Claus laugh. "He was printing hundred-dollar bills when he got caught!

"Get this—Auggie's novel is about a boy whose uncle is a

small-town bookie," says Cappy, and gives me a nudge. "But he insists that it's not about us."

"Maybe it's not," I say.

"Did I tell you that Sheila and I are getting hitched?" asks Cappy.

"No way!" I say. "You have a different girlfriend every single week!" And that's being generous.

"That was the past and Sheila is the future. There's no luckier man than I!" says Cappy.

He can see that I'm doubtful about the idea of his settling down.

As we head toward the kitchen he leans forward and whispers in my ear. "Hey, kid, you remember what I used to tell you about all the tipsters at the racetrack?"

"Yeah, even a blind squirrel occasionally finds a nut," I answer.

Auggie is standing near the door all ready to go. I move toward him and wave good-bye to Cappy and Texas.

"Get along, little doggies," says Texas.

"Don't take any wooden nickels," adds Cappy.

A peacock squawks nearby, and I swear it sounds like a woman having her throat slit.

"Those birds are giving me the jimjams," says the normally calm Cappy. "Seriously, do you know anyone who wants four peacocks? It's illegal to assassinate them—can you believe that?"

"I think we're pretty full up at my house. But if you can find a way to relate them to Chinese history, then I'm sure Bernard will take them," I joke. "He's on this huge kick to make sure his adopted daughters relate to their culture."

"*Really?*" says Cappy, brightening for a moment. "And how's it going so far?"

"Not so good," I say. "There's a slight chance they'd be interested in a Chinese Barbie doll."

SIXTY-EIGHT

Lolita's restaurant is a refurbished paddlewheel boat that plied the Ohio River in the late 1800s, taking passengers and mail back and forth between Cincinnati and Louisville, and is now permanently docked on the south shore of Lake Erie. Most everything is painted white, and there are mannequins of men and women in period dress leaning over the railing. The women wave good-bye with lace handkerchiefs while the men hold decks of cards in their hands.

The maître d' leads us to a table by the water where we can watch the sun melt into the horizon, just far enough away from the band so it's possible to enjoy the music and still hear each other talk. Auggie says that the chicken Marsala is the house specialty, so we both decide on that and he orders some wine. The waiter writes this down without even looking up at us, forget about asking to see some ID.

Lolita's is not exactly a cool young person's place. The diners are mostly older couples, and if teenagers or young adults appear, they can usually be traced back to a table shared with their parents or in-laws. But everyone seems to be having a good time.

"Cappy told me that you wrote another prize-winning story," I say. "Congratulations."

"It was just a contest held by a newspaper," he says modestly.

"What's this one about?"

"A young guy who falls in love with a Russian woman and follows his heart—moves to Moscow and tries to find a job. I know it sounds autobiographical, but it's really not."

"Of course not," I say. "Just out of curiosity, how does it end?"

"The story or my relationship?" he asks.

"Either one," I say.

"She marries the son of a rich banker because they'll have a big apartment."

"I see. And uh, what about the bi thing?"

"I think I was reading too much Sergei Aleksandrovich Yesenin at the time."

"Huh?"

"A Russian poet whose works lament the passing of rural life. He was a drinker, exhibitionist, revolutionary, and bisexual. For a while I was really into his 1916 collection *Commemoration of the Dead*. So I thought the secret to becoming a writer was to be free and open to all experiences. But to be honest, it didn't really work out for me."

"You mean that you're not bi?"

"Not right now, at least," he says. "Does it matter to you?"

"Me?" I can't help but laugh. "I practically live at La Cage aux Folles."

"But you don't date them," says Auggie.

Is that what this is, an actual date? I suddenly feel a little nervous.

"What about you?" asks Auggie. "Are you straight?"

"I think so. Bernard is pretty much gay enough for the both of us," I say.

"Then why say you think so?" asks Auggie, but his tone is one of curiosity and not as if he's trying to trap me.

"There's this movie I watched with Bernard called *A Street-car Named Desire. . . .*"

"Sure," says Auggie. "It was a play first. By Tennessee Williams. And he was *really* gay."

"Right . . . well Blanche talks about the word *straight* and says something like a line can be straight, or a street, but the human heart is curved like a road through mountains."

Suddenly a band featuring an accordion, tuba, and piano strikes up a particularly robust polka and Auggie asks me to dance. He must be kidding.

"Auggie, I can barely dance free-style—forget a polka."

He takes my hand and before I know it we're sidestepping across the wooden floor in 2/4 time with eight other couples. It feels more like a soccer warm-up exercise than a dance, but everyone is laughing and the mood is rather infectious. During the crossed hands stomp we become hopelessly lost, but no one seems to care.

On the way home I reach over and touch the clump of electric-blue fur attached to Auggie's key chain.

"That's my lucky rabbit's foot," he explains. "I found it on the steps of the Hermitage Museum in St. Petersburg."

"Doesn't appear to have worked for the rabbit," I say.

Auggie digs through a pile of stuff on the floor behind my seat. "Do you like Afro-Cuban music? Because I have this cut of a new group."

"I don't know much about it. I've been listening to a lot of Raffi lately."

He laughs and starts singing: *"Did you ever see a goose kissing a moose, down by the bay?"*

I cover my ears and pretend to be in pain.

Auggie abandons his search for the CD. "It must be inside with my stuff. I'll play it for you back at the house."

Back at the house? Then I suddenly remember that's where my car is parked.

"What's wrong?" asks Auggie. It's weird, as if he has ESP or something.

"Nothing." Then I decide that I may as well tell him. "The past hour I keep thinking about what's going to happen—if you're going to park somewhere, just drop me off, kiss me good night, I don't know."

Suddenly I start to sob. Which is strange, because I was having a really nice night up until five seconds ago.

"Did I do something to upset you?" Auggie pulls the car over.

"No, no." Gosh, I feel so ugly. If my skin was blotchy before, now it probably looks as if I have the measles.

"It's been all kids, Mom, and diapers, and I don't know how to live or date in the real world anymore. Plus my hair is a mess." I cover my head with my hands and can hardly catch my breath now.

"I think you're having an anxiety attack," says Auggie. "It happened to me once in an airport."

"Anxious about what? Nothing is happening in my life. I have no life!"

"Maybe you just don't feel in control. You're worried about what's coming next because you don't want it to be bad," suggests Auggie. "It's completely understandable after everything that's happened."

As long as he brought it up—"What are we doing?" I deliver this question as if I'm seven months pregnant by Auggie, we're not married, and he's joined the foreign legion.

"Gee, Hallie. We're just on a date," says Auggie. A little bit of helplessness creeps into his voice. "I mean, you can't always know everything that's going to happen, right?"

I dry my face with my hands and turn away so that he can't see my swollen eyes.

"I suppose we could outline a plan—decide to go to third base or something like that," he helpfully suggests.

"What exactly are the bases?" I ask.

"I'm not sure. I thought only girls knew that."

"All anyone seems to agree on is that kissing is first," I say.

"If you want to kiss, then we can. And if you don't, then we won't."

"I suppose it does take a bit of the fun out of it by making a schedule ahead of time," I say with a hint of a smile.

"You can change your mind at any moment," he adds.

"It's time for some sort of *change* or else I'm going to end up taking the bed at Dalewood that Mom recently vacated. Eventually they'll name a wing after us."

"You know what I'd like to do right now?" asks Auggie.

"Move to Zanzibar?" I guess.

"Go in the Jacuzzi and then wash your hair."

"Wash my hair?"

Auggie runs his fingers through my hair. "You have really beautiful strawberry blond hair, but *what* have you been using on it?"

"Whatever is family-sized and on sale."

"I have this incredible organic conditioner with lots of natural protein."

His hair does look really good. Not a split end in sight. Gee, Craig never wanted to wash my hair. In fact, I don't think he even uses conditioner.

SIXTY-NINE

BOTH THE MAIN HOUSE AND GUEST QUARTERS GLOW PALE PINK IN the darkness from spotlights hidden in the dense shrubbery. On the coffee table is a stack of literary journals. The front cover shows Auggie's name listed next to the title "Goodbye, Chekhov."

"Wow!" I say. "First prize—congratulations."

"Yeah, there's my prize," he points to the ten copies of the journal.

Auggie goes over to the bar and makes us drinks. The process appears to be very complicated, involving sliced fruit and a shot glass.

"What *is* all that?"

"I'm making rum runners." Pointing to the array of bottles he reels off their names, "blackberry brandy and crème de banana, a splash of pineapple and orange juice, and a dash of grenadine." Only when he gets to an aged-looking bottle at the end of the line he slyly adds, "And old Great-Granddad's secret recipe."

"Well, I won't ask you for it because the whole town recently heard about what happened to *him*. Though I wish you had been here to see everyone out fishing for the whiskey."

Auggie pours the brew into a silver shaker and strains it over ice cubes into ceramic tiki glasses rimmed with salt. "Why don't you grab a robe from behind the bathroom door? It's getting chilly out."

"I didn't bring a bathing suit."

"I could lend you one of mine," jokes Auggie. "We're about the same size." This second part is actually true.

God, I've suddenly turned into a forty-year-old. "It's fine." I take another sip of my drink. The "rum runner" is cool and perfectly sweet. I'm trying to remember what we discussed in the car. Did I agree to go skinny-dipping? And what did we decide about third base? What *is* third base anyway?

"What the hell," I accidentally say out loud.

"Huh?" Auggie pops up from behind the bar.

"Jacuzzi—robe—right!" I head toward the bathroom.

When I come out Auggie has a beach towel wrapped around his waist. He's smooth and not that tall or large, but his muscles are well defined. In an art museum I wouldn't be surprised to come across his figure as the statue of an ancient hero.

We head outside and the thrum of insects merges with the gentle trickle of the fountains. The peacocks must have finally gone to bed.

Standing at the edge of the Jacuzzi in a bathrobe I sip my drink while gazing up at the stars etched onto the dark page of night. Closing my eyes it's possible to feel the cool stillness of the shadows and the mysterious embrace of moonlight.

Suddenly the water begins to bubble and gurgle and come to life. Auggie drops his towel, steps into the Jacuzzi, and sinks back, letting out a big sigh.

Looking up to the main house I see that all the lights are out. "Around what time does Cappy get home?"

"Cappy's in bed by ten unless there's a poker game. He used

to watch a few quiz shows, but he says it's not fun like in the old days when contestants had to sweat it out in a hot soundproof booth and the games were mostly rigged."

"Oh," I say.

"Cappy claims that guys who've done time in prison are just like women who've had kids and tend to be early risers forever after."

I remain standing at the edge of the frothing water.

"Hallie, I'm allowed to have girls over."

I remove the robe and quickly slide into the water. It feels warm and welcoming, and Auggie doesn't try anything weird with his feet.

"Are you sure your car is going to make it to Iowa?"

"No," he says. "If it dies along the way I'll just catch a bus."

"Why don't you get a new one?"

"I wish!" says Auggie, and then he takes a mouthful of water and spits it up over the edge through his teeth so that it resembles a fountain. "My parents gave me money for my first year of school, but after I blew it they bailed."

Sitting in the midst of Cappy's sprawling estate, it must be obvious what I'm thinking.

"Cappy doesn't give any of us money," Auggie states matter-of-factly.

"He doesn't?" I say.

"That's not entirely true," Auggie corrects himself. "Cappy will give his kids and grandkids money for school, but if you flunk anything you're obligated to pay the money back within a year. You have to work for housing and books and whatever else. Cappy doesn't even leave us the money when he dies. It goes to dogs."

"You mean the SPCA?"

"Retired greyhounds from the dog tracks in Florida."

This is certainly news. I mean, I know Cappy has his funeral planned, because he's told me more than once that all he wants read are the race results. And I always figured there's a will, because whenever a person is overly attached to his or her money, Cappy is fond of asking if they've ever seen a hearse being followed by a U-Haul. But retired greyhounds?

"Really?" I ask.

"I guess it's not so bad. My mom is a doctor, and her brother David, my uncle, has a successful car dealership. Cappy helped set David up, but after that he had to make it on his own."

I can't help thinking about how Craig had everything on a plate and then dropped out. Maybe a bit of struggle isn't so bad. Then you appreciate things more than if they were simply your birthright.

It's quiet except for the burbling of the water.

"So what about your dad?" asks Auggie.

"What do you mean?" I ask.

"I don't know—how did you feel about his dying?"

I want to tell him that I'm sad and it's been really hard, but that seems stupid and also obvious.

Eventually I say, "To be completely honest, it feels as if I'm living an alternate reality and that at any minute things are suddenly going to return to the way they were. The present doesn't seem real. Does that make any sense?"

"A parallel universe," says Auggie.

"Something like that," I say.

"What about that guy Ray you were going out with?" asks Auggie.

"He dropped me like a bad habit," I say.

Auggie laughs. "You sound like Grandpa." He tilts back his head and gazes up at the stars. "And wasn't there somebody named Craig?"

"You like to ask the hard questions," I say.

"That's why I get paid the big bucks to be a writer."

"We broke up. Actually I broke up. I didn't think he should drop out of school. I'm a controlling witch. That's what I've become."

"I've read that most people start out as Democrats and end up Republicans." Auggie stands up and announces, "Time for your hair."

SEVENTY

AUGGIE RUMMAGES AROUND IN A DUFFEL BAG FOR HIS MAGIC conditioner. "Oh, here's that CD I was telling you about." He puts on the music and then goes over to the great stone fireplace, turns on a gas jet, and after a moment there's a roaring blaze.

We head into the bathroom where Auggie drops his towel and turns on the water in the shower. "Do you like it really hot?" he asks.

"Sure, that's great." But all I can concentrate on is the fact that Auggie is standing in front of me naked.

"Okay, go on in," he says.

Apparently he wasn't kidding about tackling my hair. After the shampoo, Auggie slowly works in the conditioner starting at the ends and eventually reaching my scalp.

"I can feel the difference already," he assures me.

When we exit the steamy bathroom wrapped in fluffy towels the room is warm and cozy. The large oven of a fire causes shadows like moving pictures to rise and fall on the walls.

"You remind me of a Botticelli painting when your hair is down like that," says Auggie.

My heart suddenly beats a little faster.

"Come lie down and I'll give you a brain massage." He plops down on the bed and invites me to do the same.

"A *what*?"

"It's how people in Russia cure headaches when they don't have any medicine. But you don't need to have a headache. It just feels really good."

His gentle smile is full of possibility and pleasure. The little voice inside my head says, "Put on your clothes and go home." Only I feel more relaxed than I have in a long time, possibly ever, and so I lie down on the bed and my towel falls away. It no longer matters that we're naked, because I'm imagining that we live on a commune and at dawn we'll venture out to roam the fields gathering wheat and berries.

Auggie leans against the backboard and places a pillow across his knees so that when I lie down my head is in his lap. The tin knights and papier-mâché masks hanging on the walls shimmer with firelight, and I feel that they're trying to tell me a story with Auggie's CD as the sound track. Trumpets blare with fat fullness, combined with group vocals, and merry flute solos are bombarded by big brass riffs.

Auggie's fingers massage my temples, and I close my eyes.

"What's this music?" I ask.

" 'Quizas, Quizas,'" says Auggie. "That means 'Perhaps, Perhaps.' It's a bolero cha. Bolero is the name for the great Cuban ballad, and 'cha' is added to the end as a way of saying it's got a little more rhythm—a little more cha-cha-cha."

A sinking feeling washes over me, and I drift back and forth across the borders of consciousness. Auggie delicately moves the tops of his fingers down my cheeks and onto my neck. A little part of me wakes up again. He lifts my arms until they're touching his and then takes my hands and slides down next to me.

Facing me with our noses an inch apart, he softly says, "Hello."

"You've cast some sort of spell over me, haven't you?"

"It's the organic conditioner."

Auggie touches his lips to mine and though it's incredibly delicate, his kiss burns into my entire body and rouses me from a long slumber. For the first time since Dad has been gone I want something.

My brain is no longer sending full messages, just a sort of code or possibly spam—Auggie is smooth where Craig isn't . . . must stop thinking about Craig . . . shouldn't make love with Auggie . . . leaves in morning . . . we'll just kiss . . . kissing is nice. Across the black canvas of my closed eyes flashes a snapshot of Bernard helping himself to an enormous piece of homemade lemon meringue pie while happily declaring, "I feel a sin coming on!"

Auggie stops kissing and I think he's going to press himself close up against me, but instead he moves his mouth down, down, down. He pays attention to me in some interesting places along the way, which is strange at first, but slowly becomes okay. For a moment my heart falls into my stomach and continues to beat there, until suddenly a roaring hurricane of desire wells up in my chest and I hear the click of the night-table drawer. Barely a moment later Auggie is inside of me. It's as if the entire night were foreplay leading up to this single moment. There's a rush of delight followed by a tingling sense of pleasure, and when I finally shout out, I'm not embarrassed. It seems like it's part of the music.

Auggie rises to go to the bathroom and when he returns we don't curl up together but lie next to each other with just our hands touching. I shut my eyes with a deep luxurious sigh. In my dreams gardens of roses bloom, children laugh, and strong arms hold me safe.

SEVENTY-ONE

I CONTINUE TO SMELL ROSES EVEN AFTER I'M PRETTY SURE THAT I've woken up, though their heavy perfume makes me wonder if I'm still dreaming, or else just dead.

Upon opening my eyes, I find that the bed is blanketed in the petals of yellow, magenta, and orange roses. I'm alone and the room is quiet. A note on the night table says, "Had to leave early to make orientation. Didn't want to wake you—you look so beautiful." There's the letter A with a little heart drawn next to it. And next to the note is the bottle of conditioner that Auggie had used on my hair.

Okay, what just happened? I ask myself. Self slowly answers, *I think it was a terrific one-night stand.* It would appear that love and luck both struck unexpectedly, thrust me into a state of euphoria, and then burned off like the morning fog.

My dress is neatly laid out on the table. After putting my clothes on I strategize the best way to reach my car without running into Cappy—whether to make a run for it, or to move slowly, staying low and close to the walls. The dress and shoes cast the sprint in a dangerous light and so I hunch over as I walk briskly, leap into the driver's seat, and head down the driveway without seeing anyone at all.

The next problem is entering my house while looking like I spent the night at the no-tell motel. I briefly consider climbing up the tree that hangs over the roof and going through Teddy and Davy's window. That still doesn't solve the problem of where my car was parked all night. I finally decide there's no alternative but to use the front door, turn myself in, and throw myself at the mercy of the court.

Mom rushes out of the kitchen when she hears the front door open. "I just phoned the Stocktons', but they hadn't seen you since yesterday afternoon." She looks more than a little worried. "I-I didn't know you were going to be gone all night."

"Neither did I." I stare down at Louise's shoes. "Sorry. I thought to call, but by that time it was already late and I didn't want to wake you." It's an old excuse and a lousy one, but nothing else comes to mind.

"So long as you weren't in an accident."

More like a group shampoo.

Surprisingly, Mom hugs me close. "Mmmm. Your hair smells wonderful. And it's so soft!"

I show her the bottle of conditioner.

Mom glances at the label, though I think she's more interested in what kind of night out involves getting your hair done.

"A friend was going back to school and we went to Cleveland and then slept at their house." I'm extremely careful with the pronouns.

"You should consider going back to school, too," says Mom. "We'll manage to get by."

Only it's not just about money. Mom is interactive and user-friendly these days, but she doesn't run the house and keep track of all the kids' schedules. However, I don't want to say anything that makes it sound as if she's not fully recovered or can't handle the family the same way that she used to.

"Pastor Costello thinks he can get you a church scholarship," adds Mom.

"Please, Mom, I'm not going to study to be a minister or a missionary."

"You can stay with your graphic design. No strings attached!"

"That's very nice, but you know that I wouldn't even be *going* to church if I wasn't taking the kids."

Mom nods her head as if this is where she figured the conversation would end up. "I've been meaning to ask you if you want any counseling," says Mom, heading in a slightly different direction.

"*What?*"

"Counseling. You know, the kids have it available to them at school and Eric at college and I . . ."

We both realize there's no need for a review of Mom's period of intensive therapy.

"Thanks, but I'm going to be fine," I say. I don't mean one hundred percent, but as of this morning, for the first time I actually believe that at some point I might just be okay after all.

SEVENTY-TWO

"WHERE HAVE ALL THE WINTER SWEATERS GONE?" MY MOTHER asks from inside Francie and Lillian's closet.

I'm going through their drawers to inventory socks and underwear. "Maybe they never made it back up from the laundry room last spring."

"I used to keep them all in a box up here," says my mother. "I don't know what happened."

What happened is that Dad died and you had a nervous breakdown. However, I don't say this. "I'm sure I can find some inexpensive ones at the factory outlet store in Timpany."

The first few days of September pass in a flurry of organizing the kids to start school. Lillian has another year to go before kindergarten and so a popular refrain for things that don't meet Darlene's style standards or Francie's tomboy requirements are, "Save it for Lillian." The boys tend to ruin most of their clothes, and even with Mom's constant patching there's not much to pass on. Their discards are mostly slated to become cleaning rags, and when those get enough holes Mom turns them into rag rugs.

Louise has given up cheerleading for good, lost her fascination with science, and now wants to become a social studies teacher. Mom is happy to see that Louise has college applications scattered about.

As for me, my nineteenth birthday turns out to be very much like my ninth, with the family gathered around the table eating mom's homemade lasagna. Pink-and-white streamers running from the wall clock to the light fixture are up and the HAPPY BIRTHDAY sign is strung in its usual spot just below the black metal plaque with GRACE etched onto it in gold letters.

The only difference is that Dad isn't here to place his hand over mine and guide the knife while making the first good-luck slice into the chocolate birthday cake. And Pastor Costello adds a round of "May the Good Lord Bless You," to the usual "Happy Birthday," which causes the candles to burn down extremely close to the cake. As always, Mom instructs me to "make a wish" before finally blowing them out.

But I don't wish for anything. Life appears to have plenty of its own ideas, and at this point I'm just clinging to my little raft. My own loneliness seems necessary somehow, like the tiny knots on a necklace that keep the pearls in place.

SEVENTY-THREE

BERNARD IS PLOTTING A GARDEN FOR NEXT SPRING WITH A
Moulin Rouge theme and the bulbs have to be planted before
the ground freezes. He's discovered a tulip called Carnaval de
Nice that has white petals flamed with dark red, which is serving as his inspiration. This is welcome news as it signals he's
wearing down on the Chinese culture program. Because I know
that the rest of us are. Particularly the CD of the Beijing Opera.
For one thing, the word *shrill* comes to mind. Bernard insists
that it's an acquired taste, much like chiffon.

Rose has started preschool, but Gigi still has another year at
home, and so she and Lillian and Rocky play together while
Bernard works on his Web site and newsletter. My mom says she
doesn't believe in preschool, though what I think she actually
means is that she doesn't believe in *paying* for preschool.

I must say that I'm not surprised to pull up one October
morning and see a glint of blue move behind the bushes, peacock blue to be exact. Sure enough, a closer inspection reveals
four peacocks strutting about, with Rocky and Gigi following at
a safe distance to observe the exotic creatures.

Inside the house Olivia, Bernard, Gil, and Ottavio are all
gathered around the dining room table. Gil explains that he's

taken the day off to prepare for his new play. Stacked in front of him are a dozen books open to various pages. Bernard is working over some plans to convert the basement into a playroom. Ottavio talks about building a shelter for the peacocks near the rabbit hutch.

"Are the peacocks supposed to save on fertilizer?" I ask.

"You'll never believe where they came from!" Bernard sounds like he's on his tenth cup of coffee. "Your friend Cappy called me the other day to see if I wanted to buy a crèche. Anyway, as I was leaving I heard the most unusual sound, like a cry for help. And Cappy said, 'Those are peacocks. They bring me a tremendous amount of good luck, but my fiancée doesn't like them. I suppose I don't have to tell you that peacocks are considered to be sacred in China.' "

"Of course I'm aware of that!" Bernard is positively self-congratulatory as he says, "I told Cappy they were an emblem of the Ming Dynasty and the peacock feather was awarded to show imperial favor and high rank. I immediately offered to buy them and said that we have a Chinese tea garden so the peacocks would be incredibly contented living here."

It's apparent that Bernard believes *he* talked Cappy into parting with his unbeloved birds. Cappy says that no one appreciates a gift nearly as much as they welcome paying for the pleasure of being swindled. I can't help but smile as I picture Cappy playing Bernard like a violin while Bernard considers himself to be the master wheeler-dealer.

One of the peacocks lets out its signature *help* and Gil says, "If they're so happy here, then how come they keep screeching like that?"

"They're adjusting," says Bernard.

Gil looks doubtful. "I think you got flimflammed by a bird trader," says the man who grew up on a famous horse farm.

"Why don't you do something by Samuel Beckett?" suggests

Olivia, who has been paging through one of Gil's books of plays.

"I think a few more people were counting on landing parts," says Gil. "I never thought anyone cared about these little community theater productions, but when there wasn't a play this past spring everyone called wanting to know what happened."

"Didn't the Moose Lodge put on a variety show?" asks Olivia.

"Hardly anyone went," reports Gil.

Bernard pretends to be aghast. "You mean they missed old Mr. Exner playing the washtub and Brenda Kolatch clog dancing?" Bernard places his hand on his chest and dramatically exclaims, "My heart be still!"

"Luigi Pirandello," suggests Ottavio. He's like having a representative of the Italian tourist board on hand, always promoting things from his home country.

"Not if they're recovering from a variety show, darling." Olivia gently places her hand on his arm. "I don't think Gil is after *more* realism so much as an escape from reality altogether."

"What about *The Sound of Music*," Bernard says enthusiastically. "We can use all the children. Rose would be adorable as Gretl."

"And you'll star in the role of stage mother?" asks Gil.

"Then how about *Mame*?" Bernard begins singing the title song. " '*You coax the blues right out of the horn, Mame . . .*' "

"Are you auditioning for the lead?" asks Gil.

"Of course not," says Bernard. "I'll just be the understudy."

"Try again," says Gil.

"You've never done Tennessee Williams's *Cat on a Hot Tin Roof.*"

Gil rolls his eyes because the play involves alcoholism and homosexuality.

"We can do a double feature with *The Roman Spring of Mrs. Stone*," suggests Bernard.

"Isn't that the one where the old actress moves to Italy and dates young gigolos?" I ask.

"Yes," says Bernard. "Mother would be perfect for the lead. Don't you think?"

Olivia ignores him and says, "How about *Rutherford and Son*?"

"Never heard of it," says Gil.

"It's by a British woman named Githa Sowerby. The play premiered to excellent notices back in 1912 and was never heard from again. It's not included in anthologies because women's work was ignored until recently. The story revolves around a family business and the patriarch's ruthless attempts to sustain it. This leads to the psychic and moral destruction of everyone involved."

Gil doesn't appear very keen, but he's always polite, and says, "If you have a copy, I'll take a look."

Bernard sniffs. "It sounds more like some socialist tract written back in the days when British industry was buckling as a result of competition from the United States."

"It doesn't hurt for people to be reminded that capitalism comes at some expense," admonishes Olivia.

Gil stops in the middle of one book and says, "What about *Our Town*?"

Bernard uses a nearby linen napkin to strangle himself. "*Our Town?*" he chokes out, as if Gil has just suggested featuring a beheading on the stage rather than a show. "There are no accents, no tragic southern belles, no nervous disorders, and worst of all—no big tap number!"

"We *never* have a big tap number," interjects Gil. "The stage is too small."

"There isn't so much as a feather boa!" Bernard is now lying prostrate on the dining room floor waving his napkin in the air like a distress flag.

Olivia appears enthusiastic. "A good production should provide a sense of the rhythm of our own life as it touches those around us."

"*Life?*" moans Bernard. "It's about *death*!"

SEVENTY-FOUR

IT'S TWO IN THE AFTERNOON AND I'M PREPARING A SNACK FOR THE kids while my mother sips her tea at the kitchen table.

"We received the most unusual postcard," she says, and hands me the piece of mail in question.

There's a picture of a woman in a bikini on the front and at the bottom of the reverse side are the initials U.L.

"Uncle Lenny!" The postmark reads St. Lucia, wherever that is. "Remember, I told you how he stayed with us while you were away?" Though I certainly didn't tell Mom *all* the details.

"Oh, right—one of your dad's crazy twin sailor uncles," she says. "He's the one who got the cat."

"That's Uncle Lenny," I say.

"What do you think it *means*?" she says.

I study Uncle Lenny's scrawl on the back of the postcard: "50 miles out and down with high fever. Coma. Left for dead in deep freeze with 80-pound blue fin tuna. Awoke cold but cured. How the mates were surprised when Charley the Tuna started pounding on the hatch!"

"I'm sure it's just another one of his wild stories," I say. On the other hand, you could never be sure with Uncle Lenny.

"Do you know what the leading cause of death is for women aged twenty-five through forty?" Mom asks.

"Stroke?" I guess as I stack peanut-butter-and-jelly triangles onto a plate.

"No. Halloween."

I can't believe that Mom actually told a joke. On the other hand, the dire look on her face doesn't indicate that she means it as a joke.

Admittedly, organizing the kids and all their costumes for school this morning was a bit hectic. Especially because Davy's lion tail kept falling off, though I haven't ruled out that Francie was yanking on it. That would have been when she wasn't whacking us all over the head with her plastic machete, which was not as light a grade of plastic as it could have been. And Darlene's tiara wouldn't stay on no matter how many bobby pins I jammed into her hair.

Then there's the candy corn that's stuck in all their pockets, and melted onto the clothes in the dryer. The kids love the stuff, especially making fangs on their teeth and sticking it up their nostrils. Sorry, but give me chocolate anytime. As far as I'm concerned, candy corn is the fruitcake of Halloween—it tastes disgusting, lasts forever, and the best thing you can do is find someone to give it to.

Pastor Costello is off visiting a church member in the hospital, Louise is at her SAT prep course, and so it's just Mom and me in charge of preparing the troops for trick-or-treating.

"It won't be that bad," I assure her. "I'll take them around the neighborhood while you stay here and give out the candy."

"The temperature is dropping fast. They're going to have to wear coats," she says ominously.

"I'll put their coats on," I say like a cockeyed optimist.

My mother gives me a look that indicates I obviously have

no memory of what it's like to put a coat on a child wearing a Halloween costume.

Lillian races into the room half in and half out of her witch costume, following a nap that lasted all of five minutes. Not having experienced the thrill of a school party, she's raring to go.

When the kids arrive home, it's obvious that they've already had *way* too much sugar—their voices are shrill and they run helter-skelter through the house searching for their buckets. Francie's machete was taken away at school and apparently the teacher "forgot" to give it back. Darlene's tiara is in two pieces and the bottom of her dress is torn from tripping over it in high-heeled plastic slippers.

Davy's the real winner. His lion got in a fight with a bear and is torn from top to bottom. The costume is ruined, and I have to go down to the basement to look for something left over from last year. After much searching I find a suit for Batman's crime-fighting partner Robin.

When I come back upstairs, Teddy is making scorch marks on the walls as he burns a cork to blacken his face for his hobo costume.

"Aren't you a little old for trick-or-treating?"

He scowls at me. "I'm going to a party."

"Sounds like a kissing party," I say in a teasing voice.

"Shut up!"

I make kissing sounds in his ear and he ducks to get away from me.

Darlene starts wailing in the other room. When I go into the living room her coat is on the floor and she's stomping on it while screeching that her costume will be ruined.

"No it won't, sweetie." I pick up the coat. "Everyone will know you're a princess because you're carrying a magic wand." I don't mention the tiara because it's being held together with tinfoil and ready to fall off again. Or the fairy princess slippers that have to be replaced with boots now that a light snow is beginning to fall.

Davy begins yelling when he sees the Robin costume I brought up from the basement.

Mom looks as if she's about to start sobbing and sits down on the couch with a faraway look in her eyes.

I go into the kitchen and grab Teddy, who is now dressed in oversized clothes, carrying a bandanna on a stick, and exiting through the back door.

"Help me!" I plead with him. "Or else Mom is going to have another nervous breakdown."

That gets his attention. Teddy goes in and looks at the mess—kids crying, fur and fairy dust everywhere. Fortunately Teddy, who has recently become an official teenager, is now viewed as a God by the little kids, whereas I am an official grown-up pain in the neck, someone to be avoided at all costs, being that I cause misery in their young lives by serving vegetables and insisting on baths and bedtimes.

They gaze up worshipfully at Teddy in his hobo outfit, which looks pretty good.

"Why do you guys want to go in those stupid little-kid costumes?" he asks. "If you want I'll make you into bums like me."

The kids are very enthusiastic. Mom appears relieved.

"Great, what do we do?" I ask.

"I'm afraid we'll have to raid Dad's closet," says Teddy.

"Mom, can we use some of Dad's things?" I ask.

"Sure," she says. "I was just going to box it up for the church after Eric takes whatever he can use."

I put a few layers of regular clothes on the kids and then we add one of Dad's jackets with the sleeves rolled up. For the bottoms we cut the legs short on his pants and tie the waists with twine. Teddy makes hobo sacks out of red-and-white dish towels and darkens their faces with cork. The overall effect is superb and Mom even gets out the camera to take a photo, the first one since she's been home.

Bernard arrives at half past five with his girls. There are only eight houses in their neighborhood, so I told them to come trick-or-treating over here after they finished. Gigi is dressed as a hippie and Rose is a little bumblebee. I think they're adorable, but Bernard is still recovering from the fact that his idea for their going as Joan and Jackie Collins was firmly rejected.

SEVENTY-FIVE

On SUNDAY MORNING I DRIVE OVER TO THE COMMUNITY THE-
ater in order to work on the scenery for *Our Town*. The Palace
was built as a movie house back in the 1920s. The façade is covered with large black and white tiles arranged to form an elaborate diamond pattern around three sets of chrome double doors
that look as if they were ripped off an airplane. A triangular
marquee juts out over the pavement above the ticket booth, a
pillar on each side, and backlit silver stars encased in bricks of
glass make up the lobby floor. In the early 1980s, after people
started driving to the multiplex cinemas at the mall in Timpany,
the movie theater slowly went bankrupt. Finally the Town Council took over the property and had it refurbished as a venue for
special events.

The theater was still empty most of the time, so Gil worked
out a deal where he doesn't pay rent but gives half the ticket
sales toward upkeep. And thus were born the Cosgrove Community Players.

Louise has offered to help me with the scenery and shows up
at exactly ten o'clock. She'll do anything to get out of church.
However, I'm pleased to have another painter, at least until I

discover that Louise has been working on the same six inches of soda shop background for the past hour.

"Impressionism was created to save set designers a lot of work." I take the brush and demonstrate.

Louise sits back and appears happy to let me continue.

"So what's going on with you and Brandt?" I ask.

"I don't know," says Louise.

"Are you still going out with him?"

"I guess so," says Louise.

"You don't sound very enthusiastic about it," I say.

"It's just kind of boring," she says.

"You mean the abstinence thing?" I ask.

Louise looks up sharply.

"Brandt told me about it when he declared that you were his soul mate."

"He works and studies most of the time, and what they call a party is a bunch of guys making organic chemistry jokes and talking about what happened in the lab. We're supposed to do this for the next five years and then get married and, I don't know, have kids, I guess."

"Wow. You've got it all planned out."

"Yeah. I'm sixteen and it feels as if my life is already over."

It's quiet in the back except for the sound of the narrator speaking a few hundred feet away on the stage.

"Think you'll get back together with Craig?" asks Louise.

"He's with Megan now."

My name is being called from the auditorium, and suddenly Gil is standing above us, rather harried and with his script flapping around. "Hallie, please fill in for Paula—she's out sick *again.*"

"And stay up until midnight painting your backdrops?" I reply. "No thanks. Get Bernard. He loves to read."

I turn to Louise and say, "Bernard was doing the lighting for a college production of *Guys and Dolls,* and after he performed "Adelaide's Lament" while the pianist was warming up, the director shouted, "Put Bernard in the dress and let *him* do the part."

"Bernard is working on the costumes and in quite a *mood,*" says Gil. "Apparently a few of the cast members were overly conservative when e-mailing their measurements."

Gil's eyes fall on Louise. "Let me borrow you for Emily. In fact, you're exactly the right age."

"I don't know anything about acting," says Louise.

Gil guides her off and a moment later I hear, "Okay everybody, Act One, page thirty, Mrs. Webb and Emily are on stage next to the trellis. Emily, please begin with 'Mama, will you answer me a question.' "

Normally I block out whatever is happening on stage, because they end up repeating the lines a million times and it drives me crazy. But I listen now because it's funny to hear Louise's familiar voice.

"Mama, will you answer me a question, serious?" asks Louise as Emily.

A woman replies, "Seriously, dear—not serious."

"Mama, am I good-looking?" asks Emily.

"Yes, of course you are," says the woman.

I stop what I'm doing and walk around to the back of the auditorium. Bernard and Gil are obviously having a similar epiphany as their eyes are fixed upon Louise, dressed in acid-washed jeans and a fitted T-shirt, but nonetheless poised, glamorous, and exuding star quality.

Heading back to my scenery I have a sneaking suspicion that we won't be hearing the name Paula Malone again anytime soon.

SEVENTY-SIX

By the first of November I'm finishing up with the yard. After a solid week of raking, the house and garage are no longer engulfed by a tidal wave of dead leaves. It's not so pleasant to be outside anymore with sharp gusts of wind from the east and low, slate-gray skies that are nature's version of a hangover.

With not much left to do, I decide to set up the little greenhouse, which we've basically ignored for the past two years. Only when I go into the shed to see if that stack of small clay pots is still tucked away in the back corner I discover that the lawn mower is gone.

I can tell from all the cars with their engines waiting out front that Bernard is finishing up one of his Girl Scout meetings, and so I go inside to see if he knows anything about the missing mower.

Troop Bernard is gathered in the living room, and he's announcing that the next three meetings will be dedicated to holiday meals, music, and traditions. "Everyone wear skirts next week in order to practice sitting down properly."

Bernard points to his one boy participant and says, "Andrew, you'll of course wear a suit." This comes out not so much as reminder than a polite note of caution. The girls giggle and Bernard chastises them, "Wait and see, you'll all be fighting over Andrew soon enough." Though if it will be as best friend, emergency date, extra man, or future interior decorator, Bernard doesn't make clear. "And on Saturday night everyone is welcome to come over and learn how to make cranapple pie and watch Grace Kelly in *High Society.*"

The kids pack their bags and put on their coats. However, Bernard suddenly claps his hands as if he's forgotten something important. "And ladies, how long should our skirts be?"

"Knee length," one girl offers, though there's a note of uncertainty in her voice.

"Anyone else?" asks Bernard.

Andrew raises his hand.

"Please proceed to enlighten us, Andrew," says Bernard.

"Long enough to cover the parts but short enough to keep it interesting," the boy states with conviction.

"Well done," says Bernard. "Forget what all the magazines are showing and work *with* your natural figure, not *against* it."

Following Bernard into the kitchen I ask him, "What's the story with Andrew? Is he an F.O.B.?" That's our code for Friend of Bernard.

"I'd hazard to say more of a B.I.T.—Bernard in Training. With the way the world is these days, a little more gaiety might be just the thing."

"You didn't by any chance borrow the lawn mower to use it as a centerpiece or something?" I ask. "I'd hate to think that I misplaced it."

"Ottavio must have taken it into town," says Bernard. "He has so many speeding tickets that they finally suspended his license."

I guess I'm not surprised by this news. The only driving laws that Ottavio seems to follow are the laws of physics.

"So these girls don't mind that you've hijacked their Girl Scout troop and turned it into some sort 1950s cooking and etiquette class?"

"There's now a waiting list to get in. Although one child's grandmother pays her twenty dollars for every meeting she attends. *Grand-mère* feels it's a bargain for finishing school."

"But aren't they supposed to learn how to tie knots and survive in the woods?"

"I think flower arranging comes in handy considerably more than *knot tying*. Why, when I took the poor creatures under my wing, they couldn't tell the difference between silver and silver plate! And I hardly think they'll need to know how to find what side of a tree moss is growing on so much as when to use oregano versus paprika."

Olivia enters the kitchen from her den and says, "I see that Bernard is describing some of the new badges he's added to the scouting curriculum."

"But aren't there existing guidelines?" I ask.

"Scouting is very much up for interpretation," says Bernard. "Just look at Robert Baden-Powell, the founder of the Boy Scouts. He specialized in putting on Gilbert and Sullivan operettas, loved playing women's roles on the stage, for which he made his own dresses, and designed embroidery patterns for the wives of army officers."

"You've forgotten the most important thing, Bernard," says Olivia.

"That he was an early fan of scented soap and enjoyed choosing fabrics and furnishings?"

"No, silly." Olivia places her hand on Bernard's arm. "He gave his mother the credit for all of his success!"

"Very funny, Mother," says Bernard and carefully lifts her hand off his arm. "Now if you'll excuse me, I have to work on the Thanksgiving menu."

"Oh Bernard, please don't have a turkey this year," says Olivia. "Poultry animals are excluded from the humane slaughter laws."

"Not to worry, Mother," says Bernard. "We'll have plenty of vegetarian dishes for you and *your kind.*"

"That's not the point," Olivia states firmly. "Massive animal factories produce those turkeys. Thousands of them are crammed together in a single shed with less than three square feet of space apiece."

Bernard flees toward the basement with Olivia shouting after him, "Gandhi said a nation's progress can be judged by how they treat their animals!"

"Well, I say that if you eat too many natural foods, then you'll soon die of natural causes!" he calls up the stairs.

SEVENTY-SEVEN

THE THIRD WEEK IN NOVEMBER ERIC ARRIVES HOME WITH HIS girlfriend, Elizabeth, for Thanksgiving. After great hesitation, Mom has finally accepted the invitation to dinner at the Stocktons'. Now that the basement playroom is finished, Bernard is planning to have a separate table for the children down there.

When all twelve of us pour through the Stocktons' front door, the scene is not unlike opening day at a Six Flags amusement park. Because dinner isn't until half past five, Pastor Costello joins us after he finishes presiding over the church supper in the early afternoon. Bernard has organized it so that my mother and Pastor Costello will sit in the dining room with the grown-ups while he and I take charge of the basement.

The new playroom is an explosion of Hello Kitty, from the wall coverings, beanbag chairs, and throw pillows, right down to the toilet seat and tissue holder in the bathroom. Bernard's plan for a more Chinese feel of "pastels and peonies" was heavily vetoed, though he claims that Hello Kitty still counts as Asian culture because it's originally a Japanese design. Yeah, and Euro-Disney is French.

Once all the kids are gathered in the basement it's a madhouse. My little brothers and sisters are faced with a whole new array of toys, while Rose and little Gigi have a fresh set of rambunctious playmates.

"Don't worry, it's all childproof," Bernard reassures me.

"Oh really." I point to where Francie is climbing the side of the hot water tank. "Including that?"

"Whoa!" Bernard races over and gently brings her back down to the floor.

Bernard has set a nice table for the kids with ceramic turkeys as centerpieces, and we serve from warming trays plugged in underneath the stairs.

The kids dive into their turkey, as they can't wait to get back to Bernard's indoor jungle gym complete with a slide. Just as they're finishing up, Gil calls down the stairs, "Pastor Costello will be there to say grace in just a minute."

Bernard and I look at each other as if to say, Oops!

I run up the stairs and fetch the baby walkie-talkies. Placing one on the dining room table I tell Pastor Costello that he can just say one grace and we'll listen from downstairs. That way his food won't get cold.

"Ah, like we put the speakers in the narthex on Christmas Eve." He nods approvingly. Anything to help spread the word more efficiently is viewed as a welcome innovation.

When I arrive back downstairs, Pastor Costello launches into how thankful we should be. There are two pauses when I think he's finally finished, but it turns out he's just catching his breath. If this were an award show, the band would have started playing him off a while ago.

Finally Pastor Costello concludes by saying, "We make a living by what we earn, but we make a life by what we give. Amen."

Through the intercom I'm pretty sure that I hear Olivia conclude with, "Ah-women."

Bernard says, "I'm impressed—Winston Churchill."

"What?" I say.

"We make a living by what we earn but we make a life by what we give."

"I just assumed it was Jesus."

Now that the kids are done, we fill our plates. Bernard's food is a real treat. He's made pumpkin dip with pita toast, mushroom bisque, arugula and goat cheese salad, sausage and sage stuffing, maple-glazed butternut squash, baked leeks in mustard cream, mashed potatoes with roasted garlic and fresh horseradish, and, there's no escaping it, Chinese eggplant purée on daikon rounds. There's also a vegetarian dressing of apple and walnut for Olivia and any other vegetarians, though I don't know what she's supposed to dress since she doesn't eat turkey. We're just lucky she hasn't started in with her description of how faster assembly lines cause more fecal material to get on the carcasses and so thirty-six percent of turkeys are infected with salmonella.

When Olivia attempted to feel out Pastor Costello for his views on the unnecessary slaughter of animals, he happily replied, "I love all of God's creatures, especially with mashed potatoes."

I wouldn't have thought that Pastor Costello would be such a hit as a dinner guest, but when I go upstairs to the kitchen, more often than not he's telling a story and everybody around the table is laughing like crazy. At one point Bernard and I happen to be listening in on the baby walkie-talkie while Pastor Costello is speaking, obviously after enjoying more than a communion portion of wine. This story is about how he did a funeral where the deceased fancied himself quite the woodworker and made his own coffin, only to have the bottom fall out as the pallbearers carried it out of the church. Everyone upstairs erupts into gales of laughter. Bernard is splitting his sides as well, though I think it's more from Pastor Costello's use of the word *folderol* and describing the body and casket as "the whole shebang."

Bernard tells me about a funeral he recently attended for one of his customers, an avid collector of Art Nouveau ashtrays, who died at age ninety-nine and was a chain smoker since the age of fifteen. "Guess what music her children had played after the service?" he asks.

"'Memories'?" I guess.

"No," says Bernard. " 'When Smoke Gets in Your Eyes!' " He pounds the table as he laughs at the thought of it.

Finally we bundle the kids up against the cold and head for home. Thanksgiving worked out okay, and I wasn't constantly imagining Dad standing at the head of the table carving the turkey. It's Christmas that I'm really dreading.

SEVENTY-EIGHT

To the kids, Thanksgiving being over means one thing and one thing only—Santa will be here soon.

"How long until Santa comes?" Lillian asks first thing the following morning.

"A month," I say.

"What's a month?"

I sit down with the younger kids and we write letters to Santa. Lillian draws a picture of herself surrounded by dolls. According to the rest of the letters, this past year I've had the pleasure of living with model children, i.e., *Santa, I have been very very good!*

"Since Santa knows everything, don't you think an honest appraisal would be better rewarded?" I ask them. "What if Santa calls and asks me if you've been good *all* the time? I just don't think I could lie to him."

They all take back their letters and add a postscript in tiny letters saying that they've been bad sometimes.

"But there's a middle category," announces Francie. "Right, Hallie? It's not *just* naughty or nice."

"Let me say that I have known children to be very far down

on the nice list at the beginning of December and by Christmas Eve they were at the top. So yes, there's still plenty of time to be good, if that's what you're wondering."

"What are you asking Santa for?" Francie peers over at Darlene's letter.

Darlene covers her letter with her arm. "You're not fupposed to tell, other than when you whithper it into Fanta's ear."

"Just remember what I said about the twins," I remind them all.

"There were lotth of twinth born thif year and tho we can only athk for one thing a piece," recites Darlene.

"That's right. If you ask for more than one thing, Santa won't have enough gifts and somewhere a child won't get a present."

Davy says, "I don't believe in Santa anymore."

"Don't be stupid," says Francie. "Uncle Lenny is Santa. That's why he left—to go back to the North Pole and make toys for Christmas."

"Once there was a boy in my class who didn't believe in Santa," I say. "But I'd rather not tell you about him since the story has a very sad ending."

"What happened?" Darlene and Francie both demand to know.

"Well . . . he woke up in the morning and there were lots of presents for his brothers and sisters but none for him."

"I was just kidding," says Davy.

"You were not!" says Francie. "Santa is going to *know*."

Davy frowns and appears worried.

"No, he won't, because he'll get Davy's letter." I scoop up the correspondence addressed to the North Pole for "mailing."

Together we choose a tree from the lot at the edge of town and set it up in the usual place in the living room. Then on Sunday after church the kids string colored popcorn and cranberries to decorate it and add the various handmade ornaments that have accumulated over the years. There's a tendency to eat more popcorn than we string, and most of the cranberries are used for wars. Meanwhile, the cat becomes infatuated with a snowball made out of tinfoil and knocks the entire tree over while attempting to play with it. The kids scream and I hoist the pine tree back into place.

I decide against the outdoor lights this year. They'll only make the electric bill go sky high. And the neighbors appear to have us covered. It's like the arms race out there—the Lochlans installed a sleigh with reindeer on the roof while the Kozlowskis have what must be the entire North Pole on their front lawn, complete with a sound track of toys being hammered and elves (actually the Seven Dwarfs) singing "Whistle While You Work." A pilot would be hard pressed to tell the difference between the Kozlowskis' yard and the municipal airport a few miles away.

SEVENTY-NINE

G IL WAS CERTAINLY RIGHT ABOUT EVERYBODY COMING TO SEE
Our Town. On opening night I'm backstage adjusting the scenery as the house fills up.

While Louise worries about her makeup, I worry that since
the Catholic Youth Organization has started rehearsing their
Christmas pageant here, the little town of Bethlehem is going
to suddenly drop down onstage, rather than Grover's Corners.

I'm straightening the map for the opening scene when I feel
a hand on my shoulder and turn around. Bernard is in his
tuxedo.

"You look like a groom!" I say.

"Bride or stable?" he asks.

I'm in my denim stagehand overalls, and Gil is wearing his
director's outfit of a black turtleneck with black wool slacks.
The stage manager shouts for everyone to take their places and
the houselights dim.

"There isn't one empty seat," I tell him excitedly.

"That doesn't change the fact that it's *Our Town,*" says
Bernard. "The theater is supposed to help us *escape!*"

"But practically the whole town is here," I say.

"Of course they are," Bernard says grimly, "it's about the horrible pointless lives of people in a small town."

Bernard wishes us all luck and heads out to his place in the audience. He likes to sit in the last row so that he can see how the costumes work from far back.

The orchestra strikes up and the audience falls silent. The curtain rises and the Narrator begins his speech about the predictable rhythms of the town. That's when I spot Mr. Phillips fumbling around near the props. Mr. Phillips plays the drunk choir director Simon Stimson, and he's been getting more convincing with every rehearsal, to the point that tonight I could actually smell whiskey on his breath. Suddenly he trips and sends the baby Jesus, which has a skateboard as its base, flying out onto the stage.

Fortunately the Narrator is on his toes, literally, and stops the skidding baby Jesus by extending his boot and, without missing a beat, continues, "Right here's a big butternut tree, and over here is the baby Jesus from the annual Christmas pageant put on by the CYO." Then he goes right back to the script, talking about how no one remarkable has ever come out of the town. It's such a masterful transition that at least a few audience members must think it was part of the play.

Peeking out into the audience during intermission I spy Craig along with some local guys. Great, we've both become townies. Only, damn he looks good. His wavy butterscotch hair is down past his ears, and he's laughing good-naturedly at something one of the guys must have just said. Well, at least he's not with that tart Megan.

I don't get many compliments on the scenery because it's pretty minimal, but Bernard and Gil insist that the sets work perfectly. Louise, on the other hand, receives a standing ovation, and guys in the audience release ear-piercing whistles when she walks out onstage to take a bow.

EIGHTY

THE SANTA FRENZY AT MY HOUSE IS APPROACHING ITS ZENITH, with the consumption of sugar adding to the tumult. Traditionally the Christmas Eve festivities include smearing cookies with red and green icing, most of which goes directly from the bowls to the kids' mouths.

It takes ten stories to get them into bed, forget about falling asleep. Teddy finally comes to the rescue by announcing: "Santa cannot come if you're awake. It's the law. He'll fly right over this house."

Pastor Costello and I clean up the baking mess and remove Santa's snack from the mantelpiece so the cat doesn't get it. After Mom double-checks to make sure the kids are finally asleep, or at least faking it really well, we sneak the presents out from the garbage cans behind the furnace and arrange them around the tree. It's not as big a pile as in previous years, but there are two things for everyone. Pastor Costello brought a few dolls and matchbox cars over yesterday, and whether they were left over from the church toy drive or he went out and bought them, I'd rather not know.

Louise goes downstairs to watch all the holiday specials we

were deprived of as children without cable TV. She gives her usual nighttime sign-off, "May the force be with you."

"And also with you," Pastor Costello answers reflexively, as if it's part of the Christian liturgy.

"Don't stay up too late," Mom cautions Louise. "There's no going back to sleep once they're awake!"

It's a quarter past ten and I say good night as well. If history teaches us anything, it's that tomorrow is going to be a *very* early morning. Once in bed I can't help but replay Christmases past, and the excitement of being a little kid, having the hiccups eight times in one night. I'm half asleep when I remember the fire in the fireplace. We hardly use it since more heat is siphoned out of the house than put into it, but Mom always loves a fire on Christmas Eve. Certainly she'll make sure it's out. But what if when Pastor Costello leaves for midnight mass she walks him to the door and forgets? I imagine the entire house going up in flames, kids trapped upstairs, presents burning, cat forever lost in the woods.

I traipse back downstairs to make sure the fire is out. Mom and Pastor Costello are sitting on the couch in the soft glow of the tree and watching the dying embers.

"I was just checking to make sure—"

And that's when I see it. They're holding hands.

"Oh my God! What are you doing?" I practically shout.

Pastor Costello leaps up, and Mom also appears startled.

"You worked yourself into this family by acting all helpful just so you could hit on my mother!"

"Of course not, Hallie," shoots back Pastor Costello. "My intentions were pure. And . . . and nothing has happened, I mean we—"

"What? You were just giving my mom the lonely widow a little comfort and consolation on Christmas Eve?" Tears burn in the corners of my eyes.

"It's not that way at all!" insists a confused-looking Pastor Costello.

"How could you *do* this to us?"

"Hallie!" my mother whispers, though her eyes flash with horror.

"Plus you're supposed to be gay!" I storm out of the room only to find myself in the kitchen. Fortunately my boots and coat are right by the door to the garage. The good thing about wearing sweatpants and a long-sleeved T-shirt as pajamas in a cold house is that you're basically ready to leave at a moment's notice.

I hear Mom and Pastor Costello talking in low voices, and then he appears in the kitchen. "Hallie, where are you going at this hour?"

Only I'm halfway out the door.

"I'm not gay," Pastor Costello calls after me. Then he quickly adds in *Seinfeld* fashion—"Not that there's anything wrong with it."

EIGHTY-ONE

I<small>T'S ELEVEN O'CLOCK WHEN I COME TO A SCREECHING HALT IN</small> front of the Stocktons' house. The lights are on downstairs and I can hear carols playing as I approach the front porch. The door is unlocked and so I march inside. Olivia, Ottavio, Bernard, Gil, and Craig are all gathered around a Scrabble board, surrounded by candles, drinks, and cookies, apparently having a grand old time.

They look up at me wearing my coat pulled over sweats and the shitkicker boots I haven't bothered removing in my rush to locate Gil.

"Oh Hallie, how wonderful that you've come by," says Olivia.

"It's a come-as-you-are party," Bernard says as he looks at my outfit.

"What are *you* doing here?" I say angrily to Craig. He is absolutely the *last* person I want to see right now.

"I was invited over, if that's okay with you," Craig retorts just as angrily.

Olivia senses a bit of tension and remarks about the carol playing. " 'It Came Upon a Midnight Clear' is such a lovely song. I'll bet you didn't know that it was written by a Unitarian minister."

Now I turn on Gil. "You said Pastor Costello was gay!"

"I said you should confirm it with Bernard. He's the one with the gaydar," says Gil. "But why on earth does it matter?"

Bernard laughs. "Pastor Costello isn't *gay*. For pity sake, he wears rayon! And look at those orthopedic shoes! Don't even get me started on that aftershave. Goodness Garbo, no!"

Olivia sees that I'm upset and doesn't treat the matter as lightly as Bernard. "If memory serves, Pastor Costello was engaged about fifteen years ago, when he first took over the church. But the young woman died of leukemia. Why is this suddenly a problem?"

"Was he caught trying to audition for a gay men's choir?" jokes Bernard.

"He was caught holding my mother's hand!" I inform them.

"I'll call the Council on Churches immediately!" jokes Bernard. "Try some of my incredible baba au rhum. It's the pièce de résistance!" He thrusts a plate of spongelike cake steeped in rum syrup toward me and practically falls over in the process. Apparently Bernard has been enjoying the rum as much as the cake.

Gil begins to laugh heartily as well, as if I'm making a mountain out of a minister.

Craig stares at me as if this is final confirmation I've lost my mind and that insanity runs in the Palmer family. Next thing I'll be seeing Jesus in the garden rake.

At least Ottavio looks concerned when hearing about a man of the cloth being accused of having designs on a woman. He's not yet managed to get all the different religions in the U.S. straight.

Tears start to flow down my cheeks. "It's not funny! He—he worked his way into my family and now . . . now *this*." I play to the hilt my role as a woman destined for the darkly fated life of a victim in a Gothic romance.

Olivia rises and steers me into the kitchen. "Goodness gracious, from the way you're acting one would think that he's taken advantage of your mother. It doesn't sound as if she was trying to release herself from his grasp."

"No." I sniffle, as if the tears could go either way at this point. "They were sitting in the dark in front of the fire."

"Just holding hands, right?" asks Olivia.

Before starting to sob, I manage to say, "My life is ruined!"

Olivia goes to the stove and ladles out a cup of hot mulled cider, adding a cinnamon stick. She places it in front of me at the table.

"Sometimes when I'm upset I think how different the world might be today if John F. Kennedy hadn't been assassinated and lived to win a second term," Olivia says softly. "Or if his brother Robert hadn't also met with an assassin's bullet while trying to get the nomination in 1968. I was impressed by Bobby Kennedy because he was one of the few politicians to publicly change his mind about Vietnam when it could still make a difference. And after his older brother died he seemed to care so much more about civil rights and poverty."

I stop crying. It's hard to keep a full sob going when someone is discussing public policy.

"There's a quote on Bobby Kennedy's grave at Arlington Cemetery. Bobby said it after his brother John was assassinated. Though it originally comes from Aeschylus. Jackie Kennedy encouraged Bobby to read the Greeks after John's death. Anyway, it goes like this: 'He who learns must suffer. And even in our sleep pain that cannot forget falls drop by drop upon the heart, and in our own despair, against our will, comes wisdom to us by the awful grace of God.' "

Olivia gives this a moment to sink in and then says, "You realize what this means, don't you?"

I wasn't aware that there was going to be a test. "That we learn by suffering?"

"Well, yes . . . but I was referring to your mother and Pastor Costello."

"That Father Costello is probably going to be Stepfather Costello before long!"

"Perhaps in time. But I think what it means right now is that you can go back to school in January."

"We can't afford it."

"Hallie, I don't mean to sound as if I want you to take advantage of the situation, but your family currently has no earned income, and so your tuition will mostly be covered."

Oh my gosh. I hadn't thought about that. The sticking point with financial aid was always that my dad earned a decent salary. What they never understood was that his income just barely paid for the family to survive.

As I absorb this information I'm reminded of something said not by a famous Greek, but another very wise man by the name of Cappy. *There are two sides to every coin, plus the edge.* The past has loomed large up until this moment, but suddenly the future appears slightly larger.

"You know, if I take a job in the cafeteria to cover living expenses, it could probably work." After all, hadn't Craig said that doing dishes in my house was like working at a restaurant?

"Yes, of course it will," continues Olivia. "And now your mother has someone to lean on. You've shown tremendous courage under fire."

"Yeah, if you want to redefine courage as not letting anyone else know that you're scared to death inside," I say.

"Hardly," says Olivia. "But either way, I'm sure your mom doesn't expect you to stay home forever. And this way you're not abandoning her in a difficult situation."

"I would have had to sign up for classes weeks ago," I say. "And find a place to live."

"Surely it's still possible to organize a schedule. Plus a few students always drop out at this time of year. As for housing, worst case is that you go back to living on campus for a semester."

I remember a girl in my freshman dorm whose mom had died in a car accident and she was issued a free meal plan.

"So you see," says Olivia, "Pastor Costello has actually done you a favor, and you'll realize it much more as time goes by."

Despair briefly returns. "But I'm just not ready for this!"

Olivia places her arm on my shoulder. "I remember the first day I met your father. He arrived huffing and puffing on the front porch, all angry and worried about you leaving school and running away. It was so obvious how much he cared for you! I think that hope is the hardest love of all to carry, because it so often means letting go. I'm glad you didn't see him the day he signed the legal guardian papers. It wasn't that he didn't understand you so much as he was too well aware that the road less traveled is rockier. And I suppose it is, but it's not something you ever consider, for there isn't really an alternative."

"I guess not," I say.

The CD finishes in the other room, and we can hear them all arguing about what to put on next. Bernard is in favor of French carols.

Gil can be heard saying, "It's a shame Led Zeppelin never made a holiday album."

Craig chimes in good-naturedly, "Turn on all the appliances and that's what would it would sound like."

Upon hearing Craig's voice, Olivia whispers in my ear, "Are you sure this is *all* about your mother finding someone? The British author Jerome K. Jerome once said that love is like the measles, in that we all have to go through it."

Then she says loud enough to be heard in the other room, "We mustn't leave the men folk unsupervised any longer or they may attempt to turn on the Super Bowl."

"Ha ha," says a tipsy Bernard as we enter the room. "The only bowls around here are used for serving soup and salad."

"The Super Bowl isn't until the end of January," Craig informs us. "But there's a big football game on tomorrow."

"Bocce is best ball game," offers Ottavio.

"I'm going down to the basement to get some more wood for the fire," says Gil.

"Save yourself the trip and just toss in the collected works of Theodore Dreiser from Mother's study," says Bernard.

"If you knew Pastor Costello wasn't gay, then why didn't you tell me?" I ask Bernard.

"Are you asking me for a straight answer to a straight question?" He laughs uproariously at his own marvelous sense of humor and sways slightly.

"Oh, just forget it," I say.

Bernard becomes serious for a moment. "Hallie, I had no idea that you didn't *know*." But his commitment to solemnity quickly dissolves. "Or else I would have outed him!" Bernard cracks up again and Gil returns with the wood.

"The moon has crossed the yardarm, gentlemen," announces Olivia. "Why don't we go upstairs?" She gives a nod indicating they should leave Craig and me alone.

And I suppose that I do owe him an apology.

Gil is the last one to head upstairs. "Guess what?"

I've had enough surprises for one night and nod my head that I give up.

"I'm quitting my job," he says. "The community theater has managed to scrape together a modest salary for me."

"Congratulations." And I really mean it because I know how much Gil hates his job.

Gil goes over to the stereo. I think he's turning it off, but as he goes upstairs Percy Sledge's greatest hits album begins playing softly in the background.

"So . . . Merry Christmas," says Craig.

"Not really, no," I say, and flop down on the couch. "I'm sorry I yelled at you. I was upset."

The song "A Whiter Shade of Pale" is playing and I hear the words, *We skipped the light Fandango/Turned cartwheels 'cross the floor.*

"Remember that New Year's Eve we left the party right before midnight and you walked me back here?" I ask him.

"Of course," says Craig, and a faint smile plays across his lips. "It was the first night we kissed. Out in the snow."

"I'm sorry for being such a jerk about you not wanting to finish school," I say.

"I don't blame you for being upset, especially with everything that was going on at home. Looking back, maybe I could have expressed my feelings a little better."

"I'm returning to school in January," I say. "Surprise!"

"That sounds like a good idea," says Craig. "I have a surprise for you, too."

Wow. I can't believe that Craig would actually buy me a gift after I've been such an idiot. I glance over to where the presents are stacked up alongside an almost life-sized soldier that looks as if it starred in a 1950s performance of *The Nutcracker* before it was promptly killed and stuffed.

"It's at my house," he says.

I follow Craig's car in mine. It's like driving through a celestial city. Christmas Eve is the one time everyone leaves the outdoor lights on all night. A full moon illuminates the sky with phantasmagoric splendor and winter's frost makes the snow-crusted earth glisten.

EIGHTY-TWO

THE LARKINS' PALE YELLOW ALUMINUM-SIDED HOUSE IS TWO STO-
ries high with a two-car garage. It's basically the same size as
ours, except they have three people living there instead of ten. I
consider them pretty lucky, because in addition to all this space
they have three fairly new cars, nice clothes, and plenty of
money in the bank. But I guess you don't ever really know how
another person feels about his or her luck.

We remove our boots in the front hall, which is lined with a
soft tan-colored cloth. "Wow!" I say. "Is this real suede on the
walls?"

"I guess so." Craig barely looks at it. "My mom always says
that it's better to buy quality because in the end it actually costs
less."

"Yeah, if you can afford it in the beginning," I say.

"Come downstairs," says Craig.

Downstairs? I thought we'd hang out in front of the Larkins'
big tree in the living room, which has a train that runs around
the base. Or else go up to his room.

Craig leads me down to the basement, where two large tanks
sit next to each other. Once he turns on more lights I can see big

goldfish swimming around, and also koi, the fish that Craig used to stock the Stocktons' pond last summer. In one tank the fish are fairly small and mostly pale orange, but in the other they're large and all different colors.

"Cool," I say. "Are you raising fish now?"

"That's only part of it," explains Craig, and there's excitement in his voice. "I'm going into the pond-building business. It's becoming very popular—not just for private homes but in malls, parks, restaurants, museums—almost any open space you can think of. I'm building a Web site, and my dad is going to back the business."

"That sounds cool," I say.

"I have an appointment to meet with a bank in Cleveland next Wednesday. They want a pond in their lobby!"

We go upstairs to Craig's room, and I hardly recognize it. There are big drawings of ponds lying across the bed and reference books scattered all over the floor.

"You're really into this," I remark.

"Sometimes I wonder if I'd have discovered all this if Bernard hadn't asked me to design that pond for him last summer. Talk about serendipity!"

"Yeah, one never knows where a day with Bernard is going to lead," I agree.

"The Stocktons said they don't mind if I put pictures of their pond on my Web site," says Craig.

"So what's up with you and Megan?" I suddenly change the subject.

Pause. "Summer fling, I guess." Craig sounds mildly disheartened.

"What do you mean, 'you guess'?"

"She's engaged to some guy at her school."

"Engaged? Really! I've never thought of us as being old enough to get married."

"What about you?" asks Craig.

"What *about* me?" I say. "I've become the old woman who lived in the shoe. Who would ever look at *me*?"

"I would," says Craig.

He clears the drawings off the bed and we sit down on the edge of it side by side. Craig kisses me on the lips, tentatively at first, and then we begin to lose ourselves in becoming reacquainted.

"Isn't this sort of weird with your parents at the other end of the hall?" I whisper.

"They respect my space. And besides, you'd better get used to it. I'm going to be living at home for a while. Though don't assume it makes me gay."

Craig and I both laugh.

"Don't worry, I won't."

From then on we remain in the limbo of unspoken words. Touching Craig is like entering an enchanted garden where you're overwhelmed by the scent and want to lay a hand on every petal, feel every leaf, and dig right down into the earth. I hear the sound of breathing but can no longer tell if it's my own or his, and soon become aware of a torturous desire for not just sex, but magnificent intimacy. Whenever he kisses or touches me, I know just how to answer. Likewise, he anticipates my desires and makes love to me until we shudder in each other's arms. I find myself sloping toward sleep wanting to capture the moment forever in a line of poetry or a painting that I can imagine but feel incapable of realizing.

EIGHTY-THREE

MORNING ENTERS THROUGH THE CHINKS IN THE BLINDS AND IT takes me a moment to remember where I am. Craig is lying next to me and smiles in a way that says we're back together and that this *wasn't* just a one-night stand.

While leaning on his left elbow he uses his right hand to examine my shoulders and face as if searching for pimples. "Hey, where did your freckles go?" he finally asks.

"They had to be sold in order to buy Christmas presents for the kids."

"What a shame," he says. "I always thought it would be fun to play connect the dots."

"I guess I'm getting old," I say. "Which is another reason it would be nice not to have to worry about stupid condoms. What if I were to go on the Pill?"

"Really?" Craig asks excitedly. "I never wanted to ask because, you know, it's your body and everything. But I fully support whatever decision you make."

"It's probably a good idea anyway around my house," I say. "Sometimes I'm afraid that I'll get pregnant by touching a doorknob. But, well, it would mean that we should both get tested and then only see each other."

I can't believe I'm hearing myself correctly. It wasn't a thought or a blinding flash of inspiration that made me open my mouth, just a feeling that it was right, that he was made for me and I for him.

"At least, that's the only way I would feel comfortable," I add. After the word *comfortable* I'm suddenly thinking about the look on Herb's face when he sees *this* prescription. Maybe I can have it filled at school instead.

"That would be great. We'll be exclusive," says Craig. After a pause he throws out the line, "Do you think you want kids someday?"

"Huh!"

"Not now." Craig chuckles. "I just meant someday."

"Please don't ask me that right now." I'm envisioning the long slog that lies ahead over the next ten days, known to children as *vacation*.

"Maybe you could live at home and commute to college?" suggests Craig.

I think about that for a moment and it doesn't provide me with a warm feeling the way that Craig's arm across my chest does. "I don't know if that's such a good idea. There's stuff to do in the art rooms and computer lab. It's only an hour. Why don't you come visit one or two weekends a month and the other ones I'll come home?"

"That could work for now, at least until my business gets going," says Craig.

Happiness floods my heart, and everything bad seems to be in the past while I finally hold the present right in the palm of my hand.

We go downstairs and Craig's mom greets us by saying, "Merry Christmas!"

Whoops, I'd almost forgotten about that. It's Christmas morning!

Mrs. Larkin ties on an apron with a big snowman on the front and invites me to stay for breakfast. It's tempting, especially since I see that she's having the really good kind of sausages that come frozen in a box. But I tell her I'd better head home to wrangle all of my brothers and sisters, who by now will be zooming around the house with their new toys.

"Well, it's fine to stay over anytime," says Mrs. Larkin. "Craig's father and I really admire how you've handled things this past year."

Just as I'm walking out the front door, Mom turns her mini-van into the Larkins' driveway.

EIGHTY-FOUR

"BERNARD THOUGHT THAT YOU MIGHT BE HERE," MOM SAYS AS SHE gets out of the car.

"Sorry about last night," I say. "It's just that . . . with Dad, you know, and everything."

We stand outside in the cold facing each other, and for the first time I notice the fine latticework of wrinkles on my mother's face.

"I understand," says Mom. "You know, Arthur and I haven't been together or anything like that." Her cheeks flush, and she looks down at the tire tracks in the driveway.

"It's none of my business, Mom."

"But I want you to know that, Hallie. We haven't even really kissed, other than on the cheek or the forehead when he leaves."

"Honestly, Mom, you don't have to tell me any of this."

"I know I don't. But please hear me out, Hallie. Right now I can't even imagine sharing my bed with another man."

If my life were a movie, this is the moment where Mom and I would bond together as adults. Only it's not the multiplex in Timpany, and I'm finding this conversation to be increasingly icky. For some reason I prefer to think of my mom as the maker of wonderful birthday cakes rather than a regular woman with . . . well . . . *needs.*

"I'm not independent like you," continues Mom. "When I was your age and your father was my boyfriend, I was writing my name on scraps of paper to see how it would look after we married, and daydreaming about the wedding. I never bothered to get my diploma, which was foolish, because if I did I might have a good job now, or at least in a few years when the twins start school. You don't know what's going to happen in life. That's why I became so upset when Louise had trouble. And you, my goodness, I'd lost control over you by the time you were ten years old, though I tried not to show it."

"I'm not strong, Mom. Be serious. When you were sick, I was the first one down the rabbit hole."

"What do you mean? You kept the whole family together."

"I hardly visited you."

"That's because you don't like to feel helpless—and there wasn't anything you could do at the hospital. But at home there was, and you did it all."

Mom is being extremely generous if you consider Louise taking off, one of the twins almost buying the farm, and all the kids now whispering "tits like a basset hound's ears" to one another during church.

"So we're just different, that's all," I say.

"My point is, Hallie, that I need someone. I'm sure you will, too, but I don't think it will ever be in the same way. Do you understand?"

"I guess so," I say.

"I'm not as brave," adds Mom.

After my experiences this past year I currently think that the bravest thing in the world is to be a mother, especially to ten children.

"You know how you found out about my age and Eric being, well, somewhat premature?" asks Mom.

"Yeah."

She looks off into the distance before continuing. "What I'm saying is that Eric wasn't an accident, Hallie. I knew there was a chance I'd become pregnant. Looking back, I realize that it was the easy way out. If only I'd had the confidence and the courage to do it the right way at the right time. And who knows, maybe your father could have been a professional football player."

Wow. So Eric was what you might call a planned accident. I let this piece of information sink in. There's not much to say other than to promise to have safe sex, but it doesn't seem the right time for that. "I thought I'd start school again in January. If it's okay with you."

Mom finally smiles. "Yes, I think that's an excellent idea."

"If you can handle things at home." And then I remember she's not exactly alone. "I mean, I guess you'll have some help."

"I hope so. If it's okay with you."

"Is Pastor Costello at the house now?" I ask.

"No. I invited him, of course, but he feels uncomfortable."

"I'll see if I can find him," I offer.

She nods as if that would be nice. "I've asked the children to wait to open their presents."

We both get into our cars. Only she turns right at the end of the street and I make a left. The silent empty yards are dotted with frosted pines and naked gleaming birches beneath a calendar blue sky. Everyone is at home celebrating Christmas or else enjoying a quiet day off.

When I arrive at church, Pastor Costello's van is the only vehicle in the lot. I find him up on a ladder in the sanctuary taking down decorations and carefully packing them away for next year, all except for the poinsettias on the altar, which will remain there through Epiphany. The church feels lonely compared to the way it was last night during the five o'clock children's service, all lit with candles, every pew jam-packed with families singing "Silent Night."

"Isn't it a little early in the day to be taking down the decorations?" I ask.

Without looking down from the ladder Pastor Costello replies, "The holiday is over for me."

"Not really," I say. "You can't spell Jesus without the letter *u*." This is one of the things Pastor Costello famously tells the graduating Sunday school class every spring, knowing there's a good chance he'll never see them inside the church again aside from Christmas and Easter.

My entreaty is about as effective as his annual speech. Pastor Costello reaches up high to remove some garland surrounding a plaque honoring the previous minister.

"Some kids are anxiously awaiting your arrival so they can open their presents," I try again.

"And what kids might those be?" He still doesn't look down.

"Well, there are two babies, but they don't care so much about presents. Then there are some little kids who might pass out if they don't start tearing open wrapping paper soon." I pause and stare at the front of the sanctuary where Dad's coffin sat almost a year ago. "And then there are some bigger kids who would just enjoy your company."

Pastor Costello finally glances down at me.

"I'm sorry I was such a jerk," I say. "If it makes you feel any better, I've been doing a lot of apologizing the past twenty-four hours. You're just one on a long list. It's basically my full-time job now."

He gives me a little smile, and for some reason I'm more relieved than I thought I'd be.

"Why don't I meet you over there a bit later?" he asks.

"Why don't you come with me now and I'll give you a ride home later? Craig and I can even help you pack up the rest of this stuff."

"Amen to that," says Pastor Costello, and finally comes down off his ladder. "It sounds like an offer I can't refuse."

EIGHTY-FIVE

When we pull into my driveway there are about seven faces pressed against the big picture window and an audible whoop goes up inside the house. The front door flies open to reveal a room that is bright with Christmas morning.

Inside the living room I see Brandt standing next to the tree, looking more grown-up than ever. Sitting nearby are Louise and Eric and Teddy. It's pretty clear they're thinking the same thing as me, that it's the first Christmas without Dad. But the little kids don't share in this preoccupation. Dad was a long time ago, and the presents are right here and now.

It's hard to tell what is on Mom's mind. She busies herself with picking up wrapping paper and empty juice glasses, a study of constant motion. She must be thinking about Dad, too. I catch her looking at his photo on the side table. He's here. And yet he's gone.

Finally Pastor Costello interrupts Mom's frenetic cleanup and says, "Come and sit down for a moment." She hesitates. There's an empty plate with Danish crumbs in her hand that's pulling her toward the dishwasher. I take the plate and she sits down next to Pastor Costello, takes a deep breath, and for the first time focuses on her surroundings.

Pastor Costello opens my gift to him—a trilogy of murder mysteries with gruesome covers—and Mom looks at me as if this isn't a very appropriate gift. But Pastor Costello quickly rescues the situation for us both. "I've been meaning to start reading mysteries. They offer some excellent insights into human nature."

"Can we open it *now*?" Davy begs Mom.

Everyone knows that *it* means the box from Uncle Lenny, which is so big that it's been stored in the garage all week.

"Yes," agrees Mom.

With help from Eric and me, the kids drag the heavy box into the living room and start to tear at it. Before long there's a big floppy piece of bright orange rubber emerging, and I say a silent prayer that it's not a blowup doll. The kids are going crazy shouting and tugging from every direction. The last third appears to be stuck and so they yank on the free end until suddenly there's a loud *whoosh*.

"It's a boat!" calls out Teddy.

While the little kids are being pushed over by what appears to be the front end of a rubber lifeboat, Eric is frantically trying to find an off switch. Pastor Costello, Louise, and I jump up to help him. But the boat keeps getting larger and so Louise and I turn our attention to moving things out of the way—the coffee table, a lamp, presents, and finally Lillian. The cat is long gone, and my mother carries the twins to the kitchen. It must be a total of fifteen feet in length!

Finally Eric yells "Got it!"

"I hope you mean the plug and not the card," I say.

We hear a giant hissing sound and the dirigible stops expanding just short of the Christmas tree. Pastor Costello snaps some pictures of the kids and Mom in front of the slowly deflating lifeboat. He asks me to take one and Pastor Costello stands behind Mom with his hand resting on her shoulder.

The kids continue to laugh and talk about how they're going to sail around the world as soon as school finishes. When enough air is out and the boat fits through the archway, Teddy and Eric drag it back to the garage, with the little kids excitedly trotting behind them and Mom yelling for everyone to put their coats on.

"Leave it to Uncle Lenny to be the life of the party even when he's not even here," I say. "And make for one heck of a good story in the process."

Not five minutes after they've gone out to the garage, there's a huge racket and the kids come tumbling back inside. Glancing toward the kitchen I see Bernard arriving with Gigi and Rose, and carrying presents. Once again, the kids are absolutely dizzy with anticipation.

Bernard gives Darlene a karaoke machine that has two microphones and a number of Broadway showstopper discs. She excitedly plugs it in to a nearby wall socket. I assume he thought it would help with her lisp. Musical theater is Bernard's solution to most of life's challenges, much the same way Jesus is the answer according to Pastor Costello.

Bernard shows Darlene where to read the words, and together they stand up to sing a song. Bernard introduces "The World Goes Round" as if he's a nightclub performer. "As you all know, I rarely perform a Liza number, but she, as am I, is enormously fond of the Kander and Ebb catalog, with its ingenious lyrics and perfect melodies." They begin crooning *Sometimes you're happy and sometimes you're sad—but the world goes 'round."*

The karaoke machine is a huge hit, and the singers have barely finished when all the little kids are clamoring to try it. Bernard relinquishes his microphone and sits down next to me on the floor by the tree. He hands me a card and says "Merry Christmas."

When I open it, a hundred-dollar bill falls out.

"That should be good for a facial," he jokes. "Or more likely, five pizzas and a dozen chocolate Yoo-hoos." Olivia must have shared my intention to start school again after the holidays.

"Thank you so much!" I give Bernard a kiss on the cheek. "I don't have an actual gift for you, but you're entitled to some free baby-sitting when I'm home for vacation."

Looking at the kids singing and running around, Bernard says, "I think you've had your fair share of child care for the time being. Just promise you'll come home and be my yard person next summer."

Bernard has more than a hunch that Craig and I are back together. I swear, sometimes he can tell what's going on with me just by examining a single strand of hair. DNA testing has nothing on Bernard's finely tuned senses.

Speaking of which, he glances over at Mom and Pastor Costello seated together on the couch, and then back to me. I'm well aware that he's dying to know what has transpired since I stormed out of the house like a lunatic last night.

"I guess it's what they both want," I say to Bernard. And it's not so terrible imagining them as a couple. I mean, so long as I don't think about them having sex. Mom and Pastor Costello can celebrate their fiftieth wedding anniversary and the two of them in bed together is a thought I will still *not* be having.

"As long as I don't picture them . . ."

Bernard reads my mind and nods in agreement. "Always fully clothed."

There's no chance anyone else can hear our conversation as the kids are now belting out "If I'd Known You Were Coming I'd Have Baked a Cake" at top volume, two on each microphone.

Bernard leans toward me. "You know what Judy Garland used to say?"

I shake my head, indicating that, in fact, I do not.

"Give the people what they want, and then go and get a hamburger."

My eyes settle on the photo of Dad. I perform a quick mental check to make sure I still remember everything about him—the way he walked and talked and smiled and even smelled. Yes, it's all safely there.

Then I glance at the little kids playing with their toys and starting to sing the theme song to *Chitty Chitty Bang Bang*. They don't remember as much about Dad. But I suppose they'll collect other memories. For instance, this might eventually become known as the Year the Cat Tipped Over the Christmas Tree or the Year That Uncle Lenny's Lifeboat Blew Up in the Living Room.

Regardless of how we all might end up remembering it, one thing is clear—no amount of thinking about the past can erase the fact that a new year is upon us, one without Dad. An arrow had been shot through our lives. Yet time marches on, and we live in the present. So it's at this moment that I finally decide to plunge into the future. And a lifetime of tomorrows.

Acknowledgments

With ongoing gratitude to my agent, Judith Ehrlich, for contributing her time and imagination to another novel. Special thanks to Johanna Bowman at Ballantine for her keen editorial eye and unlimited patience, and to Christine Cabello and Patricia Park for their promotional efforts. I'm also extremely grateful to Carol Fitzgerald and Wiley Saichek at Bookreporter .com for their marketing wizardry. A big salute to Master Mariner and salty sailor Neil Osborne for helping to channel Uncle Lenny. Continuing appreciation for my constant helpmates: Willie Pietersen, Aimee Chu, and Cecilia Tabares.

THE BIG
SHUFFLE

Laura Pedersen

A Reader's Guide

A Conversation with Laura Pedersen

Julie Sciandra and Laura Pedersen have been friends since their potato salad days as teenagers during the energy crisis in Buffalo, New York, back when you had to keep moving in order to stay warm.

Julie Sciandra: Where exactly is Cosgrove County?

Laura Pedersen: Well, how do you want to go there—by car?

JS: Say that I want to drive there from Buffalo, New York.

LP: That's easy. You get on the thruway going west, drive through a chunk of Pennsylvania, and eventually you're in the northeast corner of Ohio. Get on Route 45 heading south. After about twenty minutes you'll see a dairy with a big plastic cow on top and a faded red barn behind it—make a left at that corner. Go through the covered bridge—it's a shame about the graffiti, but it does make you wonder whatever happened to those couples, especially the ones who declared True Luv 4ever. Drive about two more miles, until you see the old mill where they sell apple cider and maple syrup, and then bear left at the fork in the road. Only slow down because a lot of Amish folk live around there and they don't like to use those orange triangles on the back of their buggies. They also don't care to have their picture taken. But if their farm stand is open you definitely want to stop and buy a cherry pie—absolutely delicious. Anyway, after approximately three more miles you'll come to the edge of town. There's the train station and then the park. If you make a right onto Millersport it will take you up to Cappy's place. Otherwise go left on Swan Street and that takes you to Main. Main Street is about eight blocks long and you'll know you're at the end of it when you pass the town hall and see the gravel road that leads to the cemetery. On a nice day the cemetery can be a great place for a picnic. I actually prefer it to the park.

JS: So this town is a real place?

LP: It is to me. But then I'm an only child and we're known for creating not just imaginary friends but entire galaxies.

JS: Throughout the first three Hallie Palmer books you make it sound as if the town has been hurt by the advent of outlet centers and superstores.

LP: Cosgrove has certainly known its ups and downs, like so many towns in Middle America. Back in the 1800s the land around there was a good place for a farmer to settle, since the soil is rich and you had not only the railroad nearby for transporting your crops but also the Great Lakes. The Erie Canal was completed in 1825, and so your grain or lumber or whatever was sent by train to Buffalo and then got loaded onto mule barges that went past Albany on the Hudson River, to New York

City, and could then go on to Europe. Similarly, after the transcontinental railroad was completed in 1869, your goods could be easily transported to Chicago and the fast-developing Plains, Rockies, and California.

JS: Do you want to start singing "Erie Canal"?

LP: *"Low bridge, everybody down. Low bridge, for we're coming to a town."*

JS: Did you have to sing that in elementary school as many times as we did?

LP: More. Sweet Home is a public school.

JS: I'd forgotten that the name of your school system is Sweet Home. My condolences.

LP: It definitely caused more than a few fights. Our mascot was the panther, but at basketball games the opposing team liked to snarl, "Sweet Home Sweeties." This didn't go over real well. No matter, I'm just glad they finally got the asbestos out of the ceilings.

JS: So the town where Hallie lives was going gangbusters back in the 1890s. What went wrong?

LP: As farming became increasingly mechanized, people began working and living in town. But by the 1940s they'd started migrating to the cities for work in the factories, steel plants, stockyards, and granaries, at least until the 1950s and 1960s when many of those jobs went overseas. Then the oil crisis and recession of the 1970s hit the area pretty hard. However, this past year the town is becoming more of a bedroom community for Cleveland, and if they go ahead with those plans to start a commuter train it's really going to revive things.

JS: And exactly how is it that you know all of this? Do you have a seat on the town council?

LP: Actually, I'm the town historian.

JS: Sure you are. Now back to the story. Do we finally find out the name of Hallie's mom?

LP: No.

JS: *The Big Shuffle* seems darker than the first two books in the Hallie Palmer series. Has anything happened to make you more pessimistic since you wrote those?

LP: I don't find it so, but then I thought *Last Call*—a love story between a roguish Scotsman living in Brooklyn and a nun who has run off from the convent—was optimistic when a good portion of that book was about dying from cancer. I tend to stick with the themes of life, love, and death. So basically in every book someone is going to get it. It was a greater tragedy because Hallie's father is a relatively young man and leaves behind this enormous family. On the other hand, the Palmers have experienced plenty of new life, with a total of ten children, and so every once in a while the pendulum has to swing.

JS: But was it necessary to go that far for Hallie to become an adult?

LP: Good question. No, I don't think anything was needed to help Hallie along, and that she was going to arrive on her own just fine. She didn't have to be snapped into reality by a major event. I suppose I was harkening back to the past. There wasn't really such a thing as "childhood" until about sixty years ago. Children were regarded as small adults. Furthermore, if you consider that back then the average life span was shorter, families were larger, and the number of women who died in childbirth was much greater, Hallie's situation as temporary head of the household wouldn't have been that unusual. In fact, I often think that teenagers today don't feel all that challenged by their roles and fantasize about being able to do something heroic in a tough situation. I'm not advocating such circumstances, simply saying that most teens can and will rise to the occasion when put to the test, rather than just play sports, start rock bands, do homework, work at the Tastee Freez, and roam the mall. On the flip side, I know a lot of teenagers who do community service, whether it's through school, a religious organization, or on their own, and this is a great way of learning about what type of adult they'd like to become.

JS: I've noticed that you seem to kill off at least one man in every novel?

LP: A few women have stepped on a rainbow—Denny's wife in *Going Away Party*, Hayden's wife in *Last Call*, and Pastor Costello's mother was called home sometime between *Heart's Desire* and *The Big Shuffle*. But you're right to ask since these deaths occurred offstage and were more plot devices than the demise of developed characters. In my defense, Olivia takes a bad fall in *Heart's Desire* and Hallie's mom spends several months in a hospital during *The Big Shuffle*. Overall, you're correct and I appear to be a man killer. Please don't tell my husband.

JS: Where did Uncle Lenny come from? He must be one of your more bizarre characters.

LP: I think Uncle Lenny comes off as being eccentric only because he's been temporarily transplanted to a small town in Ohio and we don't encounter him in the port of Marseille. Which is what makes Uncle Lenny so much fun to have in the book—he has a different vocabulary from years at sea and is not familiar with typical suburban family life. However, he's practical in the way that most sailors are, has a big heart, and ends up being an enormous help, which is more than we can say for Aunt Lala.

JS: Why is Bernard afraid to travel? Is that supposed to be symbolic in some way?

LP: I think we all have our fears, some more rational than others, some more acceptable or explainable than others. I never meant for it to be symbolic of anything. Bernard is just a home-and-hearth kind of guy and has hung on to that worry so many of us have when we're young about going into the woods and not coming back. Or worse, a loved one leaving and not returning. Bernard feels that nothing bad can happen in the safety of one's own home, surrounded by the people you love, aside from the occasional kitchen accident.

JS: What's Hallie's biggest fear?

LP: Aside from dropping one of those twins on his head, I guess it would be to make the wrong decision about something important—which man to marry, what job to take, where to live. I think that Hallie is in many ways overwhelmed by the amount of freedom she has to make choices regarding the direction her life will take. And that's why she keeps circling her safe places—Officer Rich, the Stocktons, her family—always on the lookout for clear answers. To a good card player there's almost always a right move—at least the odds favor it fifty-one percent and so you make it. But in real life the probabilities, decision trees, and possible outcomes can't be calculated as accurately. This drives Hallie crazy, the fact that the world isn't a math problem that can be easily solved with a pencil and paper. And that unlike work done with a pencil, life choices can't necessarily be erased.

JS: What are you most afraid of?

LP: Dying one of those long, slow, horrible deaths from a disease they don't know much about, you can't pronounce, and none of my friends have heard of, so between monthslong hospital stays I'm on the Internet searching for cures and ordering guava pulp concentrate from South America, lighting lavender candles, and forming healing circles with the dogs. I'd much rather the M4 bus come barreling up Madison Avenue on a winter day when there's a bad glare and the curb is slippery and performs the Grim Reaper's job lickety-split. As soon as the passengers look out the window and see that the driver has killed a woman wearing a fuzzy pink bathrobe and silver moon boots, they groan and immediately start shouting, "Give us a refund!" and "Is there another bus behind this one?"

JS: Good luck with that. Why is *Best Bet,* the next book, going to be the last in the Hallie Palmer series?

LP: At around the age of twenty-two I suddenly became very boring, basically the person I am today.

JS: So what's next?

LP: I'm working on a stand-alone novel called *Fool's Mate* which is a bit edgier than this series. It takes place in a newsroom and there are some political machinations, which I've mostly avoided in the Hallie Palmer books, aside from Olivia's protests and editorializing. I'm also working on a new series where two women open an animal hospital in upstate New York. One is a veterinarian and the other has an MBA.

JS: Wait a second. That sounds like my life.

LP: It is. But I had the idea first. Remember—I showed it to you years ago when you lived in Manhattan and then *you* went and copied it with your life. Same with John and Kelly adopting a baby from China. They stole that from *Heart's Desire*.

JS: Will a lot of men die in the next series?

LP: I suppose it depends on whether or not they're good drivers. The winters in upstate New York are very icy.

JS: What's your ultimate goal as a writer?

LP: Ideally, I'd like to get my books banned. That seems to be the best thing for sales.

Questions and Topics for Discussion

1. When the Palmer family is in crisis, it's decided that Hallie will leave school to take over and not her brother Eric, who is a year older. Was this the right decision? In your family, are tasks typically divided into what is considered "men's work" and "women's work"?

2. The neighbor lady, Mrs. Muldoon, has a daughter in Arizona who wants her mother to come and live out there. Only Mrs. Muldoon has spent her entire life in town and doesn't want to leave. What are some of the pros and cons of having family members living nearby?

3. Do you belong to a community, organization, or close circle of friends who can rely upon each other when in need?

4. What do you think is the worst possible age to lose a parent?

5. In the Palmer family the girls tend to have major difficulties during their teenage years while the boys stay the course. In your experience, is it more common for boys or girls to have a rough patch as teenagers, or the same for both?

6. Do you think it's possible to forecast how your friends or family members would react to a family crisis like the one Hallie experiences, or is it impossible to tell with people until they're actually in such a situation?

7. Louise leaves home shortly after her father dies. Have you ever had a relationship or a bad experience in a particular place and felt that the only solution was to leave?

8. At a certain point Hallie wonders if something she may have done has caused tragedy to strike. Do you believe that good and bad things happen in life based on our behavior?

9. When Craig drops out of college, Hallie worries that he's jeopardizing his future. What would you advise Craig to do? How important is a college education today?

10. Olivia's boyfriend Ottavio turns out to be the jealous type and flies into a rage when she strikes up a friendship with a man. Did you feel Ottavio acted appropriately, or was his reaction out of proportion with the situation?

11. When Olivia takes up with a younger man, her son views this as being scandalous. Is there a double standard in society that allows for men to date younger women but not vice versa?

12. Going out with Auggie seems to help Hallie realize what she really wants in a boyfriend. Do you believe in love at first sight? Do you think that your first love is your only true love? Are you rational about the qualities you look for in a partner or do you base decisions purely on attraction and emotion?

13. Hallie and Craig finally decide to have a serious one-on-one relationship. How old must a person be to recognize true love and function in a mature relationship?

14. Hallie holds much of her grief inside because she's trying not to upset her younger siblings. Are there times when it's best to try to conceal your emotions, or is this almost always unhealthy?

15. While going through some papers Hallie discovers that her mother married and gave birth to her older brother earlier than she'd led the family to believe, largely because she regretted having dropped out of school. Is it okay for parents to keep some secrets, or is honesty always the best policy?

16. Even though Hallie cares very much for Pastor Costello, she's extremely angry when she discovers that he has feelings for her mother. In your experience, do most children react negatively to the prospect of a parent striking up a new relationship after a death or divorce?

Laura Pedersen grew up near Buffalo and now lives in Manhattan where she volunteers at the Booker T. Washington Learning Center in East Harlem.

Visit her website at www.LauraPedersenBooks.com.